The Wanderess

by Roman Payne

THE WANDERESS

1st Edition

Official Website:

www.wanderess.com

About the Author:

Roman Payne was born in Seattle in 1977.

He left America in 1999 and currently lives in Paris.

For more information about the author, please visit:

www.romanpayne.com

Acknowledgments & Legal Statement:

ISBN 978-0-9852281-3-2

This first edition is published by Aesthete Press.

Cover model photography by Elena Ray. Cover landscape photo by Leoks.

Cover design/art-conception by Roman Payne.

I *designate* this novel to my little sister, *Stefanie*. While I *dedicate* it to my *Heroines*, my *Patronesses*, and to the *Wanderesses* of the world. To my Heroines and Patronesses, for their support during the novel's creation; to the Wanderesses, for their inspiration and the poetic beauty of their lives.

Special dedication goes to *Mimi* of Chantilly, France for her selfless and undying support. Without her, this book would have died in Valencia. Special thanks as well to *Guillemette* of Paris, to *Nausica'a* of Lagonisi, Greece; *Carolina* of São Paulo, *Claire* of Paris, *Choteuse* of Marseille ...and to my *Mother*. As for the men, my gratitude extends to the XVIII century adventurer, Abbé Prévost, for his classic novel *Manon Lescaut*, which served as the inspiration and architectural model for *The Wanderess*. Most importantly, this dedication extends to my close friend, the famed writer and scholar, *Pietros Maneos*, for his heroic support during the writing of *The Wanderess*, and for his *'Bramabella'*—both the literary movement, and the land.

— Roman Payne; Chantilly, France;
November, 2013

"I sleep, but my heart waketh: it is the voice of my beloved that knocketh, saying, Open to me, my sister, my love, my dove, my undefiled: for my head is filled with dew, and my locks with the drops of the night."

— Song of Solomon, 5:2

"...And where is my gypsy wife tonight?"

— L. Cohen

Chapter One

W*ANDERESS, WANDERESS, weave us a story of seduction and ruse. Heroic be the Wanderess, the world be her muse.*

...I jot this phrase of invocation in my old leather-bound notebook on a bright, cold morning at the Café **** in Paris, and with it I'm inspired to take the reader back to the time I first met and became acquainted with the girl I call *The Wanderess*—as well as a famous adventurer named *Saul, the Son of Solarus*. It was because of these two that I would come to know one of the most beautiful and touching of all love stories I could ever invent or imagine, a tale to inspire the heroic soul. But that will all come later. Now let us go back to the beginning. It all started three years ago, in Italy...

I had left Paris in the fall to roam the countryside in Europe and the islands, as the book I was writing at the time required some literary research that obliged me to travel. There were details to be learned about several locales. A specific garden in London to visit. A provincial inn in Calais, in northern France, to investigate. As well as a property in rural Tuscany where I planned to set the scene of a lovers' retreat, reminiscent of Boccaccio. Finally, a tragic ending to be staged in Corsica and Mallorca made it necessary that I visit these enchanting islands.

It was with considerable regret that I left Paris that month, for autumn is my favorite time to be in the capital. When in September the last of the Parisians have returned from their homes in the country, we collectively throw ourselves back into the joys of city life and the voluptuous season begins. Autumn: the season of parties, banquets, ballets and festive balls; the time when the luxurious *parisiennes* are the most luxurious, the virgin *demoiselles* the most virginal, the fragrant *bourgeoises* the most fragrant, the *courtisanes* the most divine. Still, although I love elegant parties, dancing and dining and spending the night with a sweet woman in my arms, my life belongs to literature. And so I left Paris that autumn to do my research and am now glad I did, for I have the most fascinating story to tell of my experience.

Arriving in Pisa, I hired a driver to take me to the village of Petrognano where I had to check on some facts and spend a few days. There was a certain country inn where I'd planned to lunch, stay the afternoon and sleep the night. In the days to follow, I would inspect the layout of the area for literary purposes.

Riding in over the countryside, the hills were burnished gold and copper. The black forms of the peasants who worked collecting chestnuts and olives in the fields dotted the landscape. And with their bulky capes, and their large harvest sacks, they resembled those great European bison that graze in the Caucasus.

Arriving in Petrognano, we rode up a winding road and stopped in front of a quaint little inn: La Locanda Villa B***[1]. This

---

[1] LA LOCANDA VILLA B***: The use of asterisks to disguise proper names, (which Payne has already demonstrated on the first page of this novel when naming the 'Café ****' in Paris), may not be familiar to readers who are not accustomed to reading 18th century European novels. This technique, which is found

was the inn I had travelled from Paris to find, and it was in front of this inn that I saw a most touching scene. A scene I will relate to you now...

A man with a very handsome face, not by any means old, although no longer in his first-youth, was preparing to leave on a journey. His driver was urging him to give the authorization for the two to depart so that they would reach his destination by nightfall (I found out later that he was going to Florence). The reason he was being held-up was because on his lap there was seated a young girl. She was not a child, no, although she was not yet quite an adult. She was somewhere in her teens, perhaps sixteen, maybe seventeen. She sat on his lap shedding an abundance of tears, making it clear that his leaving her was the source of her sorrows. My vision wasn't too great from far away, and so I approached closer. I had a better look and noticed that the girl was of extraordinary beauty. Despite her extreme youth and the fact that her hair was in complete disorder, despite too her wild show of emotions with tears spouting from her eyes, she had the air of a fine and noble lady about her, so that I didn't doubt for a moment that she was a girl of first rank. No doubt this feminine creature would grow even more beautiful and noble as the years advanced her into womanhood. The man too, who seemed equally miserable to be saying goodbye to the girl, although it was obvious his masculinity kept him from visibly crying quite so profusely a flood of tears, was so fine in the build of his body, and the sophistication of his dress, right to the elegance of his face, that I didn't doubt for a minute that he came from the highest class of citizen. So that the two together, this handsome and elegant gentleman, together with this unbelievably beautiful child, made for the most awe-inspiring couple I had ever seen in my life. I initially took the girl for his niece or his baby sister. He certainly was not old enough to be her father, though she was closer to the age of a daughter than that of a peer. The way they hugged and cried in each other's arms, I was sure they

---

throughout *The Wanderess,* has a history of use in literature where it censors names so as to protect the reputations of places; as well as of people who might not enjoy the fame of being named in a work of fiction, albeit of literature. [Editor]

were brother and sister, sharing some family tragedy. I thus became very curious, yet I watched their scene of farewell from as far as I could without distancing myself to where my vision would blur and my hearing be naught.

Between tears and embraces, the handsome gentleman whose face was quite pale as though torn by a grief that had been aching him for some time, promised the girl that he would return at daybreak the following morning, swearing that only one night would ever separate them again, that after this night they would be linked for life. The girl kept asking him to give her one last kiss before he left, and kissed him so passionately, abandoning herself to him completely, that I no longer had any doubt that he was anything besides her lover. Over and over she cried that this was surely the last time they would see each other, that something *could happen*—perhaps something *would happen* to him on the road?—and spilling ever more tears, she finally allowed herself to be freed from his lap so that the man's driver could set off on the journey.

As the gentleman started riding away, I could see him choking heavily on his own tears, now that the two were actually separated. He called back to the girl that he would waste no time and soon would return to find her at the inn and the two would never again part company for as long as they lived. Although the girl wept at this, spilling a flood of tears that seemed never to end, she was not so generous in words, and offered no response to his hopeful vows. This is something that surprised me, as if she knew something that he did not know. I would soon find out that my suspicion was right, that there was a secret between them—or *dividing them*, rather. And so, with my heart torn by this touching scene between two handsome people I'd chanced upon in the yard, I bid my driver take a break from his duties so I could eat a meal in the restaurant of the inn, take some notes on my surroundings for literary purposes, and relax my body that was weary and sore after such a long journey. I fancied that in sleeping at this same lodging where the girl would be sleeping while she waits for her lover to return the next morning, I might chance upon a discussion with her and find out what such an enchanting-looking creature was like in person.

It was then while I was in the dining room, sitting at a table near the hall where guests at the inn check-in and out, that I heard something that startled me: this young girl who had just been swearing her eternal devotion to the man who was at this time travelling to Florence, was now at the check-out counter whispering to the innkeeper that she would need to leave the inn that very moment, *and not a moment longer*; that she would be travelling on—"alone, and far"—and needed her bags brought down in the instant. When they asked what they would tell Signore when he returned from Florence, she made the sound of money piling on the counter and I gathered that this money would purchase some desired response. I could tell by the sounds exchanged once they had accepted the money that Signore would hear simply: *that* she had left, and *how* she had left, but nothing as to the route or destination of Signorina.

I, who had been so touched by the scene of affection shared between these seemingly perfect lovers as the gentleman was leaving, became horribly disturbed that this little angel who had spilled so many tears then could now be heartless enough as to abandon her lover without so much as a word as to where she was going! I quickly signed for my meal and went out to find her and inquire about the situation. She had gone out into the yard. I was determined to get to the bottom of the matter, even if it meant following her wherever she was going, or else, by seeking-out her lover in Florence. It was true, I had my literary research that obliged me to stay and inspect the Villa B*** and the surrounding countryside, and even to interview some peasants, read vernacular books, study local plants and the like, but I decided that if such a tender scene of romance and affection between two lovers could be followed immediately by a scene of such deceit and betrayal, well then I didn't need to concern myself with literary research—or literature at all, for that matter!—since this scene of deceit and betrayal was proving that the world didn't have any meaning or purpose, and therefore literature had no meaning or purpose, and so the world didn't even deserve literature! Deeply disturbed and unhappy due to all I'd overheard, I left the dining hall and went out into the yard to see where the girl was going with the porter who hurried after her with her bags.

Once in the yard, the porter left the girl and placed her bags in the shade of a tree so he could go check on the status of the transportation to Rome, (it turned out she was going to Rome). When the porter came back, he told her with great regret that there had been some problem with the courier to Rome, some delay. "What kind of problem?!" she demanded of the porter. Her face paled completely. She looked horrified. "What kind of delay?!"

"The driver was trampled by a bull in Certaldo, Miss, his skull is smashed. The replacement driver won't be arriving here before very late in the evening." To this the girl sobbed ever more despairingly as she tugged with her little hands at the lace hem of her skirt. She looked up and flashed her pair of eyes betraying extreme worry. The porter offered to give her a room where she could wait till evening and have an excellent meal prepared at the inn's expense, but she told him through her veil of tears that she couldn't stay another moment at the inn, and that if fate had dealt her such a miserable hand as it appeared it had, she would suffer the road alone with her shoes scuffing in the dust. Although how was she to carry her bags?! In despair, she plopped herself down on her luggage and told the porter to come find her in the yard the moment the transportation was ready to leave for Rome. With the porter gone, she began again to spill an endless flood of tears into her cupped hands.

I who was meanwhile still a discreet witness to this scene was so incredibly touched to see a girl so young and beautiful crying so magnificently that I decided to approach her in a gentle manner. When she heard the crunching of my shoes on the gravel beside her, she stopped weeping and looked up at me with great modesty. Her tender cheeks were steaming with hot tears. I introduced myself, and not waiting for her to reply, I told her that I'd overheard her request to go to Rome, as well as the response that the transport to Rome wouldn't be leaving until late in the evening; so to save her waiting the entire day and evening in the yard, I would take her there myself, we would leave in a few minutes. After all, I had some important research I needed to do in Rome and was going there myself. This latter remark was a lie, as the only literary research I had need of in Italy concerned Tuscany, but I was anxious to find out the story of this matchless girl. Needless to say, she accepted my offer, her face beamed with relief and gleamed with hope. So within a quarter of an hour, my driver was around loading her luggage in the rear with my own, and everyone climbed in and we were off! ...me, myself, and the loveliest girl in Europe. My joy knew no bounds as we wound around the burnished gold and copper hills of the Italian landscape. We dashed down roads, and my heart expanded with joy.

The poor girl cried so uncontrollably for the first part of the journey, pouring endless tears onto her shoulders, soaking her little shirt, that it was impossible to find out anything from her, or about her. We spoke for the first time when we reached Siena. I asked her where she was going in Rome, if she knew the city and had someone to meet, someplace to stay, or if she would be travelling on from Rome. She pressed a cloth to her eyes and said that she was travelling on from Rome immediately by boat. She needed to catch a boat to leave Italy, to leave Europe entirely, all as soon as possible. I laughed through my nose at this and replied that it was very fortunate to learn this now, in Siena, as this was the point to turn off for all port destinations. "There is no port in Rome," I told her, "and to get a boat one has to go to Civitavecchia, which is on the coast, about three leagues closer to us than Rome, about seventeen leagues from Rome, should I have taken you there first." She thanked me for being a good guide, apologizing that she only knew the north of Italy and that she would very much like my driver to take us to Civitavecchia so she could take a boat and leave the country. She then resumed her crying.

I continued to be fascinated by this weeping, and by all of womankind. How is it that a woman lets a man go to Florence as he swears his love for her, saying that he will be back at daybreak the following day so the two can never again part, and while she doesn't exactly swear a promise to be there to meet him at daybreak, she gives him all the reason in the world to make him believe that she *will* be there, her love and passion for him being so strong, her tears being so numerous. Then finally the moment the hopeful gentleman leaves, the woman turns into a cold and calculating absconder who pays-off hotel staff-members with gold to make sure that they deceive the poor devil who will return at the point of day only to have his heart completely shattered. Then she finds she can't get to Rome on her own that day, so she allows a masculine stranger to shuttle her across the wide, strange earth, on roads she doesn't know, to places with names like 'Civitavecchia'; and all the way she sobs, spilling liters of tears as though *the one who was truly broken-hearted* by this whole affair was *she!* — 'Oh, womankind! You will never cease to confuse me!'

Not being able to handle it anymore, having the whole future of literature as dependent on the answer as my own well-being, I finally turned to the girl on the journey and said:

"Mademoiselle... or perhaps, *Madame*... Please just instruct me on one thing... This handsome gentleman you just abandoned in Tuscany... I could see by your tears you were shedding back at the inn, and continue to spill in my car just now, that he is no simple companion nor casual affection, but a great lover and friend. And no doubt from his appearance, and from his own sorrowful face and shedding of tears—which although were fewer than your own, were just as potent and showed to come from a heart just as broken, for no doubt his masculinity restricted some of the tears he would have liked to shed, for I as a man myself know that whatever didn't pour from his eyes in the way of brine, poured in his heart in the way of blood, and so he was ever deserving of your love and pity... So why on earth should you abandon a man so deserving?! You will let him come back tomorrow at daybreak to a cold Tuscan inn filled with strangers to find his one true love is gone! The hotel keepers will keep the truth from him for the gold that you filled their pockets with. Please tell me why you left him."

"Dear Sir," responded the girl with a voice so clear and light and so very feminine that hearing it sent shudders of joy through the masculine chambers of my heart; she looked up at me modestly, soft as a lamb, and her tender cheeks shone with fresh stains of the tears she neglected to wipe, she spoke thus: "Please, Sir, I will tell you all that you ask, for I am deeply indebted to you for driving me down to the port where I can set sail and leave Italy alone, anonymous, and unfollowed... I will surely tell you all and I will not lie to you about whatever you ask of me... never will I lie to you! ...for I always acknowledge the generosity of others; only I *beg* of you that you *do not ask me* where I am going, *nor why!* For if I tell you the truth, it will put you in a terribly awkward position. The story is so sad, and its participants are such undeserving victims, that you will certainly feel obliged to tell Saul—('Saul' is the name of the man with whom you saw me this morning)—you will feel obliged to drive back to Tuscany to find him and tell him all that I told you and where I am sailing to, for he does not deserve the fate that awaits him, neither do I. So please, Sir, again I will tell you the truth if you ask, only please... please... *do not ask!*" With these words spoken, she resumed spilling tears. I kept my silence, and remarked to myself the rare nobility of this remarkable girl for the fact that she begged me not to ask her about her secret for the mere reason alone that she would refuse me no favor and tell me no lie, but that she thought it better for the outcome of her story for me to remain ignorant. She and I continued down the Italian road, as the golden evening sun made its heavenly fall.

Only once more did the girl and I speak before reaching the port at Civitavecchia. It was a moment she had stopped crying and was looking sadly out at the landscape passing by. I took the opportunity to ask her name, and she turned her big eyes to me which were still soft with tears. She fluttered her eyelashes, her eyes sparkling—a slight hesitation—then she answered: "Saskia."

I, who am a seasoned studier of characters, took this hesitation and fluttering of eyelashes to be a sign that she was deciding whether or not to lie to me about her name, but in the end she had told me the truth. Saskia, I knew, was a name that belonged to the Saxon people. The only Saskia I'd ever heard of was the wife of the painter Rembrandt. She smiled after she told me her name, as though she were happy she had not lied to me, that she had told me the truth after all. She then asked me my name. I told her.

"*Enchantée*[1]," she replied in French, and then turned back to look out at the road and the world passing outside the window.

---

[1] ENCHANTÉE: *(Fr)* "Nice to meet you." (Feminine form. Root of English word "enchanted")

We arrived at Civitavecchia where all kinds of ships were present, large and miniscule, ready to take passengers and fishermen here and there over the girth of this great and pleasant earth. I asked Saskia if she did not want me to help her find the ship that was going where she wanted to go, but she again begged me to remain ignorant. She turned to me and called me with familiarity by my first name and clasped my hands and with tears in her eyes she asked that I demand my driver to stop far up from the piers so that she could wander alone to her ship. She would find the right ship alone. There were porters and guides who carried bags for two sous lining the streets. I told my driver to stop and help the girl get her bags, and as soon as a uniformed porter came to help her with her bags, she paid him some coins and he helped her disappear into the crowds of the seaport, off in the direction of the water.

I who had the whole sphere of literature on my shoulders the way Atlas bore the earth on his, needed to find out the secret of this couple named Saul and Saskia. I refused to let it end there. My curiosity was eating my insides. I told my driver to wait for me, and slinked off into the crowds towards the port.

It wasn't difficult to find Saskia again, walking with a hired porter, as the porter had quite a lot of bags to carry and so walked slow enough to be overtaken quickly. I lurched in the throngs of passengers and laborers so as not to be seen should Saskia have the intuition to turn suddenly around and look to see if she were being followed. I soon saw her walking with the porter straight for an enormous vessel that was preparing to leave the harbor. Her little feet stepped up the ramp and the ship captain's crew took the bags from her porter; then, in an instant, the country of Italy lost its most beautiful inhabitant as Miss Saskia stood on a surface that had no nationality but belonged to the holy blue sea.

Once Saskia's boat was out of sight, I approached the dock where the boat had launched to enquire about its destination.

"Yes, Sir? That boat, you ask? It is bound direct for Tripoli, Sir, in Libya."

"Tripoli?!"

"Yes, Sir! First and final destination!"

With that, I turned on my heels and walked back to the car with an imagination that swam wildly in my head. I had no doubt about where I was headed next.

Chapter Two

Excited by the intrigue, I ordered my driver to take us quickly back to Tuscany, back to the inn at Petrognano.

"Wouldn't it be more reasonable, sir, to find a hotel here and stay for the night? We could leave at the point of day."

"I'm not interested in *reason*, but in *literature!* Thank you, though, for your input. Off we go!"

I was hoping to make it back by daybreak the next day, but my obedient driver pledged to do his best so that we would arrive sooner, in the middle of the night. With that we were off with great speed back to Petrognano. While the scenery passed outside, I thought about the girl's voyage to Tripoli. What would she find when she arrived in Africa? Who would be greeting her? What, *or whom*, was she seeking? I wondered about her story. A beautiful child like that travelling alone to Libya? I was certain that this story had an unusual mystery, and it wouldn't be too long before I would find out that I was right. There *was* a mystery—one stranger than I could imagine.

In the darkest hour of night, we arrived back in Petrognano. The inn looked different on this moonless night, illuminated only by the numerous stars. The black forms of the olive trees rustling in the wind seemed to pass like ghosts over the elusive landscape. The air smelled of dying grass. A weary porter came in the silent yard to usher me to my room. I bid him goodnight and requested to be woken a half-hour before dawn. He said of course, that he would be seeing me very soon.

I read a little bit by a candle and then blew it out and fell asleep. The room was still dark when I awoke, and the bluish light of dawn was soaking into the blackness of the night sky as I entered the cold yard where the dew was dropping down on the fence, the lawn, the tables and chairs. I asked that my coffee be brought to me.

The coffee was strong, and despite the lack of sleep, I felt strangely refreshed. I enjoyed taking notes about this beautiful country in my leather writing-book at the onset of dawn as the autumn birds sang timidly in their dark nests. A half-hour passed, the sun began to rise, bold and beautiful. I saw golden dust picking-up on the horizon with the arrival of a car.

Saul returned to the inn at daybreak as promised. His driver opened the door and Saul's tall figure stepped out and began to walk towards the inn. His suit that had looked elegant the day before was now wrinkled as though he had not changed out of it during the night. I gathered that he hadn't slept at all. His face was puffy and white, like the skin of a cadaver. The only color shone in various splotches of red on his cheeks. Now that he gazed at the inn where he mistakenly believed his beloved lay sleeping, waiting for him, his face grew hopeful, his eyes widened, a uniform complexion filled-out his cheeks and he beamed with health and joy. While Saul walked through the yard to the Villa B***, the porter chased after him with his luggage. I watched Saul disappear behind the front door of the inn where the reception desk was. The door closed. I heard a moment of silence. My eyes made a cursory inspection around the entryway to the inn and I saw various workers, porters, attendants, maids and valets and the like, all busy at simple tasks as they began the day of work. As soon as everyone heard the sound of a human body fall and thump loudly against a hollow wooden floor, these valets and attendants and porters dropped their tasks, their buckets and ladders, and scurried in to see what had happened.

I too joined the bustle at the reception. We were quite a crowd. We saw the gentleman had lost consciousness, had fallen on the floor and hit his head. He looked quite dead. The porters scurried to find a nurse. I asked the concierge what had happened. He told me that he had informed the gentleman that the young girl who had been staying with him at the inn had left the day before and that she had given no word as to where she was going. She had checked out, taking all her luggage with her, and left in the car belonging to some, quote: 'other man.' He apparently didn't recognize *me* as that other man. The concierge said the gentleman suffered some kind of seizure, then fainted. This whole scene gave me a feeling of disgust. I looked at the calm expression of the concierge to whom these events meant nothing as the girl's gold clinked in his pockets, and with the greatest sorrow and pity at seeing the unconscious gentleman lying on the ground, I thought of how sorrowful he would still be when he would wake up and learn from me that the news is true, that his mistress is no longer in the country, that she is sailing away from Europe, coasting along over the hot, blue sea.

Chapter Three

Before the gentleman regained consciousness, he was carried by four porters into an empty bedroom that was down the hall from the concierge. I went into the café to drink another coffee and asked that I be informed when the man's health allowed that I pay him a visit. When I was told that he was awake and receiving visitors, I walked down the hall and stationed myself outside the door of the bedroom where I overheard the owner of the inn repeating to Saul that the girl had definitely left the inn, that she had left with some other man, and no one at the inn had any idea where she had gone to, although it was certain that she wasn't coming back. I heard a groan so horrible in pitch; I stepped back and watched the owner of the inn appear in the doorway before me, clutching his hat, looking pensive and unhappy. He glanced at me, bowed deep with respect, and passed. I followed him with my eyes and then introduced myself into the room that was empty except for a single bed upon which Saul was sprawled-out, fully-clothed, a nightstand beside him. He looked as though he would die at any moment. His face and neck were flushed bone-white except for the lump of pink on his neck where his Adam's apple rose and dropped as he took feeble swallows of air. The rest was white and lifeless, except for the rims of his eyelids, which were purple with sleeplessness and an excess of tears.

I approached the bedside, "Forgive me for entering unannounced. (I recall we spoke in French, as he didn't speak Italian.) I heard about your situation with your charming companion, and since I was present yesterday when the two of you said your touching farewell in the yard before you left for Florence, and was witness to the strong emotions and vows of love exchanged between you two, I cannot help taking a great interest in your case, and the outcome of your affair."

"It's awful," he said to me, "It has to be a lie! She is not this cruel... *Is she* this cruel?! It is true then! This woman is going to kill me..."

"I myself have been witness to the cruelty of women," I told him, "and am constantly amazed at womankind's threshold for cruelty; however, I was also a witness to the tears and amount of love and devotion this particular young creature showed for you as she left here yesterday. And in my experience, when a woman's cruelty is combined with love and devotion, it is almost always without exception an act performed not out of treachery, but as a painful self-sacrifice for the good of her beloved, to obtain for him a future bounty where he would not know how to obtain it for himself, or have the courage, patience, or foresight to obtain it. Womankind always seems to be able to see a dozen steps into the future, far ahead of what men are able to see. And they have strength where we do not."

The poor devil's face did not react positively to what I was saying. He remained pale and lifeless. "I just came back from Florence," he told me, "where I learned that I had lost all that was important to me in this world, other than my mistress. Last night was the most painful... I spent the night in a graveyard, trembling beside a small tomb where there were no flowers, only a simple stone etched with a phrase that tore my soul to pieces every time I read it. I read it and reread it thousands of times until nothing remained of my soul except tiny scraps that were held together by the consolation that my beloved was here at this inn waiting for me. Then in the dark hours before dawn, I left that tomb and that person who lies beneath it forever and I returned here to find my beloved mistress has left me too. It appears she went away with another man. I don't understand how it is possible...."

"*I* am the other man she went away with."

When I said this, Saul shot upright in bed. He shook violently. His face that had been pale turned red and his eyes burned like fire. His lips curled with both the hope that there now stood before him someone who knew where his mistress might be, and the rage that he was now looking at the devil who stole his beloved. He reached into his pocket, muttering about a knife, then a pistol, "I'll kill you!" he shouted. But finding neither knife nor pistol, he tore the blanket off his body and leapt from his bed, "I'll strangle you!"

"Settle down! Listen to me carefully, please lie back in your bed. I'll tell you the rest of the story..." I approached the bedside, sat down and urged Saul to listen calmly. "This is the reason why I came back to find you: Yesterday your mistress was determined to leave this inn *by herself* as soon as you left for Florence. She arranged for a car to take her in the evening to go to Rome...

"Because I took a liking to you two, at noontime yesterday when I observed you from afar as you told her you would be back for her in the morning at daybreak, whereupon you two would never again part company—you see, sir, I have a tender heart for such romantic moments, even when I am not a lucky participant—so, because I took a liking to you two as a couple, I decided that I needed to take her to Rome *myself*, so that I could find out where she was ultimately going, and why, so as to return here and report this information to you. Don't you realize, if it hadn't been I who had taken her, it would have been someone else? And that someone certainly wouldn't have come back to tell *you* about it—for very few men have tender hearts when they have nothing to gain, but much to lose. And that girl of yours is much to lose."

"What do you say? She is in Rome?"

"No, she is not in Rome because there are no boats in Rome. Your mistress wasn't sure exactly *how* to leave Italy. In Civitavecchia, I told her she could catch a foreign-bound boat, and so to Civitavecchia I took her. The whole trip down, she cried, and cried. She appeared no less miserable than you do now. And the reason for her sorrow was simply because she was leaving you. This I promise. Oh, women!—you *are* mysterious creatures! I did find out *to where* she was leaving you to, but I did not find out *why*. She tried to conceal from me her destination, asking me not to inquire for she did not want you to know. She foresaw that should she tell me her destination I would be inclined to come find you and inform you of the fact. She knew I wouldn't hide this information from you because she said that you were undeserving of the misery of which I would judge you an unfortunate victim upon hearing the story. She tried to hide her destination from me, but my duties to humanity obliged me to investigate. I found out that she was going to Tripoli; and it is to Tripoli she is now travelling at this very moment we speak."

"Tripoli!" Saul cried. His face contorted with the awful realization of what the world was doing to his poor life. "Insane gods have written this story!" he cried, "Ô, why?, I ask, why would Saskia have gone to Tripoli of all places?!" Hearing Saul rant like this, I couldn't help smiling. 'It just keeps on getting better and better,' I thought. The miserable man then quit his bed and ran for the door. Before he could escape, however, I grabbed hold of his shirt... "Don't rush, old boy—I'll help you! I helped *her*, after all, so I can equally help *you*. Now tell the porter to ready your bags. I will have my driver take us to Civitavecchia this very instant." I turned away and shook my head wondering why I was getting involved in such a drama. It had already been a long week of travel for me. I turned back to Saul and said, "I should really stay off the road, but... I'm a foolish romantic at heart, and a literary man besides; I want to get you on the next boat to Tripoli so you can reunite with your beloved Saskia."

When I said this, Saul stopped weeping and embraced me. "That's right!" he trembled, "Her name is Saskia! How did you know?"

"She told me!" I laughed, charmed by the simplicity of his question, "And she told me that you are named Saul. But don't worry about me. Come, let us drive you to the Italian port. We must set you to sail, old boy. You are on your quest—and I am on my chore; you will find your girl again—down on the African shore!"

Chapter Four

Combining mankind's love of habit with the frequency of the déjà-vu phenomenon, it seems like we are creatures of repetition. Here I was again on the road from Tuscany to the seaport at Civitavecchia. Inspired by love and compassion, we traveled *ventre à terre*[1], kicking up dust. This time, I didn't have a beautiful young girl crying beside me. I had a handsome gentleman crying beside me—and how he cried! My Italian research trip was certainly taking an interesting turn. I begged Saul to tell me his story and that of his mistress, but he was in no condition to talk. His sadness brought him a fever, and I had to order my driver to fetch cold compresses for him at several intervals during the journey. Only one time did he speak on the way to the port, when he swore on his honor that he would remember his debt to me until he saw me again and could repay me. "We are certain to

---

[1] VENTRE À TERRE: *(Fr)* "Belly to the ground," very fast.

meet again," he said, "I will pay you then all that I can. Remember my name is my word of honor. *I am Saul, the son of Solarus.*"

The devil set the table that day when Saul told me his patronymic: *The son of Solarus.* "The son of Solarus?!" ...Where had I heard that name before?! I couldn't place it. It sounded so familiar! Unsure of the reason, although haunted by the unsettling feeling that this story concerned me more than I initially suspected, I sat pensive and turned my eyes to look at the countryside as we rode along.

Arriving at the port of Civitavecchia, I helped Saul find a boat to Tripoli. I paid for his ticket and asked if he had much money to get him by. He shrugged his shoulders and said that all the money that they had, he and his mistress, happened to be in her purse at the moment. I took out fifteen *sequins* to offer to get him by. He politely refused saying that he could accept no further favors from me. His pride and nobility made him too polite to accept even the smallest banknote as charity, let alone a handful of gold sequins. But I forced the money on him anyway with the argument that should all my efforts to first bring his girlfriend to the port and find out through spying where she was going, then to return to Tuscany and pull him from his deathbed to drive him down to the port and get him on a boat so he could follow her to another continent; if somewhere along the way his efforts to reunite with his mistress met with failure because of a lack of money, I would feel that all my charity work would have been for naught, in which case I'd be greatly annoyed. One doesn't risk one's life to save a cat from a burning house only to take him down afterwards to the cat-kennel where he will die from neglect a month later like the strays that share his lot. After he is saved from the flames, one must find him a loving old widow to adopt him. This winning argument convinced the unhappy gentleman to accept the fifteen sequins; then, praising me to the fullest extent that his energy would allow, he swore he would never forget the, quote, "sublime generosity of my heart." Then, embracing me, the poor devil said for as long as he lived he would remember me, anticipating the day when he could return the fifteen sequins I gave him, and perhaps save my life as well.

We both said goodbye and Saul reminded me of his name fearing I would otherwise forget. Once more hearing his patronymic made my shoulders tighten-up. I felt confusion. I racked my brains trying to remember where I'd heard his title before: *The son of Solarus.* Meanwhile, the porter helped steady Saul as he walked up the plank, his luggage trailing behind him, and all disappeared into the ship. As the horn blew and the sun shone, and the waves turned up on the beach, and a tear rolled down my cheek, I watched the departing ship for Tripoli and hoped in my heart that this miserable man would soon reunite with his beautiful princess. I hoped too that that girl wasn't the treacherous and vile creature that she had seemed to be that morning, rather that she was faithful and virtuous and would have a good excuse for having left him the way she did. I hoped that she was good and pure, and their future be a happy one.

Marveling on the nature of love, I headed back to find my driver so he could take me up that now-familiar road to Tuscany. This adventure had cost me a little money and a couple days of my non-infinite life. I was exhausted from lack of sleep, but overall I was happy to have taken part in this event that would have turned out differently had I not been there.

Chapter Five

I didn't hear anything else about the matter, and had almost forgotten about Saul and Saskia, when, back in Paris a couple months later, I ran across the reason why Saul's name had struck me with such familiarity. I'd just returned from Corsica and Mallorca, and was back home in Paris on a late winter day looking through some old novel notes from several years back. Attached to these notes was a newspaper clipping from *The Spy Telegraph.* (The reader will note that in my literary research, I often scour police reports and espionage newspapers such as *L'Espion* and *The Spy Telegraph*, as detective and criminal accounts often provoke interesting ideas for characters.)[1]

---

[1]Payne describes this mania for scouring newspapers for character ideas as a trait common among certain novelists, the best of them being Fyodor Dostoevsky. The reader will note that Payne doesn't uses this method and takes almost no interest in current events. He relies almost completely on his imagination for character invention. If a woman or friend in his life doesn't supply a character, then it might be a stranger, but never a newspaper. [Editor]

...And there it was!

In a newspaper clipping I had saved from over three years back, there was the following announcement:

> ENORMOUS BOUNTY TO BE PAID FOR THE DELIVERANCE TO TRIPOLI, ALIVE OR DEAD, OF A CERTAIN OUTLAW, A MAN KNOWN AS 'THE SON OF SOLARUS,' GUILTY OF CRIMES COMMITTED AGAINST THE KING OF THAT LAND. THE REWARD: 25,000 LOUIS D'OR, (CURRENTLY VALUED AT: 600,000 FRANCS).

"Good God!" I cried, "Twenty-five thousand gold louis! Why, that's enough to make the wealth of an entire family!—oh, that poor, handsome young gentleman, he couldn't have been guilty of anything that bad..."

The announcement then went on to describe this "son of Solarus," and it even showed an artist's depiction of the wanted-man that resembled Saul more or less. The happy announcement concluded by saying, "Should the son of Solarus be brought-in alive, he will be promptly executed in one of Tripoli's fine public squares for the enjoyment of all citizens present."

Attached to that saved newspaper clipping was a note where I jotted a reminder to myself to "someday" write a story about this "son of Solarus" character, as his sort interested me. Needless to say, I never got around to writing the story, and over the years I had completely forgotten about him; but now I realized why when back in Italy on the road to Civitavecchia, hearing his name startled and unnerved me.

I read the clipping again and pounded the surface of my writing desk with my fist. "I put him on the boat, damn it! I therefore led him to slaughter! ...He couldn't have known there was a warrant for his head—or else he wouldn't have gone to Tripoli the way he did!

"...Maybe he did know," I further mused, "and it was the love of his fair Saskia that drove him there despite the risk? Could it have been so?! Nonsense! How could Saul anticipate lying in a bed with his beloved without a head?! No, he certainly couldn't have known about the bounty on his head. When I put him on that boat, he didn't know I was sending him to be butchered..."

I then buried my head in my hands... 'Now Saul is dead. That fine, handsome young man with such beautiful manners is dead... *and I am to blame!* Why didn't I remember this newspaper clipping when I was in Italy? My generous altruism combined with my lousy memory brought an ignoble death to that most noble of gentlemen! If anyone deserved to live to a happy old age, it was he. Oh, I am a foolish, old monster, etc...'

While lamenting my goodwill, I tucked that newspaper clipping away from my sight and went on with my life. Remorse passes quickly in winter and nothing was further from my thoughts when, a year and some months later, while the spring flowers were in bloom, I ran into both Saul and Saskia again together in the French town of Calais.

I'd mentioned that I'd had some literary research that was calling me to the north of France. A mysterious inn called *Au Bras d'Or*, where the adventurer Casanova claimed to have lodged while laid-up with venereal disease in Calais after his ten-month sojourn in England, has stumped scholars for years.[1] I planned to solve the mystery by finally locating this elusive inn and detailing its surroundings. So after the autumn in Tuscany, and the winter in Corsica and the Balearic Islands I went back to Paris and worked on a new book for another year. At last, when the first rays of the glorious spring filled my cheeks at the beginning of April in the year ****, I collected my literary notes to record my travels and made my way across French soil to the northern tip of this illustrious country.

It was a fine day. I had only been in the town for a few hours when, while strolling down by the piers where the ferries and freight ships come in and out, I caught a glimpse of England across the Strait of Dover. The day was bright and the white cliffs of Dover shone like a shield on the water. I thought how I would soon need to cross that body of water to meet with the English ambassador to France and visit a specific garden; but I still had a few days in Calais to wander around the town, to visit the taverns

[1] *Histoire de ma vie*, Jacques Casanova de Seingalt, Vol. 10 – Ch. II, Ed. Robert Laffont.

and meet local people and travelers, and to fathom the mystery of *Au Bras d'Or.*

It was while I was gazing on Dover that I noticed a ferry some twenty meters down from the elevated deck where I was standing that was ready to disembark for England. It was the same ferry that I would take in a few days; so with the aim of reading the timetable, so as to know when to arrive at the dock to catch my own boat to England, I wandered down the steps. It was then I saw something that made me rub my eyes with disbelief:

The crew was about to untie the ropes so the boat could set sail, but they were waiting for a couple—a young woman and a man, both very well-dressed—to stop kissing and caressing each other where they stood on the passenger plank, so that the crew could pull the plank onto the boat. It became clear as they tried to separate from each other a half-dozen times, always unsuccessfully, that the man was going to return to land and the woman was going to stay on the boat to cross the Channel to England. She obviously didn't want him to go, and kept holding him with all her might as she smothered his face and body with innumerable kisses. He likewise demonstrated a distaste for her departure as he returned her kisses with a million testimonies of his own love. Finally, the captain announced that the plank absolutely needed to be pulled. The gentleman acquiesced and stepped down onto the land so the boat could disembark. Squinting my eyes to see more clearly, I noticed that this man was the same man I met in Italy a year and a half before! It was Saul! He was alive!...

As you remember... the last time I saw Saul, I was putting our dear adventurer on a boat in Italy bound for Tripoli—(Tripoli: where it had slipped by me that there was a twenty-five thousand louis d'or bounty on his head [some six hundred thousand francs...] ...where I believed he'd been arrested, tortured, and finally executed...). But now it was a fine spring day, and Saul was alive!

Then I saw *her!*—it was Saskia! She was standing on the ship, separated from her love by a few meters of sea-water, beautiful as a goddess—Ô, Heavenly Saskia! And to tell how she had changed in only a year and a half... She was no longer a gypsy child, now she commanded her full femininity, she had bloomed into the beautiful perfection of womanhood!

I recall the day I put her on that boat in Italy to sail to Tripoli, her eyes were then filled with tears of despair. Now her tears were of love and hope. She blew one more kiss to Saul as the boat made to disembark. The last time I had seen Saul, it was the day after a terrible tragedy; he was miserable and disheveled. Now, he was happy, elegantly dressed in a fine, tailored suit. He observed Saskia who was still just a few meters away. She was leaning over the railing, blowing him kiss after kiss, crying, *"See you soon, my love!"*

"À bientôt!, mon amour!" Saul called back to her. As he said this, Saskia's face lit-up as though struck by a sudden, wonderful idea. I squinted to see. What was she up to? I then watched the clever girl reach into her purse and pull out a handful of money. I could not tell how much money as things were a little blurry from where I stood, but it appeared to be no small sum. The gold gleamed in the sunshine. Money in hand, she ran over to the captain who was ordering that the last rope connecting the boat to France be untied to set sail. Saskia stood on her tip-toes and put her little gloved-hand to her mouth and whispered something into the ear of the captain. I saw him then glance down; and seeing a handful of silver coins in her palm, he smiled to his ears. She pressed the money into his hand and he called aloud to his crew: "Throw 'em ropes back to shore! Send back yore boardin' plank!" With these orders, the crew re-connected the boat with the shore. Saskia laughed with joy, as her plan was ingenious; she ran across the plank and leapt back into the arms of Saul so that she could embrace him one final time. With adoring hands, she gave him a hundred caresses. She kissed his face all over. She rubbed her eyes against his forehead, her lips against his arms, and wherever there was skin, or no skin, clothes or no clothes, the couple embraced and shed happy tears that flew from their eyes and spilled all over the place.

As soon as the two were satiated to have said yet another loving goodbye, Saskia cried a final time, *"See you soon, my love!"* and ran back up the plank, and onto the boat, and stationed herself at the rail to watch her love while the captain and crew once again pulled-in the ropes, cables and planks. Now the vessel began to sail, and I watched from afar the beautiful figure of Saskia growing smaller and smaller, her boat becoming as subtle as a whitecap on a distant swell of the wild sea. Thus the vessel made its voyage for the country of England.

As you can guess, this tender scene between a couple whom I last saw in despair made me curious and very happy. I couldn't wait to ask Saul a million questions: What happened after Italy? How did they reunite? What happened in Tripoli? Why is Saul's head still attached to his body? What the devil are they doing they in Calais? Why is Saskia sailing to England? How come their goodbye is so joyful this time? When is she coming back? ...With these and more questions nagging at my heart, I made my way towards the pier, where Saul was walking with a great smile on his handsome face. As soon as he saw me, he recognized me immediately. His eyes grew large and he embraced me. "Dear old friend! What are the chances of seeing you here? In *this* town of all places?"

"I have some literary research to do here in Calais."

"Fortune is back on my side, I'm happy to say! Today I am in a position to pay you back for the kindness you showed me in Italy... that kindness saved my life! Here, first take this..." He dug into his pocket so fast that he nearly tore the fabric. He pulled out ten gold louis d'or and pressed them into my hand.

"What pleasure to be able to pay back this debt!" He then tried to give me more than the value of the fifteen sequins I had given him, but I refused any profit on goodwill. "Let me invite you to dine," he said, "Are you hungry? I have so much to celebrate. How is it that we're both in Calais? The chances of this! I am so *happy* to see you! I'm happy for so many reasons!"

I replied to Saul that it would be the greatest pleasure to eat with him and hear all the stories that had gone on between himself and his beautiful mistress. I told him I was staying at the *Lion d'Argent* and to meet me there in a quarter of an hour, I would just go wash-up first... I also wanted to get my leather-bound notebook, as I had a feeling I would want to take notes on what I heard. And I was right, for it was there at the *Lion d'Argent* that I would hear the most remarkable story I had ever heard.

Now, dear reader, it is with great pleasure that I retell the story to you....

Chapter Six

Saul and I took a private dining-room at the *Lion d'Argent*; its windows looked out over the sea, and at all the boats in the port. From where we sat, we could see everyone who was leaving, or coming into, the port of Calais, right down to the clothes they were wearing; although I told Saul I needed my new eyeglasses to see anything in detail. I informed him that this elegant restaurant where we were dining used to be a cabaret where ambassadors and ministers passing between England and France could enjoy the most expensive French and English girls in the North of France. Saul informed me with a laugh that he was glad his days of debauchery were past. "My *wanderess* cured me of my transient heart," he said, that used to need to go wandering itself to find those short-lived pleasures and the mediocre love among *les filles de joie*[1].

[1] LES FILLES DE JOIE: *(Fr)* Literally: 'Girls of joy' (Prostitutes).

Saul and I dined on the fine delicacies fished from the coast of northern France, and washed our feast down with champagne and white wine from *Sancerre*. After we had stayed desire for food and drink, I pressed Saul to tell me his story. He began telling me of the events that followed what I knew: After he went to Florence without Saskia, after he came back and I drove his miserable soul down to the port at Civitavecchia to sail to Tripoli. I knew when I heard the start of his adventures in Tripoli that it was going to be an amazing story, so I begged he stop his tale, that the dishes be cleared, that the wine be finished with haste, and a good bottle of cognac be brought.

I asked Saul to tell his tale in full, and to tell it right. And since I am a literary man, I begged permission to transcribe all that I heard. He gave me his word that he would tell me all from beginning to end, and leave nothing out.

"Spare me no detail!" I said, "Just, for all that's holy, tell it true and don't leave anything out... And you needn't talk slow, I am a fast writer. My pen is ready!" So while the sun beyond our window made its slow and colorful descent over the curve of the earth, and the candles on our table chugged their tall flames, and with no worries to worry me and no hurries to hurry me, I transcribed over the next twenty-four hours, in my new leather-bound notebook *The Story of Saul and Saskia* from beginning to end. Before we began, Saul took a pipe from his coat and filled it with a smoking mixture[1] and he lit the pipe and offered it to me.

"No thank you," I waved my hand, "I gave that up long ago. But I *will* toast the cognac with pleasure...

"À votre santé[2]!"

"Santé!"

And so we sipped the beautiful liquor while Saul settled into his chair with his pipe and glass, and began to tell the

[1]SMOKING MIXTURE: Although the narrator never specified the contents of this 'smoking mixture,' some sources claim that while Saul was in Calais, he regularly smoked a blend of opium mixed with smoking agents, while others claim he mixed tobacco with hashish; still most sources suggest it was simply pure, honest tobacco that was being smoked. *[Editor]*

[2] À VOTRE SANTÉ: (*Fr,* formal/polite-tense [*vous*]) "To your health!"

fabulous story which I recount to you now, word for word as he told it to me that day in Calais, with not a single syllable left out, nor changed. Here is what he said...

Chapter Seven

Saul tells his own story...

"I am Saul, the son of Solarus. My mother was the niece of the Christian king of Tripoli. My father grew up at court in close proximity to the king, but his forbidden relations with my mother brought a death sentence upon him. He was forced to commit suicide—obliged, like Socrates, to drink hemlock. My mother meanwhile, pregnant with me, escaped into exile. She relinquished her wealth at court to raise me herself, living by her own hands as well as the generosity of an old peasant couple, far from the city in a small fishing village on the sunny coast of Libya. I grew up there, tall and strong, with a vigorous spirit; I reached the age of manhood with a good constitution and a curious mind.

Biding my time in travel and adventure, for these were the ways I knew to fill the heart with joy, there came a day when the *call to adventure*—that mysterious call that arrives to certain young people—beckoned me to set out on a journey to Europe.

Now please understand... I am going to tell you this story as I felt it at the time... If I offend you with mention of past vices—although I do not believe that I could offend you—please realize that these were *past vices*; vices that belonged to a spirited creature who had to go through many troubles to become the man he is today. Back in those days I loved too many things in abundance. Women, wine, and opium were the delicacies I devoured in large quantities, for with them, I did not feel like a mortal man, but like a god. Fortunately, since then my manhood has matured. I have tamed those old appetites. Perhaps I could *almost* even be called "virtuous"? Well!, you will be the judge of that from my tale...

Yes, today I am faithful to one woman. She is my morning, she is my evening; we have a love that blooms over and again, more beautifully each time than the last. You will see that we are not lovers like others, for whom love is both a punishment *and* a gift... Our love has never punished, only rewarded. Such love therein lies the *eudaimonic life*[1]. But when our story begins, I hadn't known anyone like her. I was just a reckless adventurer. *"Pleasure!"*—that was my only concern as I embarked on this voyage to Europe several years ago. Then I met the woman of my heart... true, she was then young as a girl, though she was wiser than all women of age who have never ventured out into the world on their own. As a child, my love carried a roadmap in her hand the way other girls her age carried handkerchiefs. And so she knew the way, and it is thanks to her guidance that I became a man. And it is thanks to her that I am alive today to narrate this tale. *But let me begin at the beginning...*

It was in the 3—[th] year of my stay on this, our fruitful earth, while traveling through Cataluña on my way north to a country whereto Fortune would never bring me, that I met a brave, young orphan girl who was like me, *a wanderer*. With her enchanting songs, her rare beauty, and clever tricks, this wild "wanderess" ensnared my soul like a gypsy-thief, and led me foolish and blind to where you

---

[1] EUDAIMONIC LIFE: (Ancient Greek) εὐδαιμονία: "The flourishing life" is perhaps the best translation. In the works of Aristotle, *eudaimonia* is considered the highest human good and the aim of practical philosophy.

find me now. The first time I saw her, fires were alight. It was a spicy night in Barcelona. The air was fragrant and free. But my adventures began shortly before that. Here is how...

It was the new moon, the night was pitch black. My clothes were dirty from sleeping in a ditch since the inn near the boat docks was closed when I arrived too late at night. I had some money in my pocket: two hundred silver *piastres*, a few pieces of gold, as well as some banknotes. I'd been acting like a rascal for a period of time but I blamed it on the season.

I had crossed the Mediterranean on a boat, from Egypt to Crete; and from Crete I sailed to the Greek island of Hydra on the invitation of an old and rich export-merchant who asked me to be his guest at his home. And having arrived and dined at his house with him and his young daughter, as well as the ugly man his daughter was engaged to marry, I inquired about the quaint little island where I had come to find myself. Later, after dinner, while wandering alone up the long road that wound high over the sheer rocky cliffs, with the Aegean Sea on one side and the lonely white-washed houses where mules were roped-up on the other, I spied a plump pigeon on the dusty road happily munching a piece of cord. I thought how even he was free to take flight and sail away. He could fly to Athens, or farther yet—whereas I was bound to this barren island, and no boats in the harbor were scheduled to sail that night.

I wandered back to the house and could hear my host talking loudly with his daughter's pock-marked fiancé in the dining-room. They were busy smoking after-dinner cigars and clinking their glasses of *digestifs*. I passed to the kitchen and found his daughter wearing a short sleeping-robe, reaching for something on a high-up shelf. I came behind her and pressed my hand to her bare calf and felt that her skin was burning hot. The sensation of her skin made me forget all about her husband-to-be who was coughing in the other room while her father was telling him a story in an overloud voice. I lifted the light fabric of the daughter's sleeping-robe and put my hand under the steamy mound of her groin, and I could feel moist liquid dropping from the hairy mound like steam that shoots out of the spout of a piping-hot wine keg.

"Let's go into the spice-room," she suggested, urging me to take her by the waist.

Amid barrels of saffron and white pepper, I nestled with my host's young daughter and pulled her happy buttocks over me and drifted in and out of her moist groin—my throbbing sex rocking languidly inside her own sex like a docked skiff that rocks languidly against the piers lapping the salty waters in the dark night. When she came, she uttered a little screech and I could see the whites of her eyes disappearing in her head in the dim light of the spice-room; and a few minutes later, I was alone in the upstairs room securing my valises to travel on in the morning.

While I tried to sleep that night, still excited from my sexual adventure, the source of my pleasure snuck in to kiss me good night, and I once again cupped her smoldering sex in my large hand and she uttered a pleasurable screech.

I don't know how it happened, whether a servant betrayed us, or if the tearful girl confessed all after the lunacy and passion of night had left her, but I didn't meet with happy-breakfast the next morning, neither welcome words-upon-parting. The father and his future son-in-law somehow discovered that I had had intercourse with the girl of the house in the spice-room the night before, and it being rather impossible to marry a girl off in that part of the country without her being a virgin, the men decided to hunt me down and, quote, "lop off my head," unquote. (I learned this from the driver who took me down to the pier.) I bribed the driver well so he wouldn't betray me to the merchant or to the girl's ugly fiancé, and a few minutes later I was alone and free, sailing from Hydra to the mainland of Greece. My valises were safe by my side and I marveled at my luck for having escaped from that island without losing either property or obtaining bodily injury. Success!, I cheered—for I had both health and possession, along with the blessèd memory of the merchant's young daughter to make me smile and look forward to glorious nights to come—for when you see the first sprouts, I think you know the grain that follows. My luck in the past was always good. True, there was no *ligne de chance*[1] on my left hand, but I didn't believe that that mattered.

After arriving in Piraeus, I traveled up to Athens; then into the country of Albania, meeting no hardship, and took the boat from Vlorë to the sunny shores of Italy.

I soon arrived in the town of M****, and found lodging and explained the business of my filthy appearance to the innkeeper. I gave her a large tip to show her I wasn't some vagabond without money and she gave my bundle of dirty clothes to the blind washerwoman to be cleaned. After eating a meal of cold eggs, I stretched out naked on the bed in the room I'd let. My eyes drifted from the ceiling to the window. Beyond the window stood a pleasant courtyard square, adorned in the center with a fountain. The courtyard wasn't large, but the walls on either side were tall and they both had arched doorways that led away into the common streets of the town. In the back was a portico supported by stone pillars. The courtyard seemed rather ornate considering the humble, almost plain, character of the town surrounding it; the bubbling fountain beneath my window seemed to me rather peaceful and overall I liked the room and the inn, although the meal was bad.

Lying naked on the bed, I chewed a piece of leather for want of something to put in my mouth; all the while I thumbed through the only book I had in my possession. It was a copy of *The Odyssey* in Greek. I was having the damnedest time deciphering the Greek. I'd had a perfectly good French translation of *The Odyssey* when I was in Alexandria, but I traded it for this Greek copy while on the ship crossing the sea because it was to be an even trade—book for book—and it seemed to me that I was getting the more 'authentic' item in the bargain.

I slept all evening and only awoke when the innkeeper brought the dinner. The meal was a bland stew *gratiné* with cabbage. I didn't complain about the cooking, but asked that she knock next time before entering, as I had been asleep naked on the bed, and my sex grew hard when I awoke—as naturally happens to men when roused from sleep; but she informed me

[1] LIGNE DE CHANCE: *(Fr)* Luck line

that such things didn't bother her—she grew up in a house with eight brothers; and, anyway, her curious years were, quote, "dried-up," as she put it, and the handsome sight of a nude man stirred her heart no more than the sight of two dogs playing in the yard. This bit of news didn't interest me, and I begged she leave me alone after dressing the table and setting the stew down along with a half-liter of red wine. I read from Homer all evening—keeping to the passages I knew by heart to relieve me of having to know each word of the Greek—and when night came, I saw the full moon rising outside the window: a magnificent silver disc hovering in the black abyss of sky. I thought of a vision I'd seen recently before in which the ocean at night had been as black and as deep as that eternal night's sky, and I fancied my luck to be witnessing yet another full moon. True, I'd seen hundreds of full moons in my life, but they were not limitless. When one starts thinking of the full moon as a common sight that will come again to one's eyes ad-infinitum, the value of life is diminished and life goes by uncherished. 'This may be my last moon,' I sighed, feeling a sudden sweep of sorrow; and went back to reading more of *The Odyssey*.

Around midnight, I met my neighbor in the inn. He was a skittish specimen, dwarfish and emaciated, who'd been staying there for two weeks. He also had issues with the moon—though his weren't positive like mine. The full moon made him a basket-case, he told me. It shook his nerves and boiled his blood and he couldn't sleep a wink during a full moon without taking drugs to calm himself down. I invited him into my room, and to make acquaintance we each drank a glass of Spanish brandy together and talked. Never had I seen a man's eyes bulge so much as he spoke...

"That goddammed moon!" he cried, "All I do over there in that room of mine is pace the floor—all night long!"

To this, I smiled and bared my teeth.

"How does one get a good night's sleep in this world?"

"It's like this," I told my neighbor, "I met this Chinaman once, and we practiced yoga together, although neither of us had been to India. He was actually from Singapore, but we all called him 'The Chinaman.' He had come from Asia in a train baggage car with a sack full of opium that he was going to sell in Europe for a good profit (this was the first time I ever tasted that pernicious, though unbelievably beautiful, drug). He was an adroit yogi and the two of us spent hours balancing on our heads, letting the muscles in the faces slacken, our heart-rates deepen. The Chinaman bragged that he could concentrate on whatever he wanted to such an extent, that everything else ceased to exist. You know, they say not to practice yoga much during the full moon because people get excited during the full moon and one risks going too far with the poses to the extent of injury you see...

"Anyway, to the point, this Chinaman was able to 'forget' the full moon. Such mind power he had, that his 'forgetting the moon' actually caused his eyes to *not see it!*—you see what I'm saying, neighbor? The Chinaman looked into the sky and saw a pit of blackness, whereas we other men on the ship—(I met him on a ship in the Mediterranean on my way to Malta)—we other men saw the moon and pointed it out to him. But he had forgotten the moon to the extent that his eyes couldn't see it any longer. You see what I'm getting at? All you need to do, my good neighbor, is 'forget' the moon! Then you'll be able to stop your pacing at night and get a good night's sleep..."

My neighbor drooled a little, then lathered the drool on his chin with his fingertips, forming a froth, like shaving cream. "Ah!" he replied, "worth a try! You see I believe in that stuff too: yoga and mystical powers. I once knew a man who could kill himself on command. Can you believe that? Why do you laugh? Believe it! By will of his own mind, he could make his heart stop beating for good..." My neighbor poised and looked seriously at me, searching in my eyes. "You laugh!" he repeated once more... "You laugh, but he was a master at it! He could commit suicide at his own will!"

Indeed, hearty laughter streamed through my nose.

"Could he do it perpetually?" I asked.

"Perpetually...?" My neighbor rubbed his waxy chin.

"I mean, is he still able to do it?"

"I'm not sure I understand."

"Well? Then is he dead...?!"

My neighbor's puzzled face slowly began to transform into a look of realization. "But sir," he said, "Of course he's dead! I mean to say... this man could *kill* himself on command, you see. And you don't come back from the dead!"

The two of us found ourselves crossing to the door so I could let my visitor out. I slapped him with friendliness on the shoulder.

"No, you don't come back from the dead," I agreed.

"Thank you for the brandy."

The two of us had finished on friendly terms and parted company. I had no intention of meeting this character again, as I hoped to leave the inn early the next morning and travel on, and sure enough, that is what I did.

Chapter Eight

When I left the town of M****, I chartered a boat called *"La Belle Étoile"* piloted by an Irishman, and we rounded the Iberian Peninsula and docked in the Andalusian seaport town of Málaga. It was evening and the pier was full of arrivals. The bustle of passengers arriving from abroad with their foreign commotion and the *click-clack* of luggage carts met with the sound of the local Andalusian chatter coming from the smoky *tabernas*, the brash cries of Arab children begging for coins, the whistles of men offering their services as guides. I was thirsty for a drink of fresh water, and made my way up to a bar where bright lights showed a lot of young people hanging around to enjoy the mild night. Only the patios and bars had lights in the port city because the moon was just a tiny sliver and waning. The moon was the reason I wanted only water to drink, no wine. Being superstitious, I abstained from quantities of wine, most carnal joys and earthly delights whenever the moon was waning or absent from the sky. I call it superstition because somewhere I'd heard, or invented perhaps, that the only pleasures found during a waning moon are misfortunes in disguise. Superstition aside, I avoided pleasure during the waning or absent moon also out of respect for the bounty this world offered me. I profited from great harvests in life and believed in the importance of seasons... Enjoy figs and sweet tomatoes in the summer months; yet suffer a watery soup in winter. There are hours for rest, and hours for wakefulness; nights for sobriety and nights for drunkenness, (if only so that possession of the former allows us to discern the latter when we have it; for sad as it is, no human body can be happily drunk all the time)... Finally, there are times when a man should sleep entwined in the warm flesh of a woman, his flanks plummeting into the perfumed bedding while she lovingly rolls her sweet shoulders into his chest. Whereas, there are times to be stoic and solitary—sleeping alone on a wooden board with twill sheets and splinters that scratch the skin. For this strengthens the spine, the soul, and give dreams of courage and heroism. I believed in heroism, and still do. It is said that Alexander the Great slept with *The Iliad* beneath his pillow. Though I have never led an army, I am a wanderer. During the waning moon, I cradle Homer's *Odyssey* as if it were the sweet body of a woman.

During the shrinking moon: books, scholarship, astronomy, mathematics, literature, philosophy, botany, pharmacology, chemistry, scientific inquiry, these are my occupations. When I used to live in Tripoli as a young man, my friends would come to me at night...

"Saul!" they would sing merrily, "Our festive friend! Wild and charming Saul! Ô, charismatic prince! How are you this night? Why don't you come down with us to Pasha's Garden? There will be music, and loose women eager to be made love to! Come on!..."

"Nay, friends!" I would reply, and my head would plunge back into my books. I would read until my face was blistery and I could feel the skin on my eyes cringing—as cringe the limbs of an octopus when he is thrown onto a roaring fire. Once they were gone I would put my books aside and drink a steaming tea of quieting herbs. I would press a hot steam cloth to my face to let the pores open and breathe in the solitude and the night air. I then might retake my books, and finish my scholarship; then off to bed—goodnight!

All that during the waning moon.

During the *waxing* moon, however... well that is another story! A wildebeest, a tiger, a satyr, the god Dionysus, all these I resembled more than a mere man, and still do when the holy moon grows. In general I strive for greatness and rational achievement, but I admit to you I will always have a terrible fondness for women, a tendency towards drunkenness, and a weakness for the fumes of the poppy and other miserable beauties. But I don't blame myself much, as intoxication, like sexual euphoria, is the privilege of the human animal. Sexual frenzy is our compensation for the tedious moments we must suffer in the passage of life. "Nothing in excess" professed the ancient Greeks. 'Why, if I spend half the month in healthy scholarship and pleasant sleep, shouldn't I be allowed the other half to howl at the moon and pillage the groins of Europe's great beauties?' ('...that is the attitude I arrived in Europe with; for drunk on wine and ecstatic from the 'black smoke,' I am a demigod. My father was close to the king. He was a wild-thing, adopted by royalty—therefore, *adopted by society.* Moral obligations—also *mortal* obligations—don't apply to me. I do as I please!

"I will do as I please..." I muttered quietly aloud while thumbing a coin on the counter.

There I was: standing at a brightly lit counter in a *taberna* in Málaga, Spain. Some old customers, mostly obese types with greasy faces, were seated talking and playing dominos and drinking the local yellow wine. The young people were all outside drinking beer and sangria on the patios in the cool of the night. I recognized a few customers who had been passengers with me on the *Belle Étoile*. They eyed me with curiosity and whispered gossip amongst themselves. I kept to myself at the counter drinking water and thought about ordering a cold soup. It wasn't long before I was disturbed...

The bathroom door swung open and out came a little runt of a man, shaped like a turnip, with scaly skin and patches of rash over his eyes. He practically stepped on my heels as he stood beside me at the counter asking the barmaid for his "merchandise case." Surveying him, he appeared to be a huckster of the commonest sort one finds littering all dirty port cities. His dull eyes tucked under a shiny tall forehead darted left, then right. Saliva gleamed on his lips. The shoulders of his ill-fitting suit slid off down his arms, giving him the appearance of a down-and-out colporteur who doesn't make an adequate living selling goods—either because his goods are of poor quality, or because he invests his earnings in a pernicious habit. I was surprised to notice, however, that his shoes were nice—polished and made of good leather. The barmaid gave him his case, saying, *"Aqui, Pulpa!"* The huckster looked up at me from where I towered over him, and smiled and said, *"Monsieur..."* assuming I was a French traveler, and then he told me, "I am not a huckster, if that was what you were thinking."

He grinned and I noticed his teeth were very brown, almost black. He took out a watch from his pocket and looked at the time. The watch was real gold (I have an excellent eye), and finely made. The fact that this misfit could acquire such a handsome watch yet not engage a tailor to fit his suit jacket to his shoulders made me curious. "It's getting late," he whispered to me in a hushed tone. "If you want, I can show you a good place to eat, not too expensive, and comfortable. A place locals go. I notice you were looking at *la carta*. You seem to be a traveler."

Always up for adventure, so long as they don't waste my time, kill my spirit, or deplete the happiness in my heart, I agreed to follow the runt who said he was not a huckster. We walked to a restaurant where he promised I could have an excellent fried meal cooked by a real Andalusian *freidurías*[1] cook. It would cost me only two silver piastres and my guide would drink a glass of wine with me. The wine was included in the price of the meal.

The two of us headed up *Calle de Barroso.* I walked three paces behind my guide to be proper. My hands felt for the buckles of my travelling satchels to be sure that they were well-

---

[1]FREIDURÍAS (or "freiduría"): *(Sp)* Establishment (such as a cafeteria or restaurant) in which food, especially fish, are fried and sold (or else consumed on premises).

secured. In the moonless night, a solitary streetlamp, very tall, choked a burning flame; its light gleamed on the edges of the cobblestones and on the doorknobs of the stoopy little houses lining the street. It gleamed as well on the skin of my guide's scaly bald head, on his shiny polished shoes, on a puddle of urine where a man or a beast had emptied its bladder.

Customers were spilling out of a brightly-lit restaurant in the middle of the deserted street. The restaurant seemed an oasis of life in a black desert. Music and din poured into the empty and silent cobblestone lane and my guide led me into the restaurant and we took a small table. The old *freidurita* with sagging breasts knew my guide apparently well, she called him "Pulpawrecho" and quickly sat a carafe of table wine down in front of us, as well as some egg-tortilla which we could eat while the food was being prepared. I mentioned I wanted to abstain from wine; but I'd had a long voyage, and as the wine was included with the meal and already on the table, I decided to have a glass and served my guide and served myself. Then, after spilling a splash of wine in a saucer on the table as a sacrifice to Dionysus (as was my custom whenever wine was drunk), I pulled the bitter red juice through my teeth and let it pour into the well of my mouth. It had been a couple weeks since my last drink, the wine tasted bitter and bad at first. My guide sat across from me at the little table and sipped his wine happily through glossy brownish-black teeth, and smiled stupidly at me. I again considered the likely reason for his stained teeth.

"I'm not a *guide*, in case you're wondering," said my guide, munching a piece of egg-tortilla I'd torn off and flopped in front of him to eat.

I wasn't wondering, but had simply assumed he was a guide, and told myself as much.

"No, I'm not a guide at all. I'm a servant—the personal servant of a very important man in Málaga, a notable man, though he's not old. Forty-one years. He is a *voyant.* Many people travel from far to have him tell their fortune as well as their future."

"And you live at his house, I take it. You stay at his home most of the time," I went on to guess... "but tonight you went wandering to the pier to accost me, a traveler, for amusement?

Or because you wanted me to consult your fortune-teller and fill his pockets? Or because you wanted to bring me to this *friteria* to eat egg tortilla?"

"Oh, I don't want you to consult him. Although he doesn't live far from here. Just past the bridge. And yes, I live with him."

I drank some more wine and considered the servant. His black teeth interested me. They made me hungry with that old craving. Hungry, you see, because I could tell they were black from opium smoke. I thought of the moonless night, but yet, my muscles were sore from the boat; the thought of sweet opium to numb me sounded too good to pass up. Besides, the next day the moon would start to grow again.

I was angry at myself for my inclination to vice, I longed for the day when a state of frenzy would lead my mind to sober pasture, just as it had for Saint Augustine. I longed for the day when the love of one woman would be sacred enough to forget all the rest.

'Yes,' I thought to myself back then in Málaga, licking the lips of my soul, 'I could ingest just a little opium tonight. One little pipe-full.' I knew it could be obtained. Yes, my black-toothed servant friend was a servant of opium, so much was obvious; he chattered his charred teeth and his teeth made me hungry.

"Does your master have something *soothing* I can buy to smoke? You see, I'm a foreigner. I've just arrived on shore. I was told there are no pleasure-dens here, and it's not always easy to find a quick connection in a foreign town..."

"Something soothing to smoke? Strange question! How would you think to ask for that? I mean, a clairvoyant mightn't have such a thing to smoke."

Ignoring his reply, I went on to say, "I'm a traveler after all, new to this country. Arrived tonight. My muscles are sore. I don't know anyone here, etc."

The servant surveyed me closely with caution, eyeing the plump satchels I had seated on the chair beside me in the food house. The cowhide straps of the satchels were wrapped around my leg to avoid a thief snatching them and running off. I scratched my bristly chin and pulled the last sip of wine through my mighty teeth, deciding to drink no more alcohol that night.

'You're no gendarme,' he was probably thinking. No, the fortuneteller's servant realized I couldn't possibly be a Spanish gendarme—if for my accent alone. After some more persuasion, he agreed to take me to his master to see what could be had in the way of opiates. "Make it clear, I don't want to know the future! I don't want any *bonne aventure*!"[1] I hollered after him while we paced down the black, cobbled lane upon our leaving the restaurant.

* * *

Meeting the clairvoyant, and obtaining some opium for future travels...

The servant and I crossed a bridge and came to a house where outside a wooden plank was hammered to a wall and a name was burned into the wood in large lettering. It read:

DRAGOMIR, STANISLAS V. — CLAIRVOYANT

The hunchbacked servant slid a key into the door and the two of us entered a dark stairwell. Before starting up, he turned to me and begged some money. "You wouldn't have one or two piastres to lend me, would you?"

I reached into my waistcoat and pulled out a silver two-piastres coin and handed it to the beggar. He snatched it up and said, "You are a saint, Señor. Just, please don't tell my master I asked you to lend me money, I ask you kindly." I shook my head and he bade I wait at the bottom of the stairwell while he gained permission for me to enter. Just then, a fat old woman appeared

---

[1] BONNE AVENTURE: French expression dating from the 15th century, meaning: "Fortune-telling"

on the stairs with hot tears streaming down her face. She pressed a rag to her mouth, and sobbing, she came towards us and passed us. She didn't look into our eyes while she exited out into the Spanish street.

"She's been to see the master," the beggar whispered, "and obviously she wasn't happy about what she learned."

I waited in the dark stairwell as the wretchedly small figure of the beggar-servant climbed the steps to the door high at the top of the landing. He knocked twice; the door crept open. He disappeared inside.

I meanwhile waited, clicking my tongue, dreaming of the Spanish woman I hoped I would meet and love now that I was in this new and strange country. She would be like a flower, I thought, fresh and soft, but not too young; she would be mature in years, old enough to know how to arouse me, and be versed in the arts of conversation, seduction, and sensual love. Such was what I dreamed to find in Spain, but my pleasant dream was interrupted when the servant appeared at the landing, holding a fiery candle. He signaled to me to climb the stairs. And soon I found myself standing in a room of gothic design, spacious and richly-dressed, with high-vaulted ceilings, dim like an old library, tall ironwork windows, and tables piled with papers. Smoking candles were everywhere.

"A foreigner? Welcome, foreigner..." came the voice of the man who cut an impressive figure behind a mahogany desk beneath two high-arched windows. He seemed extremely tall, although he was seated, and was extraordinarily thin. He removed the hat on his long pointed head—seemingly out of politeness—and a torrent of dark hair swirled like a storm around his ears. "My name is Dragomir," he announced with authority, "You are in my home." The two eyes in his long face shone like a pair of hazel-colored stones, or like distant fires burning in the darkness. I approached to shake my host's hand. "Excuse me for not standing," he mumbled in a low voice, "I hurt my leg yesterday. It will heal."

As the master of the house greeted the stranger, the servant hopped around like a mad fool on springs, lighting the various plates of candles, filling the curious room with blazing light. The odor of myrrh resin entered my nose, and through it, I detected the sweet smell of opium. I was aching with desire. *"Chit, chit, chit,"* my teeth chattered while a saucer of porcelain clattered beneath a cup of tea that was brought to be swilled or sipped.

"I can tell you've come from far," the fortune-teller said, staring steadily at me. "You have a strange past. A very curious past..." I waved my hand at this in annoyance. I disliked *bonne aventure* since I believed what these fortune-tellers had to say was probably true, and pity the man who knows his fate! The servant meanwhile was perched in the shadows of the room like a stone gargoyle on a medieval cathedral.

"I didn't come to have my fortune."

"I don't *have* your fortune!" laughed the fortune-teller, which surprised me entirely. "No, not tonight, I don't have it at least..." He stood and walked over to the window and opened the drawer of a wooden chest and stayed there a few moments. When he came back, he had a slender pipe of brass with a decorated ceramic bowl. "Are you hungry? There is some Spanish cheese. As well as wine. You are a guest. Whatever you'd like . . . Pulpy, go make a plate of cheese..."

The servant's lip was dripping with saliva as his master set a ball of brown opium on a plate. "Wrecho!" demanded Dragomir, louder this time. "Fix the stranger some food to eat!"

The servant leaped up to obey his master until I said: "No, please, I thank you. Kind of you. We just ate; and I'd prefer to taste that opium, as my muscles are sore from travelling." I glanced to the high ironwork window and saw the night was completely black outside. No moon lighted upon the world on this night. I knew I would eventually have to go find a hotel room or a bed of some sort. There would be rooms to be had down at the port. You can find anything and everything at the docks of a port city. Especially where the climate's sultry, where criminals and vagabonds abound.

Dragomir stood tall beside me packing a *pastilla* of opium into the ceramic bowl and lit the wick of the lamp. "For the stranger," he said.

I took two fast and long inhalations as the pill of opium vaporized in the bowl. The sweet black smoke flashed me back to a memory of that market stall in Turkey where I met a pretty young lady walking hand-in-hand with a little boy when the sun was burning my neck. She was from my city and was very pale, with white arms and delicate hands. The rest of her body was covered in a disguise, so as to smuggle the child. The kid belonged to her sister. The two were waiting for a boat. I felt this sudden urge to go find that pretty lady in disguise, to join with her, to join with the entire world and all of its people. I felt an incredible lightness and joy carry me away. The pain in my joints vanished, then I returned to the room where I had been. I reveled in this newfound lightness and bliss. A hearty laugh escaped me: "Oh, it's been a long time!" I said.

"Pulpawrecho?" the clairvoyant called to his servant, while I handed him the pipe and he passed it on to his slave. Pulpawrecho collapsed on the opium with avarice and sucked up the sweet smoke. Dragomir took a long puff when it was his turn. He asked me again did I want food or wine? I said no.

"More of the pipe?"

"No. But some for later, for which I'll pay. I'd like to have some while I travel..."

"Of course, of course..."

We were all silent a moment.

"Do you want some wine? A liqueur?"

I told him no, and begged myself to leave them, to return to the port to find some lodging.

"Now may I ask you your name?" Dragomir sat back down in his place. Pulpawrecho squirmed and uttered sighs of ecstasy as saliva dripped from his face. With an exalted grin, he smacked his lips and cried out to himself: "Ah! Pulpawrecho!—aye-aye-aye!—Pulpawrecho!" and floated neatly on his perch.

"My name is Saul, the son of Solarus of Tripoli. My father was an adventurer like me. He disappeared somewhere in the east, in Asia. Now I, in my generation, am headed to London where I have business with a merchant." I had no reason to weave lies and untruths as I was doing, but I did so for the sheer pleasure of telling a good lie. Some of what I said was true, though some was invented. I wanted to tell untruths also because I was conducting an interview with a clairvoyant and I yearned to see if he could detect a lie. My father had been an adventurer, like me. So much was the truth. His name had been Solarus. I hadn't lied about that. Though he didn't disappear in Asia, and I wasn't going to London.

"Solarus of Tripoli?" the clairvoyant turned to his servant, "We met a Solarus, did we not my fine Pulpawrecho?"

Pulpawrecho nodded his doglike head. Dragomir took another inhalation of the pipe and smiled with pleasure. "I do like that," he said. "You noticed I didn't ask *who you are* before first taking care of your needs? I am very Homeric in that way. A stranger should always be offered food, wine, or whatever he needs to be comfortable before being asked who he is, and from where he comes, before asking him to tell his identity."

I showed Dragomir the copy of *The Odyssey* I was carrying with me and he smiled knowingly as though it is natural that we should both have Homer on our minds. I told him then that I'd always wanted to own a great library. "But since I was born to be a wanderer," I sighed with regret, "I think I will never have a great library."

"Hmm..." said Dragomir, leafing through the book, "I can't read Greek. Though I do know five languages well. Pulpawrecho brought me my first copy of *The Odyssey*, in Spanish, a long time ago. I had asked him for it. He's a good servant. You see I keep him dressed well, he has nice clothes. His watch is his nicest possession, but that he procured himself." He turned to his servant, "You are so quiet tonight, Pulpawrechito, you have nothing to say tonight? The devil chomped your tongue, eh?"

"Squawk!" cried Pulpawrecho. Then gathering himself, he said that all his clothes were nice, and even his suit, though it was ill-fitting.

"But that is not *my* fault. It's not *my* fault his suit is ill-fitting,' said Dragomir, 'I even engaged the finest tailor in Málaga for him; but *all* clothes are ill-fitting on Pulpawrecho. He has a weird body. His shoulders slope oddly. You see he looks like a fiend with the shoulders of his jacket like that, but he is no fiend. He is very clever, my little Wrechito. You should pose him some questions.'

"Pose him? Alright, how did you two come to meet?" Feeling anesthetized, comfortable in my new surroundings, I forgot completely about the world outside, the city and country I was in. All that existed was this room with the tall, gaunt figure of Dragomir, and the hunched-over gargoyle of a servant on a stool, and my own self sinking lower and lower in my chair.

"How did we meet? How did I meet my master? Oh, that is a fascinating story! Oh, it's splendid, that sweet opium! ...Master, let your Pulpawrecho have one more little puff. Another little puff. Then what a story I'll tell!"

Dragomir handed the pipe to his servant and his servant bared his black teeth as he blew out hissing smoke.

"Saul is a nice name. Does its meaning have to do with the sun?"

"It means *prayed for*."

"Does somebody pray for you?"

"Pulpawrecho," said Dragomir, "Why don't you ask me that. I am the clairvoyant, aren't I? Give me your hand...' Dragomir snatched at my hand like a street artist and scanned it momentarily and then dropped it in disappointment, 'Ach!' he said, 'I see nothing in your hand. Neither a past nor a future..." He turned to his servant... "Then again, I never was reliable at reading people's hands. No, that was never my talent, was it!" Dragomir roared with triumphant laughter.

The candle flame flickered, the laughter dimmed in the room, and Dragomir dropped my palm limpidly on the wooden desk. He promised that he would pray for me when our ways parted. He then laughed with unease.

"So, then, how did you two meet?" Curiosity was nagging me about this strange pair.

"May I please, Master? May I tell the story?" Pulpawrecho squirmed with his question. The master nodded and the servant began spilling words ever faster; his hands flew and fluttered, trembling lightly like dragonflies that hover near a flower but never quite land, nor do they go off, so did the servant's hands hover around his body without settling anywhere, nor going off anywhere.

"I was down at the seaport three years ago," Pulpawrecho began to explain, wringing his hands, "doing my trade—buying, selling, trading, whatever I could to make money. I had a pocketful of stolen watches—you see, I'm a thief." He paused to smile a sinister smile at me, "Watches of all kinds—silver, brass, steel, I even had a gold Breguet! I was waiting for the hour to strike twenty so I could get into Gordita's *freidurías* and get a meal of crispy fish. I was licking my lips with the thought of that fish meal. Then I saw this young girl heading up from the sea. At first she appeared very small, and I thought she were just a little child. She wore a hood over her head that covered her hair completely, except for one lock of golden brown hair that fell from her hood and curved around her chin. Details like this always strike me. I miss nothing."

'No, that's true!' interrupted Dragomir with a laugh, 'Pulpawrecho misses nothing. Although he seems simple at times, nothing gets by him...'

'Right,' continued the servant, "so here in the humid night was this girl coming towards the street in the port; and I thought it was too late for a young girl to be alone, walking up from the sea. Then as she came close I saw she wasn't a baby. She was adolescent at least. Maybe thirteen or fourteen. Let's say she was thirteen. How beautiful she was! I had never before seen a beautiful creature like this. She seemed to be hurried. Hurried and baffled. Why do I say *baffled?*

"The young girl looked left and right, as though she were afraid of someone coming to snatch her. I admired her perfectly formed and smooth beautiful face, and my groin began to burn with the erection that was growing. I'm Pulpawrecho, you know, so my penis turns purple when it's hard. My penis grew hard and purple in my pants and my thighs burned with scorching heat and I wanted to catch this pubescent girl and succumb her and press my lips all over her. She hurried past me, her neat little bottom (a bottom the size of two fists of a man) rubbed its cheeks together, and I saw her torn skirt ruffling in the speed of her walk, and the tissue rising-up revealing the base of her cotton underwear (you see how descriptive I am! That's how I see the world!); her cotton panties rose up revealing soft and tiny butt cheeks down to her thighs, until reaching very thin and beautifully-formed calves—smooth as the white meat of a fresh market chicken. What legs she had! I began to follow her, those legs, that tiny bottom, never leaving my sight. 'Yam-yam!' I smacked my lips. Of course, me being nothing but a sorry Pulpawrecho, I knew she wouldn't want me like I wanted her. I could never *have* her... still, I *wanted* her!

"...We turned down many streets, narrow streets smelling of urine and rotting food. Finally she came to the street where we are now (this, Master Dragomir's street). She stopped as though stunned, frozen before the wooden plaque that's posted outside the gate with Master Dragomir's name stenciled in the wood. The sweet girl stopped and brushed her little hands on her ruffled skirt as she studied the sign for a moment, all the while, anxiously looking around her, desperately almost. I hid in the shadows like a wolf, watching...

"Then, in a swipe of her hands, the little girl let the hood fall from her head and a magnificent bouquet of hair toppled down over her shoulders. She was dark-haired, but golden at the same time, both pale and dark! I rubbed my hand over my groin to settle the stiffness that was growing bigger and more uncomfortable. I had to settle my desire! The girl's desire meanwhile stayed on that wooden sign over the gate. What did the sign say?, I wondered. I saw her kiss her hands then. Why? I don't know, but she kissed her own hands. All the while, she looked around with a way I can only describe as *baffled.* Dropping her dirty hands, she pressed the latch on the gate. The gate opened and she hurried into the courtyard and was gone!

"...I fled from the shadows and crossed the street and planted myself where she had stood moments before when she kissed her own hands. 'Clairvoyant,' I read on the sign, 'A clairvoyant? Very curious!' . . . I pressed the latch as she had done and entered into the courtyard. There were many doors leading to stairs, I couldn't tell at first *which stairs* she had taken to enter into the building (the entrance to this building wasn't exactly then as it is now). Alone, the courtyard was silent and empty. I heard tiny footsteps far off, but they belonged to an alley cat that was pouncing down a drain pipe. I knew she had gone up to visit the clairvoyant, why else would she have been looking at the sign? The problem was that there were many stairs and I worried if I went up one, she would come down another at the same time and be gone forever. I decided to wait for her in the courtyard. Was it fear or patience? I didn't want to confront her in the lighted room of a clairvoyant. I wanted her alone, in the dark, *like the predator I was....*"

Pulpawrecho stopped his story to smack his lips and take a breath. I was poured some water and began to drink. The wretched servant went on talking...

"While I waited for the little girl to come back down, I backed into the shadows in the courtyard and masturbated. I was so flushed with excitement, I ejaculated immediately all over the brick wall and stuffed my throbbing sex back into my trousers. Still panting, having not yet recovered, I then spied that the girl leaving out the gate from which we'd entered. I looked at one of my watches and realized she'd been upstairs an entire half-hour! Now she was leaving, hurriedly; she looked even more baffled then she had when she had come. Do you realize what I'm saying?! . . . The girl had looked so baffled a half-hour before when she'd arrived. Now, leaving the clairvoyant, she seemed *even more baffled* then before!

"...So, this sweet girl went scampering down a side-street. I left in pursuit of her, but I was too far behind and she was too quick. I'm a speedy little man. But something was driving her in haste. She had a purpose, I could tell. I lost my love to the narrow winding streets of the town. I knew that the only way I stood a chance of finding my beautiful pubescent goddess again would be if I went back to the building to find the clairvoyant myself and ask him. He would know where she was headed. He of all people would know what was on her mind—or *in* her mind, rather. A clairvoyant knew the future, right? He could help me catch my prey...."

"Ah yes!" Dragomir interrupted with a chuckle, "I remember it as if it were yesterday. You tell a story well, little

Pulpawrechito, as if you were reading from a book. You talk just like a book! You see, Saul," he turned to me, "This little man *climbed the stairs* that night, a stranger then to me as you were tonight, and he buzzed on my door..."

"No, I *thundered up the stairs!"* Pulpawrecho broke in, "and buzzed on Master Dragomir's door. Master answered right away and admitted that there had been a girl to see him—a young adolescent girl with a hood—only moments before. I pleaded to come in and said that I would pay for a consultation. I would pay for his help. How much would it cost? I had money and gold watches in my pocket. I didn't care how much it would cost. I was ushered inside...

"Master Dragomir permitted me a visit and let me sit in this very chair where you are sitting now. 'This beautiful girl who visited you,' I asked while trembling, 'she looked baffled. Where did she go? Did you send her off somewhere? You read her fortune to her and then she left? You should have detained her!' (I was almost in a fever of desire as I spoke to him that night. I couldn't control myself, it was as if I were drunk.) 'She was so beautiful!' I cried to the yet-unknown clairvoyant," Pulpawrecho inclined his head towards his master as he said this, "'Yes, she was a cute girl,' Dragomir replied, 'if you like... *children*. So what's the big deal?' . . . 'The big deal?! You let her go!" I gripped the table in fever, 'without trying to keep her here!' . . . 'Why should I have tried to keep her here?' Dragomir asked me, 'I don't abduct *children!'* . . . I remember he put particular emphasis on the word 'children,' as if my girl didn't arouse him sexually because of her tender age. Meanwhile, in my groin a heated fire was scorching what remained of my store of semen. My sex was growing hard again with the thought of that adolescent girl with her pale dark and golden hair that tumbled out of her hood, her tiny breasts pressed against her little shirt, and her baffled face turning left and right as she skipped through the shadows in the Spanish street. I was growing enflamed and excited. Master Dragomir, however, was calm. He reclined in his burnished leather chair and took up a newspaper and put a pair of glasses on and began to read to himself it as if I were a nobody, and wasn't here altogether."

"'Can you tell me at least where she went?' I begged in desperation. 'I will pay for a consultation. I will pay dearly!'

"'I don't normally *offer* information to people I don't know and don't care about.' . . . 'Will you let me *pay* for it? I'll pay! I'll pay!'. . . 'The important part of my phrase,' he replied, 'was the *people I don't know or care about* part. You can pay me, if you'd like. I'll take your money and tell you this or that, but what I tell you may lead you nowhere. She is a young child. You are a middle-aged man. You are old and she is in her first throes of puberty. Why do you want her so badly? You can bribe me. You can give me gold. Still, your little girl may never be found.'

"'Yet *if you knew and cared about me,*' I asked him, 'you'd tell me more? Who this mysterious girl is? Where she went? Where she is likely to be found? How I can have her?!' I wrung my hands as sweat dripped from my face. I looked left and right. My memory flashed back to when I'd been spying on her outside and her little bottom, those butt cheeks like two little fists, clenched with indecision, and she removed her hood and those beautiful locks of hair poured down over her sweet face. Now my consciousness returned to where I was. I looked with my beady Pulpawrecho eyes around this room of Master Dragomir while I gripped his table with my fingers that started to bleed from the pressure... 'Let me be your servant then!' I cried suddenly. 'Let me be your servant!'

"Suddenly the pressure was released. I looked around the room in confusion. Why was there nobody around? Did he not have a servant? No one had opened the door for me to let me in. Dragomir was all alone in this musty room. 'Why,' I asked, 'is there no one to open the door for you?' ...My words seemed to barely register with Dragomir as he sat in his leather seat with his reading glasses on, scanning the newspaper. I, meanwhile, was frenetic. I would have committed any act, no matter how irrational, to know where my thirteen year-old girl could be found. I would have eaten my own stool if Master Dragomir had asked. Anything to find that child! '...Let me be your servant then!'

"Dragomir said nothing, but continued reading silently.

"'Let me be your servant," I pleaded with torment, "Until *you know and care about me* enough to help me find my girl!'

"A seeming eternity followed. Finally, Dragomir broke the silence... 'This is most interesting! A ver-ry in-ter-est-ing story,' he issued to me in a calm voice, his eyes focused on his newspaper; he spoke in his strange accent (at that time, he still had a strong accent. He was new to Andalusia then, three years ago)."

Pulpawrecho continued narrating his story to me as I listened quietly in the chair, wondering why a shrewd, seemingly intelligent runt like Pulpawrecho would entrust such a scandalous story to me—a complete stranger. It was the opium, I knew—that terrible truth serum. Dark secrets guarded for a lifetime can be divulged with carefree folly after a sip of the *black smoke.* I took another inhalation from the pipe when Dragomir insisted, and felt the opiate stupor renew itself. Pulpawrecho finished his interesting story...

"'Please, Sir! Let me be your servant!' I was unable to stand the silence of my master reading his paper.

"'This is a story you should hear, Señor... I'm sorry, what is your name?' ... 'Pulpawrecho,' I told him. ... 'Señor Pulpawrecho, there is this interesting story in the paper here, about the famous Juan Gomérez trial that's been going on. Have you been following it? No? Surprising! A man like you who enjoys following strangers, one would think you would know all of the gossip. Oh well. It's a fascinating case. I'd like your opinion on it. I'll paraphrase...

"'There's a famous court case that is happening right now in Spain. The story is on everyone's lips, surprising you are ignorant of it. A man, a Spaniard by birth, of very fair complexion, is to be hanged for killing a baby. Infanticide, you see. Many citizens say he should hang or be burned alive, while others say he should be set free. The people who say he should be set free, interestingly enough, are the upright citizens, many of whom are women, people of high birth and moral integrity. It's a scandal and I'd like your opinion of the matter...

"'The story goes as follows: A certain pale-faced Juan Gomérez, who is skinny and very short in stature, was living in a poor barrio of Sevilla with his newlywed wife. She was a beautiful negress—enormously tall, with chocolaty skin and a round and mighty rump. They say she had, or *has* rather, penetrating eyes that will cause fear in a man, and sharp white teeth that shine between her dark lips. She had come from the Ivory Coast and has been living in Spain for ten years...

"'Juan Gomérez is a good Spaniard, dutiful and patriotic. As for his tastes, he found the most beautiful race to be the black race. 'Black women alone,' he decided, 'have the exotic allure mixed with the feminine power a man loves.' When Juan was first love-struck by this great negress, he asked her to move in with him, share his bed, etc. Eventually, through his earnest vows to be her slave in all matters, he talked her into marrying him. And so they were married. He did all the work around the house. He trolled around with his little mop and broom, cleaned and cooked and pleaded for sex; and she took advantage of him most of the time, but she felt some affection for him, so she shared his bed and ate the meals he cooked. Once her mother came to visit from the Ivory Coast. The two women drank on Juan's money and went carousing. They would come home late at night with all sorts of odors on their skin, their big black breasts hanging out of their blouses. The mother only stayed a week or so as she couldn't stand our dear Europe, she said the European customs were filthy; she missed her home in Africa, missed the food there, etc., etc., so off she went...

"'...Later, the first cousin of the great negress came to stay. He was a mighty tall negro with arms of steel and a voice as low as the thunder of hell. He ate all that Juan could cook and he spread his heavy body out on the floor and took up so much room, that the poor Juan Gomérez with his apron and frying pan hid quivering in the kitchen most of the time, asking his wife in a trembling voice if she or her cousin wanted more to eat or more wine to drink. Fortunately for him, that nightmare didn't last long as the great negro cousin had some altercation with a conscript soldier in the street, and not having had all his papers in order, he was deported back to the Ivory Coast. Juan was relieved, and more in love with his wife than ever....

"'Soon this great beautiful negress found herself pregnant. Now while woman gives her body as an incubator to her child and risks her life in childbirth so that this child may grow and her genes may live on after she is dead, continuing her legacy and creating a sort of immortality of her personal species; so does a man give his labor and time and resources to the child born of his genes, so that his own genes may continue on into the future and result in his own immortal legacy. A man is biologically wired to consider his life successful if he has nurtured the woman pregnant with his own child and has raised his own child. He has wasted a portion of his life, however, if the child is not his own...

"'And so, some months later, the grand negress gave birth on the floor in the couple's shabby apartment. For all her size and strength, the poor new mother was made weak from childbirth and suffered a fever, so it was up to the father to cradle the infant, wash it, etc...

"'You can believe the horror suffered by Juan Gomérez when he first saw the child and looked at its face and saw how black, how very coal-black, the baby's skin was. You see, his wife was an African negress, but she was sweet-chocolate in color. While Juan was extremely fair, almost blond, being a pure Spaniard of entirely European descent. So the baby should have been a mixture of white milk, and milk chocolate. But he wasn't, he was coal-black! His color matched the color of the great negro cousin that had stayed with the couple up until seven months prior when he was sent back to Africa. Little Juanito, you see, was not Juan's child. The baby began to cry the moment he was born and didn't ever stop. Now a babe just born, his crying resembles nothing in this world; while this little baby's crying voice sounded just like its mother's husky cousin, and nothing like her gently swooning husband. That, and his face was darker than a sky without moon or stars. Nothing so black could be born of a light cheese-colored man and a toffee colored woman. No, this could not be Juan's child. And yet, Juan had given nine months of his life to feeding that strange baby inside its mother. Our little pale-faced Spaniard was horrified. While his wife was in a fever from child-birth, Juan went to the kitchen and took a large carving knife, the kind that is used to carve pork-ham, and in order to prevent his having to toil sixteen-hour days any longer to put food in the mouth of that creature whose genes didn't belong to him, he went and sliced the newborn baby through the chest twice with the knife. His eyes gushed tears, spilling over the iron carving knife and the infant's corpse—meanwhile, as Juan served-up tears, he saw his wife looking at him through her own eyes veiled in fever that bulged with horror—horror, for they knew what had happened. She squealed with terror and fell unconscious.

"'Juan, aware of his guilt, and of his own accord, walked to the police station and gave a clear testimony of what he had done. He was promptly arrested and a picture of the crime was portrayed for the citizens of Sevilla and all of Spain, and surprisingly, many people took Juan's side—*especially the women!* Those in the courthouse saw how small and fearful and trembling this man was. His lawyer explained how long he worked day and night to feed the gluttonous, loose-legged woman who went boozing and carousing with the little money he earned. While Juan had slaved in the kitchen cooking food for his pregnant wife, she had sat at the table patting her stomach in full awareness that the baby inside wasn't his, but rather her cousin's. Still, she let her poor husband slave to nourish the child that was conceived in incest and out of adultery. So when the child was born and Juan discovered the truth, he was overcome with rage. He was like a man who was drunk. He ran for that carving knife and sliced the baby up and that is all that he could have done. The press and the public were undecided. The majority of 'sensible' citizens wanted to see Juan set free. He was dying in prison—almost dead from fever, you see, his moral suffering was killing him. Night and day, Juan trembled in his cell in terror from the fact of his own crime.'

"When Master Dragomir finished telling me of the crime," Pulpawrecho went on, lowering his tone and slowing the pace of his story, putting his newspaper down. He looked down his strange nose at me. He asked me then what I thought of the court case. "Should Juan Gomérez hang? Or should he be set free?"

"Enough, Pulpawrecho! Let me tell our guest a little of the events that followed..." And Dragomir continued the night the two of them met...

"So I set down my paper after telling Pulpy here about Juan Gomérez and asked Pulpawrecho what he would do if he were the judges. 'Would you have him hanged? Would you set him free?' . . . Pulpawrecho all the while sat trembling in the chair you're sitting in now, his fingertips white as all the blood had left them. He gripped the edge of the desk. I heard the clock on the wall tick: *tock, tick, tock.* Just then, Pulpawrecho darted off out of this room and down the stairs. I was sure I'd scared him with my story. I heard him out on the street a moment later, his shoes slapping on the stones as the sound grew fainter and fainter...

"So I went on reading my paper. And to be honest, within minutes, I forgot all about this strange visitor; and I was surprised when he later returned. It's easy to forget such little men as Pulpawrecho until they do startling things! Pulpawrecho returned an hour later and rang the buzzer quickly, impatiently. I went and opened the door myself—of course, *myself,* I had no servant then! So, I opened my door and Pulpawrecho entered into my study and held out a bundle wrapped in a wool blanket.

"'Master,' he said to me, 'Please, let me call you *Master*... I found what you were asking me for.' He outstretched his arms with a frenzied look on his face. I looked at the bundle and realized it was an infant child, all bundled-up.

"'A baby?" I inquired, "I asked you for a baby?' ... 'More or less,' panted Pulpawrecho, 'You asked me what I would do in this situation, in this court case, how I would handle the adulteress and her cuckolded husband, the murderer of the child. Well, here is my response...' Pulpawrecho thrust the baby into my arms. Its little infant feet stuck out black, like two lumps of coal, from beneath the wool blanket. His little hands flopped out of the blanket and I saw that even the fingertips were midnight black. It seemed only the bottoms of the feet were a little rosy. They were rosy and they quivered lightly as the wind blew.

"'I brought you *the* baby,' said Pulpawrecho.

"'So you did.'

Dragomir turned to me, delivering the final blow to the story, "So then I drew back the blanket. I drew back the blanket and saw that the little black baby was dead!"

A cold silence fell over Dragomir's study, here and now in the present moment where we found ourselves; the clock ticked on the wall and it caught my attention and I wondered if it was the same clock that had ticked back on that first night when Pulpawrecho had entered this room with a dead infant wrapped in a blanket.

"Do you understand, Saul, what this all means?"

"No, Dragomir."

"I knew by Pulpawrecho's gesture of bringing the child, (and *he* knew that *I* knew), that if he would listen to my story about a dead child and hear me ask him what he would do in such a situation, and then immediately run out and come back within an hour holding a dead child that is very much like, *if not the exact same child* as the one in my story, then I knew that he would do anything for me—*anything!* Pulpawrecho proved himself in that one hour to be..."

"To be...?"

"The perfect servant!"

Upon hearing this, I recoiled with a mixture of revulsion and awe.

"*...El sirviente perfecto!"* he roared with laughter.

I turned to the side and spat. Pulpawrecho looked at my reaction and rubbed his moist palms together, grinning with wet teeth and eyes that shone with self-satisfaction, for he knew that he *was* the perfect servant, and that he would stop at nothing to serve his master.

When I looked back up, Dragomir was gone from his chair. He came up behind me and placed in my hand a ball of sticky black opium.

"Give me fifty *reales*, unless if you prefer to pay in gold."

I examined the opium and smelled it. It appeared to be the same that we had just smoked; yet looking at the ball in the light, I noticed there was a strange green shimmer to it. I had never seen opium with a similar green shimmer, although it smelled fine and I just smoked some with them without ill-effect.

I gave the green shimmer no more thought and placed three gold *escudos* on the desk where the opium had been.

"Where else in Spain are you going to go visit?"

I told him I was going to Madrid, then to Valencia, then to Barcelona, before heading to France. When I said Barcelona, he lit up and grew very spirited.

"You're going to Barcelona? When? In one month you will be there? Here, I have an idea. Give me your opium back, I'll give you a bit more."

I gave the drug dealer back the two-gram ball of opium he had sold me and watched him slice and weigh a larger block equaling four times what he had originally sold me. Those eight grams, he cut down the center. "Here is for you," he said, presenting me with one four-gram block. Before I wrapped it in a piece of vellum paper I inspected it again near the candle and saw that this piece too had the same strange green shimmer that the last piece had. I gave it no more thought, though, and put it in the vellum paper and tucked it into my pocket. Green, I would find out soon enough, was my unlucky color.

"Why don't we make this a proper commission?"

"What sort of commission?" I wasn't interested in business. I had the money my old business partner Juhani sent me in Alexandria, and I would have much more money as soon as I got to Madrid.

"First, take your three escudos back."

Dragomir took the other four gram block and placed it inside a silver snuffbox. "Have a look beneath the lid." I opened the box and saw a portrait of Dragomir's face in miniature. It was a shocking portrait. Dragomir looked grim and haunting.

"I compliment your portrait artist. The resemblance is truly startling."

"Please put that snuffbox in your pocket. I want you to take it to someone. You see, Barcelona is a city I know well. I lived there for six years before coming here to Andalusia. The mistress I was in love with then, she is still in Barcelona now. I haven't written or visited her in six years but lately I cannot stop thinking about her. Please honor me with this commission, my friend Saul, and when you fulfill my request, I will reward you handsomely with money."

"As I told you, money doesn't interest me."

"Well then please, for the sake of your honor and elegance, return the favor of tonight's hospitality by swearing to me that you will take this commission to my mistress in Catalonia. I'm entrusting you with my only remaining portrait, and my last silver snuffbox. Make sure that she gets it. I don't want anything from her in return, and you might enjoy her company, she must still be very beautiful. Her name is Penelope Baena, she is still at the same address, I verified this recently, it's right in the center of the city and you just have to give her the box and maybe have coffee with her, and pay her my respects."

"Why don't you send it by courier? It's a safer bet. I might eat up your opium and melt down your silver."

"Surely Saul is joking! You would never do a thing like that! Certainly not a Homeric man such as yourself. And certainly not to Dragomir, anyhow!"

I was puzzled why he trusted me, and why he didn't send his present via courier. I would find out.

"Please, no jokes, damn it! For the sake of your honor and your elegance, return the favor of tonight's hospitality by swearing to me that you will take this commission to Señorita Baena. The opium, the snuffbox, and my portrait, you must deliver them into no hand other than that of Señorita Baena's. The other four grams is my gift to you for your troubles. Señorita Baena is a lovely creature, she lives in a tiny apartment on the first floor in Barcelona's Barrio Gòtico, and she runs the *herborista*[1] downstairs on the ground floor at street-level. I did some checking and she is still there. She sells herbal blends for magic spells, purges, anesthesia, health tonics and the like. I left all my old mistresses for her and was completely happy until one night Penelope had a

---

[1] HERBORISTA: The Spanish word for a person who practices pharmacognostic medicine—or, the practice of using medicines and drugs as they are found in a natural state; in plants, herbs, mushrooms, resins, etc.). Pharmacognosy is known commonly as 'herbalism.' Herboristas may be known in English as 'herbalists.'

vision that I would contract a plague within six months and die three days later. All the people who were near me when I had the plague would all die within three days of my death; according to her vision, I was doomed.

"She'd closed-up her shop early when I came one night to see her and a man in the shadows approached me and begged me to come around the corner to talk to him. I put my hand on the handle of my gun in my pocket and followed him. When we reached a dark place, he opened his hands and showed me a roll of gold doubloons. He said this was a gift from Señorita Baena. He told me of her vision and said that she was too cowardly to tell me in person because she didn't want to catch my sickness and die. The man in the shadows told me to go down south and cure myself with heat and a good diet, and to return to Barcelona if I wasn't dead in no less than a year's time. I loved the crazy woman and I dropped a tear on the roll of money as I handed the messenger a doubloon and told him to tell her I was going to Andalusia and that I would never return, for I would certainly die within the year. That was five years ago.

"...Knowing that that crazy woman is still in Barcelona, I am charmed that you are going there. Revenge is gentle when the wronged-one seeks to avenge what was done out of madness, and the victim didn't lose his fortune. That woman gave me enough money to set up business here in Málaga. She did me a favor with her stupid *vision*. Now you may fall in love with her. I don't *want* you to love her; but if you do end-up loving her, please treat her well and love no others. She was the only woman good enough for me in all of Barcelona. She was a genius at this, clever at that, stupid at nothing. An ardent temptress with a beautiful body, she put spells on all men around her. So please, travel with the snuffbox, and when she sees my portrait and numbs herself with my opium, tell her that I am alive and in perfect health, that I am well-known in Málaga and I speak fondly of her. Remember her address..."

I admit that Dragomir had charmed me with his story of Señorita Baena. Were it true that she was the only woman in Barcelona worth loving, I would've been happy to give as well as receive her presents.

"You're leaving so quickly?" Dragomir asked.

Behind me I could hear a small roar. A roar?, *a snore*, rather. It was Pulpawrecho. The servant who had been so lively only moments before was now scrunched up on a bench in the far end of the room. He now slept and snored loudly in an opium daze.

"I'm going to the port to find a hotel for the night," I said.

"There's a good pension above *Gordita's Wine Shop*. Not too many roaches or bedbugs, although it's a bit noisy."

I gathered up my satchels and as I was doing so I cast an eye on Pulpawrecho on the bench.

"Why is he gnawing on his wrist like that?" I curled my lip in alarm. Pulpawrecho was scrunched-up in the fetal position devouring his own wrist the way a dog lying in a corner gnaws on a bone or a piece of hide.

"Poor Pulpawrecho was taken from his mother's breast too soon, it seems. He used to suck his thumb when he first entered my service. I found it unseemly for a servant of mine to suck his thumb like a baby, so I disciplined him. He needed to suck something though, so I let him chew his wrist while he sleeps. Won't you sit back down a minute? When are you leaving Málaga?"

"You are the clairvoyant," I said, "you should know when I'm leaving!"

"Ha-ha, no please sit down... I am no clairvoyant. At least not the 'S.V. Dragomir, Clairvoyant' people take me for. That is only one of the hats I wear ...and the one I am wearing now. You see, I've worn a lot of hats over the years... Heaven's, you are all flushed! Please have some water... Okay, you look better now. Do you know how old I am? I'll be forty-two in a few days. Yet I've worked in many trades, I've lived many lives. I've been an actor, a magician, a *contrabandista*, a pawnbroker, a hired sharpshooter, a priest, a gambler... I even tended bar and worked as a fry cook. Yes, *a fry cook!*, if you can believe that. I've been to jail a few times, but I was born an honest child like we all are. The road shakes you up. You know the road, Saul. You've traveled your fair share. I like you and you interest me, this is why I am telling you this. That I am a charlatan and not a clairvoyant, that is no harm to my ego. I pay dear little Pulpawrecho who is sleeping over there an honest wage for all the services he offers me, and I live as I please. I had a large shipment of Turkish opium arrive in Gibraltar two weeks ago, and that is why I am able to help you with the stash you have in your pocket. Your meeting miss Baena will be of personal use to me. People are around to help other people in this world. Do you believe that? I really will pray for you, Saul, once our ways part. As I said: *You do interest me.*"

I wanted to leave, I was dizzy. But curious about one thing, I asked, "This story you and your servant told about how you met, I know that he was following this poor girl in the street. She looked 'baffled' as he put it. And once he saw her leaving through the courtyard, she looked, he put it... 'even more baffled' than before. It was no doubt because of something you told her that she looked even more baffled than when she had arrived. You read her fortune, of course... *so what exactly was the 'bonne aventure' that you told her?"*

"Oh, I *did* read her fortune—or rather I *guessed* at her fortune. But it was because she sought me out for that and paid me."

"Sought you ought? How? Your servant said she was running through the street and stopped in front of the sign stating your profession, and she kissed her hands. She must have been hoping for answers in life, and she stumbled on your house by chance."

"Certainly not. A lot of people come to me from the port. My services are advertised down at the port where the boats come in and directions are given to where I can be found. Wherever one finds a port city, one finds travelers coming from abroad from somewhere or another by sea, and everyone who is traveling from abroad by sea seeks two things: to first find land, and then to find their fortune. She was no exception. Once she gained land, she wanted then to gain her fortune. She came to me and I saw her vulnerable state and her young age and thought to refuse her a consultation. But she offered to pay me and even insisted on it, emptying her little purse of five gold *pistoles*. I'm not one to refuse five gold pistoles! This is a hard world for one with money in his pocket. For one without, it is impossible!"

"Yes, yes," I was impatient with my desire to know why she had left this man in such bafflement, running through the streets as she did, "So she paid you and was obviously was in need of some information. So tell me then, what was the information you gave her?"

"You are obviously curious about this little girl," chuckled Dragomir.

"I could give a damn. I'll just leave..." I again gathered my travelling satchels and then made to stand, "I was just curious to put the pieces together, you must have told her an interesting fortune. You must have been able to read her life."

"Read her life? Eh, no, actually I simply *guessed a few things...* a few things correctly. And when a complete stranger guesses correctly your life, you are ready to believe anything they tell you. It is strange how that works—or not really strange, actually. First, I simply made some obvious guesses based on her accent and physical features; then I took a leap and told her that her first name meant something like: *'clear, bright, and celebrated.'* I didn't know her name, of course, but she was stunned when I said this. She told me I was right, that her name meant exactly that: *'clear, bright, and celebrated'*—a lucky shot in the dark!, I admit it. Although there are good odds in guessing names since most girl's first names tend to revolve around words such as *blessed, beautiful*, or else *clear, bright*, and *celebrated*. These qualities seem to be an obsession among those about to give birth. I was just lucky, I chose from those five words and happened to pick the right three. Yet I won her over completely after another guess that was a safe-bet after looking at her fingertips. All this was after she'd paid me; and of course having made a few such lucky guesses, she was now ready to believe whatever nonsense I told her. So I had a little fun with her, told her this and that. I told her where she needed to go and what she needed to do to, quote, 'realize her destiny,' unquote. I made a few more guesses and played with her mind a little..."

"You played with her mind?" I asked, "...played with a very young girl who was travelling alone? I would have taken you for a man of honor. You'll do what you will, I just hope you didn't tell her anything that made her leap off a precipice."

"A precipice? Why? I am not a *mean* person, Saul. I'm a charlatan, yes, but I am not *mean*. Don't worry about the poor little girl. She was already running very quickly, I just gave her a little direction in life. I gave her a kind of roadmap, if you will, which she is now still probably following. We are very susceptible at that age. Is that all?"

"It is all very interesting. The only thing I still wonder about is your servant. He wanted to be your servant so as to find out where this little girl ran off to. Did you ever explain to him the 'roadmap' you gave her?"

"What for? To see him run off on her trail? To *lose the perfect servant?!* I told you, Pulpawrecho is the perfect servant! I wouldn't risk losing him by telling him where to run off to..."

"At least by giving me this snuffbox, you are telling *me* where to run off to."

"Of course!," Dragomir said, "I can't risk losing you either! No, I couldn't do that!" He doubled his laugh with a roar that I joined in on out of nervousness. We both quieted our laughter. "Anyway, it's too late, I see you're already going. You're already standing by the door. Anyway, that nonsense with the little girl was a long time ago. Three years have passed since then."

With these words, the fatigue and opium overtook me and I soon found myself out in the street, walking up the desolate stone lane, making my way more or less in circles as I hoped to stumble on the road that led to the port. "How do I get to the port?" I wondered aloud, mumbling to myself in the darkness.

"You just have to walk to the end of this street. Then cross the bridge, and you're there..." This response had come from a figure who had appeared suddenly in the street.

"Excuse me?" I turned in surprise, squinting to better see the stranger.

"...Just go to the end of the street, cross the bridge, and go straight and you'll reach the port," he repeated. And it was then I recognized the long pointy face of Dragomir who stood staring at me in the dark road. In haste, I clutched my satchels and hurried away from him. I hurried across the empty bridge, and paced quickly towards the black waters of the ocean that lay before me.

Chapter Nine

Saul interrupts his story...

"Perhaps I am boring you," Saul said to me, bringing me back from his tale, "There is so much to tell, I don't want to leave out details that will enlighten you to the mystery of this story."

"Boring me? Heavens no!" I picked up the bell that was on our table and shook it to make it ring. That was to signal to the waiter that we wanted something, and that he had permission to enter our private dining-room. Both Saul and I agreed that our empty bottle of cognac had been too small. We told the waiter to bring more liqueurs, a larger bottle of cognac, and enough candles to last until morning. When these arrived, the waiter left for good.

"Boring me?—a ridiculous idea! I could stay awake for a week listening to your story, I've written down all you said so far. Please do go on, I am looking forward to hearing about Saskia."

"She will come soon, fortunately. She is the hero of this story. This cognac is very good. The candles are fresh and tall. The room is warm. I'll go on with my story...."

Chapter Ten

Saul resumes his fascinating story...

" The ship horns were calling in the port of Málaga the next morning, waking me earlier than was decent. From the window of the pension where I'd spent the night I could see the stream of passengers getting thinner as all were now aboard and waiting to leave the harbor. I gathered my two valises and went downstairs to the dining hall.

I had left nothing remaining behind me in the room, my valises were by my side, and it was during my breakfast in the dining hall that I discovered the first unpleasant event of my European odyssey: my gold watch was missing! That Breguet watch was the last sentimental treasure I owned. I remembered I'd had it the night before at Dragomir's. I was so scattered in my brain after leaving his home, perhaps I lost it *en route* to the hotel. Nothing to be done though, I had to leave Andalusia seeing as I was already late to get on the road to Madrid.

Andalusia is riddled with gypsies of all ages and tricks, and as I was leaving this beautiful country, I came across an old *gitana*[1] with thick skin like leather and knotty black hair outside the station where travelers were filing past. "Hola guapo," she slithered up to me, "Give me your hand! Oh, ho! There are two pretty girls in your life... I will tell you all, etc., etc...." As I was in a rush to leave, and wanted to keep my hand away from this servant of the devil, I withdrew it firmly. Though being superstitious, I felt in my pocket for some silver *piastres* and gave a largess to the old fortuneteller. I knew these gypsies were capable of snatching a soul the way a juggler snatches a scarf, and I wanted to keep my soul for myself. Appeasing the old woman with money, I passed unhindered and felt safe, body and soul, for my journey to follow.

I arrived in Madrid early in the morning and went straight to the address that was given in the letter I received in Alexandria. There I would find my friend and old business partner, Juhani, who was a banker in Madrid, an entrepreneur, and an oil-painter of much talent. He and I worked together in Malta organizing parties until I had to flee the country, first returning to Tripoli and then fleeing there to live in Egypt. I lived in poverty in Egypt until I received Juhani's letter announcing that he too had left Malta and was living in Spain, and that he had saved my share of the profits from our last party in Malta. He announced that he'd saved ten-thousand scudi for me from our last event, which was an incredible fortune for an impoverished adventurer such as myself to fall upon. That letter found me in a miserable situation; it announced my fortune and made me rich. I set off for Europe immediately when I received it.

---

[1] GITANA: *(Sp)* "Gypsy"

Chapter Eleven

I'll tell you that no feeling resembles that wonderful sensation of when I would leave a city behind me with all the luggage I owned, all the things I care about inside, nothing left behind except the old acquaintances I was happy to leave behind along with the experiences I'd learned, and time. Thus, I left Madrid exalted! Suddenly rich, with letters of introduction to the best houses in Europe. I had letters of introduction to Juhani's friends in Paris, to his noble friends in Bavaria, in Bohemia, and Finland.

Finland was not my final destination, though I looked forward to seeing Juhani's home country based on the collection of oil paintings he had painted, and which he hung on the walls of his magnificent house in Madrid. My real goal was to get to Saint Petersburg before the summer solstice in June so I could witness the famous *white nights.* After Saint Petersburg, I didn't really care where the wind carried me. I wanted to see Poland and Petersburg; after that, I could let the earth swallow me up. I didn't know then what was going to keep me from ever reaching my goal. I would have killed anyone then who tried to prevent me from seeing those white nights (which I've still yet to see!). If you had told me what would happen to me in Barcelona, there is no way I would have believed you...

In Valencia, I almost lost my life. Yet that is a story is for another time. I arrived in Barcelona on May—nd, the anniversary of my birth. That year it fell on a night of the full moon and there was a festival in the city; there were parties in the street when I arrived on my birthday. If only that night had gone well!—where would I be now?...

The one intelligent thing I did when I arrived in Barcelona was to get a hotel room before anything else. When I arrived in the Barrio Gòtico I bought a case of wine. I walked then through the night with poetry in my heart, singing odes to the full moon above. I stumbled then on a place called the Plaça Sant Felip Neri: a stone oasis in a discreet sanctuary, unreal in that otherwise filthy and foul city. The square was both clean and fresh to the nose. I noticed two balconies of beautiful iron work on what appeared to be the second floor of a hotel overlooking pleasant trees and a fountain in the square. I looked at this charming fortress; if it was a hotel, I wanted to have a suite overlooking the square, no matter what the cost.

"You're in luck that a suite is available," said the concierge, "It never is, but tonight there is a vacancy. How many nights would you like?"

"Just one for now."

"Just one? You are then traveling on in the morning?" the concierge asked me, "Shall I book you a driver?"

"No," I told him, "I'll be in Barcelona tomorrow night as well, but I want to see how this night goes... I want to see if this charming little square isn't too noisy at night. If it is quiet, I'll stay longer, perhaps two weeks, perhaps a month. I wouldn't mind spending a month in Barcelona. But I need a room that is quiet, so I can read, engage in scholarship, et cetera..."

"Fine, Sir, but I must warn you that the town is filling up fast. You'll have a hard time booking a room for tomorrow." The concierge showed me to my suite. I locked up all my money in the safe except for a few gold escudos to buy whatever I might fancy that night of my birthday. I also saved Dragomir's silver snuffbox with the four grams of opium and his portrait for Senorita Baena, as well as my own supply of opium. I was looking forward to meeting Miss Baena.

I hired a driver to take me to the *herborista* that Dragomir told me about. It was nighttime and the full moon glowed like a shield in the sky. The herborista shop was closed but a light burned in the apartment above. I introduced myself at the door to a woman who seemed very concerned about me being there.

"Señorita Baena?"

"Yes, that's me... Who are you?"

"Saul," I said, "I've come on behalf of Dragomir, your old friend."

The woman stuttered but invited me in. She was not yet middle-aged, and still had freshness in her features, though she wore no makeup and her hair was in disorder. Her apartment was as shabby as Dragomir's home was rich. I heard noises in her kitchen but didn't pay it any notice. Before she offered coffee, I gave her the silver snuffbox containing opium and Dragomir's portrait. The sight of both made her tremble and her eyes flashed at me. This alarmed me, I wondered about the real reason why Dragomir sent to the home of this poor woman. Before one could speak to the other, two men came from the kitchen: bald and burly fellows, unkempt and rude. One shuffled behind me and the other grabbed Miss Baena. "Penelope," one shouted at her, "What did this man give you?!"

"It's a present from Dragomir," she said.

"From Dragomir?! What is it?!"

"It's opium," I told the rascal.

The two men seized me and held me down on the sofa. It was a dirty sofa, and I remember it smelled like mice. "So you came to poison Penelope on behalf of Dragomir?" the one grinned his dirty teeth at me.

"It should be good opium. I have some for myself. I would hate to find out it's poison," The two thugs then began rifling through my pockets, one thieved my gold escudos and then rejoiced after he stole my diamond pinned wallet. The other found my personal stash of opium and blamed me for trying to poison Señorita Baena as part of Dragomir's revenge. The two thugs took Miss Baena's opium, as well as my own, and forced me to eat it all. At the moment, I didn't care how much those bald Spaniards were going to force me to eat; I didn't think there was enough to harm me, although the opium tasted 'off.' There was that green shimmer and a strange metallic taste; I wasn't happy that I was forced to eat this on my birthday. I would have happily smoked it alone with Penelope Baena.

Once the thugs had stuffed the opium down my throat, they threatened to poison me. I dissuaded them. They the dragged me to the door, saying a lot of things, such as: "You tried to assassinate our friend." And "You are lucky we didn't beat you to death!"

Didn't they realize it was my birthday? I asked them this. And I asked if they realized that the moon was full. They took no interest in my questions, thus I soon found myself out in the street with a torn jacket and some scratches here and there. Good luck that I'd left my fortune in the safe in my hotel! I would get a new *tabatière* and another wallet soon after. I wished I'd been allowed to keep my opium, though; yet it occurred to me that the amount of opium they forced me to ingest was plenty to make me high—*if only that's all it had done!*

Chapter Twelve

Back at my hotel, I cleaned my wounds, redressed myself in a new, handsome suit and silk foulard, with ointment in my hair and polished teeth to parade around on my birthday night. During this exercise, I drank a bottle of Spanish wine that I'd put on ice before I left my hotel the first time to go get robbed. At least I performed my duty as an honorable gentleman as far as Dragomir was concerned. I did my commission. His portrait was delivered. Still, the fact of things was that I'd only been in Barcelona for a couple of hours and already I had been robbed of my purse and forced to ingest a quantity of opium laced with a green toxin, both of which were going to make themselves felt at any moment. I thought to go find a doctor; though the thought of passing my birthday night in examination!, being bled and all of the patient's duties... and on a full moon!... No, I decided, let me die first—this is the night for me to die—the universe couldn't have chosen a more aesthetic night. Sweet glassy moonlight soaks the sand on the Mediterranean shore, dripping moonlight on the Spanish palms, wet moonlight on the silvery arms of the ladies, of the Catalan night...

With those visions fresh in my mind, I went to the safe in my hotel to take a roll of gold doubloons. Then I suffered a delirium... I started thinking that the men who robbed me had followed back to my hotel, and that should I leave, they would enter and steal all that I had. This delirium convinced me to take *all the money I had in the world* out with me out on my birthday night!—Ô, unfortunate me!

My worldly fortune amounted to several rolls of doubloons and some *lettres de change*[1] of an equal value drawn on a bank in Barcelona. I put this money in my pocket, along with my jewels; and so impeccably dressed, poisoned with a large dose of opium laced with some mysterious green substance, I hit the streets on my first night in Barcelona, for my private celebration.

Festivities were abundant in the streets—I believed it had all been organized for me, in honor of my birthday. Nothing tame interfered with the wild creatures all around me. I tried to keep my cheer although all I could think of was that substance that was meant to kill Penelope. Dragomir surely didn't mean for *me* to eat it—why would he?! You know what they say: "*When the poison is in the snuffbox and the snuffbox is for Penelope, it's Penelope who dies, not Saul.*" Damn you fate! *My* opium wasn't green. It was black as the cemetery, untainted and wrapped in vellum. I was just going to smoke a little black opium to ease the pain in my limbs—moreover, *to take me away from the shock of experiencing the present moment.* Instead I ate four grams of toxic green opium, but at least it was opium underneath! And so, I decided to just enjoy the four grams of green opium I had already eaten while I still had the consciousness to do so... How did Socrates know after he drank the hemlock that he'd been poisoned to death? He was a skeptic, after all. Should a follower of Marcus Aurelius commit suicide if he cannot abstain from dangerous passions?

---

[1]LETTRES DE CHANGE: *(Fr)* "Letters of Credit," "Promissory Notes," "Orders for Payment," etc. The modern *Lettres de change endossées** (*endorsed) were in use in Europe from 1610 onward (beginning in Antwerp), and are still in use today. They were created for travelers and foreign transactions, permitting money to change hands from debtor to creditor, via banks or agents, without requiring the risky transport of funds to other cities.

As the opiate took effect and I had yet to feel the poisonous aspect, I started to enjoy my birthday celebration. Everywhere in the streets, people drank and cheered, danced and kissed—and all to celebrate my night! I saw this moment as attached by threads to eternity and woven between all the other braided moments of my past and my future. The human brain is so puzzling. If I can explain the change that happened in my brain when I turned off Las Ramblas to walk through a deserted part of town, you will have the portrait of the rational man instantly metamorphosing into the disassociated schizophrenic.

I was still half-sober when a man—a very tall man, he was dressed to his eyelids in black crêpe—stopped me on the street to tell me I looked deathly pale. Having seen me for the first time at this moment, I took offense. How the hell could he have known what my complexion *normally* looks like? And what if I were *always* deathly pale?! I asked the monster these questions. He replied that he couldn't know, but that if I needed a hospital, one could be found at the end of this side-street near where we were standing. I don't know if I thanked him, or cursed him to Hades. But I *did* take his advice. I went vagabonding down that side street where the hospital was said to be... just in case.

My vagabonding took me into a seedy part of town that I found out later was called El Raval. The street where the said-hospital was located branched-out into sinister alleys, apartment squalors, everything the color of soot. The quarter smelled of poverty and dirt. In this dirty quarter, I thought, in the fine clothes I'm wearing, all it would take is one crazy thief with a pistol to rob me of my entire fortune and make me a pauper. But no, I would take a bullet before surrendering to any thief.

"Why on earth am I following this street that leads to a hospital?" I screamed this question over and over in a very loud voice, so the passersby thought I was mad. "Why am I following a street that goes to a hospital? Do *I need* a hospital? *Well, do I?* Damn-it, I *am* a hospital!"

By now, the opiates were in full effect with all the sweet pleasures opiates bring, my head tingled, my body too. I enjoyed the high until I felt something else, something new, something very *unlike* opium. It was that green death... that unknown chemical, it frightened me at first! 'Why frighten you, Saul? Of all people, *you* are not afraid to die. Take it as it comes...'

Next effect to shake my brain, what made me truly certain I had been killed with a chemical poison, and not some *douce tueuse*[1] like our Lady Opium who is natural and holy to medicine. First I suffered twinges in my head where, for the space of a several moments, I didn't know where I was in relationship to the world: An intense self-depersonalization schism, I believed I was standing by myself, watching myself walk down the sidewalk; then my chest tightened and breathing became strained. The leather of my head started tightening in the strangest way, I was sure that at any moment I would die of a brain aneurysm, or else my heart would give up...

Then comes a moment when the panic disappears and I feel numb again. I am at peace. Now, no longer at peace, my depersonalization fever strikes again and rises to a level where, *not only* was I autoscopic[2], but I was also *teleautoscopic!* My Watcher-Self was not near to my body like the first time; rather, I was *far away from my body* this time, about ten meters up in the air, and away, looking down at the pathetic figure of my carcass walking along without a soul, trying to fight off death, and trying to make sense of what remains of his life. Wherever could he be going on this sidewalk he was sent to stroll?

Fortunately, these crises of autoscopy lasted only moments and I would soon come back to myself enough to register my surroundings. I passed a young couple kissing away on the street. Between embraces they whispered to each other; they giggled pleasantries, and they laughed away *that world* that was outside of *their world*, the world of their love. And I heard what they were saying between kisses. They were discussing *me!*

---

[1] DOUCE TUEUSE: *(Fr)* This phrase can either be translated as "sweet killer" or "soft killer."

[2]AUTOSCOPIC: From the Greek αὐτός ('self') and σκοπός ("watcher"). Autoscopy is a mental phenomenon experienced most often through mental illness or drug abuse, where a person hallucinates that they are outside of their body, watching their body (often from an elevated position) perform the same tasks that the person was engaged in when the hallucination began. Autoscopic experiences are reported to be very brief, and often very terrifying.

Those stupid animals! I, *Saul,* who is *after all a human being,* yet a human being who has lived his whole life with a great respect for philosophy, while striving to live the eudaimonic life, was now in the process of giving up his soul, of dying. Meanwhile, these lovers were amusing themselves by painting my death into their tryst as some sort of ornament to the scene.

"You will not have it!" I growled, loud as I could as I passed the two lovers, "*You* will not have it, and *I* will not have a banal ending by going out *here,* like *this*... and with *you*!" So I spoke as they huddled in fear. Though I did not understand it then, that the end had not come yet, that it was now the very beginning; and that my poisoned body was struggling to bloom, and not to die.

The sound of my new life began, as begins the sound of a solitary Spanish guitar. Imagine if you will, a classical guitarist who is highly skilled in his art, and who strums the one guitar he loves, and has had for most his life; he strums from his solitude, a single soul lost in the Spanish night. His song is in a minor key, it speaks of travel, of loneliness, of love.

As I walked that night, and *wherever* I walked, the sound grew stronger and more beautiful. Gone were all the symptoms of my, *malaise;* I no longer travelled from my body and I no longer feared to die. I simply walked and listened to the classical guitar, imagining the scene of the player who was playing.

A scene formed itself in my imagination... It was one of some handsome, olive-faced youth playing beneath the balcony of some lady, who may fall in love with him, he hopes, if he plays well enough. He is perfumed and is wearing his finest suit for the occasion. The lady may listen by the window with eagerness, or she may fall asleep in her bed if his singing voice doesn't match the charm of his rosewood guitar. So the youth will play his song and she will either be enchanted or annoyed by his nighttime serenade. It will all depend on the condition of her heart, and the direction of its affections.

I was meanwhile floating along in my own universe—a cloud of anesthesia, a euphoria of harmony. The guitar piece was progressing nicely and I knew I would soon overtake the youth in the street. I would stop to watch him play his song, guitar on his knee, his face tilted amorously, upwards!—towards his one love's balcony.

I was soon to be brought to light, though, and shown the falseness and foolishness of the idyll my mind had conceived. As I gained pace and the guitarist played on, keeping his great wheel of a song rolling along in the minor key, and when his song came 'round again, and the wheel came 'round again, that would be the moment I would pass the trees that blocked the part of that house where the balcony was, where the player was playing.

Two, or perhaps three times in a person's life, usually not more, does it happen that everything aligns together in poetic perfection to allow his and her destiny to become for a time, as beautiful as we say, it *had to become.*

That was how it was this night. When the singing began, not a moment later or a moment sooner, was when I caught sight of the guitarist...

It was that it was *her* voice, that it was *her* touch on the strings, that had seduced me up until I caught sight of *her*: I saw a young girl sitting alone on a balcony, at a moment when she began to sing. No other way to describe her voice other than: *It was feminine.* It was feminine and healthy, without a blemish though not over-practiced. The songs of Orpheus may have moved rocks and snakes, and killed his lover, but this goddess' song moved my heart to a kind of love that ten-thousand vipers could never poison. Here is my impression of seeing her for the first time:

A very young girl was seated on a balcony, a mere two floors up from the street. She finished her song on the classical guitar, and now she's stopped and sits still, as though caught by a sudden idea. She is the very portrait of youthful perfection, including all the charming defects of youth. Her feet were bare (I noticed them first), and were smudged with dirt. Her legs dangled over the balcony's edge. Both were tanned, and her knees had scratches on them. Her skirt was the color of cracked-cream. It was bunched-up and was dirty at the hems as though she'd been out tramping in the streets. Now she was apparently at home and at her ease, certainly at her father's house. I imagined they were a rather poor family. Husband and wife were asleep in bed, while their daughter had decided to fetch her guitar and step out onto the balcony to serenade herself in the light of the full moon...

On her small thighs sits her Spanish guitar. Her fingers resume plucking the strings. Her song resumes on the minor key. Her head is lowered in concentration, her face is obscured by long falling hair. A simple cotton nightshirt, two straps on tiny, bronzed shoulders, clings to the forms of her body, a body that has just begun to show the first early, promising signs of an upcoming womanhood. Her small breasts tremble slightly over the pumping of her young heart. Her ballad turns round-and-round, the great wheel that always falls on the same low refrain, only to rise again. Each time the cycle turns, I expect her to resume singing.

It was only when she prepared herself to sing again—raising her chin, letting her forehead ascend, bathing her face in the moonlight, an act which sent her mass of hair tumbling back over her shoulders—that I saw her face for the first time... it was the most sensual, holy, and angelic face that heaven or earth e'er did create. The first sight of her face made my heart evaporate in my chest.

Could I neither die then nor gaze at her face every day, I would need to recreate it through painting or sculpture, or through fatherhood, until a second such face could be born. It was a face at once innocent and feral, soft and wild... Her mouth voluptuous, eyes deep as oceans, her eyes as wide as planets. I likened her to the slender Psyché and judged that the perfection of her face ennobled everything unclean around her: the dusty hems of her bunched-up skirt, the worn straps of her nightshirt; the blackened soles of her bare feet, and the soot-covered balcony on which she perched. All this and the pungent air! Ô this night, sweet pungent night! Hébé[1] *may come but a season. But this girl's season would know a hot spring and an Indian summer.*

---

[1] HÉBÉ: *(Greek)* The Greek goddess of youth, daughter of Zeus and Hera. The word "hébé" (ηβη) is also used to describe the time at which a girl or woman has reached the climax of her beauty, in contrast to the masculine version: "Aristeia" (ἀϱιστεία), the time when a Greek man fights his 'best fight' in battle.

When I achieved to separate my eyes from my angel, I looked around at the street that was otherwise dark and deserted. I felt then a strange heat penetrating my body, and the pleasure I had felt from gazing at my girl turned into an intense fear. The poison in my blood made itself felt again. My heart pushed at the cage of bones in my chest. The vertigo that one experiences before losing consciousness increased to overwhelm me. My vision failed me—now the world was blurry, now it was black! And what if I am to die now? Oh, no! Don't make me die just now!

I felt myself sleeping while standing, I wanted to look at my guitar player again. But eyes fluttered... between blackouts and blizzards of blur... I couldn't focus on her anymore. All I could see was myself: my own dead body dressed in funereal clothes. I was keeping vigil over it. The girl with the guitar was gone from my life, but I was happy! I had died, but I was happy... For I had died the sweetest death of my life!

I didn't wake up until very late the next day. Or maybe it was two days later. I was in a small, unknown room, dimly lit, lying on a small, unknown bed. The room was warm and smelled fresh and sweet, like amber and sugar, like teenage perfume.

I was numb and at peace. Although I seemed to not be in command of my body, I was not afraid. I strained to move my eyes so as to look around and understand my environment. At first I thought I was alone in the room. I flashed back in my memory to think where I could be. Was I back in Malta or Alexandria?, I wondered. Then I remembered I'd arrived in Spain. I felt myself smile as I remembered the vision I had had on the street, watching that girl playing and singing on her guitar.

The schism I'd experienced out on the street replayed itself in my memory with great clarity. I had separated saint from devil in myself out in the street. From now on I would live the ascetic life. This thought made me laugh. It was a small laugh, but it sounded giant in that bedroom. What room was I in? I rolled my head and felt a pillow propped beneath it, a pillow that smelled sweeter, fresher, better than anything I had ever smelled before. I rolled my nose into the pillow, tasting it with my mouth.

I realized the mobility of my head. Then a sudden fear came and I shot my head up and looked around.

Girl's clothes were scattered everywhere, strewn all over the chairs, the floor, an old trunk stood in the corner. It was then I noticed, sitting in a small chair of light-colored wood, several paces away from me, a young girl. She was staring at me with great intention, her two fists plopped in the lap of her crumpled skirt. Her eyes were wide open. Her lips trembled slightly and were glossy and pink. She said, "Good then! You are awake now!"

"I am awake?!" I asked her, surprised. But *who was I* to be awake?! So, it seemed when we die, we meet no agèd man with a white beard seated on a throne in the clouds. Instead, we meet a young girl sitting in a chair of light-colored wood, in a room where feminine clothing and girlish possessions lie scattered around; the air is filled with the enchanting smells of teenage perfume... this is death.

As though someone were handing you clues to a riddle, which becomes ever more clear each clue you are given, so did my memory piece itself together as the moments flit by. I remembered arriving in Barcelona, the commotion in the street, buying wine in the Barrio Gòtico, leaving my money and jewels at my hotel, being poisoned at an herborista's house. I remembered dressing for my birthday and going out and seeing this same girl, this soft adolescent, who seemed to me *an angel dancing on glass.* then to be carved in ivory or white marble. My angel was dressed in ivory and white marble, and sat on a balcony in a poor quarter of town on a road where I was told I would find a hospital. Now, to-night, the light was different. Everything in this scene now was more real, more sober. The girl with the guitar, now my guardian, was still a creature of youthful perfection. But she was no deity. A nymph, yes. But she was no goddess holding her womanhood before man as honey and poison, the gift of life, and the gift of death. I didn't have to fear for my life, I knew, for my guardian was just a young girl wearing a little pale-yellow summer shirt: all damp from the Barcelona humidity, its straps clinging to bronzed shoulders rolling down into the fabric covering a young girl's chest, breasts small as two ripe apples, a small little tummy. Bunches of white lace on her cotton skirt shone bright against smooth, golden legs bearing only a down of fine, light-colored hair.

I gasped and had a flashback from that night on the street. I remembered, as I stood there, my blood pumping poison into my heart; my wild heart pounding with insanity—her clothes were a little dirty that night. Just as the exquisite angel in the graveyard where many storms and foul days leave their filthy imprint in the folds of marble cloth, sticking in the cracks of stone; so this girl with her guitar appeared that night in my intoxication, perfect then too as now—except now she was no ivory goddess, no immortal angel, she was merely a young girl who had recently bathed, and whose face was fresh and charming, who sat on the edge of her seat in a very small and cluttered little room that smelled of sweet perfume.

She asked me the most bizarre questions: "How did you come to fall in the road in fine clothes? You were sleeping..." She sat patient and seemed to look inward at herself; until suddenly she cried out: "So it's true! I knew that you would fall in this road, I knew it had to be in Barcelona, and on this road!"

Was she crazy? I of course had no idea what the girl was talking about. I let her go on talking about how she found me in the road—"sleeping in fine clothes," as she put it—and I said nothing.

"Did you know you were going to fall there?" her face kept searching in mine, "*How long have you known* you were going to fall there?! Do you know Adélaïse? You've never heard of her? Neither Adélaïse from Marseille nor Adélaïse from Paris?"

I had never been to either Marseille or to Paris, and I didn't know about falling anywhere and I told her as much.

"I was poisoned. It wasn't planned. They forced me to eat the opium. It has a strange green shimmer. I wanted to find the hospital to get an antidote. I was close, I think. It seems there is a hospital at the end of your street. A man wanted me to find it, a tall and thin figure; he said I looked like I was dying. *And I knew then that I would fall—and I did fall!* ...I guess I did, who really knows ...Listen, I won't trouble you anymore. I'll leave now."

I tried to get up out of her bed.

"Don't!" She rushed to me and threw herself against me, which caused me to fall backwards on the bed. I felt then an incredibly soft body and the sensation was so sweet that I let her breathe against me, her chest on my chest; her scent was some soporific drug that I breathed until I fell into a deep sleep.

Sometime later, the room was very dark, the girl was gone. Her chair was empty.

I sat up in the small bed, weak from fever and fearing it had been a dream, and that the girl had never been there. While travelling, I occasionally lodged in inns where I was put-up in the bedrooms of my hostess' young daughters, during the time they were away studying or doing something. I was probably at one such inn now, I was sure of it. As I considered this, the sound of breathing caught my ear. I rolled and looked down over the edge of my little twin bed and saw that there on the ground, curled up and sleeping softly like a squirrel in a pretty little ball, was the young girl, my guardian.

Chapter Thirteen

"My dear," I said to the floor in the darkness, "You cannot sleep on the wood. Take your bed, I will sleep down there."

The girl rolled a little and opened her delicate eyes. "No, no," she purred, "you need the bed. You were sleeping on the hard stones in the street. So I get the hard wood. Let's sleep, both of us. Goodnight...."

"Goodnight." I rolled onto my back in the dark and contemplated this magical child who had taken me unconscious into her home and sacrificed her bed. Her parents were no doubt asleep in a nearby room. I worried about them entering. Her poor old father would bring his sword, and I had no such weapon to meet him with. How was this my fault? I was recently sleeping in the street. This bed came by surprise.

Daylight flooded the room and the warm Barcelona sun cracked the mud on the windowpane where it had rained in the night—it was the only window in the little apartment and it went out to the little balcony. The window was behind my head. The girl brought me coffee and was surprised that I took sugar. This was the first day we spoke as two people. "Somehow I thought you would take it black," she said.

"I am a man. I like to taste sweet things: honey and rose-oil, a woman's skin scented with amber, vanilla and myrrh, and other things that are feminine. You are a woman. You enjoy musky men, and black coffee."

"You are right," she laughed. Her clothes were changed now and she wore a pink dress that was so short that I noticed she had on underneath white cotton panties with a pink trim. There was no jewelry on her fingers, neither on her wrists, although around her neck she wore a golden locket shaped like a heart. It appeared to be fairly precious. After she brushed her hair by the mirror, she sat beside me on the bed, showing perfect confidence.

I asked her, "Are your parents in the house?"

"Nope. They are... They're not here."

"Then how did you get me up into your room?"

"Golya, the maid, she helped me. We both carried you inside and undressed you."

"Undressed me?" I looked past her and noticed my suit of evening clothes and silk foulard; they'd been ironed and were hung on the wall behind her empty wooden chair. "Golya and I carried you, then I sent her away. She won't be coming back. I sent her to her parents in the country. She usually sleeps here though."

"Here, where?" I looked around the room. There wasn't so much as a cubby hole for a maid to sleep in. Near the wall where my clothes were hanging, a limp curtain was strung to conceal, rather poorly, a makeshift kitchen. "So there are many other rooms in this house?"

"No, no! Not many! Not even one more! This is it! It's just a room in a building with other tenants. But Golya sleeps in the common stairwell. There is a little closet with a bed only so big. See that door over there? In it is a little bathroom. And behind you is the window that goes out to the balcony where I play my guitar at night."

"Hmm," I said, "How long have you lived here? And, dear girl, excuse me for asking, but you don't seem to be of any great age—*where are your parents?*"

"I've lived here nine months! Can you believe it by looking around the room? So you know, every night these last nine months—that is to say *every night since I've been in Barcelona*—I've spent every evening, and most of every night, playing my guitar on my balcony. And every night sleeping in this tiny bed you're in. But now I can stop and give this room back to the landlord because I found you, just as I knew I would find you: *sleeping in the road in fine clothes.*"

With this last phrase of hers, I became convinced that the girl was mad.

"My parents, you ask? That's a long story—a story for another time. Just don't think about them. Don't trouble yourself about anything. Except don't forget one thing... don't forget where you were born! Where *were* you born, anyway? Your Spanish is good but I can tell you're not Spanish—just like I am not Spanish. How do you feel, by the way? The jaundice is finally leaving your skin...."

"Jaundice?!" I stood up so quickly that the poor girl rattled on her bed. Grabbing at my skin, my hands trembled. I looked in the mirror... So terrified I was! My entire skin was dark yellow!

"I believe you were poisoned with copper," she told me, "'*Vert-de-gris*', I think it's called in French—in English I believe it's called 'verdigris.' I read about this poison in a novel once... that in itself is a funny story... I was walking home to this room one evening when a strange man came from the shadows, a very tall man in a black suit, and he handed me a novel... a book, you see... and he said, 'I think you dropped this, Miss.' Well I hadn't dropped it. It wasn't even mine; but before I could say so, the stranger disappeared. I looked closely at the novel. It looked new, like it hadn't even been on the ground. I think he lied about the whole thing. Anyways, I took this novel home and read it cover-to-cover in one night. It *was* a strange novel indeed! When it began, the hero had been poisoned with copper vert-de-gris. I was so shocked by the descriptions of the poisoning, and so afraid that such a thing was possible, that I went out first thing the next morning and bought all the proper antidotes for copper poisoning—you know, chelating agents[1] and such. I was horrified that I might need them someday; and I did end-up needing them... to help you! So, you *did* eat copper!, didn't you?!"

"I ate opium," I said, "Poisoned opium. It was green."

"Oh!" She then blushed as much as a girl can blush, and she hid her face in the blanket that was against my legs. I felt a warm tingling vibration rise through the limbs of my body.

"No," I said, "you are probably right about your diagnosis of vert-de-gris. In any case, you'd better get back in your chair. You're too beautiful of a girl to be lounging next to a grown man naked in a bed—even if he does have a blanket over him."

"Oh, Monsieur! You *are* naïve!" The child patted me on the forehead as though *I* were the child. Then returning to her chair a few meters away, she said, "In any case, Mister, I'm the one who brought you here—to Barcelona, I mean—*and* to this very room. *It is now that you are found! Do you hear?"* ...This statement made me paranoid, then she added, *"Now I am found too!* Oh, I'll worry about you, Sir! ...but don't you worry about me..." She then tossed her head back and laughed. "You *are* a naïve man—yellow skin and all!"

With these strange words of hers, I knew now for sure the girl was mad.

---

[1] CHELATING AGENTS: Used to detoxify the body of metal poisoning by converting the metals to chemically inert forms.

Chapter Fourteen

The Gypsy and the poison...

The poison wasn't finished with me. I had a high fever the next morning before dawn. I thought I had recovered from whatever I'd ingested, the dizziness was gone, my jaundice had disappeared. Then the fever returned: sweat, delirium, and ranting.

The previous day had been joyous and gay. After I decided that the girl was crazy, we giggled a lot together, and seeing that I was in good spirits, she played songs for me on her guitar. She plucked a haunting Spanish piece in a minor key; then she sang a song that she wrote in English, which she'd sung on her balcony the night of my accident: "Ceylon," it was called. She then played a Romanian gypsy song. Her voice was enchanting, melodic, it pranced from note to note with ease and fluidity.

Now it was night. The moon outside her window was half-full and waning. *'That moon says I've been here a whole week,'* I said to myself, *'Do you remember the fullness of the moon on my birthday? Now the moon is cut in half. In a week there will be no moon at all. When it starts to grow again, I know I can begin drinking again; and I can begin seducing women again! ...I won't be here with this little girl at that time...*

'Although she is certainly lovely!—one can't deny it. No, one couldn't find a more exquisite youth anywhere. Although, she is just that, a youth—and nothing more...

'Yet where does she come from, this sweet child? She strums her eastern songs as though she's been singing them since she was a babe... I'm sure she grew up with a tambourine at her feet to collect tips from the passers-by. It seems she has no parents. I've heard her speak several languages—and all with a mysterious accent... I can't place her anywhere. Doubtless, she is a nomad of sorts, like the gypsy in that Romanian song she sings: the one about that female drifter who is a pickpocket, and who amuses herself by stealing the souls of men. A "vagari vulgaris[1]*,"* I told myself, *"that's what she is, and nothing more!"*

'No, I didn't come to Barcelona to meet a transient. I came to Barcelona to devote myself to pleasure. To carouse with black-eyed beauties, Latinate she-wolves, fire-eyed Spanish seductresses with snakelike bodies and an equal devotion to pleasure, women well-versed in matters of love... I dreamt of Spain while I was unconscious tonight. Now that I'm awake I ask myself: What am I doing here?! Why am I lying in the bed of this teenaged Calypso[2]*?, this young, guitar-strumming girl who escaped from a gypsy encampment!'*

...Thus ran my thoughts as I drifted to sweet sleep in the girl's little bed that night. While she, dear self-sacrificing angel, slept on a pile of her girlish clothes on the floor.

---

[1] VAGARI VULGARIS: *(Latin)* Meaning a 'common vagabond.' This phrase is of Payne's coinage: Construction of the Latin verb 'vagor' ('to wander'), and 'vulgaris' ('common').

[2] CALYPSO: The name in Greek (Καλυψώ) means "I shall hide," which is what the nymph-goddess did when Odysseus shipwrecked on her island in *The Odyssey*. She hid him from the world for seven years.

It was then about four in the morning that I awoke with a terrible fever. She awoke too and spent the rest of the night boiling herbal infusions to drink, to bring my fever down.

With the attention she paid me, I felt shame for having dismissed her the night before as a mere runaway gypsy-child getting in the way of my fun. Carousing with mature Spanish women was the furthest thing from my thoughts as I lay with a fever, an invalid, fortunate to have someone to take care of me. The fever started with my hallucinating of strange things: animals that looked like men, the presence of ghosts in the room, looming monsters, and the like. The poor girl had become afraid by my thrashing-about, screaming nonsense: *"Do you see them?! Do you see them?!"*

"See what?!"

"Those beardless fish! Why are they building fires in the room?! Where are we now?! Greece?! [And so on....]"

Sleepy-eyed, and docile as a lamb, she went and boiled water. She gave me to drink a bicarbonate solution. She fed me chelating agents. Then she put a cold compress on my forehead. She declared I had a 'dangerous temperature.' And the next hours were spent with her cooking me hot teas and infusions to sip, preparing poultices for my back, my stiff arms, and my legs.

"Drink some tea," she said to me, "and tell me where you were you born."

She pressed a wet washcloth to my forehead.

"Drink some water."

"I am going to die," I told her.

"You are not going to die. You were meant to fall sleep in the street dressed in fine clothes. And *right now,* we are meant to be here in this room, you and I. Soon you will take me to the town where your father was born. We will travel together."

"Don't you think it is weird to speak to a man like this?"

"No, I need to help you."

"How do you know *it is you* who needs to help *me* and not the other way around?"

"You are in greater need than I am at the moment. And it is important that you stay alive, since your life is an important one—although right now, your life is a puzzle to me."

"Right now 'my life' is a puzzle to me as well."

"That is why I need you to help me. Give me information so I can put the puzzle together."

"Why?"

"Why?!" Suddenly she was filled with exaltation, "Because everything depends on it! Our destinies are entwined, yours and mine!"

I waved my hands in annoyance. She had begun to sound like one of those young girls in a convent who reads too many novels. She went on...

"Do you really think I would have spent the nine months of my life living in this tiny room in Barcelona if I weren't waiting for you to appear as you did? I like Barcelona well enough, but I like Paris better. I could have spent these last two years in Paris looking for Adélaïse. But instead I spent two years playing my guitar to an empty street at night, waiting for you to stumble into view.

You would think from these strange words of hers that my hostess was a complete fanatic, a gullible nutcase who was madly in love with me, (or *'the idea of me'* at least); but I would soon learn that this was not the case. *The truth of our situation* was much more interesting than my intuition had picked-up on. She knew what she was doing. She was a clever child, crafty and wild—*but not at all crazy...*

"Who is Adélaïse?" I asked.

"Oh, Adélaïse! She is my best friend! We haven't seen each other since we were eleven. We were classmates at the boarding school in London, we were inseparable. I loved her and she loved me. To know about her, you have to know about my life... I grew up in Holland, in a small city not far from Amsterdam. My parents had one goal for me as a child: they wanted me to learn English. So when I was very young, (only six years old), they used all of their savings—making tremendous sacrifices, and depriving themselves of all of life's comforts so they could afford it—and they sent me to a private boarding school in London. During the five years I spent at that school, Adélaïse and I had a perfect friendship. We discovered together what it meant to be *girls* ...to be *people* of all things—and of all things, what it meant *to be alive!* ...This sensation lasted until my final spring at the boarding school: That sad spring. *Oh, it was the saddest spring one could imagine!*

"...At the end of winter, my parents travelled down to see me from Holland. They had an accident on the road. Both were killed. When I was told the news, I cried so hard that I had to be watched day and night for a long time. People at the school thought that I would choke to death on my tears ...or else they thought I might simply kill myself...

"I remember my obsession with the last two letters I received from my two parents. They each wrote me these letters separately—my mother *hers* and my father *his*—which they often did. Neither of them had any close friends, and I was their only child, so they were both very intimate with me and sent me letters about their private lives that often resembled confessions. The only letters I received written by both of them on the same stationery were the inevitable cards sent for Christmas and Easter. Those are times when one is supposed to act joyfully in spite of everything. The rest of the year, they wrote to me secretly and in private. They never hesitated to pour their hearts out, sharing their lives and private thoughts with me. From those two final letters written while they were alive, I learned from both my father and mother that each had been suffering in private for years. So, I knew when they died just a few days after their letters arrived, that both my father and my mother died poor and alone. All of a sudden, I found myself, 'alive and alone,' and 'an orphan' to boot, all in one single day. It's true that I had spent the previous five years living without my parents, but they were always a 'constant' in my life. I knew their death would change my life, but I wasn't certain *how* it would change my life. Because my parents died penniless, consequently leaving me penniless as well, the only thing that I was certain of right away when they died, was that I would have to leave my boarding school...

"'*To go where?!*' I asked myself over and again. The answer came from outside. I had an uncle, the brother of my mother. He was a bachelor of about fifty years, living in Italy, in Verona to be exact. He was wealthy, but his health was starting to turn bad. He learned of my mother's death, and learned of my situation, through some indifferent relatives of ours. So just two days after my parents died, this uncle took legal custody of me. Being wealthy, he could have easily paid for me to stay at my boarding school in England, but he liked my company so much in the two days we spent touring around London to visit the monuments, that he wanted me to come live in his mansion. It was a beautiful converted-monastery atop a hill, overlooking the city of Verona. So at age eleven I moved to Italy. That was the last time I saw my best friend, Adélaïse."

"You never went back to London?" I asked.

"Yes, yes... after I stopped living in Italy, I would go to London when it was more convenient than going to Italy. I had to go to one of those places... You see, my uncle was a very generous man. And he adored me to the heavens. I would certainly still be with him in Verona if he hadn't died 'all of a sudden.'

"...Unlike my parents, who had no will, my uncle's will was complete and he updated it every six-months. He had arranged things in it so that when he died, I would benefit from an annual income of two-hundred pounds sterling, which I could draw from every three months for the rest of my life. You know the value of two-hundred pounds... it's a respectable income even for somebody with a family, so just think how a young person on her own could benefit!

"...Before coming to Barcelona, I sought a new life by travelling to new cities, destinations I chose according to the caprices of my wanderlust at any given time. All my wanderings were funded, thanks to my dear, loving uncle, without whom I would only have an eleven-year-old kid's education; and I would be working as a waitress in some miserable café in London, or back in Holland...

"...But just as my uncle was generous in his protection of me, he was also generous in his jealousy. He had his lawyer add it to his will that should it ever be discovered that I live with a man, or were to marry a man, or do anything with a man, I would no longer receive my two-hundred pound income. His will explained it in nice enough terms: when a girl is a *demoiselle*, her parents or guardian should take care of her, be they living or deceased; but once she is a lady, a *dame*, it is her husband who must take financial responsibility. That was the legal, rational, explanation, although it only covered marriage. Elsewhere in the will it explained—always in well-intentioned terms—that his estate was free of obligations to pay me my income after his death if it were discovered that I was 'involved in any romantic way' with a man."

"Your uncle was in the unfortunate position of being in love with you," I told her, "But what if word gets around that you are keeping me in your apartment?"

"I would lose my income."

"Doesn't that scare you?"

"It's not something of importance to me right now. It's just an income, and nothing more."

I envied her that statement. I too have said phrases like, "It's just money, nothing more." Although it was always something more. I was an adventurer, living an adventurer's life. It was always of great concern to me, and of great uncertainty, where the next money would come from, and where it would get me. Sure, I was an adventurer, but she was not an *adventuress*. She was a *wanderess*. Thus, she didn't care about money, only experiences. Whether they came from wealth or from poverty, it was all the same to her.

Chapter Fifteen

The days that followed were filled with fever and nausea, and during the nights I suffered tormenting dreams. After one such night, I woke up in panic. I had recalled that when I left the Hotel Sant Felip Neri on my birthday, I'd filled my pockets with my entire fortune: all my savings and all my jewelry. I had left nothing behind me at the hotel. I was awake now and the girl was standing over me, her hands trembling to press a wet cloth to my forehead. I panicked, and cursed in French, (French is the native-language of my mother, as she grew-up in royal and diplomatic circles; thus it is also my native-language in a sense, it is the language that comes easiest to me when I panic)...

"Putain ! Mais il est où, mon argent ? Je l'ai perdu !" [1]

"De quoi parles-tu, mon cher ? [2] What money?

[1] PUTAIN … PERDU ! : Translation: "Fuck! Where is my money? I lost it!"

[2] DE QUOI … MON CHER ? : Translation: "What are you talking about, my dear?"

"My money! It's gone!"

"What money?"

"In the pockets of my suit! Before I fell in the street... I had several rolls of gold coins and some bank exchange-letters..."

"Oh?... several rolls of coins and bank exchange-letters...?" she tumbled her head, then burst into laughter, "Don't worry, my little paranoiac, your money is safe..." and crossing the room to where my suit was hanging on her wall, she took from the pockets the many rolls of gold doubloons and an equal amount of money in *lettres de change* for a bank in Barcelona. I looked it over, it was all there. Nothing had been lost. I was still rich. I exhaled with relief and felt better all in all, though I couldn't understand why she'd called me her 'little paranoiac.'

"Don't panic, Saul. Everything is in order. When you fell in the street, I was the first person that came to you. No one stole so much as a button from your jacket before I took you inside our apartment."

"Wait, girl..."

"What?"

"How do you know my name?"

"You told me."

"I did?"

"You don't remember? When you first thought you were going to die, you told me your name was Saul. 'I am Saul,' you said, 'the son of Solarus. Please remember my name and patronymic to pass them on to those who will have survived me.' ...I asked you then to tell me about your father, Solarus, but you wouldn't tell me. Will you tell me now? Where did your father come from?"

"Did the money and jewelry fall in the street when I fell?"

"No, it stayed in your pockets. Will you forgive me for going through your pockets while you were unconscious? I thought I might find in them the reason *as to why you were unconscious*, and that it would help me to revive you."

"You are a good girl. Take half of the money. It's yours."

"No, I don't want your money." She put my gold pieces and exchange letters back in my pocket and her cool body fell on my feverish limbs and I felt a great peace with her on top of me. There was no sexuality in her embrace, only friendship. She asked me again in which country I was born, and about the home where my father was raised. Again I dodged the question. This will come up again. My father's origins were an obsession of hers. You will see why in time, I still didn't know why myself.

I remembered then what Dragomir had said about the mania parents have about giving their children names that mean *bright, shining,* or *famous,* or all three. I had to agree. Over the many years of my amorous life, I had had intimate relations with such creatures of the sweet-smelling sex who were called Alina, Brigitte, Claire and Clarissa, Eleanor, and Ellen, Helen, Lucy, Phaedra, and Phoebe, etc., which all meant more or less: *clear, bright,* and *celebrated.* This is the trick that Dragomir had used to guess correctly the meaning of the name of the pubescent girl whom Pulpawrecho had followed through the streets of Málaga. With that in mind, I scrawled: *'clear, bright, and celebrated'* on a piece of paper, and asked my young hostess what her name was.

"Saskia."

"Saskia?!"

"Yes... Why...? Why do you sound so shocked?"

"Does Saskia mean *'clear, bright, and celebrated?'*"

"What?"

"Is that what Saskia means?, *'clear, bright, and celebrated?'*"

"Nope, not at all. It means: *'from the Saxon people.'*"

Defeated, I wadded-up the paper where I had my divination written down, and I tore it into little shreds and threw the shreds into the stove.

A sadness fell over me then. It was not that I hoped to amaze the girl by guessing the meaning of her name. I just wanted to relate my new friend in Barcelona to the same whimsical girl who visited Dragomir and Pulpawrecho years ago in Málaga, but there was no correlation. I guess I was sad because *that* story didn't have an end, and I wanted it to. I wondered where *that* girl was, and if our paths would ever cross.

I looked at Saskia after my eyes drifted away for a while. I tried to lighten-up. "Saskia was the first-name of the wife of the painter Rembrandt."

"It was! I'm impressed that you know that. The only reason *I* know that is because she had my name."

"Both you and his Saskia are Dutch."

"No, I am Dutch, but Rembrandt's wife was from Friesland. They are like Dutch people, except they speak funny."

"So Rembrandt's wife... that's where I've heard your name before. Saskia is a beautiful name." It was no use. Finding out that Saskia didn't mean *'clear, bright, and celebrated'*, made me depressed. I was sullen after that and went to sleep for an hour. When I woke up, Saskia was touching my forehead: "Your fever has broken, my dear friend. You have recovered. Now we can go to sleep and not worry."

You can imagine how I hated it when she called me 'dear friend!'

Saskia spread herself on her nest of girlish clothes on the wooden floor beside my bed and covered herself with a wool jacket to sleep.

'It's too bad she insists on sleeping on the floor,' I thought as I drifted to sleep, 'It's also too bad her name doesn't mean 'clear, bright, and celebrated.' If it did, we would have a lot to talk about.'

Chapter Sixteen

Waking up abandoned...

I woke up in a clear, lighted—*and empty*—room. I saw no girl, received no coffee. Nevertheless, I felt my strength returning—that renewal of health which healthy men take for granted. I got up and walked the four steps to the bathroom. It was the first day in over a week that I got out of bed without help from Saskia. I looked back on the floor to the nest where she slept, and saw not a soul, only clothes. I was used to her by now. Where had she gone? I was suddenly 'alive and alone'—as hopeless as an orphan!—"Saskia!"

She was gone.

"Saskia!" I screamed again, "Where are you, my little gypsy girl?!" I looked for her in her bathroom, then in the empty hole of a kitchen that was partitioned from her bedroom only by a curtain. I looked for her on her balcony, though since I'd been there she hadn't gone out even once to play her guitar. She played it several times each day, but always by my bedside. I started to get dressed, and while dressing, I noticed a slice of paper on the table, written in neat, legible handwriting:

Dearest Saul, there is absolutely nothing for us to eat at home. So I went to buy provisions. Back soon! Your friend, Saskia.

'Hmm... eat!' I thought, 'food...' I rummaged around her kitchen looking for a scrap of something. I was very hungry. But more than hungry, I was thirsty for a drink of coffee. I also was thirsty for wine. True, I told myself, the moon was in its waning phase and I always avoid alcohol when the moon is growing smaller or not in the sky at all, but this was a special occasion. This was the first day I was well after a particularly messy convalescence. I was well, yes, but I knew I could increase my wellness with a bottle of strong, bubbling wine! I continued to rummage around her kitchen assuming the girl must have stashed *at least one bottle* of wine. I was wrong. No wine, no food, no coffee, no whisky, nothing. "Back soon," she says, "...went to buy provisions." I looked in the pockets of my suit and found in each the rolls of doubloons and my *lettres-de-change*. "Poor girl, she could have at least used *my money* to buy the provisions. Why didn't she use *my* money?!" I suddenly felt bad for her.

"After all, what are you doing here, Saul?" I asked myself "Saskia suffers every night on a nest of clothing on a wooden floor. She would probably like her bed back. She has been suffering in silence for over a week on the hard floor. She is just like her parents were, with their habit of 'suffering privately.' She has taken care of me, she cleaned my suit, she bathes me with a warm washcloth, she depleted her kitchen by feeding me broth when I was weak; and when I was strong, with large European meals she cooked with care. And now she is buying us both food with her own money. I feel bad."

I decided then that I should leave. I was a burden on the young girl. It was lamentable. Nothing to do but leave. So I finished dressing in my fine suit, tied my silk foulard around my neck, found my shoes, and made to leave.

"Perhaps I should leave her a note?" I wrote a brief explanation in French and left it on the table...

"Saskia, ma chère amie, je suis parti. Vous m'avez beaucoup aidé et, grâce à vous, je suis à nouveau en grande forme. A présent vous devez retrouver la jouissance de votre lit, de votre espace, de votre vie privée. Ainsi, je vous la rends. Adieu, Saul." [1]

With that, I made for the door. I went out into a corridor I'd never consciously seen before, and made to close her front door which, if it clicked, it would lock. But before I closed it I thought, 'Perhaps Saskia would like to know where I'm going. Would she? Perhaps. Who knows. So I went back inside and amended my note, writing this postscript in English:

"PS: If you want to see me again, for whatever reason, I am staying at the Hotel Saint Felip Neri."

With that I left Saskia's home and wandered through the bright morning streets of Barcelona, gaiety in my heart for I'd survived yet another misadventure, no sense of direction as my mind entertained only visions of soft, bubbling wine and a hot bath in a real tub at my hotel suite. I crossed Las Ramblas with haste and felt my money and my future bulging brightly in my pockets. I was healthy again and wore my destiny like a flower in my buttonhole. Little did I know then that dark winds of trouble were brewing on the horizon and they were soon rip my destiny's petals clean off its stem.

Being lost, I stumbled on Hotel Sant Felip Neri by fluke, and greeted the concierge. He was shoveling snuff into his nose and looked at me strangely, as though he at once knew me but had never seen me before. I asked for the key to my room and he stumbled into the back and returned with my two valises and my case of wine.

"You were gone a week, sir. Certainly you didn't think your room would still be reserved for you."

I was stupefied; I stared at my valises, at the case, and all I could think of to say was, "At least you didn't drink my wine."

---

[1] TRANSLATION: "Saskia, my dear friend, I left. You* really helped me and, thanks to you, I'm healthy again. But you need your bed, your space, your private life back. Thus, I am leaving them to you. Farewell, Saul." (*You [vous]: Non-familiar form of address hints that Saul is demonstrating his distancing himself emotionally from Saskia's care and the intimacy of her bedroom [at least in the modern usage of the French vous/tu.] [Ed.])

"No, sir. I have my own wine."

I asked him for another room, he said "Impossible. It's high-season. We are all booked-up."

This made me angry. I waved my arms. I insisted he evict some other guests to make room for me—no avail. He told me that the entire town was booked-up and I would have a hard time finding a room anywhere. This made me absolutely furious and I contemplated beating him across the face. I wanted my bath and my wine in peace.

The concierge apparently gauged my anger and thought it was in his interest to cool me down. He said, "There was a messenger stopped by this morning. He was from the Urquinaona Hotel, not a very nice hotel... rather precarious place. He stopped by to say that their hotel had several vacancies and that if we had to turn any guests away it would be most kind of us to send them to the Urquinaona. Here is their card."

I took the card which read nothing other than a street address, and room-rates which were very cheap. "How far is it?"

"You can walk there. Just go up this way..."

I mumbled some insults at the rat, gathered my valises and my case of wine, and took leave, my mind set on catching the next ship out of Barcelona. Dismissing the idea of taking new lodgings, I walked the opposite direction of this so-called Urquinaona, going instead towards the Mediterranean. I was hoping to leave immediately for Florence, via Corsica.

I'd mentioned my plans were to visit Helsinki and then Saint Petersburg for the white-nights; but in Madrid, my friend Juhani described to me how fast it is to cross the Balearic Sea and the Mediterranean from Barcelona by way of the French *paquebots* that sail between Corsica and Barcelona; and Corsica and Italy. I had a very good reason to visit Florence...

Already fifteen years had passed, from this time I narrate, since I had last seen my mother. Last time we were together, she was already white-haired and nostalgic. While there I was, in the first flower of my youth, in prime physical shape, and was preparing to leave home to go live in Tripoli to become a fresco painter and work on the side for money as a gold-leafier, gilding the city's mosques, Christian churches, and temples. My mother would stay behind with the old fisherman and his elderly wife who long ago delivered me from my mother's umbilical cord and raised me, and who continued to help provide for my mother, and for me my entire life up till that point. My mother fell into my arms and cried. She wished me luck in Tripoli but begged me for both of our sakes to save my money and set my sights on Europe—the continent where life was healthier and a man could easily reach old age. She specifically wanted me to go to Florence, the city of art, for at that age I wanted to be a painter.

When she was a child, my mother travelled with the royal family to Florence and she said it was the most magical city on earth. While raising me, she often talked of the day I'd be grown and wouldn't need her anymore. She would travel alone to Florence, she said, to finish out her own days in the one city she loved. When I left for Tripoli, she warned me of the intrigues in that place: "Saul," she made me promise, "Remember to never tell anyone in Tripoli who your father was. But all the while, have inward pride in the fact that you are *the son of Solarus*—noble Solarus—for he was a great and charismatic man, a leader of men, and his greatness cannot be exaggerated. But in Tripoli, your father has many enemies, and you will be punished wrongly if they learn you are his son. When you are abroad, however, you should reassert your self-awareness and spread your *kleos*[1] far and wide, telling one and all that you are Saul, the son of Solarus. Be proud, my son. It's a shame you never knew your father." My mother always amazed me with her heroic temperament. She'd had an aristocratic education, and believed in *kleos* as she believed in Homer.

Afterwards, my mother talked more about Florence. She said, "And if you decide to leave Tripoli and you come back here to our village, and this house still stands but I am not in it, come to look for me in Florence. I will surely go to Italy come the day that, from my humble work here in the village, I can afford the

---

[1] KLEOS: *(Greek:* κλέος): Eternal fame, renown and glory. A Greek concept, preliterate in origin, that stresses that one's life has meaning if their name is "sung" for generations yet unborn to hear. Along with *timé* (earthly possessions, bounty), *kleos* is the central theme to a hero's purpose in Homeric myth.

trip." My mother wove nets that were sold to the fishermen of the village, earning a few coppers a day.

I embraced my mother then and I vowed to myself to help her when I earned money in the city. Unfortunately, I was washed away with personal ambition, circumstance, folly, and the vanity of youth, all which took me to Malta and kept me from returning home for a long time—my mother had already left our village by the time I back-tracked through it. Yet looking in retrospect on my life in those days, I sigh; the caprice of youth goes with the wind, I've no regrets.

Thus not having seen my dear old mother in fifteen years, and the *paquebots* being so fast from Barcelona through Corsica to Florence, I decided to put my Russian dream of daylit-midnights on hold for a year and venture to Italy to see if my mother had realized her own dream and was living there, happy.

Thus cursing Barcelona to hell, I walked along the boardwalk towards the boat docks, where a tall, sun-burnt seaman informed me that a shipwreck in Corsica would delay all travel. There were not enough *paquebots* for the demand. Other travelers had tickets and were waiting. The captain of the sea-route confirmed his statement. Since I had no ticket, I would have to wait longer than the others. I tried to bribe my way ahead of those honest passengers. No use. Too much impatience all around, even among the poorest ticket holders. So I bought a first-class passage to Florence via Corsica; but because of that damned shipwreck, I would have to wait three more days and nights in Barcelona. What games fate would play with me under that Catalan sun! At least I had money, and plenty of wine. The weather was good. I turned on my heels and returned to the statue of Cristóbal Colón, and headed up Las Ramblas, asking here and there for vacancies with no luck whatsoever, until I reached the bleak quarter of Urquinaona. There, on a shabby side-street, beneath a dingy awning, I found the Urquinaona House, which was apparently the only hotel in Barcelona with *nothing but* vacancies.

The man at the desk was suspicious. I was too finely dressed with my evening party suit and silk foulard to be seeking a room in such a place. He asked for three nights in advance and I paid them, collected the key, and since there were no porters, I dragged my valises myself, and my case of wine, down the hall, had a look at the scene, and came back.

"Can you give me a better room? Or two adjoining?"

"We've got what we've got," he frowned, "And nothing adjoining. We are a poor hostelry."

Intolerable filth, insects buzzing in the stale air, and only an old animal skin flopped on the floor to serve as a bed. Bathroom down the hall. This adventure put me in a foul mood.

Alone, I bolted the lock, tossed my valises on the floor, looked out the tiny window at the street, and opened a bottle of sparkling wine from the case; and, spilling the first sip on the windowsill in honor of Dionysus—as it is my custom to pay respect to this god when I drink, lest one day the holy grape cease to grow—I toasted to myself: "Well, Saul, here's a drink to drinking during the waning moon. May the next moon bring better lodgings." I swilled the bubbling wine from the bottle, not caring for how fast, or to what condition, it intoxicated me.

I sat down on the animal skin and drank more, and more. With the first halos of inebriation, I thought about sweet little Saskia... 'It's good that I gave her her bed back. She would never have suggested that I leave on her own. She was too polite for that. And all that nonsense about me 'having to stay there'; and of us 'travelling together,' and the worst of it... that phrase about my *sleeping in the road in fine clothes*, which got her worked-up to no end, until she swore *I was meant to find her*—or *she was meant to find me...* and that we needed to stick close to one another... all that was either due to her madness, or else just the innocent fantasies of a young adolescent girl's mind.' I drank more wine and stopped thinking about her. I stopped thinking all together. I drank one liter of wine after the other, trying to dim my eyes so as not to look upon the wretchedness of my room. Soon I fell asleep dead-drunk on the animal skin on the floor.

Chapter Seventeen

Déjeuner chez Madame Dépression...

It was evening when I awoke with a terrible temper. The wine had done me no good. I was claustrophobic in that little room. My nerves were bad. But it wasn't as simple as to go out and wander the streets. Along with the claustrophobia, I was feeling that famous *terror of the marketplace*, agoraphobia, which I recall only experiencing after grave misadventures. It came like any transitory madness and overwhelmed me with incredible anxiety so that I didn't know how to cure myself of the claustrophobic feeling. I couldn't go outside. Just the idea of being in Barcelona filled me with terror. Going *out there*, to mingle with the crowds, *with them*—I had to avoid this at all costs! All of the life out there in the streets was too tied in my poisoning experience of the week before. I chattered my teeth; and to prevent myself from losing my mind completely, I would have to wait for the hour of my boat alone in my miserable room. To be in the streets was intolerable. My hotel room was intolerable. Only sleep or alcohol offered to hide me from my private hell. Such transitory madness is the product of *travel and experience*, a fever which adventurers don't mention in their memoirs. Surely it was *travel and experience*, and not my *folle conduite*[1]. I opened a new bottle of wine from the case and began taking greedy swallows. It made me sick. Wine during a waning moon leads to no good. I wanted to go outside to find an opium den but the paranoia was too much. I stayed with my bottles in that slum. I honestly tried to kill myself with that wine, though I had no idea why.

Morning announced the third day of my drunken frolic through the daisies of depression. The sun woke me up. I was gloomy at first until I remembered I had a boat to catch that day. The thought of it chased the madness away. As if my old brain had been replaced by a new instrument, I was fresh. Soon Barcelona would be but a shameful memory. I was free of this hotel room, free of other people. Time to leave Barcelona to the frogs and dogs—adieu!

At ten in the morning, I walked down to the seaport to check on the status of my boat. I showed my ticket to the operator at the port authority and he informed me that the *paquebot* would leave that evening at the twenty-first hour. This meant I had a whole morning, afternoon, and evening to waste before departing for Florence.

I walked back to my room, shaved, got fresh clothes out of my valise. Dressed for travel, I left around noon to stroll through the town, to see if I could get any meaningful impressions of this wicked city while I was sober and hungover.

The Barrio Gòtico is the most picturesque part of Barcelona I found. Its mazes of bright, dilapidated streets fascinated me. This is where my first hotel, the Sant Felip Neri, was. Everywhere were colorful streamers, birds in cages, dancers, musicians performing the *passacalle*, revelers and fire-blowers, meanderers and riffraff. I turned one corner and heard the melody of a guitar. I followed the sound until I came to an alley where a young man

---

[1] FOLLE CONDUITE: *(Fr)* "Reckless behavior."

sat playing. He had a deformed body and was perched on a pile of wood, old guitar in his hands. He played beautifully and I listened, though his grotesque body unnerved me. This was the first time I thought of Saskia that day. Her music was beautiful, her voice was beautiful, her body was beautiful. Even the dirty little pads of her feet were beautiful. I cursed myself then. For once, heaven had sent me Beauty in its most perfected form and I abandoned it. She might not have been a girl after all but an angel: a force to guide me on this hazardous path of life I hurry down... How can life be hazardous if it can only end in death? But she *was* life. She had nursed me and played majestic music and sang with a voice that no mortal possessed. While I had been in her bed, drinking her broth, I thought time and again of older Spanish seductresses in cabarets and dens of ill-repute.

I continued through the Barrio Gòtico until I reached a square where I was attracted to a solitary lemon tree that grew on a berm caged in stones. This vibrant tree gave me solace. I sat on the stoney edge of the berm beneath the arbor of my tree and watched the people that passed: Three women came chattering in the Catalan language, their breasts were large and their legs were long and I saw in them all the filth of the world. I used to enjoy such women. Now I saw them as vulgar.

Then came a young child in a yellow peasant dress, she pranced through the square chasing a cicada. I thought to offer her a lemon to match her dress but resisted. She too was vulgar in her naivety. She had not the knowledge of the world, of music, of life alone in a messy room, and of copper poisoning, to interest me. Was I falling in love with Saskia? I didn't know, though her memory stirred violence in my heart. An old woman passed the square, wrinkled, withered, hunched-over. She was smiling at her own thoughts though death was approaching her. She was like me, I thought. When I was younger, I would cling to life because life was at the top of the turning wheel. But like the song of my gypsy-girl, the great wheel turns over and lands on a minor key. It is then that you come of age and life means nothing to you. To live, to die, to overdose, to fall in a coma in the street... it is all the same. It is only in the peach innocence of youth, like the days in Saskia's possession, that life is at its crest on top of the wheel. And there being *only* life, the young cling to it, they fear death...

And they should! ...For they are *in* life. Now that I had passed that frightful episode of life: *Youth.* ...Now that I was in the flower of my age, I was more glorious than ever. I was a man. I didn't fear death because *I had already experienced life*—I'd lived it to the core. So why did I miss this child who was in another world. Was she the life that I so loved once upon a time?

I stayed beneath my lemon tree and a band of Romanian *gitanas* materialized in the center of the square. They had guitars and crude instruments and wore rags. I would have forgiven them that, had they played any of the songs that Saskia had played on the night she found me lying in the street—*'in fine clothes,'* as she insisted on saying. But these gypsies played no such harmonies. They played a raucous cacophony of stringed disasters—every note off-key. So, alone in a square in Barcelona, surrounded by an orchestra of diseased women serenading my tree with broken instruments, I found myself 'alone and lost.' Their faces grew uglier and uglier as they played. My lemon tree turned black as the sky grew dark with storms. Rain fell. This was the hell that Dante found 'midway through the journey of his life': she-wolves and jackals and gypsy wenches playing out-of-tune guitars. And here I was, 'in the 3—th year of my stay on this, our fruitful earth,' and I was in Dante's hell. And with my great age, *the only thing I knew was,* whether or not I was in love with Saskia didn't matter, *I had to find her!...*

"I will find her!" I gasped and clasped my hands, and turned on my heels. Then with hope in my heart, I raced down to the promenade of Las Ramblas and crossed over into the neighborhood of El Raval. I was doomed though. I should have asked somebody for the road to the hospital. But that day I didn't remember this particular detail of the night of my misadventure. It came back to me much later.

I walked a long road in the El Raval district, it was riddled with balconies strewn with clotheslines and sheets hanging to dry. All was silent except for the sounds of swearing and shouting coming from the open doorways of taverns where drunken men gathered. The balconies of the apartment houses all seemed familiar and not at all right. 'Where is Saskia's balcony? Neither this street, nor that...' I searched the entire neighborhood and never found the place where my angel sang and strummed and danced on glass.

So, I walked, desperate and depressed, turning thoughts over in my head: 'If I don't find Saskia, how can I bring myself to leave Barcelona?' In the space of a moment, she had become my twin planet in this senseless orbit I was a part of, circling around the sun, around the earth, onward towards frailty, senility, and death. 'Without Saskia,' I thought, 'the white-nights of Petersburg will shine no light; and Florence will be the empty carcass of a forgotten city.' Was I deranged? Maybe. Yet, is it not derangement that guides us to seek out those we want to love in this world?

So cursing my fortune and the winding labyrinth, black as death, they call Barcelona, I wandered back to Las Ramblas where I hoped to find Saskia carrying provisions in the crowd. My madness then took me once again to the Barrio Gòtico. It was there I saw a familiar site: the Hotel Sant Felip Neri. And outside the hotel, in its courtyard square, I stopped in horror... 'What is that? A dead body?!'

Chapter Eighteen

Death in Barcelona...

It was the corpse of a man lying face-down, naked on the stones. Around him was a great commotion of people flailing their arms and policemen jotting notes. A coroner approached the corpse and checked it for signs of life; finding none, he covered it with a sheet. Nearby, another sheet covered what was obviously the body of another man. He lay under the window of the room that I was given at the Hotel Sant Felip Neri.

The coroner and some policemen carted away the two cadavers. Some more police remained to question people who had witnessed the deaths. I passed through the crowd and entered the lobby of the Hotel Sant Felip Neri. At the desk was the same concierge as always, taking a noseful of snuff.

"Oh, it's you..." he said dryly, "I have..." But before he could finish, I interrupted...

"Interesting event about those two dead bodies lying on the street beneath the windows of your hotel."

"Yes, well, 'public death.' It is a very common sight here in Barcelona. Happens all the time. Always has." Then he said with a hint of condescension, "Oh yes, there was some... *person*... just here looking for you, a couple of hours ago, a young lady carrying a guitar case."

"A guitar case?" The thought of it made my heart tingle. "What did you say to her?"

"She was full of questions I couldn't answer. I told her you checked-out. She then asked if there was a room available here in our hotel and I said that we were full. That was before the... uh... *accident*. Before two of our guests died. We seem to have a couple of vacancies now."

"It would appear that way." Through the drapes in the lobby I could see the coroner directing the passage for the two cadavers to be carted away. All the while I trembled with rage knowing this insect of a concierge could have told Saskia where I was. "Why didn't you tell her I had moved to the Urquinaona?"

"Is that where you moved to? I had no idea... she just left after that."

No use in talking to such a creature. I got ready to go... "The young lady with the guitar case... she didn't leave a message for me?"

"No. She just left," he said, excusing himself to use the toilet. While he was gone, mumbling, "The fool!" I started up the stairs. I wanted to see what had come of my old suite in the hotel.

The door was wide open, and an elderly maid was cleaning the windows of the door out to the balcony. "Strange about the two bodies lying in the square," I said to her.

"I'll say it's strange... I can't understand how it could have happened!"

"A double suicide, apparently." I contemplated the relationship between the two men. The placement of one body had been directly below my old suite's balcony. The second body had been below another window in an adjacent room.

"Possibly suicide," said the maid, "both of 'em died with knives sticking in their chests. You see the blood stains on the balcony railings. So they fell out of the windows *after* being stabbed... *Or else they were pushed!* Seems both died at the same time."

"You don't think they planned it together?" I made a slight grin, "A little brotherly pact of suicide?"

"Damn, I don't think that," said the maid, "they sure weren't brothers. This one here's been staying in this suite for an entire week. He was a man from England, or from Ireland, or something up there. He didn't speak a word of Spanish, didn't know what he was up to. The other one, though. He was Spanish, from Madrid. He was very kind to me and said that I was the only one in the hotel he could talk to, seeing as how he only spoke Spanish and me too. Pity he had to die. Don't think it was suicide. The man from Madrid was too happy of a man. The Englishman too, he seemed all serious and oh-so-important about everything. Can't imagine someone like that just stabbing himself and leaping out of a window. Nothing stolen that I could see. The whole thing's a mystery."

"A mystery," I repeated. That was enough to leave a bad taste in my mouth. I said goodbye to the maid and walked down the stairs, slipping between two detectives who were heading up. This murder, as it seemed to me then, had no purpose other than to make those two rooms vacant. I would soon learn the drama that would create. Later, much later, all the pieces would come together. I'll come to that when it's time.

I went down through the square and out into the sunshine of the promenade of Las Ramblas. Down I walked, looking at the Mediterranean Sea bristling blue with silver filets of sunlight in my field of vision. When I came to the sea docks, I was informed of yet another delay. Bad weather near Corsica. My *paquebot* scheduled for that evening wouldn't sail until the following morning at daybreak. I cursed aloud, annoyed at having to spend another night in that roach-infested hotel at Urquinaona; I then left the docks intent on having a drink to pass the last hour of daylight.

The tavern where I stopped was at the base of Las Ramblas where the promenade empties out into the thoroughfare of seaboard comings-and-goings. It was a dim tavern. I ordered a beer, not caring where the moon was or what time of year it was, I just wanted to get to Florence and get this murderous city out of my head. While I drained my beer, my ears perked-up to the sound of a Spanish guitar strumming lightly in the background. My chest tightened and I swung my head around picturing the gypsy girl who'd taken possession of my thoughts, but there was nothing in that dingy bar save for an old man playing a pinewood instrument. His scabby fingers dialed the laments of 'Recuerdos de la Alhambra,' and with that sad song, I hung my head down and wept.

'Why are you weeping, Saul?' I asked myself. 'Because of her, and because of me, and because of all that I didn't do and left behind forever. Now it's time to take your old miserable self out of this bar and away to bed. Tomorrow you wake when the sky begins to bleed blue into the ink of night. You will walk down to the harbor and board the boat that will sail away with the gleam of the rising sun."

"You forgot something!" said a voice. There was someone behind me. I set my empty cup down, turned around again, and saw a ridiculous figure of a man grinning a toothless grin. He said to me, "Hey-hey! I thought I saw you up by that hotel where the two men killed themselves. You dropped your scarf up there."

I didn't own a scarf. Maybe he was talking about my silk foulard? That, I was sure I had left back at the Urquinaona. I felt around my neck. It was true, my foulard was gone, but I was sure I left it back in my hotel room. The man didn't know me, he couldn't have seen my foulard.

"You saw me up there?"

"I did! You dropped your scarf."

'Nonsense,' I thought, disgusted with the situation. I paid for my beer and left the bar without another word to anyone.

Of course, if it was the memory of the sad Spanish song, and the ridiculous notion that I *had* dropped my foulard up by the Hotel Neri; of course it was these and not other things that caused me to backtrack my steps and hurry back through the Barrio Gòtico, back to the place I had wanted to leave behind me forever.

Chapter Nineteen

Why do we mortals wonder if it is through *human chaos* or through *divine perfection* when the world guides us to some magical event? In either case, is not the result the same? Is the result not *divine perfection?*

Dusk had already fallen when I reached cobbled streets of the Barrio Gòtico. The lanterns were lit. I passed the Cathedral of *Sant Jaume* where a shabby red scarf was tied to one of the iron-barred windows. I wondered if the old man was right about my dropping my foulard in front of the hotel. If so, why didn't he pick it up and chase after me to return it to me? A likely story!

I was drawn back to that square where the hotel was and through the narrow streets I walked and it was now fully night. This was the first moment I realized that *I didn't have to* sleep in that filthy room at the Urquinaona at all. I *could* take one of the new vacancies at the Hotel Sant Felip Neri. I would have a bath, and sleep tonight in a good bed. Why had I just then thought of that? What is the harm in taking a dead man's room, so long as it's clean? I got angry at myself for not taking a suite after the accident, and for being so slow to react to new opportunities that presented themselves. Over the past few years, it had become a habit that was proving dangerous to my well-being. My thoughts were interrupted, I heard the sound of a guitar. Over the last couple days, my biggest disappointments had come in the shape of guitar players, and I assumed this one would be as lame and shabby as the others. I then heard the words sung as I entered the square, they were in English...

Ceylon, Ceylon... So Long, So Long...
To your far distant shores
To that long away time
When our eyes were for the heavens
And our lips were for each other
And our flesh was for the world
And our dreams kept us wandering on...

"Saskia!" I cried, my eyes falling on her standing on the iron wrought balcony two stories above the Plaça Sant Felip Neri. There on the balcony of the hotel, wearing a pale nightdress, was my friend: the lost orphan-girl, holding her guitar, singing 'Ceylon' into the night. She heard my voice cry her name. Her eyes grew wide, she looked at me; and she set her guitar down and disappeared from the balcony. A moment later, she came running to me through the square, from the hotel...

"Saul," she cried, "you came back! Just like that!" She threw her arms around me. I picked her up so her bare feet no longer touched the ground. Her feet flapped and she sobbed and between sobs she asked, "Why did you run off from me? I went to buy the foods that you said you love! And coffee, and wine too! But you left!—just like that!"

"I felt sorry for you, my dear Saskia. You were a little housecat sleeping on the floor of your room every night. It was time for me to give you your bed back."

"You felt sorry for me! You should have felt sorry for me these last few days, not being anywhere where I could find you..."

"You're crying, Saskia!... I went looking in your neighborhood for you... I spent most of the day everyday looking, but I couldn't find your balcony, I couldn't find your house..."

She pulled away from me, then looked up into my eyes, "Did you really come looking for me?"

"I looked and looked! First, I tried to take my hotel room back, so you could come to me when you wanted, but they gave it to someone else."

"I know, they told me. They told me which suite had been yours and so this morning when I found out it was available all of a sudden, I booked it indefinitely. You chose a beautiful hotel. It's ours now. We can sleep here tonight. Come on...."

She took my arm and we started walking towards the hotel. "You know that I keep hearing songs," I told her, "played on the Spanish guitar. I walked and walked this whole week through, constantly thinking of you."

"And?!"

"And... I was wondering why I ever left your apartment. I missed you. And so I listened. I hoped I would hear you somewhere, hear you playing your guitar."

"And you did hear me. Promise me you won't leave again."

I then made a million promises as we entered the hotel. The concierge was a new one whom I'd never seen. He was courteous and didn't show astonishment at a girl so young being dressed in so light a nightdress coming in from the square at night. I noticed her hair was arranged, as though she had been expecting a visitor, she looked older than she did at her apartment, and more beautiful. We ordered some food to be brought up to our room and inside the room she cleared her guitar and clothes from the dining table.

A waiter from the hotel restaurant came and placed our dinner on the table. There were Spanish cheeses, some grilled *pescaditos*, a loaf of bread, a bottle of cold wine. We drank a glass and I said that I had a strange feeling after seeing Saskia playing her guitar on the balcony of the hotel, as though there were some destiny at work after all.

Saskia's voice then turned serious, and strange... She told me that I should get used to my strange feeling, because there would always be destiny at work for us. She told me then that she would never let me disappear again. She said she needed me.

"Oh, my poor girl!" I told her, "It can't be this way—not this way!" I got up from the table and began pacing the floor with thundering feet in that enormous room... back and forth, I walked, shaking my head, blowing steam, until I took the girl firmly by the shoulders and looked her in the eyes and said, "Listen to me closely, Saskia. You cannot talk to a man you've only recently met like this, telling him *you need him*; it won't do! You will frighten him away!..."

She just laughed, "You men! You are frightened so easily!" She then freed her shoulders from my hands, "but it's good that you teach me these things," she said, "I have so little experience in these matters."

"I have quite a lot of experience in these matters. Look, Saskia, when a man meets a woman, he needs to feel like he is the *hunter*, like she is the *prey*. She is a wild prey that looks good to eat, like you... But if his prey just hops into his hunting net and says: *'I am yours, let's travel together!'* he feels like he hasn't earned his prey through honest 'hunting'; consequently, he doesn't feel like a man. When a man doesn't feel like a man, neither sexual feelings nor romantic feelings can emerge in him."

"Have you checked your net recently, my good huntsman?, because I didn't hop anywhere near it!" She laughed again and had the nerve to roll her eyes.

"Remember that this hunting expedition was *mine*, the net of concern was *my net*, and when I said *'we are going to travel together'* that was me telling you what's going to happen. You would be a fool not to obey because *your life depends on it...* But in any case, I am a long way from being in your net, Monsieur the hunter... in fact, I think your prey just outran you."

With these final words, Saskia shot me a cold, firing look with her eyes that showed both irony and condescension. In one swift move, she overwhelmed me, she blew me across the room. A thunderclap of feminine power charmed and diminished me. I remember thinking then that this was the first time in a long time—where it concerned my dealings with women—that it was obvious I needed to go back to school. I told her I was impressed. She asked me if I knew *why* she wanted me in her net. I told her it was odd that I should be so important to her.

"I want you to help me find my friend."

"Find your friend?"

"I know it is a selfish reason, but you have to help me. She is my best friend. Her name is Adélaïse..."

Saskia then explained to me her story: "Ever since my uncle died, I have been wandering around Europe. I even went to Asia. I wandered all the way to Ceylon. That is where I wrote the song I sing. And all the time I wander because I don't know why I should stay any place? What's to stop me from wandering? I haven't had any reason to do anything in this world, or *not to do* anything. Money comes to me every few months without fail—more than enough to live on, plenty enough to amuse myself with, so I don't need think about money or managing a household. I never liked that concept... what they call 'the household.' The word alone is horrible, industrious and binding. I think I am a nomad by nature... but that aside, what should stop me? I have no family, no friends whatsoever, never a lover... Adélaïse is all I've had. She is the only person still living with whom I've shared my heart. When I went back to the boarding school in London after my uncle's death, I was told that she had already left our school to return to her parents'. They wouldn't tell me why she left, but I thought I overheard the dean mention something to his administrator about how, because of her parents' divorce and all the legal fees, etc., they no longer had enough money to pay her tuition. Anyway, I did find out from them that her father was living in Marseille near the Place de Lenche, and that her mother lived in Paris on the Île Saint-Louis[1]. They refused to give me

---

[1] ÎLE SAINT-LOUIS: The smaller of the two naturally-formed islands in the Seine that are located in Paris, in the center of the city near Notre Dame. Unlike its larger neighbor, the Île de la Cité, the Île Saint-Louis is a quiet sanctuary, almost

exact addresses of either. So with that information, I went to both cities: to Paris and Marseille, and hung around waiting to run into my friend, to bump into her on the street or something, but I never did. Once, while wandering that quiet, little residential island they call Île Saint-Louis, an old gardener woman sweeping leaves in a garden apron, called to me. She wanted to tell me something. She looked like a witch with that broom and that apron covered with leaves, and her dark, deep wrinkles. She told me she could read my life. And what she told me about is *you.* She knew all about you, Saul!..."

"How could this Parisian witch know all about me? I have never been to Paris."

"She didn't know your name, of course, but she knew all about you, and that you could help me reunite with Adélaïse. She told me if I went to Barcelona, I would, quote: 'find a man sleeping in the street in fine clothes.' She said that his destiny is intertwined with mine. She said a lot more things. But don't you see how I feel Saul? I feel like I need something or someone from my past to make the present make sense to me... Adélaïse is the only person from my past I want to see again. If I don't see her, I don't know '*why it is*' that I should stay alive!"

"So that explains why you always talk about how you were meant to find me *just as you did*: *'sleeping in the street in fine clothes,'* ...You know this *'in fine clothes'* thing made me think you might be totally nuts. But Saskia, why did you choose *me* of all the people who pass-out in your street? It seems that the men here in Barcelona drink so much that on any given night, one can trip over a dozen of them sleeping in the street *...and in fine clothes too!"*

"It wasn't a sleeping drunk I was supposed to find. And I cannot tell you any more, Saul. The woman in the garden said that if you learn too much of the puzzle before it's solved, my work will have been for nothing. You and I both will be doomed. I, of course, know the whole puzzle in its entirety, but I cannot

---

strictly residential, and proudly void of noisy markets and stations, and large institutional buildings.

tell you more. I promise I will tell you all though—*just as soon as we find Adélaïse.*"

I wanted to know more about this puzzle *before* we found her friend, but Saskia wouldn't tell me any more.

"You are a crafty girl," I told her, "You know, I was once overly-confident about my hunter's net. Since I was five years old—that beautiful age when I became actively interested in the female sex—I thought my net was good enough to catch virtually any prey. But now I see that it isn't going to be enough to catch a creature as wild as you."

To this, the rascal simply smiled at me. She then said, "You can try other weapons, you know ...other than that stupid net of yours."

* * *

We both felt heavy from the food we ate. Now that we were finished, the dinner table resembled a battlefield: carcasses of fish, spines and skins, rinds of mouldy cheeses. My body ached and I felt hollow and exhausted from the past days of self-isolation and alcoholic depression. My body was like that table: a half-eaten battlefield, filled with bones and skin torn apart. I told Saskia I wanted to rest a moment. "I just want to close my eyes for a minute. It's still long before midnight. I won't go to sleep for the whole night now." But I didn't realize how truly drained I was. I fell into a deep sleep the instant I lay down, and it was well after dawn when I awoke.

The white sun flooded into the hotel suite. I glanced over at Saskia. She was beneath the sheets as I was. The bed was made when I fell asleep on it the night before, and I knew that Saskia had put the sheets over me. We were lying far apart. No one observing us that morning could say we were lovers. I was fully dressed—she hadn't dared to take off my clothes—while she wore pajamas. She on her side, I on mine, were tucked-in as innocently as two young children who've not yet learned of the existence of the sexual body.

I was glad I didn't try to kiss her or touch her the night before. And glad that we hadn't made love. For this morning we didn't have anything to feel embarrassed about. And what was better, we didn't have to worry that terrible worry: the worry that we'd begun the game too early, and that consequently, we would have to end it early. That was a worry only I would have had. Saskia was too inexperienced to have that unhappy worry about her relationship with me. I was glad she had trusted me enough to sleep in the same bed as me, instead of suffering on a mound of clothes on the floor like a cat.

I went back to sleep. And when I awoke, Saskia was at the dining table eating a pastry, drinking coffee. I stirred and got out of bed, and then I went over to her to say good morning.

"Thank you for letting me sleep."

"It's normal. You were tired," she said, "I think that your tiredness has been following you around for many months demanding a night's sleep like last night. Finally you gave in." She took her guitar from where it stood by the door and asked if I minded if she played. "Your fingers are made for the strings," I told her, "Please play me something."

"How did you know about that?!" she ask me, frightened.

"Know about what?"

"Fingers are made for strings? The... the gardener woman in Paris... she said just that... *'Your fingers were not made for keys but for strings,'* were her exact words. I had never met her, I didn't have my guitar with me, yet she said to me, *'you love song and you sing.'* How could she have known that if she couldn't read my life?"

I urged her then to sing and to play. She sat on the edge of the bed and played for me the song she wrote in Ceylon...

Ceylon, Ceylon... so long, so long...

It was then in the springtime

She explored in the orchards

Where the trees gave her fruit

and the streams bathed her body
while the sun warmed her skin
and her youth bore her dreams
then when night came a falling
Her lost lover came down to her dreams.

Saskia set her guitar aside. "I was so young when I wrote that. Do you like the words?"

"That depends on who your lost lover was... the one who came down to your dreams..."

She laughed. "I guess he was the lover that all fourteen year old girls dream about... I went to Ceylon for three months, on a whim, after my uncle died. It was three years ago, seems like forever ago. Everyone thought that fourteen was too young to be travelling alone, but I didn't care. I was a wild girl. I found Ceylon to be the most magical country on earth, I wanted to immortalize it in my memory: the vibrancy of the colors, the humidity that allows trees of all kinds to produce splendid fruit...

"...As for the lover, I certainly didn't have anyone in mind. I think girls always dream up love stories, though—no?"

Her innocence made me smile. She was innocent to the very fibre of her, and I didn't want to damage that innocence. This was the first time in my adult life that I was near a beautiful female whom I didn't feel the desire to make love to. She was too young to have the feminine charms that mature women possess and use so beautifully, for as I grow older I find that the charms of adult women ripen to perfection as they age too. Saskia was still a great beauty, and I should have lusted after her like after any woman; yet I thought that morning, waking up beside her, 'Sooner would I protect her as my child than as my wife.' This was probably for the best. Unless I was in love with her, I would often tire of a woman as soon as I'd slept with her. I did not want to tire of Saskia, and I knew that if I didn't make love to her, I would never grow tired of her. I wasn't sure then if I would ever love her like a woman, I hoped I would love her someday. I wondered if she wanted to leave right away for Marseille, and then for Paris, where we could try our luck together in the search for this lost friend of hers, Adélaïse.

"Marseille is useless," she said, "I spent one month in that city, asking all around for information about Adélaïse's relatives. I knew that Adélaïse had the same family-name as her father; I found out that there was only one Monsieur Letheux who was old enough to have a child and who lived in the second arrondissement of Marseille, where the Place de Lenche is. I found out that, if this man was in fact her father, he left Marseille during the time I was there to take up residence again in Paris. So it's fair to say that unless Adélaïse is off at another boarding school somewhere she's with one of her parents in Paris."

"So we will leave for Paris then, kid. I was just heading there myself anyway..."

"Yes, but Saul, my dear, after we finish our breakfast... I have to leave you for a little while... I won't be able to come back to see you until the day after tomorrow."

"The day after tomorrow!"

I was taken aback by her words. 'The day after tomorrow?' Was this sudden indifference to our knowing each other coming from the same girl who played her guitar every night for nine months so she could find me?... the same girl who was so obsessed with me during my illness that she never took her eyes off me day or night?... I remember, I thought she was going to be a burden to me during my adventures, and that I'd never get rid of her... but now it was *she* who was abandoning *me!*

"Today is Friday, tomorrow is Saturday, let's see... I can meet you here on Sunday night..." She went for her guitar to lock it in its case, "I have a few personal things I need to take care of, some important things."

I sat stupefied. She stood next to me, rubbing my head like I was a pet.

"So eight o'clock Sunday night? We can meet in here. The concierge gave me two keys. Here's yours. You're going to be good when I'm gone, right? You're not going to have friends over, are you?—I'm kidding, you do what you want. But you won't leave this hotel before Sunday, will you? I mean *leave for good.*

You can go out to have fun, of course... But you won't disappear from my life, will you? Promise me, Saul... I don't want to come on Sunday and find another one of your terrible notes written in French—*God, that was the saddest thing ever!*—promise me, please, Saul, that you won't disappear again."

"I won't disappear again," I promised. But all of this left me in a foul mood. I sat in a state of shock as Saskia left our hotel, leaving me by myself.

'You can go out and have fun,' she had told me as she rubbed my head like a pet—*why would I want to go have fun?!* I knew then I was attracted to her more than I had thought. The skillful hunter meets the wild gypsy girl, and that's what happens. He catches her in his net, thinks she is caught for sure, and then she jumps out and is gone. It sounds like a silly thing: her leaving me alone for a weekend was tearing me to pieces—but that's how it began.

She said I could go out... The last thing I was going to do was leave that hotel. Not even for five minutes. An obsession grew hold of me. Where was she going for two days, for two nights?! I didn't care, didn't want to know; yet I wanted to be with her. I knew I shouldn't leave the hotel even for a minute. What if she were to come back before Sunday and I wasn't there to greet her? You see what a mess that girl put me in when she turned the tables on me? It was on that Friday that I really began to *need* her, that she began to take possession of my soul. I have never been the same since.

Chapter Twenty

That weekend without Saskia was horrible. I stayed in the hotel all day Friday. I wrote a letter to Juhani, read from *The Odyssey*, and drank coffee. It was now the new moon and the moon would be starting to grow. From Saturday onward I could drink wine again...

Friday night, I stayed in the hotel and rested. A faint hope that Saskia would come by kept me there, but she never did. I slept early and woke up Saturday morning to continue the same boring regime.

Saturday the moon turned to its growing phase. It was the slightest waxing crescent in the sky. I knew this was the time to begin living again. In a week it would be a half-moon. No time to waste.

I spent Saturday in the hotel without Saskia, pacing the floor, thinking, trying to read, it was useless. I determined myself to go out Saturday night and distract myself. I asked the concierge at the Sant Felip Neri about the best entertainment and he suggested I go see a spectacle at the *Teatro de la Santa Cruz* on La Rambla. I followed his advice and bought a ticket for the theatre. It was the night of a special production followed by a costumed dance where all spectators were obliged to dress in the fashion of the last great Spanish war. I went to a tailor shop and bought finery for the evening. I went to an arms boutique where I spent fifteen pistoles on a fine sword of steal and Spanish silver, its handle decorated in emeralds. Before dressing in my royal pomp, I went to a tavern to toast a few drinks to the glory of the growing moon.

It was an ordinary tavern, I talked to no one and drank a bottle of Rioja by myself. Feeling very light, I walked back to the hotel to drink some more wine and get dressed for the theatre.

At nightfall, I left for the theatre. If it weren't for the wine, I would have felt like a fool walking by myself in such pomp with my jeweled jacket and sword down Las Ramblas. A prince, such as I was dressed, should never walk in public without a valet. But the wine I had drunk at the tavern and in the hotel was in full effect, and I arrived at the theatre to see quite a crowd dressed as I. My head was spinning when I took my seat.

The production was a bland sentimental ode to Spanish and Catalan victories. After a couple coupes of champagne I was thoroughly drunk. I kept my seat while the stage was cleared and the parterre was prepared for dancing.

You can imagine my surprise when I saw among the guests in the theatre, Miss Saskia! She was dressed as a Spanish countess! And she wasn't alone!—but on the arm of a young Spanish officer!

Her date had a very pretty face, he looked like the perfect Romeo: Around twenty years old, possessing a slender, elegant figure, a noble face with the colorations of a Greek or Italian. I was stupefied by the sight, confused... in a tornado of rage I left my box and flew down to the parterre...

On the theatre floor, I approached the couple. Their beauty was already attracting the attention of the other guests. The officer held Saskia's small hand and turned her around as the dancing begun. I interrupted their activity by tapping the shoulder of the young man.

"Yes," he asked me.

"Noble friend," I said, "I would enjoy the pleasure of a dance with your beautiful partner."

"Well of course you would," he smiled, "enjoy the pleasure. *She is after all* extremely beautiful."

I growled at this, his words drove me to fury. Nothing to do with a scoundrel like this but to drive a sword through his stomach! I touched the handle of my sword in a way that made it obvious of my challenge. Saskia fixed her eyes on both of us, remaining motionless herself. Her partner looked confused for a moment, then smiling, he said, "I think it would please the other guests more to see you dance with my partner than it would to see the two of us fight... but the decision is yours." Saying this, he touched the handle of his own sword, while I made up my mind to kill him. Saskia reacted to this scene by blowing out a violent breath. "Don't bother with this!" she shouted, "I'm going home!" Then like the queen she was, she picked up her dress and stamped out of the theatre.

"If you'll excuse me now," said my rival, "I'm going to see my companion home." Before I could react, he was gone. And all eyes turned to me. As I was quite drunk, I saw only a blurry haze in the faces of the theatre crowd. I quickly left the theatre, determined to kill him that night.

The two were far off when I entered the smoky street. They were going on foot towards El Ravel. 'And this is why she said she couldn't see me until Sunday night? She had plans all along to spend the night with this... boy?' I was stupefied. I couldn't for the life of me understand what he had to offer her. Never before had I been outdone by a man of his stature.

I stalked after the two while I debated whether I should rush the man now and dip my sword in his spine to let his guts spill on the street, or if I should follow discreetly from afar and kill him later. To this day, I do not know why I chose the reasonable act. Where women are concerned, my passion burns with ferocious heat, and I have little patience; yet today I am glad I decided then to follow them discreetly from afar.

Saskia, countess of the night, walked on the arm of her friend and no one looked back to see if I followed. I assured myself that she was walking on his arm merely to avoid tripping on the stones in her high heels or to avoid the advances of predators lurking in the shadows, and not out of eagerness to be close to him. Still I didn't know what their relationship was. All I was certain of was that this man was walking Saskia to her home late at night after a dance—you can believe this made me furious!

I stalked the two like a lion through the shabby streets around a couple of turns where bleak figures hunched and slept in doorways. I recognized the apartment house where they stopped: a gated garden beside, a balcony above the street—it was the same balcony where I first set eyes on Saskia while she was serenading the night.

After they entered the apartment house, the door shut and locked. From outside I hear the *click-clack* of four shoes walking up the stairs. 'So am I to wait out here while these monsters make love?' Cursing and drunk, I shouted up to the balcony, "I will come back and kill you both!"

Thus abandoning Saskia's house and street, I walked a very short way and turned back. I passed again by her place, looked again at her lit window over her balcony, and went the other direction towards the supposed 'hospital.' I'd only walked a few meters down this street when I saw a tavern tucked in the shadows. I thought to myself that at least there I could drink myself to death. I must have appeared foolish dressed like a prince in their ridiculous tavern, but I was so angry and drunk, I didn't care. I ordered a brandy, took a swallow and told the barman I would return in a minute. I walked back towards Saskia's apartment, imagining that this was the moment when my rival was undressing her. I couldn't stop asking myself why she would cheat on me with such a person. I would kill him no matter what the reason, I decided. Looking at her window, her room still glowed amber with lamplight. Across the street below I spotted a wretch in a doorway and tossed him a silver piece, saying, "Here's a doubloon for you... tell me, man, will you be able to stay awake awhile?"

The wretch fondled the silver piece, eyes dropping tears—clear and greedy tears, over the money he was given. "I'm at your service, *Dueño y Señor*[1]*!*"

I made signal to the balcony up yonder and the room where Saskia lived. I told the wretch to pay attention to that window, that balcony and the door leading out to the street. If he saw a young man with a sword leave that building—or with no sword—he was to run to the tavern and fetch me. There was a gold pistole in it for him.

Back at the tavern I order a full bottle of brandy and began to increase my drunkenness ten-fold. A few minutes later, the tavern-keeper approached me...

"Señor, there is a person at the door who wishes to speak with you... says he has business with you. I responded that I can't imagine what his business could possibly be—you see, he is a complete..." I didn't let the tavern-keeper finish, mid-phrase I bolted to the door, went into the street and found the wretch. He was out of breath...

"Sir..." he said, "the owner of the bar wouldn't let me in... I ran here as fast as possible... to tell you some aristocrat with a sword left that building... the building you told me to watch... not more than two minutes ago... I ran here as fast as I could..."

I was exalted hearing this. I fished in my pocket for a gold pistole and handed the money to my good messenger while he caught his breath. I then took off to find my enemy.

I ran around each street leading away from Saskia's home, hoping to see a figure walking in the darkness. I saw none. 'If that beggar lied to me,' I thought, 'inventing the story of the aristocrat with the sword to rob me of a gold pistole, I will find and kill him...' After a while of searching in vain, I gave up the hunt and made my way back to Saskia's.

---

[1] DUEÑO Y SEÑOR: *(Sp)*: Lord and Master.

The light in her window was now off. I imagined that the rascal was still there, that the two of them were sleeping in the darkness after the conquest of love-making—this made me furious! Below the balcony, I yelled out so the whole neighborhood could hear: Sah-skee-ah!"

A light lit up in her room. I yelled again a second time but by that moment she was already climbing through her window to the balcony. She wore pajamas and seemed startled. Her beautiful eyes looked at me as she shouted, although in a whisper, "Shhh! Be quiet!" Then she disappeared back into her room and I feared that that would be the last I would ever see of her. A moment later, however, she appeared downstairs, leaving the front door of the building to greet me...

"Saul! My God, what are you doing? I'm glad you came!... *but why are you such a mess?!"*

"I'm a mess? Why? Because I was drinking myself to death while you were making love to that fool."

"Making love?! Crazy man! What are you talking about? Come inside, everyone can hear us out here..."

I followed the liar into her apartment building, but stopped her on the stair, "So you know, Saskia, if *he's* there when I go in, I will kill him."

"*He* who? The man I went to the theatre with? No, he's not here. Of course not! Come on, let's go up..."

Saskia's apartment was in fact empty, and showed no trace of a male's presence—nothing hiding under the bed, no male clothing around and nothing discarded on the floor, no wetness on her bed sheets (of course I checked!). Still I was angry by all that was obvious, and I abused her with my words.

"Come, let's go into the kitchen and draw the curtain. We can talk there. I want my bedroom to stay as dark as possible. I fear there may be curious people spying tonight. I'll explain what I mean... do you want tea? I will set water to boil. It was nice to see you at the theatre, by the way. My night started to be interesting as soon as I saw you."

"Ah, interesting as soon as you saw me? So I was the start of the interesting part! The end of the interesting part was after you slept with that that fool! It seems he left your home just minutes ago..."

She didn't respond to my accusations, but merely uttered, "Hmm..."

"*Hmm* what?"

"*Hmm* meant: I don't recognize you, Saul... One would say you are jealous. Why would you be jealous of that young boy, it's absurd! Maybe you *have* been drinking, but that is no excuse. Anyway, *who* do you think you are?!—do you think I am *your woman?* I am *not* your woman, so you know. Yes, I took an interest in you. Yes, I suggested we travel together, to which you consented; but I am not *your woman* and never said I would be. Therefore, I am free to sleep with whomever I want. You can sleep with whomever you want."

With that, Saskia turned away. She went into the dark part of her apartment and took her guitar into the kitchen where I was and began quietly plucking a mournful song, but she didn't sing. I was struck miserable by her speech. She was right, after all. She never did propose that we be lovers, nor anything of the sort. The truth of the matter is that, simply put: Saskia out-seduced me. I had flattered myself over the years, considering myself the great seducer of the Mediterranean world. Now here I was, out-seduced by a gypsy girl of seventeen. Was I not ashamed? Still, anger from jealousy is a difficult anger to shed, so I kept on being angry...

"You disgust me, Saskia."

She looked shocked and put her guitar down.

I told her that I acknowledged she was free to sleep with whom she wants. "But why do you hide it?" I asked, "You told me when we parted last that you had 'personal business' to take care of. You would see me Sunday night, you told me. If you are so 'free,' as you say, why didn't you tell me Friday that you had a date to go to the theatre? You make me sick!"

"You're drunk! Do you want to know who the boy was?"

"I don't care. Light a lamp or two, will you?"

"He's a relative of my uncle—my dead uncle—and I can't light lamps, he may come around again and see shadows in the windows. "

"So he's your cousin? And apparently you are in love with him if you don't want him knowing another man is here..."

"No, I'm not in love with him! And he's not a relative of mine. He's a relative of my uncle, I think by marriage. I'm not really sure. It's a complicated mess, but I already told you most of it...

"When my uncle died he left me an income of two-hundred pounds a year. The only condition on that income is that I can never live with a man or have it be discovered that I had any kind of romantic involvement with a man; otherwise, I lose the inheritance...

"So if I lose the money, it has to go to somebody... This person you saw me with at the theatre, Andrea is his name, he's a fool and he's greedy. All he thinks about is money. His family has a ton of estates around Milan, in Lombardy. Already he has an impressive income and doesn't need any more money. His position at a bank in Milan is secure. Apparently, before my uncle died, Andrea managed some accounts for him; and the two were related somehow but I don't know how. Andrea discovered some document, or perhaps he counterfeited it; the document says that if I lose my income through the discovery that I have a lover, my income will be lost according to the wishes of my uncle, and the document says it will come to Andrea instead of me. So you see, ever since my uncle died, Andrea has a way of 'coincidentally' running into me in various cities; he checks up on me to see if perchance there is a man in my life...

"I'm better-off to agree to meet him when he finds me and asks to see me. It doesn't cost me any real effort, and it certainly saves a lot of hassle. If I were to refuse an invitation from him, he would become suspicious and snoop into my life until he found something. As soon as he learned about you, I would be disinherited overnight—poor, and without family: *Moi, qui ne suis qu'une petite orpheline!*[1] When I was little, my mother and father both worked... enough so I didn't have to realize that money existed. You can say that they tried to hide our poverty from me. I had only modest clothes, but they seemed just as nice as the other girls around me. And on my birthday every year they gave me a bottle of *eau parfumée*[2]. On Christmas they sent me new guitar strings, and materials to make my own jewelry. My parents were virtuous souls: they somehow managed to put enough money together to send me to London so I could learn English with other girls of my age. I will never know how they managed to keep me all those years in London... I know they sacrificed a lot for me. They wanted me to have a good life. And they came to visit me once a year... each and every spring!... That is, until their last trip down, when they didn't make it all the way...

"At least my parents died while in a foreign country," she went on, "They were seeing the world when they left it. Wandering is the way to die, wouldn't you agree? But one must have money to wander. Still, I believe, one can be a wanderer, *or a wanderess*, without any money at all! ...but that's no way to live, is it? Just as it's no way to live to be caring all the time about an ignorant fool like Andrea—even if he *can* lead you to ruin and make you go crazy.

"But when it comes to pass," I broke in, "that she falls into ruin, I want to be there to help my little gypsy girl know that it is only financial ruin, so that she won't go crazy. I want to help her pitch her gypsy tent by the riverbank... I will build the fire to keep her warm. And I will feed her while she sings me songs, and neither of us will weep."

"You're right," she said, "neither of us will weep."

---

[1] MOI . . . ORPHELINE: *(Fr)* 'Me, who am nothing but a little orphan girl!'

[2] EAU PARFUMEE: *(Fr)* 'Perfumed water' is similar to eau de toilette ('toilet water'), which itself is a lighter form of perfume than traditional French *parfum* ('perfume'); except that an 'eau parfumée' is *even lighter* (weaker in strength) than an 'eau de toilette.' This 'water,' scented usually with rose, vanilla, fresh scents such as citruses, or else a blend of scents, is traditionally given to—and worn by—girls approximately between the ages of seven and fourteen. In most western countries, girls younger than seven or eight are not allowed or encouraged to scent their skin. While generally at around thirteen or fourteen years of age, a girl's femininity urges her to experiment with 'coquetry' and she'll start wearing an 'eau de toilette' instead of an 'eau parfumée.'

The center of Saskia's back was covered this night in the soft-knit of her pajama top. Sitting beside her, I pressed the palm of my hand on this place—perhaps the most sacred place on a woman's body. The two of us were near the kitchen. And with my hand on her body, the world felt perfect. Life was perfect. I felt her body perfectly until, I think, she realized how perfectly I wanted to feel her body. That is when she spoke and ruined everything...

"You know, Saul, I feel safe with you. I want you to know that I will tell you everything in my life..."

"What is it?" I asked her.

"I'm sorry if I didn't mention yesterday that I had a date for the theatre for tonight... I guess I didn't think it was important to our friendship, so I didn't bring it up. I guess I was mostly surprised to see you jealous of him..."

"I don't know if 'jealous' is the right word."

"What then?!" she said, "*Saul...* how could you, man that you are, be jealous of a child like he is?! And how could you be jealous anyway, *seeing as you and I are just friends?!*" With that, Saskia left my side and went to boil water for tea.

I was blown away by all this. For a long time, I sat with my head drooped, saying nothing, feeling myself a dupe. When I first met Saskia, she said *everything in the world depended on our being together.* Was it not her devotion to our relationship that had seduced me into being with her? I had tried to leave her, but she sought me out again... checking into my old hotel and playing her siren song from the balcony. Now her devotion had turned into indifference. Her dreams seemed to fall like snow in the night, only to melt with the rising sun—and I was the dupe.

I only opened my mouth after a quarter of an hour: one, to tell Saskia she was right; and, two, to tell her that she was a ridiculous creature, a mere adolescent, and that I had expected a maturity from her of which she was not capable. I finished by saying that I could only be happy far away from girls of only seventeen years, because they are all idiots.

I couldn't believe the effect my words had on her! She erupted in tears, choked on her sobs, and trembled and made fists so tight that her nails cut the soft skin of her hands. "What I mean is that you are right," I told her, "we never did make a vow of commitment, it was I who imagined that we had a strong emotional bond—but this was a reaction to your attitude towards me. That aside, I have to tell you I can never respect you again. I suggest we go our separate ways." With these grim words, Saskia exploded into even louder sobs. I went on, "Things would be different had you cheated on me for *passion* alone. In that case, I would be jealous and despise you, but I would know it wasn't your fault because *passion* infects even the noblest hearts. But the truth remains that you took your friend home with you *not* out of *passion* but only so that you would continue receiving your money. There is a word for such women. We call them whores."

Her pan of tea water dropped to the floor. Her hands trembled and she stood in the kitchen sobbing away. As tears tumbled from her eyelids, I took a pinch of tobacco and laughed.

"You are a monster!" she said, and turned to me to let these words pour out, "Stop laughing, damn you! You have an evil heart, a black soul, etc.... So you know, I took him to my home only so he could snoop in my apartment. I hoped that he would get bored with what he found and stop spying on me. His pretext for wanting to come see my place was that he wanted a cup of coffee after the dance, and before going to his hotel. That is all! So why did you say I had sex with him, Saul? Tell me that you have never once in your life brought a female to your home at night with whom you did not have sex. Really? Not even once! You're a liar. So then you, Saul the Great, think that I am a whore? Well you are wrong! And you know what else?... who gives a damn about your destiny, or *my* destiny, for that matter! To hell with both you and me! What? I can say that if I want. I don't care what happens anymore. I think I hate you, Saul. How could you say such a thing?—that I'm *a whore!...*" Her tears kept her from saying more. She didn't run away and she didn't shout in anger, she just kept crying in her kitchen. All the water in her sweet body poured from her face, dripping down her beautiful cheeks, soaking in her pajamas, splashing on the floor. I was made tender by her crying, her sensitive heart made me ache profoundly. I felt torn, I wasn't sure.

Before I'd ever set foot in Greece, in Spain, in Europe altogether... when I was living in Alexandria, I didn't have much money and lived in a very poor quarter of the city where the prostitutes and erotic dancers were. In that part of town, one met a *different kind of woman*—the kind of woman who never took a man to her home *unless* it was to let him sleep with her. Thus, in Alexandria, I got used to thinking of *that kind* of woman; when I came to Europe and met the *other kind*, the *virtuous kind*, I didn't recognize the difference right away; so I confused the virtuous Saskia with the former kind and I couldn't work it out in my head. And so that night, with the alcohol and the confusion, I lay on her bed in the darkness and thought. After some minutes, Saskia came from the kitchen where we had talked, and she approached the bed. Still crying, she lay down beside me on top of the blankets. She didn't touch me, she just lay there. Finally, she confessed, "I have not slept with anyone since I met you, Saul." Her tone of voice was so sincere, I knew she was telling the truth. And like the wispy smoke of an opium cloud that disappears in the night once it leaves the smoker's lungs, so my anger disappeared when that phrase left Saskia's mouth. I thought then only of one thing: of comforting her until she stopped crying. I touched her shoulder. "Don't ever call me an idiot again, you idiot..." She made a small laugh.

"I am glad we aren't fighting anymore,' I told her.

"Me too... don't you think it's strange that we had a fight about nothing?—well, except that it was not about nothing, because you were jealous because I had a meeting with another man. That means you are attracted to me." She giggled again.

I didn't know how to escape from that. It is true that I was depressed without her when I was alone at the Urquinaona; and sick with longing for her when she left me alone in our suite at the Sant Felip Neri... but was I attracted to her?

When I woke up in the bed with her at the Sant Felip Neri, I felt a sort of love for her, but as I said: more than wanting to embrace her as a woman, I wanted to protect her as my child. Although, she was no longer a child. She was almost eighteen years old, and she had lived longer on her own than many women had. By experience with the world she was a woman, only in love was she a child... And so, when I became sick with jealousy seeing her on the arm of another man, I knew I was falling in love with her as a man falls in love with a woman. Now I knew, and the whole business was all-too-obvious to Saskia. She clung to me then, in the darkness, on her little bed. I bowed my head and she kissed the lobe of my ear. Her kiss was not on the lips as lovers do, but I was happy not to go deeper than that this night.

"The truth is," she told me, "in all my life, I've only slept with one person—it was three years ago, I was only fourteen. I told you about my uncle's will. They way in which he adored me was all too evident in its terms—I earn a yearly income from his estate for life, although I am not allowed to ever love a man...

"I went to live with him when I was thirteen, as soon as my parents died. He treated me as a child then, he considered me a child... and I was a child. But at fourteen he saw my body change and I developed the haughty and flirtatious character of a young woman. He was intrigued by this change...

"So one night, while I was sleeping, he entered my room and caressed me. I pretended I was asleep at first, and let him do it. I was partially afraid to show him I was awake, partially curious to know what he was doing. I continued to let him until it had gone on so long that I was too afraid to show him that I was awake unless I had anything but a look of happiness on my face. Then, I don't know what happened. I started to feel sexual myself. I was already interested in boys—and in men—and this was the first time one touched me in this way. I let him proceed and, what may surprise you, or even disgust you, is that I started to return his affection, in my own clumsy inexperienced way. He was rough with me, and he took my virginity that night. But the whole time, I thought... it wasn't awful. No, it wasn't completely awful, although I wish he had been more gentle. Can you imagine that reaction from a niece? 'It wasn't completely awful, although I wish he had been more gentle!'—I bet you think I'm deranged. I slept with my uncle, and it didn't disgust me at all... although I wish he had been more gentle."

"I don't think you're deranged."

"Afterwards, he kissed me on the cheek and told me he loved me and respected me, and that he would always be there for me, but that now he would leave me alone to sleep. I fell into a deep sleep, and by the next morning when I awoke, he had already left on a business trip to Athens.

"Every other day, I received gifts from him by the post: vases with Greek goddesses painted on them, incense, jewelry with pearls, precious stones, and seashells. I tried not to think too much about that night we were together. I knew he was a bachelor, and that it must have been hard to have a pretty girl sleeping in his house—even if I *was* his niece. In short, I forgave him. He didn't get me pregnant; and at fourteen, I felt old enough, and developed enough sexually and emotionally, so that it didn't ruin my childhood or leave scars...

"Still, although he didn't scar me, that experience with him made it difficult for me ever after. I had trusted him as a protector, as my guardian, and when he took the initiative to sleep with me, it made me distrust the protection of protectors. Do you know what I mean? A youth thinks their protector is more powerful that anything; that he can and will save them from anything. That's probably why young people think they cannot die—those who love them and protect them can save them even from death. So when your protector reveals to you that they are defenseless to their desires, it makes you feel defenseless yourself. Ever since, I have felt that if I were to give myself to a man, I would have to trust him as much as I trust myself. Now, if a man makes advances on me, I see him like I saw my uncle: a man at the mercy of his desires. And if *he* is at the mercy of his desires, and wants me to submit as well, then we are both at the mercy of things stronger than us—and this scares me. So ever since that experience with my uncle, I have been waiting to trust a man entirely, and to feel his strength and control, as well as his love for me, before I sleep with him. I hope you believe what I'm telling you...

"If you knew all that was in my heart," she continued, "you would believe me without a doubt that it is unthinkable, impossible, that I would have slept with that silly boy from the theatre. Not only could he never be a protector for me, but he is even acting as the opposite. He wants to *take* my income from me, and leave me stranded in the street. To prevent this, I have to act like I enjoy his company, and that I do not love any man. If he knew about my feelings for you, I would be disinherited. Don't forget this as well Saul... Andrea loves money more than he loves women. Do you think he would abandon his evil plan to enjoy a sensual relationship with me? No, if he ever succeeded in seducing me, it would only be so he could use *that* as the proof I was with another man.

I listened to all that Saskia had to say. She spoke with wisdom, and I felt her words deep in my body. Her head was against my shoulder where we lay on her bed—I on my back, and she on her side with her hand clasped innocently and childlike on my upper-arm. I believed everything she said; more than believed, her story was more real than life. She trembled as she spoke. This was a girl who was beautiful to the depths of her creative soul. She was innocent, yet she knew the world. She loved people as she loved the world. She had loved her uncle although she didn't ask for his passion. But her passion was abundant and free, and so she gave it... family member or not, she discovered through her uncle the sensation of being made love to. I had been a fool at the theatre. In Saskia, I recognized a sensitive female who could now as a woman only give herself to a man she loved and trusted. When she said she was 'free to make love to whomever she wants,' she was telling me that she was free in her wildness; that she was a wanderess, a drop of free water. She belonged to no man and to no city. She told me she was faithful to me because she saw something in me that I didn't see in myself. I had grown weary of myself by this time. With the advancing years, I was getting more and more aware of who I was—going on the theory that a man is no more than the sum-total of his actions, that his actions make up his character. And his character is who he is...

I used to paint when I was younger, but in recent years I lived only for my own pleasure: wine during the waxing moon, opium, and women. There is much pleasure in that, but nothing admirable. Yet Saskia saw something in me to love that I didn't see myself; and so I decided that night after Saskia made her confession about her uncle, and about the amount of trust she would need to have in a man before she could let him make love to her that, from then on, I would devote myself entirely to her. I would not treat her like those women in the past I often seduced for a single night of pleasure. No, I would in all respects be a man of virtue and honor with her. So thinking this, I smiled with pleasure and felt the softness of her hair with my hand, as her head lay sweetly on my shoulder in the dark.

"I promise," she whispered to me, "that the next time I am with a man, you will be the first to know, because it will be a very important night in my life."

"I adore you, Saskia. Thank you for trusting me with your story."

"Saul?" she asked, sliding her head up slightly to look at me in the darkness.

"Yes, little fox?"

"Well, two things... First, can we sleep like this tonight? I mean with my face on your shoulder and my hand on your arm?"

"Of course, I would like that. And the other?"

"Do you mind if we go sleep in Golya's room?"

"Who is Golya?"

"My maid, remember?, the one I sent away. Her bed is behind a door in the staircase. It's really small and claustrophobic, but I'm afraid Andrea might have a spy watching my apartment while he's in town."

I touched her face with my fingers and smiled, and the two of us stood up in the darkness and went through the stairwell to sleep in Golya's bed. Now, just as before when we were in her bed, she put her face on my shoulder and her hand on my arm. And I kissed her on her closed eyelids and she clung tight to me and said goodnight. That is how we slept on our last night together in Barcelona. As we drifted asleep, I told myself I would protect her as though she were my child, as though she were my wife. And that night, I truly began to love Saskia as a woman. I like to think that it was that night she began to truly love me.

Chapter Twenty-one

Together in Paris...

The events that happened during the short time Saskia and I lived in Paris together were strange and extraordinary. These events seemed to arrange the architecture of our destiny—assuming our destiny could have been otherwise. I often wondered why I agreed to go with Saskia to Paris and live with her there. True, I *did* want to help her with her, "assumed," plan to find Adélaïse, although I was skeptical of this mysterious "Fortune" she spoke of. I didn't go out of charity—of course not. Charity meant nothing to me then. I think it was *simply put...* Saskia had succeeded in seducing me. Without knowing why or how, I found myself in love with this strange Wanderess. Maybe I was just in love with the dream she was selling me: *a life of destiny and fate*; as my own life up until we met had been so void of enchantment. Those things: *mystery, fate, enchantment...* they are things that young people offer us as soon as we get close to them. And if we're not careful, we can be seduced by, and drawn back into, the youthful world they preside over. Regardless of how or why... as soon as I knew Saskia, I found I could no longer live without her.

It was there in Paris that the great mystery that bound the two of us together began to unveil itself. That city was our wine, our poison, our pleasure and pain. We loved Paris ...that is, until it led us to ruin. Here is how it started...

Following the incident at the theatre in Barcelona, Saskia and I departed immediately for France—it was Sunday morning. I was charged with my two valises. Saskia had only her guitar case and a large suitcase containing her favorite clothes and possessions. Everything else, she left behind in Barcelona. We arranged for a messenger to go to Andrea's hotel with the lie that Saskia was travelling to Portugal with a group of female tourists, and that if for any reason he had business in Lisbon, she would be "most thrilled" to see him there (although she left no address as to where she would be staying)... The message was scheduled to be delivered only after we had crossed the French border...

We arrived in Paris eight days later and rented a lavish apartment on the Rive Gauche[1] side. Our balcony overlooked the river Seine, as well as the tip of the Île de la Cité[2]. From Saskia's dressing table, one could see much of the Île Saint-Louis, the island where we were sure Adélaïse was living. We planned to go there every day to look for her; and in the evenings, we would go to the theatre at the Comédie-Française. We knew it was a risky affair to frequent the theatre together. It is known that Paris is the crossroads for adventurers and opportunists, and all the colorful characters of European Society as a whole; and if gossip were to travel to Andrea from anyplace, Paris would send it faster than any other town. Yet Saskia couldn't live without the theatre and society. And my greatest pleasure was pleasing her. Imagine the two of us: she, a wild spirit, and me a man of liberty; not for a

---

[1] RIVE GAUCHE: *(Fr)* "Left Bank" (The section of Paris south of the river Seine which flows from the east to the west. The neighborhoods north of the Seine form the Rive Droite ['Right Bank'].)

[2] ÎLE DE LA CITÉ: The larger of the two islands in Paris, in the Seine river, on which the cathedral of Notre Dame and the Palais de Justice are situated. The other island is Île Saint-Louis, where Saskia seeks her friend Adélaïse.

minute were we to become housebound slaves to anyone, not when the splendours of Paris were outside to be tasted.

Madame Gazonette[1], our landlady, was a flamboyant and sentimental woman of about sixty years who spent her time reading fantastic novels and creating gossip about other Parisians—from the famous to the fictitious. She said she loved what sorts of bizarre lives people lived, although most of her stories were perfectly impossible. She caught me in the hall once to inform me that the famous Marquis de G***, who supposedly lived near us, had been caught a month ago by a fish: a bottom-feeder in the Seine. She admitted that such a capture was, quote, "most-likely fiction, invented by people who wish the Marquis de G*** harm"; but she upheld that it was perfectly possible. The fish made the marquis his prisoner in the Seine, although he offered to grant the marquis one wish. The marquis said to the fish: "A wish, eh? I wish I hadn't met you today!" ...That day was a Friday; and the fish being more clever than the marquis, he granted him that wish for that day, but none the rest. So once a week, every Friday, the fish let the marquis out of the river so he could run errands in Paris and enjoy his favorite activities: that of promenading in the Tuileries Gardens, and going to the theatre at the Comédie-Française. I laughed through my nose at her story and wondered what marvel she had put in her laudanum that day.

When Madame Gazonette met Saskia, she fell devoutly in love with her. She would comment on her beauty constantly, and on the beauty of us both as a whole... "And if that isn't the most handsome couple!" she said often, clasping her hands to show how profoundly she took all of this, "and you both speak such amazing French! And with these adorable accents too!..." I informed Mme Gazonette that I had learned French before any other language, it being my mother's native tongue. Mme Gazonette was impressed to learn that Saskia learned French in London from her friend Adélaïse...

"The two of us were glued together in England," Saskia told her, "We spoke in English every day before six in the evening,

---

[1] MADAME GAZONETTE: The word 'gazon' in French means 'lawn' or 'turf.' It is also a slang word for a woman's pubic hair.

and after six we spoke in French. But this is my first time really 'living' in France." Madame Gazonette wondered why on earth we were in Spain when we met—no bother, she left our apartment after inviting us for the *apéritif* and a *souper*[1] at her home any night we wished.

I feared for good reason that the Gazonette would also fall in love with inventing gossip that involved Saskia and me. And since at least half of her stories were believable—when they didn't involve things such as time-travel, witches, magic fish, or the transforming of male facial hair into diamonds—I couldn't risk her inventing gossip about the two of us, and I knew warning her was not enough. The second day in our new place I paid Mme Gazonette a visit at her apartment beneath ours...

"Are there any vacant maid's quarters in this building that I can rent?"

"I'm sorry, Monsieur, most of the maids for our building live in the same house as their employers; but if you don't want another woman living in your house, which I can understand, I can arrange for a maid to come afternoons to clean, etc. I can find a maid who is honest... they are rare, but I can find one!"

I told her that it had nothing to do with a maid and told her firmly to remain discreet about what I was going to say. I invented a tale about Saskia coming from a very conservative household, and that her father's position in the government made it necessary that she stay out of the press. I informed Madame that Saskia's life was of nobody's business, and that as far as the public was concerned, she lived alone in our apartment. I insisted that Saskia's name was to be the only name attached to the apartment, that my name appear nowhere.

---

[1] APÉRITIF AND A SOUPER: *(Fr)* The words 'apéritif' and 'souper' now figure in modern English after having been borrowed from Classic/Modern French. As for the word 'apéritif,' neither the meaning nor the spelling were changed, whereas the French word: 'souper" was modified to become the English word: 'supper'; and with the change, went the meaning. 'Souper' as a noun in French means 'the evening meal,' which is the last meal eaten at night. The word appears more in Classic French: Used primarily by the noble, the wealthy, or the educated classes, it means: Any nighttime meal shared between friends; or if eaten between strangers, a meal shared by people of compatible values, who seek the intimacy of others present. The word is still used to refer to a 'dinner after a night out *(soirée).*'

"If anyone asks you about Saskia and me," I told her, "you say that I am her tutor in French, and that I live elsewhere. That is why I asked you if there is a vacant room somewhere in the building where I can throw a mattress. The smallest possible. I will pay an extra gold louis every month for the rent."

Madame Gazonette liked the idea of an extra louis every month and said that throwing a mattress down wouldn't be necessary, as she had a room that already had one. She led me up to the top floor of our building: a dim corridor of student flats, building maintenance closets, broom closets and the like. She unlocked a stoopy little door at the end of the hall, opened it, and I saw inside the perfect alibi: a miniscule space of three by two meters with enough dust to signify that someone hadn't been inside it for a long time. In the center of the floor sat a floppy old mattress. A nightstand of common pinewood stood by the table. There was also to my great satisfaction something that would make it believable as a place where someone might live... a foot below the ceiling, casting moonlight on the mattress on the floor, was a tiny window looking out over the city.

"I'm very happy, Madame," I reached in my pocket for six louis d'or.

"I am very happy too, Monsieur, shall I prepare the room?"

"On the instant," I told her, adding that she was to abide by certain conditions for this deal to work out: one, she and I were to remain the only two people on earth to have a key to the room; two, every day she would heat the room so it would be warm enough to make someone believe a person could live there. She would also sprinkle men's *eau de toilette* on the sheets... "Don't scrimp on quality," I said, "our tutor is a real dandy—*I think he makes extra money on the side!* Ruffle the sheets a bit then, and put a candle that has been burnt all the way down on the night table, changing it often so the room will look constantly fresh and used.

"...If someone rings at the gate," I continued, "asking after Saskia or myself, make them wait. If we decide to be available to see them, we need time to be each in our place. If someone asks for me and I am out and around town, don't make them wait; invite them up to the sixth floor, enter with your key without knocking, and let them glimpse at my lifestyle—show them into this shabby, little cubbyhole *where only I live, remember!* Prepare official rental papers for this cubbyhole for me to sign tonight; we'll have them notarized. We'll also notarize the agreement for Saskia's apartment to have legal proof she lives alone... I count on your discretion, Madame." I then gave Mme Gazonette an extra louis to find a Catholic cross for the wall and to buy some books on ecclesiastic law and theology. I wanted anyone who visited my room to believe I was an *Abbé* at seminary school studying to become a priest. I reminded her again to keep the room smelling like men's *eau de toilette* and fresh burnt wax.

Madame Gazonette was a good woman, and a real Parisian in the way that she thought neighbors, and neighbors' neighbors, should either know nothing at all, or else only things that aren't true. She grew up in the days of make-believe, and my request didn't startle her in the slightest. She was fond of the theatre; many of her friends were actors. She too would have been an actress if her husband hadn't forbade it while he was alive. So after hearing me cast her in the role of 'landlady,' Mme Gazonette swore on the soul that she swore she lost long ago that she would perform her role well. She laughed and changed her mind about her soul, "No, Monsieur, I'll swear on my health. That means more to me! I am honored."

"Very good," I said, "I will leave you to clean my *garçonnière*[1]. And remember all that I told you about Saskia's privacy."

When I returned to our apartment, Saskia was seated at the table writing something down on a piece of brown stationery, which she quickly hid from me, sliding it into the book of Homer I'd given her. She jumped-up and asked me if we would go look for Adélaïse then, or if I wanted 'to help her understand her fortune...' I told her that I wanted to take a walk. "This is my first time in Paris," I told her, "I want to explore." She could come or stay, I explained, but I wasn't happy about the way she phrased our plans: *either search for Adélaïse, or help her with her fortune.*

---

[1] GARÇONNIÈRE: *(Fr)* There is no accurate translation for this French word that refers to a discreet apartment or room (usually in the city) that a married man keeps in order to engage in infidelity with his mistress or mistresses.

"Once we find Adélaïse, you two will be in your own little world together," I told her, "Like lovers, you won't need anyone or anything from outside. You two can go abroad together. Leave me here..."

"Oh, my poor Saul... please don't be so sensitive!... I will never leave you, no matter what happens with Adélaïse. She is my best friend, yes, and my only tie to the past. But in a way, you are more important to me now... You are part of my fortune, and my fortune is my only tie to the future. It is my destiny. Just as you are helping me now, I will help you. I will always help you, Saul My Fortune. Once we find Adélaïse, you will see what I will do—once we find her!"

I took her hands in mine and sighed, "Oh, unhappy Wanderess!" It was really something to pity. "You will never navigate in this world if you talk to other people in this way. You call me your 'fortune.' You say, '*Once*' we find Adélaïse, not '*if*' we find her... Adélaïse could be dead. As for your fortune, that could merely be the ramblings of a woman who believed herself a visionary because she ate the mushrooms growing in her garden."

Saskia pleaded with me then. She said that this gardener woman *was* a visionary; that she didn't eat mushrooms—that she *couldn't possibly have*... 'It is the middle of summer,' she told me, 'Mushrooms only grow in the autumn time... when the weather is damp.' She said that she'd memorized her fortune, and that a thousand times she'd written it to paper, destroying it each time so that all that remained was the copy engraved in her memory. I listened to her tell me that she considered the words of the gardener woman as true as nature, and as inevitable as the changing of seasons. She believed in this fortune more than she believed in anything else in the world, even herself. 'Unhappy Wanderess,' I thought to myself, 'This beautiful child, wandering the world and suffering; cursed to wander and suffer ...and all for some mischief told to her once by a madwoman in a garden—sprinkling seeds, surrounded by weeds.'

At thirteen, Saskia lost everything in her world in a single moment of confusion. At fourteen she was sent off into this world; she was given her wandering shoes, some money for the road, and a premature adulthood. Now, at seventeen, the only thing in her life besides her lost friend, was this mysterious 'fortune' that was supposed to solve everything for her, and which I still didn't understand. I pitied her and agreed to tell her all she wanted to know... All, that is, except: *where I grew up, and where my father was born...*

"Why not that?" she stamped her foot.

"Because it doesn't suit me. And I'm stubborn," I told her, "Where I grew up and where my father was born are the two things you want to know most. And what I want to know most is: *why you want to know these things! Why is it,* you want this information so badly? If I can't have what I want, you cannot either."

"Child!" she exhaled with impatience, "The gardener woman said I cannot explain the puzzle to you, or else it will be ruined, the fortune will be ruined, we will be ruined, and our future will be terrible!"

"This was the gardener-woman on the Île Saint-Louis?"

"Yes."

I gave a long breath and reclined in my chair, "As a rule," I told her, "gardener-women are easy to spot—since they lurk in gardens. I will go to the Île Saint-Louis tomorrow and torture every garden-woman I find until I get one to speak up and tell me what this is all about."

This joke of mine made Saskia cry. I hated seeing her cry, seeing her soft cheeks attacked by tears. She said she was fed up. She told me how scared she was all the times she almost lost me: when I left her apartment in Barcelona after she'd healed me and I almost left for Florence without trying to find her; when I became furious because I thought she was having a romance with this Andrea boy—she was sure I would either kill him and go to prison, or else distrust her forever and abandon her; and there were many other times she was afraid I would leave her. She said to be kind to her. And even if her 'stupid fortune' was just that: *a stupid fortune,* it was all she had to grasp onto in this world besides the memory of her friendship with Adélaïse. Without her fortune, she told me, she wasn't anybody. She cried again and I hugged her in my arms and told her I would tell her everything. I would tell her everything, I promised, except of course for the name of the country where I was born and the place where my father was raised.

It was still our first day in Paris. Saskia and I had yet to share a bed together in Paris. We were on the bed together, distant. Never had we ever kissed as lovers; if we touched lips it was as brother and sister. In one moment of emotion, our lips fell together by accident, but we quickly removed ourselves as though we were children touching glass with dirty hands. We were sacred to one another. We were frightened by the influence each was having on the other, more and more every day. 'I love her no longer as a child,' I told myself, 'Since our last night in Barcelona, I love her as a woman, and I want her.' But mine was a difficult task, I knew. It was probably the hardest task I ever set for myself. Since I learned the way her selfish uncle altered her sexuality forever, just so that he could extinguish a desire that was driving him crazy... And then his trip to Athens afterwards, with the gifts he sent to try to heal his cowardice and shame... The more I thought about him and what he did, the more I thought how unnatural he was—a monster, what he did was monstrous. And so I was setting before me the hardest task of all: I would not touch her as a man touches a woman until I knew she was fully grown, heart and mind, and until I knew she fully loved me and trusted me beyond measure.

So that night after we had kissed... after I wanted her, was inflamed by her, I stopped and told her what I'd decided. She told me that she would be my sister until the day we could become lovers. We were already lovers, although lovers who do not touch are comic lovers. The comedy in our lives was those first few weeks we lived together in Paris: Our bodies desired one another, our souls opened for one another. We experienced all of the happiness and anguish of first love. Those first few weeks in Paris, we barely touched lips; yet the few times we did, it had the force of a collision of stars.

Our landlady interrupted our pantomime love affair that first evening. She came to finalize things on the apartment and offer us wine. While Saskia sat sharing stories with Mme Gazonette, I sat somber in a chair thinking: 'Why does Saskia need to know where I am from? And all this about my father?

What possible business could this young girl have with the once famous Solarus?' I was suspicious. My intuition told me something bad was going to happen. A few more glasses of wine and I became very light at heart. I stopped thinking somber thoughts to listen to Mme Gazonette. She was good company that day, giving us some interesting facts about her life:

While she was young, she told us she had the pleasure of meeting Jeanne d'Arc at a ballet[1]. Jeanne had by then acquired a nerve disorder. She was trembling when they shook hands. Regardless, Madame said she was very pretty in spite of rumors about her having been an ugly, mannish and beastly thing. On the contrary, Madame told us that she was feminine to her fingertips and even had the body of a ballerina. During their conversation, two different men and one woman approached Jeanne d'Arc to inform her that, although she chose an important mission in life, she *could have* been a ballerina if she'd wanted to; for, they said, *'You have the body!'* After Madame Gazonette described meeting Jeanne d'Arc, she announced that this night was the twentieth anniversary of her discovery that she was in menopause.

Before the good woman left, giving us back our pantomime love affair, she made sure to get another rent payment from me. I gave her thirty-six gold louis for six month's rent on our apartment (this was in addition to the six louis already paid her for three month's rent on the cubbyhole where my ghost would sleep), and I gave her three pistoles for the services to be rendered daily unto 'Ghost Saul.' With the gold still clicking in her hands, our happy landlady clasped them to her heart and sighed, "it is good to have you here! Good to drink Italian wine and reminisce of those beautiful memories of menopause! Such joy," she added, "is only achieved by Shakespearean youths who fall asleep during love making! Ô, to youthful love on hot summer nights! May you young birds make beautiful music together on your first night in Paris..." This statement made

[1] JEANNE D'ARC AT A BALLET: Such a meeting could never have occurred, since Jeanne d'Arc (John of Arc) was born in 1412 and died in 1431. The first attested ballet performance was given in 1581 at the French court. Although there may have been ballet performances before 1581, it is doubtful that there were any many years before—certainly not as early as the fourteen-hundreds.

Saskia blush to the ends of her ears. Madame Gazonette turned serious and told me directly...

"Now, if you hear pounding on your floor, like a broom handle mutilating the wood, it's because I am I'm rapping on your floor, Monsieur. This means you must hurry up to your garçonnière!" Waving my hands in annoyance, I rushed our landlady into the hall and slammed the door.

Alone, Saskia turned to me naïvely, "Saul?" she asked, "What is a garçonnière?"

With great flourish, I recounted the history of the French 'garçonnière,' assuring her it is an old national custom, very acceptable to many people; that it is a room rented by a married man where he can rendezvous with his mistresses. It can also be a room where a brave wife can visit her *amants.*[1]

"Why do you need one of those?" she asked me, "If you want to cheat on me so badly, you can just pick a time when I'm on the island looking for Adélaïse."

This response left me baffled. Was she jealous? Or did she not care? Oh, womankind, you will never cease to confuse me! To prove my faithfulness, I led Saskia by the hand up to the sixth floor and opened the door to our garçonnière.

"This is where the world is to believe I sleep," I told her, "I am your tutor only—Saul the tutor!" She lit up a smile, understanding what this was about, and threw her arms around me. We stepped into the room and since all the bare floor was covered by the mattress, we climbed up on the it, she bounced a little on it as though it were a trampoline. I saw then an honest tear roll down her cheek...

"That is touching, Saul. You are looking out for me. You want me to be safe."

"I want you to keep from losing your money."

"You are protective," she said, "You want my life to turn out well. Oh, why don't you tell me where you are from!"

---

[1] AMANTS: *(Fr)* 'Lovers,' principally used by engaged or married females to describe their extramarital sexual partners.

Then she sighed, "Oh, never mind." She put her arms solemnly against my chest. I released her to light the candle by the mattress. I lay down and urged her down beside me. She asked me to close the door. "Does it lock?"

"Of course it does. The landlady and myself are the only people with keys."

"I want a key to this room," she said.

"Why?"

"Because it's called a 'garçonnière.' I don't trust that word."

Okay, little fox, I'll have a key made for you tomorrow. But don't put it on your keychain. Hide it carefully, away from spies.

"Saul?"

"Yes, Saskia."

"Lock the door."

I knelt and locked the door. I locked the door locking the world and time outside. I stretched my body across the mattress and Saskia drew in close to me and placed her open hand on my chest, her mouth near my shoulder; her breath, my breath blew out the candle, and I held my lost Wanderess with tenderness until sweet sleep overcame us.

Chapter Twenty-two

I had to carry Saskia like a rabbit downstairs from our garçonnière to the apartment in the morning, she was so sleepy. She went out onto the terrace with her coffee, came back, and commented on how nice it was that we had this magnificent apartment, yet that we chose instead to sleep in a broom closet on our first night in Paris. She then suggested we drink champagne for breakfast, complaining that time was slipping by. I thought this the most ridiculous thing anyone could say. I learned after, while she tried to get me drunk, that she was using champagne as a truth serum. She urged me to drink again and again, but I laughed at her childish tricks. She asked me again where I was born. I told her, "In a country." She thought that was very funny. I told her my country was on the Mediterranean Sea.

"Well that narrows it down... Are you from a big city?"

"I'm from a little village. A fishing village on the Mediterranean. A village with one school and one church."

"Was your father born in this fishing village?"

"No, he was from the city, from the capital."

"Athens?"

"No!"

"Hmm... Okay, what were your favorite things to do when you were a boy?"

"I liked to paint, and make weapons out of things found around the house, and make weapons out of things found in nature... you know, normal boy-things."

"Yes, you boys are weird. More about your country, what kind of place is it. What are you famous for?"

"Making war."

"War?! What kind of war? A *peculiar sort* of war?"

"All wars are a little peculiar, don't you think?"

"This is hard, Saul." Saskia frowned and looked discouraged. I laughed at her, then I said, "We're also famous for fishing, in my fishing village. We're famous around the world for a certain species of fish that only we have."

"Really!" she cheered, "That's great! What kind of fish? Is it a fish peculiar to a certain country?"

I laughed at this. "My girl, what peculiar questions you ask! Don't you know, fish are peculiar to oceans, not to countries..."

"Darn it, Saul! Ach, I'm no good at this..."

"Yes you are, don't stop. Keep going..."

"Your father... I imagine your father was a very handsome man."

"He had that reputation," I said, "Although I never met him. I've seen paintings, and portraits... he was a strange-looking man. They say, to some women, he was considered as handsome as a god. To others, he was too exotic-looking. He made them uneasy. When I picture him, I don't picture him like the paintings, because I know paintings lie. Sometimes before sleeping or while I dream, I picture my father's face. What I see is a giant shield, polished like a mirror, reflecting the sun. But the sun is reflected so brightly that I don't know if it is a shield, or if it is the sun itself. I picture his wild hair streaming-out from all sides around the shield and sun. You know, my father lived his whole life in the capital of my country..."

"But which country?! Which capital?! Tell me, Saul!..."

"...It was fashionable at the court of my country," I went on, "for royalty to buy exotic slaves that come from around the world. These slaves become 'curiosities' of the court. Some are purchased because they are hideous, and they are treated badly. Some are put in cages so that tickets can be sold for the public to come gawk at them. Other court 'curiosities' are fortunate: purchased because they have a special talent, or great beauty. These 'curiosities,' if they are still children, are given an education at the royal school, and raised together with the royal children. They themselves are treated as nobility. Many gain their freedom as well as rank and honor. One such 'curiosity' was acquired when our navy captured a pleasure-boat on the Black Sea. Her name was Polinichka: a beautiful aristocrat from Saint Petersburg. She was blonde, white-skinned, with piercing blue eyes; and a grace, they say she walked the way snow floats down... unlike anything the Mediterranean had seen before. Just before she died, she became my grandmother.

Another such 'curiosity' arrived from the Americas around the same time. His skin was red, his hair was black. He was an Indian of the Cherokee tribe. A strong man, no one could outwrestle him. He was brave, learnèd in botany, he had wisdom in healing.

Because this Russian and the Indian were both exceptional in beauty, and each had talents and manners that were valuable and admired, each was treated like the nobility, educated at court, and eventually they were granted freedman status...

"The Cherokee never thought of marriage; as favors from women arrived to him too easily, he never had to bother with the thought, and his desires were kept on low-flame. But when Polinichka fell in love with the Cherokee, he sensed this, and his desire flamed-up to a lust he had never felt before. Yet this one time, he felt his lust dominated by something much deeper: *he admired her.*

"...And so, wanting to marry her before he spent his desire by seducing her, he left court and hid himself away and taught himself Russian. When he returned to the court, he used her native language to court her—it was their secret language, no else spoke Russian. Now while the king's brothers and cousins all were fond of the Cherokee, the king himself—barely an adolescent at this time—was jealous of the Indian and hated him...

"The Cherokee courted Polinichka at night beneath the Mediterranean stars, and described the stars of the Americas. He told her which animals they represented. She in turn described to him the white-nights of Petersburg: those nights when the sun dips barely over the horizon at sunset, and gives rise to the same sun only minutes later. I remember when as a boy my mother made up stories about these white-nights to tell to me as I fell asleep, I was at once mesmerized and hypnotized, pacified and terrified. The stories of these 'endless days called nights' so left an impression on me, that they are the goal, the destination, of this European journey I am taking now. Once I see those white-nights, I can let the earth swallow me up, I can drift out to sea alone, it won't really matter...

"It is too late in the year to see the white nights this year," I told Saskia, "but, then again, why hurry to one's own end? I will go to Petersburg next year, after we find your friend... And after I visit Florence... I need to see my mother once more. She must be old now...

"Well, back to my story," I resumed, "It wasn't long before Polinichka and the Cherokee were married. All of the royal family, except for the king and the queen, attended. They were married without the blessings of the Catholic church, but they didn't care. Polinichka was Russian Orthodox. And my grandfather, the Indian, believed in Nature and Spirits. They were happy and in love their entire life together. They had one child, a vigorous boy whom they named Solarus. He was my father."

With that, I stopped my storytelling, and I went to find some wine in the cupboard.

"Hey, go on with the story!"

"There is no wine here," I said, "Let's go to a café."

"Nope, bad plan. *First,* we go to the Île Saint-Louis to look for Adélaïse, *then* we go to a café. You can wait to have your wine."

"I can *not* wait for my wine," I told her; thinking how to avoid that island to drink some wine in a café, I tried persuasion... "Saskia, listen... when you and Adélaïse find each other again, you will want it to be an intimate moment. You should be alone together. She is your best friend, your twin."

Saskia chewed her nails, biting off flakes of polish. "Okay, go drink your wine," she said, "I'll go alone." I laughed to myself about her fingernails: a collage of colors like layers of the Earth, each color representing a different date of application of polish, a different time in her life. Yes, it was true that Saskia had the life-experience of a grown woman, but her fingers were those of a teenage girl.

"It's going to take me a couple hours to get ready... I have to bathe and get dressed... Give me two hours."

"Two hours!" If she needed *that* to bathe, I told her, then she should let me go *first* to the island. I would go drink my wine in a café there for an hour or so. Surely with my head full of wine, I would be more effective walking around looking for her friend.

"Why do you suggest that?!" Her mouth dropped open, "Why drink your wine *on that island?* You can't look for her when you've never seen her—are you crazy?! And if you were to pass her?! And if she saw you?! Not knowing what the other one looks like, you two will pass as strangers! Then she will be gone forever!"

She threw her head in her hands then in complete despair. I told her to calm down. "Go bathe and dress and give yourself time, Saskia. How's this for a plan to find her... You said that not many people your age in Paris understand English. You said this island is residential, and very peaceful. So, if I see a girl there that could possibly be Adélaïse, I will walk up and greet her in French; then I will say to her in bad English, with a terrible accent:

"'Miss, excuse me but I'm curious... I just thought I overheard you mumbling something to yourself in English before I approached you. Am I wrong?' ... 'No, Sir, I wasn't mumbling to myself in English,' she may answer. 'But you do speak English?' I will ask. 'Yes, I do.' ... 'And you can write in English?' ... 'Yes, of course, they teach us that in school.' ... 'Then you are in a position to do me the greatest favor! It will only take you five minutes and I will pay you an écu for your trouble...'

"...The girl may be too proud to work for an écu, or too rich; she may consider herself too busy to help me, but I will insist with the pitiful nature of an unrequited lover... 'You see I'm in a desperate situation! I'm from Portugal, and neither my French nor my English is good at all... My problem is, I'm in love with this French girl that lives here on this island. I have a rendezvous with her in an hour... on that bridge over there, you see. Since I cannot explain my feelings for her in good French or in good English. I would like to give her a letter expressing my love for her. Just one page, two at the most, but not more. All you need to write to her is this—it must be in English, because I won't have a chance at communicating with her if the two of us meet, if she doesn't know English...

"'Dear Adélaïse... (you see her name is Adélaïse), for many months now I have admired you from afar, etc....'"

I stopped narrating my plan and took Saskia's hands... "You see what genius this idea is?" I, at least, admired my own plan tremendously. "If the girl I ask the favor of *is* your friend Adélaïse, I will know for certain the moment I say that Adélaïse is the name of my sweetheart."

"Oh!"

"If it is *not* Adélaïse... well, it may be a friend of hers and she may say... 'Wait! I know an Adélaïse who lives near here... could your sweetheart be the same Adélaïse?'"

"Yes!"

"...And even if the young girl doesn't know a soul named Adélaïse, our écu may still have bought us a good connection with someone who knows various families established on the island..."

"It will also have bought you a love letter you can give to some French girl!"

I smiled and laughed, "I can write my own love letters in French, thank you."

Saskia laughed and agreed, adding that I did write very charming letters—when they weren't letters of farewell. She kissed both of my hands over and again. She was thoroughly convinced that my strategy would work. "Saul, you are clever beyond belief! I should have asked you to plan this with me from the beginning. Okay, please go now to the island, I will bathe and get dressed. Don't drink too much wine!"

Saskia's faith in my idea gave me enormous pleasure, so much that I convinced myself I would find Adélaïse that very morning. I was soon to be discouraged, however, when an hour and a half went by of my wandering the Île Saint-Louis and I did not see a single girl that could have possibly been her friend Adélaïse. The island was empty, except for some uninteresting characters. I would have left altogether unaffected by the island, except when leaving I came upon two figures that confused me and left me in a daze for the entire afternoon to follow...

I passed a gated garden on the occidental side of the island where a plump, old woman, with the body and face of a peasant, was sweeping debris from the stones with a thatched broom. She acknowledged me, and then resumed her loud conversation with a man at the open window of the house to which the garden belonged. The man was mostly concealed from my view by the dirty glass of the open windowpane, but I could see enough of his features and stature to know I'd seen him before, and under strange circumstances. But *where* before?, *when*?, I couldn't place it. His thin, sallow face, his dark cloak and hat. I then recalled it, and became convinced that it was the same man that followed me in Valencia, from the restaurant to my hotel... 'What a strange-looking man,' I thought. He eyed me briefly, without showing any interest or recognition, said adieu to the woman in the garden, and shut the window.

As far as Adélaïse was concerned, I would have been completely forlorn after my fruitless search on the Île Saint Louis, but one happy event happened after the encounter with the man and woman in the house and garden: I made an acquaintance while still on the island, walking down the rue des Deux Ponts to go back home where I believed Saskia was still dressing. I finally passed a girl of about Saskia's age. She was alone and I greeted her with my intended script: "Mademoiselle, pardon me... I thought I overheard you mumbling to yourself in English, etc., etc..." It turned out that it would have been impossible that the girl mumbled to herself in English since she didn't understand a word of what I was saying in English, and didn't even understand the word 'Hello.' She was friendly though, in French; her name was Sarah Lingot, and she'd lived her whole life on the Île Saint-Louis. Her father, she explained as we stood on the sidewalk, talking as though we were already friends, had just retired from a long military career where he had been of high rank, perhaps even a general. We spoke, and I was glad Mademoiselle Lingot was not Adélaïse, since Mademoiselle Lingot was neither pretty, nor very captivating in her manner. I mentioned to her that I had important business with a family on the island. I offered her an écu, which she refused; but she said that I could come visit her at her parents' home whenever I wished; and as long as my affairs were honest and out in the open, she would help me where she could.

I left delighted by the encounter and returned around noon to our home on the quai. Saskia had never left, she had only finished dressing. I was charmed to see her dressed in a way I had never seen her before. She looked like a beautiful piece of candy—color on her lips, long lacquered eyelashes, her hair back in braids. I kissed her forehead and she wrapped her arms around my neck.

"I missed you, kiddo," I said, "I found a beautiful island in the city. An island with many a bridge. And now I come back to find you in braids, what a pleasure! You know, a girl without braids is like a city without bridges..."

"That's nice. Did you find someone to help you write your love letter?"

"Nay," I said, and let her fall away from my neck, where she stayed clinging, "The island was empty. Too early, I guess."

"I kind of thought it would be. That's why I didn't dress so fast. Later it will be better."

"I met a girl, though," I told Saskia, and described my meeting with Mademoiselle Lingot, saying that we now had an entry into a good home on the island. Saskia seemed jealous, although she only replied, "That's good you talk to girls. You don't want to forget what they sound like... I'm going to the Île Saint Louis now for my own detective work. Will you be good?"

"A saint," I said, "I might go for a walk and drink more wine. Let me give you some money." I knew that Saskia was out of funds until she went abroad to draw on her inheritance. I searched through my pockets to give her a handful of écus, and in doing so I realized that our wealth was quickly diminishing. For her it was clothes and guitar sheet-music, for me in was opium and wine. I needed to think of ways to fill our purse without depending on Saskia's inheritance, which we could only draw-on abroad. Paris had us glued to it, the way that city glues so many wanderers. I knew that Paris was reputable for gaming rooms where they say that ruined adventurers often made back lost fortunes in a single day. I think we had under a hundred louis at that time. 'If only I could get my hands on two-thousand gold louis d'or,' I thought. 'With two thousand louis, Saskia and could live in comfort long enough to find Adélaïse and find my mother in Florence; it would take us all the way to Saint Petersburg to see the white nights. Just two-thousand louis d'or, and we will no longer need Saskia's uncle's money. We can live together openly for the whole world to know...'

Still, and no doubt wisely, I decided to *not* go to the gaming tables that day. As far as adventurers go, I had always been one of the more successful. But as for gamblers, I was a disaster. With my passionate temperament, I knew a day at a roulette table would leave me and Saskia in the street: two paupers without bread or clothes.

"I'll be back when I can!" Saskia planted a kiss with her candy mouth on the tip of my nose and skipped out of our apartment. Her gaiety, her freshness, made me infinitely happy. I think that this time with her, with us living together in Paris in that apartment on the quai of the river Seine, was the happiest time I had ever known up till then in my life. I stood at the window and watched her bouncing happily across the bridge over the Seine. And I thanked then the generosity of the gods for my luck, and my life, and the city of Paris, and I thanked Saskia and all that had led up to her finding me that night in Barcelona.

Chapter Twenty-three

I was indeed a saint while Saskia was tramping around Paris looking for Adélaïse. I smoked myself to heaven in an opium den on the rue Saint-Honoré. I then got lost in my fog of pleasure and explored the old streets of the Rive Droite[1]. I contemplated all the possible reasons why the sun shines. I contemplated the moon too, knowing that the day is beautiful but that night would soon come and the moon would be almost full. I knew that some adventures would present themselves in the coming days, and new adventures are always exciting when one is in a new city.

I sold my sword on the rue de Rivoli—that beauty of silver and steel with the emerald handle which I bought in Barcelona the day of that horrible night at the theatre in Barcelona—a night I hoped to erase forever from my memory. With the money I

---

[1] RIVE DROITE: *(Fr)* The "Right Bank." This is the section of Paris north of the river Seine, which flows from the east to the west. The neighborhoods south of the Seine form the Rive Gauche.

received for the sword, I purchased a pair of diamond earrings for Saskia at the Place Vendôme.

When I returned home, everything was quiet. Saskia was still out. I poured a glass of wine to drink, and before I sat down to enjoy it, I opened the door to our patio and spilled the first sip on the ground to appease the gods, as is my custom. That was when Saskia entered. She was all in a tizzy...

"That stupid island!" she huffed, throwing her purse down. "*You* go there and the people are nice. *You* meet people. One girl even picks up on you and invites you to her home! Why aren't people nice to *me*?"

"Drink some wine, Saskia."

"No, no, that won't help... First of all, the island was empty and desolate. I was desolate too. Nowhere was there anyone or anything that had to do with Adélaïse. Oh, I did see a few people! There were some here and there, and I tried your trick. I went up to each one and asked if they spoke English. They all shook their heads and said, "Français!" So I then asked them in French if they knew a lot of people on the island. One lady growled at me. *"Ça ne vous regarde pas,*[1]*"* she howled at me. One man responded to my question by sneering at me: *"Vous êtes bien trop jeune et trop jolie pour être inspectrice de police!*[2]*"* Just then I'd had enough! I decided to come home. So when I was leaving the island, I passed a yard where an woman was sweeping up leaves. Her grey hair was all knotty and she had a dirty old broom. She reminded me a lot of the old gardener woman I met on that exact same island years before..."

"The woman who told you your famous fortune that you refuse to share with me?"

"Yes, that one... my famous fortune that is the reason you and I are together. Both women had similar faces, both had icy grey eyes; although the one today looked like a mule, whereas the fortune teller didn't look like a mule. Anyway, I decided to talk to

---

[1] ÇA NE VOUS REGARDE PAS: *(Fr)* "That is none of your business.

[2] VOUS ÊTES BIEN TROP... *(FR)* "You are far too young and too pretty to be a police inspector."

her, not thinking that there was any way in the world she too would humiliate me. Boy, I was sure wrong...

"'Bonjour Madame!' I greeted her cheerfully, 'Did we not see each other here once before?' She set down her old broom and looked at me in a mean way and said, 'All I can tell you, little girl, is that you are being followed. Not just here on this island, where you've been coming every day for over a week now on some kind of unknown business, but you are being followed elsewhere too.'...

"I was speechless! The old broom-lady continued, 'You know the people on the Île Saint-Louis talk about you, don't you? Many close their shutters when you approach their houses. Have you not noticed all the closed shutters? Isn't it a little hot out to be closing shutters?'...

"I didn't reply to the old witch, she made me furious! I simply turned around and headed to the bridge to come back home, deciding never to return to that stupid island again. How come I don't have your talent for getting people to open up to me?"

"You have the talent. You just crossed the wrong people today. Happens to me too some days."

"Still, I think you should take over the job of finding Adélaïse. The only way I will ever find her is if I spot her with my own eyes, whereas you can charm somebody who might know her."

"Do you want to go to the theatre tonight?" I asked.

"Oh yes!"

I was glad to have changed the subject away from the Île Saint-Louis and Adélaïse, and Saskia was in heaven when I presented her the diamond earrings I bought for her. "No man ever offered me earrings! Not even my uncle. And these are so beautiful!" She threw her lovely arms around me and hugged me with all her might. I was thrilled that I made her happy and it was with great joy we dressed for the theatre that night.

* * *

At the Comédie-Française...

That night, Saskia was as beautiful as the sky when night's phase possesses the moon and every constellation. When she appeared at the Comédie-Française, wearing a silk taffeta gown, her shoulders nude and neck perfumed, with diamonds in her ears, she excited all of Paris. The production was Molière's *Dom Juan.* At intermission, we drank champagne, and many came up to us to pay compliment to Saskia's beauty. Afterwards, we returned to the parterre where our seats were; but before we sat down, I saw something very disturbing: Above us, in a box at the right of the stage, a man was seated alone, no lady beside him. I recognized him as the same man who had been in the house that morning on the Île Saint-Louis, talking to the peasant woman through the plate-glass window—he looked different now as he wasn't wearing a hat. But this was not what disturbed me. It was that even that morning, when he was at the window, I decided he was the same man who followed me in Valencia. That morning I made other connections, but nothing that grasped me. Now, seeing him clearly, his face, stature, the serious way he composed himself, I realized that *this was the man!* ...not just the man from Valencia, but from Barcelona too; and not just Barcelona, but elsewhere...

Watching him flashed pictures in my mind: tangible memories arranged with vague associations. I flashed-back to the night I met Saskia, remembering that strange man on Las Ramblas who stopped me when I was poisoned; and, telling me how sick I looked, he advised me to go to the hospital that was on the very street where I would meet Saskia. If he hadn't stopped me and told me about that hospital, Saskia and I would have never met. Looking in the theatre that night at that long face with those dark, gaunt features, I recalled the ship captain in Barcelona at the port who announced that all boats to Florence were either canceled or heavily delayed. It was also thanks to this announcement that Saskia and I reunited after I escaped from her apartment in El Ravel. Had the boats been running, I would have left Barcelona on the spot, damning that city to the dogs. And I would probably have forgotten Saskia.

They say that when we dream at night and see a figure who tells us the path we need to follow, the direction we need to take in life, it is always the same figure in each dream. He or she may vary slightly in form between dreams, but it is always the same figure. It seemed to me that the messengers in my life—the ones who have guided me towards unbelievable experiences, led me to the people I've cared about—these messengers all resembled the same man, a man I now saw outside of a dream. He was in the same theatre as me, seated in a box for a performance of Molière's *Dom Juan*, on my first night at the Comédie-Française in Paris: that strange city that would forever leave its mark on me.

The presence of this man in the theatre made me uneasy. "Let's go to the bar to get some champagne," I said to Saskia. She didn't reply, so I excused myself, saying I would come back with champagne. Saskia was talking to two other girls when I returned. They were about her age, both elegantly dressed. Saskia appeared very jealous when I arrived—a strange thing, considering the girls were not as beautiful as she. She didn't introduce me to them, so one of the girls introduced herself to me. Saskia stared at her with angry eyes when she did this, and without further conversation, she uttered an insincere goodbye to them and turned to face me, her back turned to them in a way that seemed very impolite. She then began to tell me how wonderful she thought the play was. This show of jealousy charmed me completely. Saskia was now more beautiful than ever in my eyes. So I told Saskia how beautiful she was to me, and how I loved her more than Molière. She took my arm and we wandered away from the two girls, and from all other people, and we found a corner of the theatre where we could be alone. Saskia hugged my shoulders, and she asked me if I was a little tipsy. Before I could answer, she said, "Not now, I meant *then*. When you said you loved me more than Molière." I tried to respond but she hushed me, saying that it didn't matter. She didn't care if I was a little tipsy when I said I loved her. Either way she said she was happier at that moment than she had ever been in her entire life. I told her that *she herself* was tipsy to say such a thing, and she admitted that she was a little tipsy... "More than a little," she said. Then she smiled in a sneaky way, and she said,

"Regardless..." and she told me that she loved me too... more than Molière, and more than Racine and more than Beaumarchais, even more than Shakespeare. Her words made me dizzy with pleasure, and I gave her a hundred caresses and covered her hands in kisses. My heart was aflame when we left the Comédie-Française that night, and I gave no more thought to the presence of my "messenger" in that theatre. I only thought of that gypsy child named Saskia.

Chapter Twenty-four

That night after the theatre, Saskia told me the first part of her fortune. It was her fortune, I came to realize, that had seduced her; her fortune that had seduced me. It was her fortune that was the true author of our lives. It was just as intangible as love, as intangible as disease; and just as love and disease are invisible entities that take over the mind and body of the infected, so did that fortune work like an invisible disease: it worked through the body and mind to construct our mysterious relationship and build the outcome of this story. You will see as I go on...

After the theatre, we found a restaurant on the quai of the Seine which looked elegant, called Chez Lefèvre[1]. Inside, it was

---

[1] CHEZ LEFÈVRE: Payne may be referring to the restaurant 'Lapérouse,' founded by a monsieur 'Lefèvre.' Located at the current 51 quai des Grands Augustins in Paris' sixth arrondissement, Lapérouse has the same approximate location ('on the quai of the Seine') as 'Chez Lefèvre' in this novel. Lapérouse was founded in 1766 by Lefèvre, a celebrated wine-merchant, and is still in business today at the time of this publication. The original name of the restaurant was 'Limonadier du Roy.' It was changed to 'Lapérouse' in 1878 in honor of the famous navigator: Le Comte de Lapérouse. [Ed.]

dim. Every single table was empty, but we didn't take that as a bad sign. There was a summer storm that night and a blustery wind had cleared the entire quai of all souls. The restaurant only had one waiter. He heard us come in and came from the back patio and welcomed us to a table. He was a small, tired-looking man: an Italian from Mantua, he told us. He explained that the owner of the restaurant wasn't in; that the chef was there, but there had been no customers all evening. The waiter showed that he was a little drunk as he opened up to us...

"I received some very bad news today," he said, "I don't want to spoil your meal... it was personal news about my family. So if you don't mind, except when you need me, I'll be out back on the patio smoking and drinking."

His frankness was endearing. Saskia, always moved by tender scenes, asked the waiter if he wanted us to leave so he could be alone... "Since we are the only customers," she said, "if we leave, you can close up and go home to be alone." The sad waiter replied that he didn't want to be alone; that he wanted most of all to be out on that patio smoking and drinking, knowing all the while that the chef was there in the kitchen and that we were here in the dining room. Saskia thanked him, with damp eyes she whispered to me that he was breaking her heart. I ordered a bottle of Bourgogne; and a moment later, she and I were alone at a table with good wine to drink.

We talked and drank. Saskia was moved to emotion by the red wine and our solemn waiter. After he took our order, he returned to the patio where we could see him drinking spirits and smoking the thin, generic cigarillos that the waiters along the quai smoke. After a while, the chef appeared from the kitchen and called to the patio, "Guido? Eh, Guido?..." But our waiter didn't seem to hear him. The chef proceeded to our table carrying two plates of pasta. Halfway to our table, he stopped and stood still, and stared at me. I looked at the chef and at our plates of pasta expectantly. A minute passed before the dumbfounded chef approached us finally and set the plates down in front of us; he said...

"Sir, I'm sorry... I couldn't stop staring at you just now."

"I noticed. Why?"

"I mean, I'm not sure we've met before. Or, rather... Have you come to our restaurant before? No, I'm sure that you haven't. Where have I seen you before?"

I told the chef that I had never been to his restaurant before tonight, and that it was unlikely we'd met anywhere considering I was new in Paris.

"It must have been a picture of you I've seen somewhere... published in the press, in some journal if you'll forgive me saying. Yes, I'm intruding. It's just that your face is unmistakable."

"Well, never mind," I said and waved my hand, "our dinner will get cold."

"Yes, excuse me please, sir. And you, madame. Bon appétit."

"Merci."

Once he left, Saskia turned to me with fascination in her eyes... "Saul! What are they saying about you in the press?"

"How would I know? I don't read the press."

"Huh, that's true," she said, "Neither of us read that rubbish. Though, I wonder what they're saying about you."

"How do you know it's not about *us*?" I laughed, "You know your boy, Andrea, he certainly has our relationship covered in the press."

Saskia smiled at this. "No, no, no! I think it's about you, and only about you... I bet they're saying fantastic things in the press about you."

I didn't know then that Saskia's guess was right. I didn't give any thought to what she said at the restaurant, not knowing how serious things would become later. Later, when she and I were apart from each other, I grew convinced that she had known all along about those articles in the press... that she knew about them that night we dined at Lefèvre's restaurant in Paris. You will see in time what I mean.

"You have your pasta and wine now," Saskia went on, "...wine always puts you in a mood to talk. Our waiter is away on the patio drinking and smoking. The place is vacant, we have the whole restaurant to ourselves. I think you should tell me about your parents and your childhood. That will solve everything. Then I will know where you grew up and where your father was born, and then I can tell you my fortune. That will help us find Adélaïse... then we can go to Florence!"

"Tell me your fortune right now, I will know why you latched onto me in Barcelona, and that will explain everything! No need to know about my childhood..."

"But *who* did I latch onto in Barcelona?!" Saskia demanded. She then went as far as to punch the restaurant table with her little fist. "I don't even know *who you are!* Here I've told you all about my childhood, about losing my parents, I made the confession about my uncle and showed you all my vulnerabilities, and you won't even tell me which damned country you grew up in! You're tremendously selfish, Saul. You watch me give away all my secrets, while your own life you shroud in all this mystery..."

"Good girl, you're right," I said, and I took her fist in my hand. And she was right. Why was my life top-secret?, when she opened hers up to me with the loving trust that I wasn't going to ruin it? Was I not being a child?, puffed-up with his own self-importance, by hiding my life story? Perhaps it was because as a child I was taught to be secretive about my family and my origins, perhaps it was because I wanted to know why she so lovingly abducted me in Spain... In any case, Saskia was right about wine inspiring me to talk. To whom does wine not give the inspiration to talk? I drained my glass again and called our solemn waiter over to get another bottle in the queue and take our orders for the next course. When I finished with Guido, I looked over at Saskia and saw she was furtively writing on a piece of paper. I ask her what she was writing and she jumped as if startled; she then handed me a piece of paper...

"This much of my fortune I'll show you," she said, "It's the first few lines..." Then she handed me the paper that read simply:

"You are a Wanderer searching for something, or 'someone' rather.

You were raised by the people of the north, but you are not one of them, as you belong to no people and have no country."

I laughed to myself, and asked her if I could keep the paper. Saskia was so sensitive this night, I didn't dare make fun of her garden-woman clairvoyant, although it seemed that she was a fraud. Obviously Saskia was a wanderer from the north. She spoke French with a Dutch accent, in phrases littered with Englishisms."

"I know these first few lines of my fortune are obvious," she said, "but you would be shocked if you knew the rest—the things it says about my life!" She then went on to say that if I knew then, at this dinner table, the rest of her fortune in its entirety, I would bet my sanity as well as my life on its "mystical authenticity."

To this, I couldn't help myself. I roared with laughter... "I would *bet my sanity on its mystical authenticity!* That is too much!" and my laughter filled the empty restaurant. I calmed myself down as quickly as possible to not hurt Saskia too much. She sat silent, blushing red to her ears with embarrassment.

"I know I sound stupid," she said.

"No, no! It's just the wine we've drunk. And... I'm very happy that we're sharing things together tonight."

She looked so sensitive, this wounded creature sitting near me in the restaurant on this night, with a pitcher full of water ready to come storming from her eyes should I laugh again. I felt great pity for her then, my solitary wayfaring girl with no country, who belonged to no people, who grew up without knowing where she was going or why. I imagined the scene that spring day in London when, as a child of twelve, she lost everything in her world in a single moment of confusion. Now here in Paris, the only two things in her life, me aside, were her search for Adélaïse, and that mysterious fortune which I had just laughed at. I told her again I only laughed because I was happy and because I loved her.

"Where should we start in telling about my family and my life?" I asked her.

"How about your mother. Where is she now?"

"In Florence, I believe."

"Hmm… what were your favorite things to do as a boy?"

"Most of all of all…" I had to think hard about that time that exists still only in fragments… "I loved spending entire days painting colorful designs on the skiffs we had. They belonged to the old fisherman who raised me together with his old wife and my mother. It was the saddest thing in the world to me when the fishermen would go fishing in the skiffs and all the paint would wash off. My mother saw my talent and encouraged me to become a painter when I grew up." I told Saskia how my mother had to go into exile when she was pregnant with me…

"She is the niece of the present king of our country… the same man who, as a youth, hated my grandfather the Indian. My mother was only a girl of your age when she fell in love with my father, Solarus: the son of the Cherokee and my grandmother, the Russian Polinichka. My father was, they say, a very charismatic man and was loved by the people at court. But my father, the son of two freedmen, was not a nobleman. He was not liked by our king, just as his father before him. The king was jealous of my father's strength and charm. So when our king found out about his niece's pregnancy, he ordered the death of my father (my father had admitted he had taken my mother's virginity). Like Socrates, my father was given hemlock to drink. The rumor is, however, that the executioner loved and respected my father, just like almost everyone at court. So loving him, he mixed in the water—instead of hemlock—barley. According to this legend, a rooster crowed as my father drank the barley water, and Solarus then slipped away to who-knows-where. The executioner then reportedly filled an empty grave, and he told the king that the job was done. A friend and confident of my mother who was there when the executioner reported to the king that Solarus was dead, went to find my mother just after. She found her pregnant with me and told her that Solarus had been executed. To avoid my being killed as soon as she gave birth, my mother slipped away in the night. She changed her clothing and assumed a false name—claiming to be a poor merchant's daughter rather than a princess—and she travelled on foot many, many days, until she reached the fishing village where she gave birth to me, and where I grew up. She didn't have any money with her, and consequently she was dependent on the generosity of others. Fortunately, my mother possessed great charm, noble graces and beauty, and a cheerful disposition... all which inspired people to assist her. She was grateful to accept the generous hospitality of the aging fisherman and his frail spouse when they opened their home to her and offered me a place to grow up and to take on after their death. As for my father, I don't know if it was true that the executioner helped him escape or not. I believe that he loved my mother very much, so I think if he were alive, he would have come to find her. Since he didn't, I hold the belief that he was executed after all."

Saskia asked me what religion the people of my country believe in and I said we were Roman Catholics, that our king is a Christian king, but that before him our country was ruled by moors. "I know it!" she cheered, "You're from Portugal!" I reminded her that my mother and I, along with most of the ruling class and the courtiers, grew up speaking French. And that French, as far as I knew, had never been the ruling-class language in Portugal. She was confused, and being confused she was solemn. I tried to cheer her up. I told her that we would find my mother in Florence as soon as we found Adélaïse, and that my mother would tell her the truth about where I grew up and where my father was from. She asked me again how long since I'd seen my mother. I told her, "Fifteen years."

"In that case," she said, "I will be so excited to be with you and your mother in Florence that I won't care if we ever make it to Saint Petersburg for the white-nights."

"We're not going to stay in Italy with my mother forever," I said, "Before I let the earth swallow me up, you and I are going to Petersburg together! Back to my story...

"When I reached manhood, my mother begged me to go to Florence to study painting. We had no money for my studies, but she thought I could find some menial work in Florence to sustain me. I informed her that a friend of mine from our village had moved to the capital of our country, to where she and my father were from, and he worked there painting gold leaf on the monuments and official buildings; and he said he could get me the same job as him. I, knowing that riotous adventures could be had with my friend in our capital, told my mother I was going there instead. My mother accepted this, but she made me promise never to reveal the names of my parents while in that city. Should I be wise enough to one day leave our country, she told me, I should sing my father's name from every rooftop, for he was a man to take pride in.

"And so, I left for the capital, found my friend, and worked for a while gold-leafing the monuments and official buildings. Eventually, I met a group of young men a few years older than me who lived in Malta. They, with their sophisticated clothes and worldly ways, seduced me into a life beyond that which was offered in my friendship with the young fisherman's son whom I came to the city to work and live with. These wild gentlemen told me glittering stories of their escapades in Malta. I decided to visit Malta immediately with them, and when I did, I met my future friend and business partner, Juhani who convinced not to go back to my home country. He and I began organizing decadent and luxurious parties together..."

I then told Saskia of the night we threw my last party: a rich event that drew important people from all over Europe. Juhani and I held an auction, where we auctioned off precious art for a large return. We had roulette tables with the largest bank in Malta. "But that same fateful night," I told her, "I made the unlucky decision to seduce the wife the Maltese ambassador to England. It was after I seduced her on the beach that shots rang out in the night. The ambassador and his bodyguards tried to kill me as I fled the island in a small boat piloted by a single man whom I had enough money on me to pay handsomely. And as we were leaving Malta, while the ambassador stood on the shore firing bullets at me, I stood like Odysseus leaving the island of the Cyclops. From the boat, I shouted at the ambassador, 'Do not forget me! I am the son of Solarus, the man who seduced your wife!' It was that moment of hubris[1] that cursed me. Among

[1] HUBRIS: *(Gr)* An important term in Homeric works meaning 'excessive pride.' It was Odysseus' excessive pride that drove him to shout his real name at the Cyclops, Polyphemus, as he was fleeing the Cyclops' island in his boat (*The Odyssey*, Book IX). With this comparison, Payne suggests that some or all of Saul's many sufferings were a result of his hubris while fleeing Malta, since, in *The Odyssey*, the cause of Odysseus' sufferings and his delayed return home was this act of hubris which informed the Cyclops of Odysseus'

other things, I learned that I would be executed should I try to go to Malta again, or should I ever try to enter England. This is why I can never go with you to London."

I continued telling my story to Saskia...

"We were lucky to have clear skies during the whole escape from Malta. The boat was too small to sail the wide sea, and I feared if we made a long journey, a police boat would catch up with us and control us. Since Malta lay midway between Italy and Sicily to the north, and North Africa to the south, I had my choice. The pilot of the boat was from North Africa and he hoped to return there; I had paid him enough so that he shouldn't have had any say in the matter. But I made him happy by agreeing to go to North Africa. The thing that swayed my decision was that Africa is cheap. The pilot had most of my money. Since I was hosting a luxurious party in Malta the night I went into exile, I was wearing all my gold and jewels. I sold them all—all, except for my gold Breguet watch that was stolen in Málaga—and they paid my way from where we landed until Alexandria where they funded my life there for some time.

We didn't see any ships on our way to Africa, and we weren't controlled as we docked. I bade farewell and thanks to the pilot of the boat and set out on land for Alexandria. There, I lived in poverty for many years. Egypt was a strange country to find myself suddenly living alone in. Alexandria was dirty, and the neighborhood in Alexandria where I lived was very poor and sad. The men of my neighborhood worked as either laborers, or criminals; and the women mostly dancers in nightclubs, or prostitutes on corners.

"It took years, but Juhani proved to be a better detective than the Maltese ambassador; and he proved to be a man of virtue, and the finest friend anyone could ever hope to have. He tracked me down in Alexandria this last winter—I don't know how he did!—and he sent me a letter to announce my fortune of ten thousand scudi. He told me he could transfer the money to a

---

identity. Once the Cyclops knew that the man who blinded him was the famous hero who sacked Troy through his ruse of the Trojan Horse, he was able to curse Odysseus to his father, the god Poseidon, thus creating the plot of Homer's great epic.

bank in Alexandria; or else, I could use the advanced money enclosed in the letter to travel to Madrid and accept my fortune in person. You know the rest of the story. Do you want more wine?"

"I want to hear more of your story," Saskia said, "Tell me about your mother. What kinds of things did she tell you when you were a little boy?"

"Well, back on the subject of executions... My mother told me the truth about my father and his execution, although she believed the legend was true about the executioner giving him barley to drink and helping him to escape. She said that everyone loved my father so much that only the king's presence at the execution could have forced someone to kill him; but that the king was too cowardly to attend the executions he ordered. She told me a gruesome story to show how cowardly and barbaric the king was: when she was a young girl, the king made her witness an execution out at sea...

The execution in the Mediterranean...

"My mother was a mere adolescent; the king, her uncle, was only a few years older. He had ordered the execution of a young nobleman for treason, and he conceived of the most barbarous way to do it. My mother was among the royal family that was brought along to witness the execution. They often brought noble children along to witness executions in my country. The children weren't told beforehand where they were going or why. The story my mother told me went as follows...

"The execution was held on a boat set adrift in the Mediterranean one early summer morning when the sun was not yet scorching the sky. Besides the soldiers, the spectators numbered only ten or so. The condemned man was accompanied by the closest members of his family: his sisters, brothers, and his parents. They were all brought onboard to see their close son and brother shot dead and dumped into the sea. The king was not present, he always avoided his own executions, although he had given instructions to his soldiers. The soldiers were a hoard of heavily-armed guards. They had the condemned man in chains.

While his family sat on boat's deck, crying, his mother and father tried to approach their son, to caress his hands one last time before they lost him forever. The guards were ordered to prevent this. The condemned man was not to be touched. My mother said, 'As soon as the boat was a ways from shore, the most evil thing imaginable in this world occurred: the chief executioner ordered the prisoner's family to draw lots. They didn't know why, but did as they were told. The loser was the prisoner's little sister. As loser, she was handed a pistol and was instructed to shoot her brother in the chest, or in the head, or anywhere else until he be dead; then his body would be dumped in the sea. If she failed to do this, the soldiers would shoot *her* and dump *her* body in the sea. After which, the funeral lots would continue and the next member of the surviving family to lose lots would be faced to kill the young man, or else refuse and be killed as well...

"His sister dropped the pistol at once. She could not shoot her older brother. The girl fell in tears in the boat. A guard shot her in the head and he dumped her body into the sea. All members of her family collapsed in tears.

"The lots fell to one of his brothers next. A guard forced the pistol into his hand. The brother, trembling, made ready to drop the gun as his sister had. Before he dropped it, the condemned prisoner stopped him and said, 'Brother, I will die today no matter what. I will never see the shore again. Salt will eat my flesh and fish will pick my bones. Tonight I shall dine in the underworld, while in this world, waves will tumble my skeleton. There is no reason for you to die as well. Save our family yet another grief and pull that trigger, Brother. Kill me now!'

"His brother stood a long time, he then crossed himself, pulled the trigger and killed his brother; but then immediately he fell onto the planks of the boat and fired one more bullet... this one, into his own brain. The cries of the family of the dead roared like the waves as they lost their minds. They had lost two sons and a daughter on this trip out to sea, and never would their happiness or their minds be returned to them. Slowly, languidly, the boat made its way back to shore."

* * *

Saskia's face retained a look of horror throughout my story. "Your poor mother!" she cried, "But why did she tell you that horrible story?!"

"I told my mother that when I was grown, I was going to go to the capital and kill our king, to avenge my father's death. She knew that such a mission would end in my own death, and that she could not survive that. So she told me this story to show how cruel our king was, how insane... she said that by forcing my father to drink hemlock, that was our king's way of 'being lenient.' No, she urged me to avoid insanity altogether, and instead to leave our country as soon as I was grown and seek a better life in Europe. It is because of stories like this that I will stay here in Europe. And why I will never return to the country of my birth."

"But you have to return!" she cried, "*We* have to!" As she said this, she fell in tears into her hands. I didn't know what to say. I didn't know then that in Saskia's mind this was the key to everything... "*We* have to," she cried again; for in her eyes, this was the key to our fortune, to her fortune, to her life.

Chapter Twenty-five

Saskia was a free bird one minute: queen of the world and laughing. The next minute she would be in tears like a porcelain angel, about to teeter, fall and break. She was brave, and I never once saw her cry out of fear. She never cried because she was afraid that something would happen; she would cry because she feared something that could render the world more beautiful, would *not* happen... She believed if I gave in to make her fortune become realized, the world would be ultimately profound and beautiful. I guess I held out because I feared the realization of her fortune would mean the destruction of us together. And each time she cried, I fell a little more deeply in love with her.

Saskia was my entire world when we lived in Paris. I lived for her pleasure, for her happiness. Every caprice she had, it was my joy to indulge her. Whatever she saw in a shop window that made her eyes light up, I would go in and buy it for her. The money Juhani had paid me was just about finished. It was now the end of August, and the white nights of Petersburg were long past and Russia was forgotten entirely. We still had twenty louis, although with our nights at the theatre, restaurants and cabarets, I knew this would not last through autumn. Still, I kept my cheerful constitution. I kept it in my head that I if we could stumble on two-thousand louis, we would be able to travel and could live on this money for the next ten years. I was preoccupied with this idea. Saskia could have gone to her bank in England for money, but she would have had to go alone. Saskia could also draw on her income in Italy, and I was free to enter Italy. But the cost of the voyage; well, we didn't have enough money left to *both travel together* to Italy.

As for Saskia, I knew that she felt actual, *physical pain* when she was away from me. She confessed this to a doctor she visited, as she said 'at random one day.' He was a general practitioner who lived and worked a few apartment houses down from us. I had told Saskia that morning that I would be gone the entire day, meeting with a friend of Juhani who was a travel agent in Montmartre. I hoped to arrange a small advance from Juhani so we could live together without being dependent on her income, without hiding. I also hoped to get Juhani to advance us tickets for Florence to leave immediately. You will soon see why I gave up hope in finding her friend Adélaïse in Paris. But first...

While I was away in Montmartre, Saskia missed me and didn't know what to do without me. She told me after the event that she went to the doctor to tell him about her pain—I was very touched by this! The doctor didn't prescribe her anything. He simply told her: "If it causes you physical pain to be away from him, then *simply do not be away from him!*" Saskia thought this was logical, and even laughed at herself for not thinking of it before. She confessed this merry story to me once I returned from my mission, and the two of us laughed together and we rolled on the floor and I gave her a million caresses and swore to her that we needn't be apart ever again.

There were only two dark clouds in our sky: one was that Saskia was stubborn in her search for Adélaïse and she didn't want to go to London or Italy until we found her. The second cloud was that I didn't yet have word from Juhani about an advance, and it was rumored that Andrea had heard about our concubinage in Paris and was coming to investigate himself. How could he not hear about us? Saskia and I were on everybody's lips at the theatre: the new mysterious couple in Paris. *Le tout-Paris*[1] believed that we were lovers, it amused itself by gossiping; and you can believe that gossip in the city of Paris is gossip to be devoured the entire world over...

As for our finances, we no longer had enough even for Saskia to go alone to London...

"I'm glad we don't have enough money to send me to London," she told me one night, "I'm finished wandering alone without you."

"Better we starve together?"

"Yes, better we starve together."

My hope rested always on Juhani sending word from Madrid that he would advance me money, after which I would book us tickets to Florence leaving immediately. I told Saskia it was pointless to stay in Paris, since she didn't want to return to the Île Saint-Louis to look for Adélaïse. Saskia was forever haunted by the words of that old broom-woman who claimed she was being followed, talked about, etc. So she asked my advice on other ways to find her friend. Our efforts weren't needed, however, as we soon learned a hint about the whereabouts of Adélaïse.

It was now late autumn. Every morning brought ice to the streets of Paris. Saskia and I were poor, and we lived only for each other. We no longer had money to go to the theatre. We drank wine at home together, and we ate only once a day, only at dinnertime, and only in inexpensive bistros. We feared the looming day when our rent would be up and we would be required to pay again. There was still no response from Juhani. I was afraid, and rightly so, that he was away travelling who-knows-where, for who-knows-how-long...

Saskia seemed happier than ever just to be in the present moment. She stopped asking me about the home where I grew

---

[1]LE TOUT-PARIS: *(Fr)* Literally: 'The all-Paris' or 'everyone in Paris' is a French expression used since the 1600s to mean the 'High-Society' of Paris, or at least the affluent, fashionable crowd.

up, and about the birthplace of my father. I was under the illusion at this time that she cared more about me than about her fortune. We dressed warmly every night, and after dinner we took long walks together around Paris. Eventually came that singular night—that fateful night that all the events in Paris had been leading up to—that night that convinced us to leave Paris once and for all...

It was the six month anniversary of the first night Saskia and I had met. Unlike when we met, the moon was only half-full and waning; but we would drink anyway. We would spend more than usual: splurge on the theatre and go to a more expensive bistro afterwards to celebrate. We were greeted by a character while we were leaving the theatre whom we knew already, he was a silver-haired man of sixty, though still very handsome, named Monsieur de Charmolit[1].

M de Charmolit obliged us to go to the souper he was hosting near the theatre. Although we had a special occasion to celebrate in private, we agreed to go for one drink. The souper was in a noisy hall on the quai of the Seine. We drank some champagne and then agreed to leave to find a quiet restaurant for the two of us. I went to the coat-check with Saskia to help her retrieve her coat and scarf. And when I came back alone to the table to say goodbye to M de Charmolit and his friends, I noticed a new face sitting with them: the Maltese ambassador to England!

He paled when he saw me. The color soon returned to his face and he left the table of Monsieur de Charmolit and came to have a word with me in private. I stopped him and said in hushed-tones, "If you want to settle this once and for all, we can take two pistols and go down to the Seine." He waved his hands...

"None of that! None of that!" he said, "I don't have a problem with you anymore, son of Solarus. I handed my problem with you over to the English and Maltese governments. Try to set foot in those places, you'll be arrested and maybe executed. I hear you will also be executed if you try to come near your fatherland,

---

[1] MONSIEUR DE CHARMOLIT: The name 'Charmolit' is rather comic, being a conjunction of the French word 'charme' ('charm' in English), and 'au lit,' which means 'in bed.'

your capital city of Tripoli... that is, you will be tried and executed if the fortune-hunters don't kill you first to claim their prize."

"So I've heard as well," I told him, feeling regret about my past. One part of the story that I left out when I was telling Saskia of my escape from Malta was my arrival in Tripoli. I didn't want to mention Tripoli or Libya to Saskia because I didn't want her to know I was from there. Before I went to Alexandria, I first went to Tripoli thinking I could settle there. It was night when I arrived and I met a beggar on the steps of a temple. He recognized me as the son of Solarus, and he warned me to leave the city unseen, as soon as possible, for the police had been after me for years. I did leave Tripoli, as I took the beggar's words as an omen, having them be the first words spoken to me upon my arrival. Though I didn't think about that beggar since. Now I had the same warning from both a beggar *and* an ambassador, so I had no reason to disbelieve them. I looked at the gentle face of the old ambassador. I had no more quarrels with him. I told him I was sorry for the errors in my youth, adding that I couldn't help myself... his wife *was* very beautiful.

"And she *is still* as beautiful as she was then, my son of Solarus. It is because of my wife's beauty that I forgive you for being a bit 'dizzy' that night. I'm afraid it's out of my hands now. England and Malta consider you a traitor. They won't forgive you as easily as I did. But Tripoli, it seems, has you on the list of top criminals. They have a desire to kill you that outshines all the rest. I would watch out for Tripoli if I were you... that is where your family comes from, is it not? Anyway, I hope you can stay out of the nets they've laid for you."

I thanked him, said goodnight, and walked solemnly to the door where Saskia was waiting for me. We exited into the street and started walking together down the quai of the Seine.

"Do you have a preference for a restaurant?" I asked her.

"I liked that place we went last summer. Chez Lefèvre, remember? The place with the sad waiter who spent the evening drinking and smoking."

Chez Lefèvre was nearby. I didn't speak to Saskia on the way. All I could think about was my conversation with the ambassador... 'The beggar said that police have been looking for me for years,' I thought, 'And now the ambassador says that I am on the list of top criminals. Fortunately, I never need to return to Tripoli again... But wait!' a horrible thought then passed through my mind, 'When I left Tripoli for Alexandria, I stopped in our village to see if my mother still lived there. Our house, the house of the old fisherman and his wife, was in ruins...' At the time, I believed that fisherman and his wife had died of old age, and my mother took whatever money she had and went to live in Florence. With tonight's warning from the ambassador, I wondered if perhaps the police didn't find my mother and arrest her. Perhaps they arrested everyone in our house and left the place in ruins... 'Impossible!' I decided, 'That is a thought too ugly to imagine. No, she is alive and happy and living in Florence.'

Inside Lefèvre's there was a crowd. It wasn't like that pleasant night in summer when we were alone except for the chef and the waiter. Guido wasn't there this night, and we didn't see the chef. We took a table in the back, I ordered apéritifs and champagne. We drank our apéritifs; and fueled by the alcohol, I decided to tell Saskia what the ambassador had said, to admit that it was Tripoli where my father was born, where my mother was exiled from, where I had lived as a young man, and why I should do all I can never to go back there. Before I could speak, however, she started fidgeting and staring around her, muttering broken phrases in connection with a nearby table. I looked at the table that had caught her attention. I didn't see much of interest there. There were three people dining silently together: an old couple, obviously married, both carrying solemn expressions, together with their daughter, who also looked solemn and didn't speak. The girl was half turned away and I couldn't see her face. The old man looked very sad. I saw he wore French military dress with a few medals of honor on his chest. Seeing their sad faces made me forget about the ambassador. When the champagne arrived, Saskia and I toasted to six months of companionship dating from the night I almost died. We drank, and Saskia said to me, "That girl at the table keeps staring at you."

"She's probably jealous because you are more beautiful than she is."

"I don't know. She is very beautiful."

I looked then to see her face closely; it is then I recognized her as the girl I met that day long ago on the Île Saint-Louis. "It's that girl I told you about," I whispered to Saskia, "Sarah Lingot." The girl looked again at me, uneasily, and I raised my glass to her and her family; then I stood up to go reintroduce myself to Sarah. After her parents showed their approval for her to be speaking to me, she asked them to be excused so she could come meet Saskia at our table. Saskia introduced herself to Sarah and for the first time Saskia treated another woman in a friendly manner in front of me. The two girls joked and laughed, and Sarah said to me, "You were looking for someone when you were on Saint-Louis, no?"

"Yes, I was. We were, and still are... it's Saskia's friend, a girl about your age named Adélaïse... she is said to have lived on the island with her parents—or her mother at least—before and after she went to school in London for some years..."

"Are you sure her name wasn't *Adélaïde*?, rather than Adélaïse... because some of my friends told me about a girl-friend of theirs named Adélaïde who went to England for school a long time ago. It must be the same person. They said she came home to Paris last spring, but she was different than before... moody and unhappy with everyone around her. Then, they said, she met a couple of strange people and left with them for Italy. They were going to go somewhere in Tuscany eventually, but Adélaïde wanted to stop in the north somewhere—in Milan, or Verona, I think..."

"Verona?!" asked Saskia, "Are you sure?! And are you sure her name isn't, rather, *Adélaïse*?"

"No, I'm not sure... not about any of it."

After hearing this story, Saskia sat pensive for a long time, not moving. I looked over at Sarah's table and noticed an empty bottle of champagne, as well as some open gift-boxes. I asked Sarah then what they were celebrating on this night. She told me they were celebrating the retirement of her father who just finished a long and honorable military career. I remarked again to myself how strange it was that he and his wife looked so sad. Saskia interrupted our conversation to ask Sarah how she knew this girl—"Adélaïde," as Sarah called her—went to Tuscany by way of Milan or Verona. Sarah repeated again that she didn't *know* any of it for certain, but that her friends told her that after she came back from England, there came a day when she started frequenting an older couple: a man and a woman, whom they called "strange," and that one day they stopped seeing her in public except in the company of this couple. "Then suddenly," my friends said, "she left her home and family. It was rumored that she went to Italy after this couple suggested she come with them..."

Saskia was sure by Sarah's account that her friends were talking about Adélaïse... the fact that their first names were practically identical, that both had gone to private school in England, and that Sarah said this girl left for Northern Italy, the place where Adélaïse surely imagined Saskia was living still... "She would have gone to look for me," Saskia said to me later that night, "just as I came to France to look for her. We were such close friends, she simply *must* be in Italy..."

When we left Chez Lefèvre, we said goodbye to Sarah's parents, congratulating the father on his retirement and his military career. We promised Sarah we would come visit her on the Île Saint-Louis. We then left the restaurant and walked home. Saskia remained pensive the entire way back. At home, trying to cheer her up, I suggested that some more champagne would do her good. She wasn't eager, but she said she would be fine to drink some. It was now cold in Paris, and since 'maid's quarters' on the top floors of Parisian apartment houses usually retain the extreme cold in winter, as they retain the extreme heat in summer, we stored our cool wine and champagne that autumn in our garçonnière. So I went up to the sixth floor to get some champagne.

As soon as I climbed the staircase, I found a young woman collapsed on the floor in front of a shabby apartment door. It appeared she'd fainted, or was only just sleeping. Once I'd revived her I asked what she was doing collapsed in front of a door, she started to cry. She said to me that her boyfriend lived in the apartment before which she'd collapsed, and that he hadn't contacted her for several days after she had told him she was weak from illness and hunger. She told him she had no money for food, and didn't know anyone else in Paris, or what to do... So having no news from him, she finally walked to his apartment that evening, determined to either find him or else to wait for him. She'd been there for several hours, she told me, waiting... then finally she collapsed from sickness and starvation among other things, though mostly from sadness. And she didn't wake up until I came and found her. I told the girl not to worry; that I would get her some food and a doctor. "In the meantime," I said, "you can sleep safe from worry in our spare room on this floor." The poor soul cried in gratitude and followed me to our garçonnière where she collapsed on the bed and went straight to sleep. I shut the door quietly and locked it so she would be safe, and hurried down the back stairs to see about finding a doctor.

There was a brass plaque in front of a nearby building stating that a doctor had his business there, perhaps he lived there too. Although it was night, I rang and roused the doctor from sleep, begging him to come out to assist a young woman who needed him. He came right away and was friendly, saying that he didn't mind waking up if there was an emergency, and asked me what was going on. I recounted the story of the sick and starving girl to him. What happened during this time, Saskia told me later that night...

Having waited for me for a long time, to come back to our apartment with champagne, she finally grew worried and went to find me. She climbed the stairs; and since she now had a key to our garçonnière, she unlocked the door and saw the sleeping girl on the bed. Of course, she became angry—and confused. At first she closed the door without waking her, locked it again, and started pacing back and forth in the hallway in front of our garçonnière, as she tugged her hair in fury. She then decided to get to the bottom of the matter and reopened the door to the room, looked for me behind the door, and then yelled at the girl to wake up and explain to her what she was doing there. The girl was feverish, and so tired, that she didn't wake up to Saskia's shouting. Saskia yelled at her that she was a stupid girl. Furious, she then slammed the door and sat down in the hallway near the door and sobbed in her hands. That is how the doctor and I eventually found her there. At first, we didn't see Saskia. The hall was dark, and we went straight into the garçonnière to attend to the sick girl. I finally found Saskia in tears when I came out alone to light the lamp in the hall. I went to her on my knees to ask her why she was crying.

"Because you said to me that you were going to get champagne upstairs only so you could come up here to get in bed with some stupid girl! You are an monster, Saul..."

"What?!" I said, "If I wanted to be in bed with that girl, then why then would I have left and come back with a doctor?"

"What doctor?!"

The doctor came out in the hall then to tell me that the girl had a fever, but that she would recover soon. He stopped talking when he saw Saskia crying before me. She looked up at him and instantly stopped crying and smiled at him, recognizing him as the same doctor whom she consulted when she was miserable because I went to Montmartre without her. He of course recognized her instantly as well, and his face grew very kind. He asked her why she was now crying, and said, "This must be the man you came to see me about."

"Yes, it is the same man. I was only crying just now because I didn't understand what this girl was doing in our spare bed. But now I'm figuring it out..."

"Yes, well, this good man came to find me because he found a girl collapsed here in the hallway. Go and see for yourself." Saskia went into the little room, and with her gone, the doctor said to me in a hushed voice, "Your young lady is a rare person. I know you are aware of this. So please, always treat her good. This is the one favor I ask of you... *always treat her good.*"

"I thank you, doctor. I am aware of how rare she is. I will always treat her good... Please tell me how much I owe you for helping the sick girl in the bed."

"There is no charge," he said.

The doctor went to say goodbye to Saskia. He also told me he gave the young woman his address in case she didn't recover as well as he thought she would.

Saskia and I went to sleep, too tired for champagne. By morning, the patient in our garçonnière was well and she said goodbye to us. I gave her money to keep food in her stomach, and she left without trying to see if her boyfriend had come back home. This was our last day living on the quai of the Seine.

Saskia and I decided that the story of Sarah Lingot probably had enough truth in it make it a fact that Adélaïse no longer lived in Paris. Without her, we were not needed in Paris. Our hopes remained with Juhani, as we were almost completely broke and had no money to leave town. We slept late that next day, waking at noon, and when we awoke Saskia and I left our tidy apartment for about two hours. Among other things, we went to La Poste to see if we had a letter from Juhani. They told us that the mail from Spain would be arriving later that day. When we returned in front of our apartment house, we both grew uncomfortable—a strange premonition came over us. We climbed the stairs to the fifth-floor and went down the hall to our door. It was strangely ajar. I opened it slowly, thinking there might be someone in our apartment. Saskia waited in the hall while I searched. There wasn't a soul in our apartment, but what I did find was bad news: our entire home had been destroyed. All the furniture was turned upside-down. Our few possessions were smashed and lay on the floor. Saskia's clothes lay torn and flung around. My papers were scattered, and some of the pages were burned. Shreds of broken glass lay everywhere on the floor. The only thing unharmed was the most important thing: Saskia's guitar. It was perched in the armoire as it always was when she didn't play it. Saskia came in to our room crying.

"I'm going to go mad!" she cried, looking through her torn clothing, "Burglars! ...although what did they steal?!—nothing at all!" It's true, nothing seemed to be missing. Everything that we had was simply broken or set fire to. The little money we had, I kept on me at all times. Saskia's joy was restored when she found her diamond earrings. Apparently the thieves hadn't seen them. She said that since her earrings and her guitar were safe, the rest of her things didn't matter, and she was happy. Since I kept my clothing and many of my things up in our garçonnière—to give the impression to visitors that Saskia lived alone—I went up to the sixth-floor to see if that little room had been broken into as well. Everything upstairs was untouched, the room was exactly how the sick girl had left it when she left at noon that day. I changed into clothes for travel, and went back down to get

Saskia... "We're leaving," I said. We still had another week left in our apartment, the rent already paid; but I knew we shouldn't stay there. "Besides," I said, "the last week of rent will help pay Mme Gazonette for the damage done to her furniture. It wasn't much to reimburse her for the furniture, but I couldn't be bothered about this. We had no more money left anyway, and how was it our fault if somebody broke in?—the locks should have been sturdier...

"Take your guitar and a your suitcase and your most important things," I said to Saskia, "We're leaving." I told her we would go have lunch in a café to calm down, and then we would go back to the post office to see if word came from Juhani. The Spanish mail was due that afternoon.

While we were eating inexpensive dishes at a bistro near La Poste, Saskia repeated again and again, "It was Andrea. I know it. He arrived in Paris just as the rumors had predicted he would, and he found out where I was living—I have no idea how he found it out. Then he came to break everything apart and read any papers he could find to have some proof that you and I are living together." I too shared her belief that it was Andrea, although this idea fell apart completely when we arrived at the post office...

There were two letters. To our great joy, the first we opened was from Juhani. He addressed his letter directly to me as though I were alone in Paris, although I had told him about Saskia in my last letter to him. He began by making extensive apologies for his delay in responding, saying that he had been away in the countryside evaluating the value of a piece of land for his bank; and he just now returned to Madrid and wrote me this reply as quickly as he could, even before taking off his coat.

Juhani wrote that he would see about advancing me money and buying me a couple tickets to Italy, although he needed three days to do this. He wrote that he was sorry if this put me in an embarrassing situation—could I wait three days? Signed, His Truly, Juhani. Underneath his signature there was a postscript: he wrote that if I wanted to be a guest at his home in Madrid, I could come immediately and stay as long as I wished. All I had to do was go to a certain friend of his in Paris and ask him for a ticket to go see Juhani in Madrid, and I would have a first-class ticket immediately. "I hope this offer appeals to you," he wrote, "It would be like old times to have you back here."

I folded the letter and said, "This gives us the hope that our financial problems will be over in a few days."

Saskia seemed sad and pensive. So much so, that I didn't open the second letter to see who wrote it. I folded it and put it in my pocket, and asked what she was thinking about.

"Nothing," she said, "I'm cold."

"Let's find a café somewhere." We took our suitcases and Saskia's guitar and walked a few streets until we found a warm café glowing amber-colored from the light of a large fireplace in the center of the room. We found an intimate table near the fire and ordered two cups of chocolate.

"It's nice here," I said. Saskia was still silent, however, appearing sad and pensive.

"What is wrong?"

"You know, Saul, you fulfilled your promise to me. From here on out we can be quits."

"'Quits?!'... Why do you say that?!"

"Because you promised me you would come with me to Paris to find Adélaïse. We found out last night that she isn't in Paris. She's in Tuscany—on her way she might be visiting Verona or Milan. Who knows, maybe she will leave her new 'friends' in Verona and stay there to look for me. I don't need your help anymore to find her. I can visit the cities and villages of Tuscany myself. I can visit Verona myself. You've done your part. I'll write you a letter of honorable dismissal. Then you can go off on your own."

"'Honorable dismissal?!' Saskia, have you gone out of your mind?!"

She didn't reply, she looked cold and unfeeling. Then she said to me, "Yes, Saul. Honorable dismissal. You have to realize it will be better for me if you're not in my life. Now we know that Andrea is in Paris. You know he has a talent for finding out my address when I don't leave any traces or any clues. It's only a matter of time before he finds us here. And then I will lose my inheritance. You see? It is better if you leave now."

I stood there, stunned. For a long time I stood there, looking at her cold, unfeeling face that was, however, trembling each time our eyes fixed on each other. I said to her then, "Saskia, what is this about? I know you are too poetic of a soul to care more about inheritance money than you care about a relationship like ours. I know you know that if you lost your inheritance, I would take care of you and offer all you need in the way of money. You know that we might even find relief if you lose your inheritance. We wouldn't have to worry anymore about living together out in the open. We would be fully alive together. No, Saskia, there is another reason why you are telling me to leave. What is it?"

"You are right," she said, and she buried her face in her hands; then she lifted her face, her hands were covered in tears, "I cannot lie to you, I see. It doesn't work. The real reason why I say we should be quits, and the reason why I say this only now—not after our conversation with Sarah Lingot, nor after Andrea came and ruined everything in our apartment and destroyed our possessions and read your papers—the reason I am sad about this only now is because the reason I am sad is because of Juhani's letter to you."

"Why, because he only wrote it to *me* and not to *us*?"

"That's only a small part of it. Of course, I wouldn't be sad if he'd invited the two of *us* to come to Madrid to stay with him for awhile. But the fact that he invited you, and he said you could have your ticket tonight... Look, Saul, if you stay with me, we are going to have to go find a cheap, miserable place to stay for a few nights with the hope that Juhani will come through to advance us money in a few days. If he doesn't come through with money, we will be stuck and who knows what will happen! This way, you can leave tonight, travel in comfort, and soon you will be with your dear friend whom you've known since Malta. You won't be obliged to hang out in dirty rooms with your little gypsy girl." At this, she broke into tears that fell like two waterfalls, "That is why I say you've fulfilled your contract, and now we can be quits."

Now that she was crying heavily, I took her hand and led her away from our table, away from the other tables. I took her behind the chimney where I could see only her. I took my sad gypsy girl into my arms, and stood there holding her, if only so her tears could soak into the fabric of my scarf and not stay wet on her beautiful face. I then stepped back to look into her eyes. I asked her then to tell me if there was another reason she wanted me to stay with her, other than simply to find her friend Adélaïse. She had said to me once that she needed *me* to realize her 'fortune'; that without me she would not find what she was looking for. I said that she knew all along that her fortune wasn't merely to find her lost best-friend. If it were just that, she could've used part of her income to hire a private detective. A private detective would be more efficient and easier to manage than trying to stabilize a capricious adventurer on his way to find the white nights of Saint Petersburg. "No," I said, "there's something that you're seeking beyond simply Adélaïse and you're not telling me what it is. You need me for this, you know that. So, what is it you are seeking, Saskia?"

"My destiny," she replied, "and I can't have it if we are apart."

"Why should we be apart? You are my sister, my love, my wife, my undefiled[1]... I will stay with you, and our life will be a good one. I shall follow your caprices, and you shall follow mine. But never will a caprice of mine take me away from you."

"I believe you," she said and pressed the side of her face hard against my chest and kept it there. We stayed silent for several moments.

When we returned to the table, she smiled. We both smiled. I took the second letter out of my pocket, which was addressed to her, and I handed it to her. She examined the sealed envelope and couldn't determine who had sent it. She opened the envelope and began to read it to herself. She then lowered the paper with a steady hand and said to me calmly, "It's a letter from my uncle's trust."

---

[1]This phrase is a variation on verse 5:2 of Song of Solomon, King James Version.

"Well, what is it?"

"It couldn't have been Andrea who broke into our apartment this morning."

"Why couldn't it have been him?"

"Because he's dead."

Chapter Twenty-six

Saskia had informed her uncle's estate that she would be in Paris for several months but she didn't give them an address where she could be reached. They sent the letter because Andrea claimed Saskia as his last of kin; although he didn't explain exactly *how* they were part of the same family—if they *were* related at all. As last of kin, they were obliged to contact Saskia immediately following his death. They wrote that, not finding an exact address in Paris for her, they made some failed inquiries about her address before finally deciding to write her via the central post office. This was the one letter they sent to the central post office: it confirmed that Andrea had in fact been on his way up to Paris from Rome on some "family business" after learning she was there; but that passing through Genoa, he was killed in an accident. His death occurred about ten days before our apartment was broken into.

"Are you a little sad?"

"I'm relieved!" she smiled, "and worried."

"Worried? Why?"

"I never really thought of Andrea as being part of my family. After my uncle died, I considered myself an orphan. If Andrea was a relation, he was a bad relation; as family members are supposed to help each other out, not try to steal money from the other family members... Still, now that he is dead. If I wasn't an orphan before, now I truly am an orphan. No one can even claim to be part of my family. I truly am a wanderess now!"

"You are a wanderess," I said, "but now you and I are part of the same family. We won't ever wander alone anymore."

"I just can't figure it out," she said, "since the estate didn't have our address, Andrea couldn't have had it either. Otherwise, I might think he hired some men in advance to come destroy our apartment. So then... *who did it?*"

"A mystery. Let's not go back to see."

We didn't go back. We walked around, bundled-up warm, carrying our luggage. We asked here and there for the most inexpensive place to stay imaginable, where we could pay by the day. People looked at us strangely when we asked this, since I was dressed like a gentleman and Saskia like a lady of the first-rank. If I judged that the astonished people were fools who didn't deserve a response, I simply laughed at them. If they seemed to be good souls who might try to help, I would point to Saskia's guitar case and tell them, "We are poor travelling musicians. We are obliged to dress in these bourgeois costumes." The worthy souls took this as a worthy explanation, and after a couple hours of searching, we were led to a place off the rue Saint-Denis that announced itself as a sort of hostelry for people with very low means. We decided to spend three nights there and no more; as we were convinced of the fidelity of Juhani, we believed he would soon come through to save us.

The outside of the hostelry gave the appearance of a prison. Residence structures on either side were loaded with barred windows. There was a closed entrance gate in the center of the structure. Once inside the gate, the place didn't look any less discouraging: ugly walls with windows surrounded a cold courtyard. In front of the courtyard, in the center, sat a stoopy little box where an attendant waited behind a grill. At the rear of the courtyard there were no windows, just a high, solid wall of stone that was as black as the gate, while the residence halls on the left and the right side were white-washed, and each contained windows that were closely spaced together, suggesting that the rooms were very small.

At the grill of the box, the attendant told us that there were rooms available, and that each room cost two francs per day. We didn't think it was possible to find a room so cheap, and had counted on paying at least five francs; however it turned out it was forbidden for women and men to share a room, so we would therefore need two rooms at a total of four francs per night. In addition, there was the displeasure that we couldn't share a bed. Even married couples had to sleep in separate parts of the hostelry. The women's quarters were in the building on the left side of the courtyard, walking in. The men's quarters were on the right side. Each building had a separate entrance, and men were forbidden to pass through the women's gate, and women through the men's gate. There was a curfew every night at ten o'clock, all tenants were required to be in their rooms, the lights automatically shut off.

We could afford more than four francs per day, but we were exhausted from looking for lodging morning till night. We didn't pay any money at first. I gave the attendant a two-franc tip when we first arrived on condition that he watch our luggage for a half-hour while we talked it over. Before leaving him, I asked, "What kind of people stay here?"

"Travelers mostly, travelers on a tight budget."

"What kinds of travelers?"

"We don't let riffraff through, if that's what you want to know. Still, I'd advise you both to lock your rooms from the inside at night."

"Thank you, we will be back in a half-hour to let you know."

Outside, the wind had died down, and we were dressed warmly, making for an agreeable walk—although the neighborhood was bad.

"If you want, I will leave you the rest of our money," I said, "I'm sure you can buy a ticket to London or Italy, since you will only need one... I could go down to Madrid today."

"I was just thinking how I don't like it that we will have to sleep in separate rooms these next few nights."

"Seriously Saskia, why don't you leave today without me and go to a country where you can collect on your inheritance? You can avoid sleeping in this prison."

Saskia turned to me with a look of horror. Her eyes went searching into my eyes. "Saul! Listen to me! I was an orphan today, till you told me we were from now on family, you and me. You are my brother, my lover, the only husband I will ever know! I don't care where I have to sleep, just so long as I am not far from you." She held her hands as if to pray, and put them against my chest. I held her, and while I held her, I thought to myself about the way she used to talk about her fortune being everything, and about Adélaïse being everything. I asked her to whom she now gave her allegiance. "Is it to me you give your allegiance, Saskia? Or is your allegiance to your fortune, and to Adélaïse?" Saskia lied to me then and said it was to me she pledged her allegiance; and I believed her and held her even tighter.

Chapter Twenty-seven

My wanderess and I walked back down the shabby streets around the rue Saint-Denis. I was torn between my honor and my wish to be with her, until finally I decided those sentiments were one and the same... "Saskia," I said to her, "a man cannot watch the woman he loves suffer to sleep at night in a miserable place. Let us then pay for only two nights at this strange hostelry. The day after tomorrow, we will check-out in the morning and go to the post office to see if Juhani came through on the money. If he hasn't, we will use the rest of what we have to buy you a ticket to Italy. I will then go to Madrid and take an advance from Juhani, and then come immediately to Florence to meet you. Can you promise me to go along with this? Otherwise, I won't be able to sleep at night..."

"I agree to this. We will both leave Paris the day after tomorrow, either together or alone."

At the hostelry, I paid for two rooms for two nights and gave the attendant one franc for a tip, telling him that I wanted our two rooms opposite each other in the courtyard, facing one another so that we could look out of our windows and see the other one. The attendant agreed to this and showed Saskia to her gate, and me to mine.

My room was cold, there was mold on the walls; but the sheets were clean and the bed smelled fine. The night was clear outside and I could easily see across the courtyard, which was only about forty paces wide, to where Saskia stood in her room waving to me, bathed in the yellow light. That night we had several pantomime conversations through our closed windows. The cobblestone bed of the courtyard was six long floors down below. At a quarter past ten at night, the gas lamps in all the rooms shut off automatically and each prisoner in that hostelry was left to the dark world of his or her private cell.

The first night there, I slept like a stone. In the morning Saskia signaled to me from her room across the courtyard as soon as she was ready to come downstairs. Just seeing her that next day was pleasure in itself, having spent the night in two separate buildings. She said she hated her room, but that it was a happy room because she knew I wasn't too far away.

That day was our last day of innocence together. That night would bring death and a new epoch. We enjoyed simple pleasures that day. We didn't want to spend any money, as we were afraid we would need to buy Saskia a ticket to Italy the next day. At lunch, we shared a single loaf of bread. This was enough, for our spirits were joined through our refusal to separate; thus our very privations became our delicacies, we feasted together on our abstinence. I was even fine to go without wine—which was for the best, as the moon was waning.

* * *

The 1st Revelation…

Ô, it matters not if I die in sorrow, ecstasy, boredom, or pain. Just so long as I die—not by day, but by night!—while the moon does wax, and not wane...

Our last night at the hostelry, everything seemed to be slipping away: from the moon that grew blacker each evening, to the mild autumn evenings that slipped one by one into the frozen nights of winter. We returned to the hostelry just before the curfew after a happy and innocent day walking around Paris. The thought of coming back to sleep was dreadful, as our rooms were lonely and miserable places. After saying goodnight on the street, we walked under the foreboding arch towards the gates. I took a final look at Saskia as she disappeared through the silent gate of the women's quarters. The attendant eyed me carefully from his station as I turned away from everything, and walked through the men's gate, smelling the sour air.

Once inside my room, after locking my door, I checked the bed for insects. I barely had time to get undressed before the gas lamps shut off. The night was clear yet the moon was thin, and the hostelry beyond my window was steeped in darkness. Only the lights in the halls remained burning, thus I could see a slim beam of light outlining the shape of my door. For a long time, I stood at my window, staring out. I tried to imagine Saskia in the pitch-black of her room. Had she been lying in her bed? Or was she at the window looking out to me, as I was looking to her? I eventually shrugged my shoulders, got into the bed, and lay on my back thinking of how Saskia and I would be abandoning Paris that next morning—*come-what-may*—whether we were together or separate, all that would depend on the whim of fortune. I was so soul-sick, I never did sleep that night. It must have been four or five in the morning, (the nights were so long, it could have been later), that I heard a short, quick knock on my door. It was a knock that belonged to a hard hand. I leapt up in the darkness, unable to determine where the door was.

"Who is it?" I demanded, loud and sharp.

"Maintenance!" called a man's voice.

"Damn you! I didn't call maintenance... what time is it?!" While I stood in that utterly black room cursing, I heard the sound of the bolt on my door being unlocked, whoever it was had a key or else picked the lock. My door began to open slowly... the light from the hall then spilled into my room cutting the black silhouette of a very tall man standing in my doorway. He was carrying a lit lantern but held it in front of his face so that it obscured his features completely. The only thing I saw around the blinding hallow of lantern light was the illumination of the man's black coat and his black hat.

I clenched my fists, ready to leap on him. The man said calmly, "That won't help you tonight, Saul."

"How do you know my name? Who are you?!"

"Sit down on the bed, Saul. We'll have a little talk."

I backed away from the intruder until my legs hit the bed frame, causing me to stumble and almost land on my back. It was then the intruder took away the lantern away from in front of his face and I recognized him... "You!" I called out, looking at that long and gaunt face that belonged to none other than the clairvoyant from Málaga.

"It's you! Dragomir! You're in Paris?!..."

"I knew you'd remember me, Saul... Relax your fists. Don't try to strike me, there are others outside."

"How did you get in here? Past the guard? How did you get a key to my room?"

"The attendant was 'tied-up,' as you would say—*still is, actually*—so I helped myself to his keys. Sit on the bed. I want to talk to you a moment." Dragomir set the lantern on a wooden footstool near the door, and he closed the door. The other stool in my room, he pulled close to my bed and sat himself down on it. By now I was accustomed to the lantern-light in my room, so I could discern clearly the features of his face, his hands, his clothing.

"Please, sit on the bed so we can talk. I have come for matters of peace, you have my word."

"Is your word good, Dragomir? Just as you said your poisoned opium was good opium? Did you come to finish what you wanted to finish by sending me to Penelope Baena's?"

"You thought that was a trap, did you? No, Saul. I did, however, hear what happened to you at Miss Baena's home, and yes, I admit I gave you poisoned opium *on purpose*... but Saul, *the poisoned opium was meant for Señorita Baena! You* were not supposed to eat her opium. *Your own opium was not poisoned!* I could not have known you were going to eat her opium!"

"...Going to be *forced* to eat it," I corrected him, "So you didn't want to poison me, alright, you just wanted me to commit murder?"

"Not murder. It wasn't poisoned to the extent it would kill the woman—only make her very sick, as you yourself unfortunately found out. But it all turned out well, didn't it? You are in Paris, and you are with an absolutely gorgeous girl as a result! *..are you not happy?!"*

"How did you know about her?! How did you find us here?! Tell me, *how did you know that I was in Paris?!"*

"Oh, Saul, come now... it's impossible *not* to know where you are these days. Saul, 'the son of Solarus of Tripoli,' lives a very transparent life in Paris, you ought to know. I see you regularly at the Comédie-Française. I also saw you once on the Île Saint-Louis... I was in a house talking out of the window to a woman in the yard..."

I felt the blood rush out of me when he said this. I realized then, that mysterious man in the window, the mysterious man on the balcony at the Comédie-Française... they were both him... Dragomir! He was the "messenger," the one who never stopped showing up in my life!...

I shook my fist at him... "*So it was you! You were the man who* followed me in Valencia... *You* were the one in Barcelona... *You* were the skipper at the docks, and *you* are the one who gave me directions to find a hospital the night after the night you poisoned me! You have been following me! You, Dragomir!... And whatever your motivation is, it the same motivation that brought you to Paris this time!... *You have followed me here!"*

Dragomir simply raised his eyebrows... "Who knows *whom* I have been following, my dear Saul... but no, to reassure you, if I *have* been keeping tabs on you, it certainly was *not* to see that you poisoned Señorita Baena. Anyways, let's forget it, please, for tonight I've come on business. I've come to help you, Saul. 'How,' you ask? I'll show you how... Come with me to the window. Let's look down at the courtyard."

I walked beside Dragomir to the window of my room. I watched his movements carefully, full of suspicion, mistrust. I opened the pane and felt the frozen chill of the late-autumn air against my face. The lights were off in the rooms of the women's quarters across the way. Down in the courtyard, four tall street lanterns were lit to keep sentry in the night. All the gas lamps were unlit, as was usual while the tenants slept. Beneath the lanterns, the cobblestones of the courtyard shone slick and dark with the rain from the evening past.

"In a moment," said Dragomir, "you will see what looks like a very short and oddly-shaped woman enter this courtyard..."

I stayed silent and watched below.

"...I say 'looks like' a woman, because in actuality, it isn't; it's a man you know: my servant Pulpawrecho. He'll be dressed like a woman. He wants more than anything to gain access to the female quarters tonight. He would even die for it.... *Do you know why?...*"

I shook my head. He continued... "Remember in Málaga when we told you the story of how Pulpawrecho and I met? It started with a thirteen-year-old girl he was stalking in the streets. And how she kissed her hands as she read my name and title: 'Clairvoyant.'

"...Because Pulpawrecho knew that she had consulted me for her fortune, he assumed—*and rightly so, by the way!*—that I could keep track of her long into the future. This is why he begged me to let him be my servant. He knew that someday—*yes, someday!*—I would have the heart to pay him for his loyal service. And so he's worked for me... waiting and waiting... Now he's decided that tonight's the night! So, tonight he has come here to collect on what he is owed..."

I didn't make the connection right away. So Dragomir continued with a twist of a smile, "Let us just say that it has taken Pulpy four years—*yes, four long years!*—to catch-up with the fee that he requested for his loyal service; but it was not for nothing—*not for nothing, you see!* Tonight, Pulpawrecho has now finally caught up with his little girl!"

At that moment a crash sounded in the courtyard. It sounded like sheets of glass breaking on stones. And then there was the sudden light of a dozen fires: the gas lamps in the courtyard lit up with the crashing sound, they chugged their flames. I looked out the window, scanning the pools of light in the dark night, wondering why the gas lamps had come on. And then, there in the center of the courtyard, I spotted a terribly deformed feminine creature. She wore a sort-of dress: mud brown, with coarse twill fabric. In all actuality, it was not a dress, but a potato sack. The woman stopped in the middle of the courtyard looking left and right, and then... upwards... apparently sizing-up the hostelry. But when her head lifted up for the first time, it sent her knotty, long hair tumbling down to the ground—you see it was a wig! Then I understood what Dragomir had meant about the creature dressed as a lady, a deformed lady entering the hostelry; it was no lady—*it was a Pulpawrecho!*

"Dragomir!..." I whispered loud and urgently, "What is your servant doing down there?! And dressed like a woman!..."

"He has special reasons to want to get through the women's gate tonight... You realize, don't you son of Solarus, that tonight is only the second meeting between us two? Even if you say you've seen me 'here and there' since then, tonight is only the second night we meet together as Saul and Dragomir. And just as Pulpawrecho stole your gold watch on the first night we met you down in Málaga, on this second night he has decided to steal your girl."

Dragomir pursed his lips silent, while below, Pulpawrecho disappeared through the women's gate. Dragomir the clairvoyant, meanwhile, resumed narrating scenes from my life, from my future... "In a few moments, you see, Pulpawrecho will be in your girlfriend's room. And once he's there..."

"Once he's there?!" I demanded, flashing my eyes from master above to servant below... *"Where has he gone?!"* I pounded the window of my room so hard that one of the plates of glass fell inside my room and shattered on the floor. I turned and started for the door… "I'm going downstairs!" I yelled furiously, "I will catch Pulpawrecho before he reaches her room."

'You will never make it on time, Saul. Too many stairs… Too many to go down, too many to go up; and by the time you make it to your girl's room, Pulpawrecho will have had plenty of time to do what he came for… to rape her."

"To rape her?!" My head swarmed with rage. The first thought I had was to kill Dragomir then and there, to strangle him with my bare hands, in my bare feet. But I knew I had no time, I had to hurry to Saskia. I grabbed Dragomir by the throat and threw him against the wall, then I turned to run out the door… I didn't get two steps, however. I heard him picking himself up from the floor and the distinct *'click-clock'* of a loading gun. Knowing that Dragomir was now pointing a revolver at me, I stopped—my palms open, slowly, softly, and most carefully I raised my hands above my shoulders. How ashamed I felt turning around in submission with my hands raised, palms outwards like a man who fears death. I had no doubt that Dragomir was going to put a bullet in my head no matter how I took it. Yet when I finally turned around to see that it was in fact a revolver that Dragomir held in his hand, you can believe my shock to see he wasn't pointing the gun at me… rather, *he was giving the gun to me!*

"Now do you see what I'm saying about there being no time to wait on the stairs?" he said, insisting I take the gun, "Here you are son of Solarus, take this gun and go back to the window—and keep your eyes peeled! Don't miss a movement…"

I was struck dumb in astonishment, but I took the revolver from Dragomir's hand, thought for a moment to shoot him, then walked back to the window where I aimed the barrel of the gun at the lightless form of the women's quarters across the courtyard. Perfect timing… a light came on across the way. It beamed from the window of my belovèd. Just as a flower unfolds to bloom, Saskia's room unfolded into a visible scene: Her door was opened, light infused within from outside. So as a dark insect creeps its feelers onto the fresh petals of a flower, so did the wretched Pulpawrecho creep his miserable feelers into the soft innocence of Saskia's room. Just like Dragomir, he carried a lantern in front of his face; and seeing his prey, he advanced slowly: short, rhythmic steps, one by one.

Saskia who had been in her bed, apparently asleep, jumped up the instant the light came in from the hall. The instant Pulpawrecho came into sight, she gave a scream so sharp, so high-pitched, that even from the other side of the courtyard, I feared my ears would explode. Back on their side, in the women's quarters, the hunched-back, black silhouette of Pulpawrecho, set his lantern down on a stool in her room to burn steady. This not only to give light to his conquest, no doubt, but to free his hands to devour his feast. Yet it also illustrated for us onlookers all of the colors, tones and shapes of the two bodies—both the human being, and the insect.

Saskia screamed again—and again—and then again. She leapt onto her bed, backpedaled her bare legs toward the wall. Her back was up against the wall at the back of her bed when Pulpawrecho let drop his potato-sack dress to the floor to reveal his own bandy pair of legs, and an erect, purple penis that resembled the horn of a curly ram.

"Shoot now," Dragomir whispered to me, "Shoot before he gets too close to her, otherwise your girl will be in danger."

And so I shot. The moment I saw Pulpawrecho drop his brown twill robe, the moment I saw his genitals from forty paces away, I fired a roar of bullets into Saskia's room, pulling the trigger: *once, twice, three times, then four!* Four bullets blew Saskia's room apart. Four bullets blew butterfly clouds of smoke in the night air, leaving such trails through the courtyard that it was impossible to see what I'd done.

There I stood with such fury, with such impatience, with *such terror!* There I stood at the window of our smoldering hostelry. I stood waiting for the smoke to clear. I stood terrified that Pulpawrecho had managed to harm the life of Saskia once he recognized that his own life was in peril. But I considered his nakedness, and saw no place he could hide a weapon. My impatience and fury were due to the uncertainty that my shots hit any flesh. Thus blinded by the smokescreens of my creation, and deaf from the powder blasts, that wicked beast: Pulpawrecho, he could have been violating the body of my friend, my child, my sister, my wife, my spouse, my undefiled Saskia... safe from anyone seeing or hearing anything.

It seemed to take forever for the smoke to clear. When finally I could see across to the women's quarters, I saw a ghost at the window. She was a pale ghost, white like a gypsy in the moonlight; though of course it was not a ghost but the body of Saskia, alive and unharmed. She was standing in her white nightgown, untorn and untarnished... She stood at her window across the courtyard looking into my eyes, nodding her head *up and down...* then again, *up and down,* then again, *up and down.* Then, keeping her head bowed, she raised her eyes to me, raised her mouth and her spirit, all to show me eternal pleasure and thanks for what I'd saved her from. The lantern that Pulpawrecho had brought to her room was still burning. Light flooded Saskia's beautiful face as she smiled and closed her eyes. Then she opened her eyes again, smiled at me more warmly than ever, and with her summoning hand, she beckoned me to come to her room. She appeared as ethereal as a cloud.

"Well done, son of Solarus... I think you just killed my servant."

I turned away from the window and pulled the curtain closed. It didn't instantly occur to me that I might have just killed a man, or that somebody might come arrest me. As far as I was concerned, all I'd done was to squash an insect who threatened to blight a beautiful flower when she was just beginning to bloom. I thought then of the smile Saskia had given me after it was over: that eternal pleasure, she gave thanks for what I'd saved her from.

I looked then at Dragomir with a face of profound confusion. I still held the gun close to me, not sure if I would need to use again. It confused and surprised me that Dragomir had helped me to kill his faithful Pulpawrecho. But what was to stop him from surprising me by wanting me killed as well? I told Dragomir that I didn't understand... "Why did you do that, Dragomir? Wasn't he 'the perfect servant!?'"

"He *was* the perfect servant," Dragomir said, "Still, I couldn't risk losing you and your girl. You two interest me infinitely more than Pulpawrecho ever could—even though, *he was the perfect servant...* Beyond that, he was my friend. But business is business, you two are crucial, whereas Pulpawrecho was disposable."

"But why is it so?!"

"You'll soon see, Saul... You'll soon see everything. But for now, let's be quick! We need to cross the courtyard. We should go upstairs to get your girlfriend, and to make sure that my servant is defunct."

"I can do it all alone."

"Don't be foolish. Take me with you. It will get messy if the police come, I can help with that... poor Pulpawrecho."

"You can't help if the police come," I told Dragomir, "Everything will be clear if the police come. I am the one who has fresh powder burns on his hand and wrist. That's proof that I am the one who shot the gun tonight. Still, that doesn't mean I am going to hand over the gun to you. I don't trust you, Dragomir. I am going to keep the gun as we go our separate ways."

"That is very well!" he laughed, "Whoever told you that you should trust me?! I am Dragomir!... a dishonest charlatan, only out for his own gain! Yes, you would be a fool to trust me, son of Solarus. And if you were a fool, I would be especially dishonest with you. I don't have the slightest respect for fools."

I put the gun in my pocket and told Dragomir to go down the stairs in front of me. Soon we passed the attendant where he was tied-up in his box. We then ran through the women's gate to find Saskia.

She was standing by her window in the same place that I'd seen her from my own window. But now she was no longer nodding 'yes' with that ethereal smile playing on her lips. Now she was standing at the window spouting waterfalls of tears. She was breathing too fast for her heart, almost hyperventilating; still in shock. Away from her view, on the floor between the bed and the door, lay the corpse of Pulpawrecho. I looked back toward Saskia and pronounced her name and she turned around quickly and threw her arms around me. She turned her face to the side and I waited for her breathing to slow down. After a few minutes of her body pressed against mine, she was as calm as a lamb. It was then that Dragomir entered the room. She looked at him strangely at first. Then her eyes glazed over. She was held in a trance.

"Come now, Clara, you look as though you don't recognize me."

Saskia, hearing Dragomir address her like this, turned to me... "What is he talking about?"

I shrugged my shoulders.

"You act like you don't remember when we met, Clara. It was four years ago in Málaga. You were only thirteen then. Yes, you've changed a lot in these four years. But your basic features are true as ever. Do you remember, Clara? You came to me one night in Málaga to have your fortune read. You were lost in life and needed help. So I gave you a sort of roadmap to follow."

"Whatever you say, Monsieur. Still, my name is not Clara. And I've never been to Málaga!"

"Oh, come now, gypsy girl!... I know you are the same girl who came to me in Spain four years ago. You needed direction in your life. So I told you what I knew about you and your future... which was, by the way: *everything!*—so you go by the name of Saskia now? That matters little to me. Today your name means the same thing it meant back on that fateful night in Málaga: *'clear, bright, and celebrated!'*"

"Hmm," Saskia frowned her brow... "I'm sorry to have to end things like this, Monsieur... you are charming and very agreeable... but I really am not your girl! My name is Saskia. It means 'from the Saxon people.' It doesn't mean 'bright, celebrated, famous, or any of that... So Please, Monsieur, Tell me why you are here... Did you shoot this man?"

"It was your lover who shot him, and at quite a distance too! He's remarkable with a gun. The man who lies dead on your floor is my servant. He wanted to rape you tonight. I knew this beforehand, thus I came to furnish Saul with a pistol so he could kill my servant. That, good lady, was one of the hardest decisions I ever had to make, please never forget that, Clara—or 'Saskia.' I loved my servant. Dearly, I did. Never will another man walk this earth who will be as loyal to me as my dear Pulpawrecho who lies here only to rot and nourish worms...

"Why did I do it?, you might ask. The answer: Pulpawrecho has already experienced enough of the world. He lived what you'd call *a life.* His death today means very little in the grand scheme of things. Clara, I know that you are young and pure. Why should I let my servant who destroys all he touches take it upon himself to destroy you too? What I mean to say is, you have never been in love with a man before; although I feel this is a sensation that is beginning to form in you towards Saul. So why should I let my perfect servant take it upon himself to spoil and tarnish the sweet innocence that belongs to you now and only at this one time in your life?—when it's gone, it's gone forever. But now, don't take me for a poet! I had other reasons why I wanted Pulpawrecho dead and out of the way. His murder was his destiny. I, myself, read it in his hand the last time he consulted me as a clairvoyant. It was written. Wrechito is gone, and you are saved ...but don't waste time, Saul and Saskia... Make haste! I urge you to both to leave the quarter right away, never to return. The police will be looking for you in this neighborhood tonight, you hear?"

"We don't have any money," Saskia said, "but we need to move, Saul! Here we are hanging around in a hostelry with a dead body that you shot, in my room. We can't discuss our plans with this complete stranger."

"He's not a stranger to me," I told Saskia, "I met Dragomir the clairvoyant at his home in Málaga. And it seems we've been seeing each other ever since."

"What?!" Saskia cried, "You met him before? ...in Málaga?! And the dead man who wanted to rape me, you met him too?!"

"Yes, him too. In Málaga as well. I met them both the same night. I'll tell you about it sometime, but not right now; we need to find a place of exile right away!."

"Saul," said Dragomir with a giant grin on his face, "When you tell your Saskia about the night you met me and Pulpawrecho, don't forget to tell her about the person who brought Pulpy to me... *that certain girl whose name means 'clear, bright, and celebrated.'"*

"My name is not 'Clara!'" Saskia screamed.

"Oh, so you admit that it was *you* who brought Pulpawrecho to me."

"I never even met that dead man in my life!"

This was going on too long. "Let's go," I said, "Dragomir, you wanted to check the body. Do it quick or we'll leave without you."

Dragomir went over to look at his dead friend and servant. "You know," he said, "Pulpawrecho looks better now than he did when he was alive.

I quickly inspected the body. I saw that three of my four shots hit him. Two bullets were in his shoulder, and one was in the side of his head. Saskia, who had a strong distaste for death, waited at the door.

Outside on the street, we started walking towards the Seine. We went undisturbed, we saw no sign of anyone having sent for the police. It seemed just as well in that quarter. The neighbors probably don't want to mix themselves up in anything when a few gunshots are heard at the hour before dawn.

Now it was dawn. Rosy and yellow patches of sky alighted over the river Seine, the air was frosty and clean. Saskia carried her suitcase and guitar case. I had my two valises. Dragomir carried nothing. At the river, we saw the tops of the trees crowned with the light of dawn on the oriental side of the Île Saint-Louis. Dragomir turned to us...

"Saul, do you remember when you saw me on the Île Saint-Louis a few months ago? I was speaking through the window to that old broom-woman. You do? Good. Well, the woman in the yard had good reason when she warned you that you two are being followed. The truth is you *are* being followed, both of you. That is why I want to urge you to leave the country right away." He reached into his pocket and pulled out two rolls of coins—each containing ten gold louis.

"Take these twenty louis, Saul, they will be of use to you."

"I don't take gifts, especially not from you. I saw what your last so-called 'gift' brought me—it was a poison that almost killed me."

"That is exactly why I want to help you get to Italy. I didn't mean for you to be poisoned. I wanted revenge on Señorita Baena... *only on her.*"

"Saul," said Saskia, "Take the money, we need it."

"I don't want anymore gifts from this man."

"It's not a gift," said Dragomir, "It's a loan."

"I'm not sure if I can pay it back."

"Oh, you will pay it back," Dragomir smiled his sly smile, "You will pay it back, and you won't even have to work for it. If I'm lending you twenty louis now, it's only because I know that you're going to pay me back a thousand-fold."

I didn't understand that morning what Dragomir meant when he said I would pay him back a thousand-fold. If I had understood... had I known the future, I would have taken every precaution to see that Dragomir would never come into my life again. As you will see, I didn't take those precautions...

"Before we part ways," said Dragomir to both Saskia and me, "let me be one last time who I truly am: a clairvoyant." So saying, he asked us there on the bridge over the Seine, to hold our hands out. We did and he put his hands on our palms, inhaled and said: "I see you both in Italy. In Tuscany you two will have the best luck, your lives will be the richest there...

"But in Tuscany you will be tempted to remain, either to live, or to stay long. But do not fully unpack your luggage. Always be ready to go again on the road. You shall not remain in Tuscany very long, for your destinies await you elsewhere."

After his prediction, I said to Saskia in a loud voice so that our clairvoyant would hear my words clearly: "Dragomir here tells us our future... though he confessed to me in Málaga that he wasn't a real clairvoyant, and that he didn't know anyone's future. He confessed he used that form of witchcraft known as 'manipulation and guessing.'"

"I told you that in Málaga, Saul, because you made it clear that you don't believe in clairvoyants. How else could I have entered your spirit other than by showing faith then in *your* beliefs? The fact that I told you that all clairvoyants are rascals, and that I myself admit to being a rascal, or at least posing as one, for pretending that I am a clairvoyant, this led you to believe that I wasn't a rascal because I made it clear who I was. Even if you did change your mind about it after the opium incident—you decided I was a rascal after all..."

"No, after the watch incident," I told him, "That's when I knew you were a rascal."

"Oh, I'd forgotten. I'd meant to give it to you hours ago... Here is your gold watch back." So saying, he handed me my dear, beautiful Breguet watch, the possession that meant everything to me! It belonged to my father, it had been in my mother's possession, and she gave it to me when I came of age. I found it missing, as you remember, the morning after the night when I met first Pulpawrecho, then Dragomir. Dragomir had told me that Pulpawrecho stole it.

"That is why I wanted to go back to visit the body of Pulpawrecho," Dragomir said to Saskia and me, "It was not to make sure that Pulpy was dead, I was sure of that; but I knew he had your watch on him. You deserved to have it back..."

"Thank you, Dragomir," I said, admiring my watch, "You don't make it easy for me to think you're a rascal. Although you still are a rascal!"

"Good luck to you and Clara in Tuscany, may you find old friends, family, and new lives."

"Mr. Dragomir," Saskia broke in, "You obviously don't know who I am. And I don't know who you are either. But since you are the one who gave Saul the gun to use on that man who broke into my room last night, well then I am in your debt. I thank you from the bottom of my heart. I will always be in your debt. Goodbye."

With that, Dragomir silently lifted his hat, bowed to us both, and turned on his heels. We watched him disappear across the bridge to the Right Bank from where we had come. Saskia and I continued on to Left Bank, and walked eastward down the quai—that quai that gave us so many souvenirs of a carefree time forever past. Occasionally, we would look over our shoulders to make sure we weren't being followed—either by criminals or by the law.

Chapter Twenty-eight

The sun was now overhead. The day was crisp and not too cold. Saskia and I walked along the quai until we were far enough away from that infamous hostelry on the rue Saint-Denis, far enough away from the Île Saint-Louis, as from the Comédie-Française.

During the walk, Saskia asked me a million questions. She wasn't happy to let that encounter with Dragomir fade into the past...

"What was his name?... Dragomir?! Had you mentioned to him that we were planning to go to Italy? How did he pick Italy?"

"No, I mentioned nothing of the sort."

"Strange that he should guess that. And to guess that we would have the best luck if we went specifically to Tuscany... 'There we will find,' he says, 'old friends and family.' Strange seeing how I'm looking for an old friend and you are looking for your family. Florence is in Tuscany, and Florence is where you believe your mother is living... strange that he should guess all of that!"

"He didn't guess it," I told her, "But he also didn't find out by magic, the way clairvoyants are supposed to find things out... he learned of it somewhere, somehow... but I'm not really sure where or how."

"Hmm," Saskia said, more interested in fiddling with my clothes than with talking. "That's a really beautiful watch. How did you come to lose in to Mr. Dragomir in the first place?"

I thereupon told Saskia the story of how and why I ended up at Dragomir's house in Málaga. I didn't, however, tell her the part about how Pulpawrecho came to meet his master—about him stalking a girl—as that seemed irrelevant. But I did tell her that Dragomir spoke that night about a certain 'Clara' girl who came to consult him years before. I found it amusing that Dragomir really believed Saskia was the girl who led Pulpawrecho to him, that she was the girl whose name meant *clear, bright, and celebrated,* and whose fortune he read to her so as 'to play with her a little,' so as to give her some 'direction in life. Then, four years later, he runs into a young woman who reminds him of this girl from his past, and whose age the girl would have now, and he figures it is she. I remembered how Pulpawrecho's story struck a chord with me with that one detail: how the baffled little girl stumbled upon the plaque that read: 'Dragomir – Clairvoyant,' and, *as if it were fate bringing her there*, she kissed her hands. I liked that part about the girl kissing her hands, and wished then that Saskia's name *was* Clara. In telling Saskia about Málaga on that famous walk away from the hostelry in Paris, she asked me...

"Remember when we first met—or rather, when I first told you my name is Saskia, and you asked me over and over again if it meant 'clear, bright, and celebrated?'"

"Yes."

"Did you ask me that because of this girl? I mean, did you ask me this because Dragomir spoke to you of this Clara girl in Málaga, and you thought I might be her?"

"Yes."

"But why did you come to speak to Dragomir of this other girl? ...This 'Clara' person? And why do *we* speak of her? What does she matter to us?"

I didn't answer her question, but simply walked along.

Our road took us to *Le Marais*, a neighborhood of dark intersecting roads, with obscure alleys behind the markets of immigrant merchants, and the busy workshops of artisans. It was a quarter we had never been in, and it seemed like a perfect place to hide two fugitives. We hoped, in staying there, that we would attract no more attention than the mice in the street, we hoped our past would not catch up with us.

There in the Marais, we rented a small apartment in an old medieval townhouse on the rue de Vieille du Temple. Dragomir's twenty-louis was plenty to live comfortably for a little while. And soon after, Juhani came through with an advance of three-hundred louis. As soon as this arrived, we bought tickets to Italy, with no date assigned to them, so that we could leave if we needed to collect on Saskia's inheritance.

Our mornings were happy, our evenings full of laughter. The murder of Pulpawrecho soon left our thoughts, along with all other unpleasant memories. Several times Saskia asked me why, if we were not looking for Adélaïse anymore in Paris, didn't we go immediately to Tuscany to look for my mother and Adélaïse there. Whenever Saskia brought this up, I would remind her that she loves Paris. I would tell her that we were not going to travel to Tuscany just because Dragomir told us we would have good luck and a rich healthy life there.

"Oh, so it's Dragomir who decides in favor of us staying in Paris now?" would be the response of the clever girl, "I should thank him for his decision."

I told Saskia that I was ready to leave Paris as well, but that travel would be easier in spring. It was already winter when we came to live in the Marais, and the months seemed only to grow colder as they progressed. We waited on, and slowly time went by.

I didn't see anymore of my "messenger" in Paris, except one event occurred in late March that made me wonder if we were still being followed or not...

There was a wine merchant at the great marketplace of Les Halles, about a quarter-hour on foot from our house. There one could find the best prices in all of Paris on the good wines of Bourgogne and Bordeaux. Maurice, the patron, was an old man with a large stomach who told nothing but jokes with his great accent from Marseille. It was already almost April, but this night was as cold as a night in the dead of winter. The moon was growing fuller, it was almost full. I left a café near Les Halles where I smoked a pipe of opium and drank a pitcher of *vin chaud*[1]; and although it was already very late, I decided to buy some wine for when I got home.

It was the first and only time that I went to this wine merchant's that Maurice wasn't in. A woman of about fifty years was keeping the shop. I asked where Maurice was and she said he was ill. I asked for a bottle of the Bourgogne that I always bought, and she told me that they had none, that the shipment didn't come in. She recommended a bottle of Bordeaux that she said was just as good, it was about the same price; I didn't want to take the time to look further. I bought a bottle of her wine and braved the cold streets home.

Outside the window of our kitchen, a single lantern burned in the alley where there was a printing shop down below. Some stray gutter cats foraged for food in the alley, above the moon burned in the sky like melted silver cooling in an almost round black mould. Saskia was asleep and didn't wake up when I came in making noise. Alone in the kitchen I uncorked the bottle of wine that woman sold me and poured a full glass. The color was deep red, with no purple in it, which meant it was old enough to drink. I was always picky about red wine... never so young that there should be a hint of purple in the color.

As was my custom, I spilt the first large swallow from my glass out for the god of wine to enjoy, as superstition says that he

---

[1]VIN CHAUD: *(Fr)* "Hot wine." Heated wine is sweetened and flavored with cinnamon, cloves and other spices, as well as fruit.

who does not honor the gods will someday find his wine keg dry and no food in the pantry. His bed will be empty of his wife or his mistress...

Since I was next to the window, I spilt the swallow on the windowsill looking out on the alley. The puddle of wine reflected the light and shape of the lantern burning. It was then, before I drank from my glass, that a stray cat jumped down from the gutter and began to lick my offering to the gods. "I wouldn't do that if I were you, cat," I said, "that wine is for mighty Zeus and Apollo." Shortly after I said this, the cat fell on its side. I pulled it in close to the windowsill so his death would not be caused by falling. The cat began to convulse slowly, his breathing was labored.

I watched that cat for sometime. He didn't grow any worse, but he didn't get any better. I wasn't completely sure if the wine was poisoned, or if it was the fact that the cat licked an offering to a god that made him sick. That bottle was all the wine in the house, so I hoped that it was a curse from the gods that struck him down. I didn't look forward to pouring the wine down the drain. I decided then to test it on another cat, from wine that was not offered to a god. I found a piece of bread in the pantry and tore a piece off. I then poured a nice swallow of wine that thoroughly soaked the piece of bread; then I threw the bread into the alley. I saw a couple cats fight for it, then one cat—having won—ate the bread, let out a little cry, and then fell on its side.

"Poisoned wine!" I decided to go to bed. But first I wrote on a little square of paper these words: "Don't Drink Me!"—I then stuck the note to the bottle, tying a string around it to make the note stay. I then put the bottle under the sink where there were bottles of various household poisons. I went to bed thoroughly disgusted with the way my evening had to go.

It was late when I woke, I had a headache. Saskia was already awake and was moving around in the kitchen. I jumped out of bed and ran to her and asked her if she had by any chance drunk any of the poisons under the sink. She looked at me with the strangest look! She asked me why on earth would she ever drink the things under the sink?! I reinforced her thinking, telling her one more time not to drink anything we kept under the sink;

then I left her alone. Scratching my head in wonder, I went down to the alley to see about my cat.

The printer's shop was open and a worker was out in the alley eating his lunch. I bid him good day and looked around until I spotted the cat. He was stiff and silent, lying on his side on the dirty ground.

Inspecting the cat, I found that he was still alive. His breathing was regular, although he looked ill and had a pained expression on his face. I thought the matter over... 'That was twelve hours ago that I fed him that bread, and he is still alive! This poison is not strong...'

Back upstairs at our windowsill, it looked as though the first cat had tumbled to his death in the night, as he was no longer on the windowsill. I eventually spotted him, however, on the ledge of the roof that sloped down beneath the window. He had apparently crawled on his own out to the ledge to sleep. I threw a walnut at him and it pounced off his body, he glanced around. He looked only half-sick. I knew he would be in fine shape, but I had to know for sure...

So I took the bottle of poisoned wine and went into our bedroom where Saskia was tuning her guitar. That was good, I told her, as I needed to hear a song that morning. Once it was tuned, she played me a beautiful song about two wayfarers travelling through a rainforest together; and after it was over she asked me if I was going to get drunk for breakfast.

"Oh, this wine? No, no, I'm not going to drink it. I'm taking it to go to poison a donkey."

For the second time that morning, she gave me the strangest look! I left her there on the bed with her guitar and walked out with the wine bottle through the cold, icy morning, down to the marketplace at Les Halles.

Once at the market, I passed the wine merchant's and noticed it was closed; so neither the woman who sold me the wine nor Maurice were there to question. It was just as well, I hadn't come for that.

I came to the *Halle des Blés*, where they sold flours and seeds, and I found a solitary donkey roped-up. Around him were piles of dried corn. I got on my knees, quickly made friends with the ass, and grabbed his snout. He resisted at first, but when I stuck the mouth of the bottle into his gourd, he obediently drank the wine.

"Now I need to wait," I said. I left the ass and went for a stroll and came back. As was expected, the ass was sick, lying on his side, labored breathing, slight convulsions, a desperate look on his donkey face. I left him there again. I went and ate breakfast in a bistro. I walked around awhile. I went then to drink a pitcher of vin chaud in a café. I took my time. Some hours later, I went back to visit the donkey. As before, he was lying on the corn. He was like before, but the desperate look on his face had relaxed—it appeared he'd gotten used to his condition by now. There was no doubt he would survive.

'He's a little donkey,' I said to myself, 'Perhaps it's a donkyesse?... anyway, she's smaller than I am, weighs a bit less than me, so she'd be easier to kill—yet she's just sick. Whoever it is who wants to poison me... first off, it wasn't that woman at the wine store. I'd never seen her nor wronged her in my life. And she alone couldn't have influenced Maurice to take the day off from work—unless she'd poisoned him too, of course...

'No, I can bet safely... whoever wanted to poison me did so not to kill me, but only to make me sick. And the last person to poison me was Dragomir. Still, the two can't be related,' I told myself, 'I believe this was just an accident; Dragomir had no motive to poison me. I haven't seen or heard from him since last fall. If it wasn't an accident, then it was those same people who trashed our apartment on the quai... they've tracked me down in the Marais—bad news..."

Thus I threw my hands up on the matter. But I did not stop giving the matter thought... it was because of this poisoning attempt that I decided we should leave our apartment on the rue de Vieille du Temple in the Marais, without delay, and with great secrecy.

I told Saskia about the drunken donkyesse. She was sad that I had to poison a donkey of all creatures, but said that I did right; and that given the recent events in our lives, it was perfectly natural that somebody should poison our wine. They failed at making us ill, but they succeeded in chasing us out of France.

"We are not being chased out of France," I said, "We wanted to go to Italy this spring anyway."

"I can't wait to be in Italy," Saskia replied.

We therefore moved our belongings from our apartment little by little, to not be suspected of moving. Each time we went out, we carried an extra bag with us, which we kept safe until our escape, in a storage attic owned by Madame Gazonette, on the rue des Fossés Saint-Bernard in the fifth arrondissement. Madame Gazonette was no longer furious with us. In fact, she loved us more than ever, since we were now in funds and we could afford to pay her handsomely to replace all that was destroyed when those people broke into our apartment. She wanted us to move back in, yet our hearts were set on Italy. And so, on the twelfth of April of that year, we took our things from Mme. Gazonette's attic, and left Paris in the utmost secrecy.

Chapter Twenty-nine

Italy...

With April, came the warm weather. It was sad to leave Paris when we saw how beautiful the city became at the coming of spring. We arrived in Florence on a Friday afternoon and came to a hotel overlooking the square my mother told me about: the Piazza della Signoria. It was right next to the bridge spanning the Arno river: the Ponte Vecchio. I knew that if she were in Florence, she would come to these places on Sunday. So, the day following the next day, Sunday, I walked the whole of Piazza della Signoria and the Ponte Vecchio from morning till night and I didn't see her.

Florence too is a beautiful city, but less amusing than Paris. I also don't speak Italian. I do speak French, Spanish, English and two other languages, I think that's enough. I wasn't going to try to learn Italian. Saskia knows just as many languages as I do, if not more, from all her wandering around the world. She knows Italian since she was a schoolgirl in Verona. So while we were in Italy, she translated everything to me.

The only person we told we would be in Florence was Juhani, and the first Monday following our arrival, a letter came from him to the post office in Florence. He had the good news that one of his friends owned a villa in Tuscany that he rarely used and was vacant then. Juhani's friend had plans for his villa the next autumn, but now was spring. So if we wanted, we were welcome to stay in his villa for the next six months. The villa was in the famous city of Siena, about thirteen leagues south of Florence. Saskia and I both agreed that only good things could come from six months in Siena, as this would help us save money, and we thought we might find those we were looking for. Had the villa been in the rural Tuscan countryside we would not have accepted the offer, but Siena was a possibility in our search.

We left Florence the next day. The road was terrible and the journey took a long time. They were building a new road, we were told, but it wouldn't be ready for five years.

The villa was a charming stone house on the Strada Malizia, just outside of the city-centre. It only had one-storey, but it was spacious and sunny, with an herb and vegetable patch outside. The house was built circular around an interior courtyard planted with lemon trees. We had all the food we needed for summer growing all around us. We were happy to have come, and our nights in that courtyard under the lemon trees were so bucolic—in the moonlight we would lounge on white cushions and drink wine, while Saskia played her guitar. I had no hobby while she played, except that of listening to her, and composing in my head verses to praise the beauty of her songs, her voice, the joy I felt beside her.

By day, we searched for Adélaïse. When at night we felt like seeing the city and its people, we walked down to the Piazza del Campo, or to another square where the moonlight was generous, and we would eat and drink wine until half-drunk and merry.

The most illuminating of these nights at the Piazza was a night when there was no moon at all and blackness shone on the earth. I could see nothing in that medieval square except for her face and hands, the contour of her neck; and in the background, the faint surfaces of the other diners on the terrace that glowed from the light of the candles on each table. Yet as Saskia and I talked, a bright star emerged from the darkness and gave shape to events in our past. Here is what happened...

We ordered red wine. It was a good wine from a nearby village called Brunello di Montalcino, and it made us easy with words. After we finished two bottles of it and were more drunk than usual, we were so light-hearted and happy in our drunkenness that we decided to keep the wine coming. As we were toasting the third bottle, a startling incident happened... A handsome young man appeared in the piazza, at the edge of the restaurant's terrace, and he looked into the crowd of diners where we sat and shouted loudly, "Clara! Clara!" while waving his hand. Hearing that name flashed me back to that fatal night in Paris. Saskia looked at the youth in alarm, I did too. A moment later a girl from a table behind us jumped up and broke into laughter, *"Marco! Bello! Sei un idiota! Sei pazzo! Mi sei mancato[1]!"* She ran towards him and they embraced for a long time. The couple then wandered off together and never returned.

I turned to Saskia and said a clumsy thing that I should never have said: "I think every time I hear someone say the name 'Clara,' for the rest of my life, I'm going to think about that unknown girl who made me kill Pulpawrecho."

It was a tasteless remark: gloomy and sad. And, as a rule, it's bad form to confess loudly to murders one's committed while drunk in Italian piazzas; but beyond that, it was just a foul thing to say. I blame it on the enormous quantity of wine that we'd drunk... that, and the quality of the night. But, oh, what a night it was!... I was happily across the sea from the home that used to be the only place I knew on this earth before I grew up to taste the perfumed flesh of travel and the beautiful body of the world. Now I was in Italy, a country I thought I would never live to see. My mother had sent me there in dreams, through many a bedtime story when I was a small boy. But now, to think that I was in that

---

[1] MARCO…MENCATO!: *(It)* "Hey Handsome Marco! You're an idiot! You're crazy! I've missed you!"

far-away place, together with my wild-eyed enchantress. Saskia too looked enraptured to be with me. And with the wine flowing freely, the night progressed sweetly. That is, until I had to go and ruin the mood by saying, 'forever will the name Clara make me think of that unknown girl who made me kill Pulpawrecho.'

Saskia became flustered—angry one minute, then pleading with me—asking me to explain what I meant by such a horrid statement. I told Saskia that it was Clara's fault that I had to kill Pulpawrecho.

"Why *her* fault?"

"Not her fault, but *because of* her... The Clara girl whom Dragomir mistook Saskia for was the same girl that Pulpawrecho fell in love with the night she came to consult the clairvoyant in Málaga. The moment that little madman saw Clara, he fell in love with her, pathologically, she became a perverse obsession. And because Pulpawrecho *also* mistook you for Clara, just as Dragomir had, he tried to rape you."

Saskia didn't say anything. She looked puzzled, confused, and infinitely sad. Finally, she said, "So what you're saying is that it is because of *me*, and no one else!, *but because of me that you had to kill?!*"

"My dear, I didn't mean that! Certainly if Pulpawrecho hadn't thought you were Clara, he would have eventually found another girl of your age who reminded him of her, and he would have tried to rape *her* instead; and Dragomir would have sentenced Pulpawrecho to death for *that girl* instead of you. What do we care about all this! Do you think it weighs heavy on my conscience to have killed an insect such as Pulpawrecho? Dragomir himself wanted him dead."

I was so drunk while we were talking about this, that I didn't notice at first when Saskia slipped-up... She made an error with words a little later in the conversation... "Tell me how this Clara girl inspired Pulpawrecho to want to rape *me, Saskia*?" she said, "I mean, *if Pulpawrecho never even met this Clara girl,* how could Pulpawrecho have fallen in love with her? It's impossible! Dragomir is the one that met her..."

Her cheeks turned fiery red then and she became flustered. I think it was at this moment that she realized where she'd slipped-up. For how did she know that Pulpawrecho never met this Clara?! ...To cover herself, she added, "But you know what, Saul, you are right. It doesn't matter who killed Pulpawrecho, or who inspired him to be a madman and a rapist... the fact is that he was *by nature* a madman and a rapist... *so why should he not have been killed?!*"

"Hmm," I said, considering everything, "Just how do you know that Clara never met Pulpawrecho? I'm just curious." I waited and waited but Saskia didn't answer me, she just sat there, nervously tapping on her wine glass. I decided to let it go. I took my own glass in hand and took so pleasurable a swallow that it made my head tingle with intoxication. I looked up at the dark sky, and over at the famous *Palazzo Pubblico* building that crowned the Piazza, then back at Saskia. "Why don't you drink your wine?" I asked her.

"I think I'm already drunk."

I chuckled at this, and Saskia began to cry. Instead of her cries growing fainter as my chuckles grew faint, her tears only increased. Then there came a moment when she broke completely. Her head plummeted into her hands and she lost all control. She cried and cried, tossing tears around, beginning sentences that had no beginning, saying apologies that had no end. Her last apology went like this... "I'm sorry, Saul, I am so sorry! You will never trust me again... I'm scared about what I have done... for six months I have lied to you—*six months!* I told you before that I *cannot* lie to you. 'It won't work,' I said, 'it won't work!!'"

"Saskia, please... settle down... Now tell me what on earth you are talking about."

"It's me, Saul!... I am Clara!... I am Clara! Dragomir wasn't confused... Dragomir *is never* confused! I was the one who was lying when we spoke in front of you. He and I both knew that I was Clara and that I was lying to him. I'm just glad he didn't insist I was a liar and an evil girl to make me confess in front of you both... But trust me, *Dragomir is never confused...*"

"So you are Clara?!"

She grabbed my hands and held them tight... "No, Saul, I am *Saskia!*... I was born with the name *Saskia*... Please promise me that you will never call me Clara. I never wanted to lie to you, Saul. I promise. The only thing was that I was forced to lie because I needed you to believe that I had never met Dragomir in my life. You, yourself, know the reasons why no one should know that I met Dragomir... So, yes. I had to tell a lie these last six months—ever since that hour before dawn at that hostel when I denied I was Clara."

"You were born Saskia?"

"My parents gave me the same name as Rembrandt's wife. I was always happy with this name. Then when my parents died, my uncle came to pull me out of a future of misery. He offered to take me to Italy, and he made me what I am today: 'Wanderess,' as you call it, an orphan, a wild girl, but free!... No need of money, no need of people, the only thing that ties me down and makes me submit is the uncertainty of it all... where should I go? What will become of me? It is my destiny that intrigues me, yet it is my destiny that rules me, unfortunately...

"My uncle put forth that I assume a role during his lifetime, and that I assume another role after his death. After his death, his wish was for me to remain faithful to him and not to attempt to erase his memory in the arms of another man. It's ridiculous, I know. They say it's incestuous, a condition like that put on you by your own family member. They say a condition like that should *make me* erase my memory of him. In a healthy situation, it would be in the arms of another man that my memory of him as my loving uncle would be strengthened. To be honest, Saul, I don't understand the taboo of incest, I never saw his love for me as a bad thing; but perhaps I don't understand life. No, I'm too young and unsettled to understand life. Yet my uncle, for all his money and all his years, he lived and he died without understanding life.

"...The role I was to assume during his life: be a good, loving niece and a perfect example of a virtuous young lady of the haute-bourgeoisie. He wanted me to lose all memory of my parents, separate myself from the past, and forget my childhood in Holland... what he called my 'vulgar upbringing.'...

My uncle had been in love once in his life: to an upper-class Spanish woman named Clara. Years later when my mother was pregnant with me, he asked his sister to name me 'Clara.' My mother said he was furious when I was born and she and my father named me Saskia instead. He thought that Saskia was a good first name for a savage girl—that was the term he used: *a savage girl.* The day I came to live with him in Italy, he announced that he was going to call me 'Clara' from then on, which is the only name I went by in Italy, and even afterwards. I asked him why he didn't name me 'Chiara,' rather—the Italian form of 'Clara.' He didn't tell me about the Spanish woman he was in love with. He just said that 'Chiara' was a suitable name for a cheap schoolgirl whore. Whereas the Spanish form, 'Clara,' he said, is an elegant name for a lady; and therefore, that is the name he chose. I was thirteen when I met Dragomir in Málaga; and at that time, I only called myself Clara. Two years after my uncle's death, at age fifteen, I went back to being Saskia."

"Clara means 'clear, bright and celebrated,' doesn't it? Dragomir guessed this. Is that why you believe in your fortune so much?, because he guessed your name correctly?"

"That's not all he guessed correctly. I don't think he guessed any of it... *I think he knew!*"

"I still don't understand why you didn't tell me the fact that you used to be called Clara when Dragomir called you Clara in front of me. It's as if you didn't want me to know that Dragomir is your fortune teller."

"I'm afraid that's exactly why. I thought if you knew it was Dragomir who told me my fortune, and you knew that the crucial part of my fortune is *you*; and if I told you that *our destinies are entwined*, you would laugh and blow me off as a ridiculous, incredulous fool for listening to a madman like Dragomir, whom you would call a 'false clairvoyant...'"

"You are right," I told Saskia, " I would have written you off as being a ridiculous fool. But why would you have imagined that I would think of Dragomir as a madman and a false clairvoyant?

You told me about this made-up 'garden woman' long before you knew that I knew Dragomir... long before the incident with Pulpawrecho at the hostelry. You told me *she* told your fortune before we met Dragomir together, before we learned what kind of man he really is... a man without morals, rotten in the head, a man who is mad ...*or else simply evil!* Why then, if this was before the Dragomir drama, would you think I wouldn't take you seriously if you told me of your fortune as predicted by him?"

"Because he is a man!" she said, "I knew you wouldn't want to follow me around while I'm following the instructions of another man. That is why I made up the story about the garden woman on the Île Saint-Louis."

"That's right!" I exclaimed, "I'd completely forgotten about that particular lie you told me... there were so many lies! Tell me Saskia, hearing all this from you now, how can I trust you in the future? Why should I trust you?"

"Why should you trust me? I never said you *should* trust me! *You can't! ... you shouldn't!*"

"Well, you have spoken... goodbye, Saskia."

With that, I stood up from our table in the Piazza, fished in my pocket for some money to pay the meal and the wine, left it on the table, and left Saskia sitting there—she looking at me, *stupefatto*[1], mouth agape. I walked then to our villa alone, anxious to sleep and forget this night.

---

[1] STUPEFATTO: *(It)* "stupefied."

Chapter Thirty

I slept alone that night, I woke up alone. Saskia had not come to bed. We always shared a bed, her body, not far from mine, although I never touched her at night. She sometimes rested her face on my bare shoulder before we slept. Sometimes she laughed and put her nose against my neck and put her arms affectionately around me. But that was the extent of our nocturnal caresses. She never cried in bed, since neither of us had ever any reason to be sad while we were together and close beside; still sometimes she would be taken by a pensive mood—when she thought about her dear friend who was lost, or about a country or city she missed, or something else that touched her from her past—and she would lie with me on the bed, rest her cheek on my chest, and with her arms around me like that we would fall asleep, only to find that in the morning we lay far apart.

On this night following our argument in the Piazza del Campo, Saskia didn't come to bed. The morning after I went into the kitchen to make my coffee and I saw her asleep on the sofa. I took my coffee through the bedroom and out onto the courtyard so as not to wake her, and to feel the morning sun on my face. I was only outside for ten minutes; but when I came back, she was already gone and she didn't come back home again until very late that night. I was in bed alone again all of that night. Around dawn, I heard her sneak into our bedroom. I pretended to be asleep but I opened my eyes to catch a glimpse of her. She was wearing her pyjamas, her hair was tousled from sleeping, and she sneaked on her tip-toes. I kept pretending to be asleep while she placed an envelope on my chest. A moment later she was gone.

I had a fearful realization as I sat up alone in our bed and tore open the envelope. I heard her leaving then. I heard her stepping out of our front door, her footsteps grew fainter and fainter as she walked away from our villa. I was afraid and I knew what the envelope contained: a letter from her saying adieu... "Goodbye forever, Saul." It was the worst fear I had suffered in years. It was with trembling hands that I finished tearing the envelope apart and unfolded the paper. When I read the first paragraph, a flood of intense happiness filled my heart. It was not a letter of farewell. It was a letter to bind us closer than ever before. The first paragraph read...

> *My Dearest, Dearest Saul, I will be back home later today! In the meantime, I wanted you to read my fortune, the one I've been searching for, the one that concerns you... You see, now that you know who gave me my fortune, there are no more secrets between us—at least there are no secrets that I am keeping from you. So, I can now freely share with you my entire fortune. I don't have to leave anything out. So here it is, my entire fortune as I received it in Málaga four years ago...*

The Fortune Of Saskia

"You are a Wanderer searching for something, or 'someone' rather.

You were raised by the people of the north, but you are not one of them, as you belong to no people and have no country.

Your name means clear, bright, and celebrated.

Your fingers were not made for keys, but for strings.

You love song, and you sing.

I see you travelling.

In three year's time, you will be in Catalonia.

There, through your music, you will make a man drunk from love and beauty,

So much so, that he will come close to dying.

You will find him sleeping in the street, in fine clothes, in Barcelona.

You must save him and protect him, for your destinies are entwined.

His death will mean your death.

You will find what you are seeking only when you enter the country of his birth and the home where his father was raised.

There you will find your true fortune, your destiny, your salvation."

Reading her fortune brought me both joy and suffering. I laughed many times thinking back on all our interactions that were obviously influenced by this... the "*sleeping in the street in fine clothes,*" especially. It showed me why Saskia had been so determined to have me in her company, and why she panics if we have to be apart. You could say that our relationship finally made sense—that is, if relationships can ever make sense. Dragomir impressed me with his talent, I admit; her fortune was extremely well-told. He'd said that he made a lucky guess about the meaning of her first-name... but how did he guess that she played a stringed instrument? That she loved song and she sang? In neither Pulpawrecho's nor Dragomir's account of that night in Málaga was Saskia said to have carried a guitar case.

The first part of the fortune astonished me because in five short phrases, he touched on the most important aspects of Saskia's life and character. He listed the essential elements of her condition, as though he had known her already. It was the first line that said she was 'searching for someone.' Of all things that drove Saskia in this life, nothing came before her *search for her lost friend.* Adélaïse was at the top of the list. I was impressed that this Spanish charlatan actually had a gift. Before I read this paper, I could not fathom how any 'fortune' could dominate a person's mind and life entirely for several years. Now I understood why she considered this her destiny. I, who disbelieved in mystic clairvoyance, would have been just as obsessed as Saskia, had I'd been given a similar fortune that described so accurately the aspects of myself and my character. I would have declared such a fortune my destiny.

As for the rest of the bonne aventure... that which begins with: "In a three year's time, you will be in Catalonia..." it was simply a self-fulfilling prophecy. Now that the fortune teller had won Saskia's faith, he was free to instruct her to go on errands. The more she accomplishes using her fortune as a guide, the more she is working to prove her own fortune correct. The fortune read that in three year's time she would be in Catalonia. Any coincidence that she *was* in Catalonia? She was given a date and was obliged to show up...

Of course, Dragomir is a good businessman. He knows that if you want the buyer of a fortune to be satisfied, you must assign them tasks to undertake to realize their destiny. Like the labors of Heracles, the tasks should be numerous and they should take years. Imagine a fortune teller who guesses things about your life, the meaning of your name, etc., but doesn't construct a roadmap for your future—just a fortune that says who you are and where you've been... No, the one thing that the people who consult clairvoyants all have in common, is that they all are uncertain or afraid of their future. They search for a symbolic roadmap to tell them that they are on the right path. And a roadmap of the future could interest no one more than Saskia, who has unlimited freedom in her life, but who doesn't know what to do with her freedom.

What caused me suffering when reading her fortune was this second part, the roadmap part. I don't know how I came to be the unlucky man who happened to lose consciousness beneath her balcony—in that neighborhood, on any given night there must be a good deal of young men who pass out in the street after leaving bars. I just happened to be the first man to pass out beneath *her* balcony, and so she believed I was *the one*... And now, according to her fortune, she was supposed to enter the country of my birth and the place where my father was raised... This made me suffer. I believed she would sooner or later find out, and she would ask me to go with her. I would say no. And she would have to go alone. I planned to stay in Europe at all costs. I told myself over and over: there was no way that I would ever return to Tripoli, to Libya, or anywhere near it. I wouldn't set foot again on the African continent. Not in Alexandria, not in Cairo, nowhere. 'She would have to make that voyage alone,' I thought, 'and if she does, I doubt she will ever come back.'

Chapter Thirty-one

I had all day to think about Saskia and her fortune, and I came to some conclusions. She returned that evening, just as she said she would. She was happy to see that I was in a good mood. She was in a great mood. There was a man with her. He was short, had bad teeth, was dressed shabbily.

"What's he for?" I asked.

"He works at the market down the street. I bought twelve bottles of prosecco, and he carried it for me."

I took the case of wine from the little man and gave him three soldi[1] and said goodbye.

"I also bought you a present," said Saskia. So saying she handed me a large package. I opened it with delight and was

---

[1] SOLDI: A soldo (plural: "soldi") is an Italian coin minted in copper (originally in silver). It's value is approximately 1/20 of a lira.

excited to find a giant tablet of beautiful 'laid paper[1],' together with a wooden box containing an assortment of pastels—every color of nature, all colors of the Tuscan landscape, from the beige of grain to the blue of azure. "It's to keep you busy when we travel ...while I play my guitar!"

"Thank you, little rabbit," I said, kissing her forehead affectionately, "And thank you for the note this morning. I was happy to receive it... relieved is the word... the mystery of your fortune has been weighing on me since we met."

"Me too, I am relieved. I missed you today."

We put a bottle of prosecco on ice and walked out to the courtyard. The moon was out and waxing, so I could be free with the wine. And we were free. We drank and we laughed and we told stories. It was not long before Saskia brought up the conversation I would have preferred to avoid. But I did my best to keep it light...

"One thing you didn't explain to me, Saul... How do you think that Pulpawrecho fell in love with me when we never met?"

"I never did tell you the story of how Pulpawrecho came to meet his master," I said, and then recounted the story to Saskia of how this common huckster, thief, and pervert, followed her in the street that night four years ago. And how, not being able to find her, and wanting her more than anything, he sold himself into slavery as a servant of Dragomir with the hopes that Dragomir would someday lead him to find her. Pulpawrecho didn't doubt that Dragomir would know *where* to find her—not because he believed Dragomir gave her a "roadmap" to follow; but simply because Dragomir was a clairvoyant... thus he could see into her life and her future.

"So it was because of me that Pulpawrecho became Dragomir's servant."

"And he was a perfect servant," I said.

"And it was because of Pulpawrecho, whom you met on the street, that you came to meet Dragomir."

---

[1] LAID PAPER: A fine-quality paper possessing a ribbed texture to hold the imprint of pastels. Used by artists since the 12th century.

"Yes."

"It's strange, this life of fate and destiny. Our meeting, for example... if one of a million flukes didn't occur, we would never have met."

"Here's to our flukes," I said and raised a glass of prosecco. We toasted and drank, and I thought about what Saskia had said: 'It's strange this life of fate and destiny,' and I felt sad again. I was sad because this fantasy of a fortune meant so much to her. Now I knew that to realize her fortune, to go to the very end of it, she would have to go to Tripoli. I remarked that I'd done well to conceal from her all this time the name of the country where I was born and the city where my father was raised. I realized though that in concealing this information, in keeping her ignorant about the place of my birth and home of my family, I was guarding a secret. I was being deceitful in the same way I considered her deceitful when I learned that the 'garden woman' on the Île Saint-Louis was a fabrication and that Dragomir was the real witch.

"I was wrong to blame you last night," I told Saskia, "I don't know why, but it hadn't occurred to me then that *I too* am hiding things from you. Since I am not telling you where I am from, nor where my father came from, why should you have been expected to tell me that your fortune teller is Dragomir?"

"So now you will tell me where you are from?"

"I don't know. Will you first answer a question for me? You have been saying to me all along that the most important thing to you in this world is your destiny. And last night, I said to you in my anger, 'how can I ever trust you again,' and you replied, 'You *can't*! You *shouldn't* trust me!' After all that's been said, I want to know where your allegiance truly lies... is it to me and your friend Adélaïse? Or is it to your fortune?"

"Saul! My fortune *is* my destiny... and without a destiny I wouldn't be alive. How can I neglect destiny? It's impossible!"

'What kind of reasoning is that?' I wondered. "You could forget your fortune now," I told her, "and you will still be alive. And all that happens to you in the future will be your destiny. We will find Adélaïse, we will live wherever you and I want to live, we will be happy. And soon you will laugh when you remember this drama about your fortune. You will laugh when you discover that you have a beautiful destiny all the same without it."

"Saul, will you help me? Will we go to your country? To the place your father was raised?"

"No, we will not."

Saskia looked at me in horror. "But you said you would help me realize my fortune!"

"I said I would help you find Adélaïse. Until this morning, I didn't even know what your fortune was."

Saskia grew flustered. "Why won't you help me?"

I told Saskia then that she would have done better to keep to her lie about the garden woman. I admitted that Dragomir was a clever man, that he was even a brilliant and gifted man who has a knack for reading people, and for knowing their weaknesses and their fears... I told Saskia that his fortune was so well-conceived that I agreed with her for believing in it. "It's a perfect fortune," I said, "you would be foolish not to believe in it! Only a true visionary could know these things about you on first sight."

But I went on to say that in spite of this, I could not support her continuing the search for this Dragomir-conceived destiny. "My opinion of Dragomir," I said, "is that he is a villain. He is a very clever and ingenious villain, but he is a villain all the same... He constructed your fortune with brilliance, but he gave you steps for you to realize your destiny that I cannot go along with because they involve me, and to what end, I don't know. He gave you instructions for you to follow so he could watch you dance—just as he came to me at the hour before dawn with a pistol so that he could make *me* dance. If he wanted to keep Pulpawrecho from raping you, he had a million ways to prevent it other than choreographing that drama with me firing bullets at him from across the courtyard. Moreover, he had some reason to have me kill his servant which eludes me. He didn't prevent the rape out of concern for you or for me. He wanted his servant done away with and he didn't want to do it himself...

"Lastly, who else would have broken into our apartment in Paris? Andrea was dead somewhere on the Riviera when it happened. It had nothing to do with your inheritance. You noticed that nothing was stolen?, that they only rummaged through our papers?... I think what happened was clear: Dragomir happened to be in Paris at the same time we were there... He first saw us on the Île Saint-Louis, then at the theatre, then he had us followed and found out where we lived...

"He had met each of us in Málaga, and knew our personalities, so we made for an interesting target. He knew he could make you dance by telling you your fortune. He saw that he could make me dance when he sent me on an errand to poison his friend Penelope Baena in Barcelona. So when he found out where we lived, he organized the break-in so that he could read our papers, diaries, letters and what-not, to have information about us that he could use to his advantage. If he knows more about your personal life, he can better tell you your fortune the next time you two meet..."

"No, no, no," Saskia interrupted, "I'm sure it was friends of Andrea who broke in to our place. But it doesn't matter. All of my fortune has come true so far... to the point where I found you sleeping in the road in fine clothes. Now I'm supposed to go to visit the place you are from, so I will go visit it."

"Again, I ask you Saskia... where does your allegiance lie? Is it to me and Adélaïse? Or is it to your fortune?"

"Again, Saul... my fortune is my destiny. It is *our* destiny. My allegiance is to you, of course; but it you don't choose to help me, don't be surprised if one day you find me gone. You asked me how you can trust me, and I said you couldn't. I said that you shouldn't... I'll never lie to you, but I have been faithful to my destiny ever since I was a little girl, as you are faithful to yours. Don't ask me to cheat on my destiny."

"You have spoken, Saskia."

That conversation ended our happy time in Siena, although that was not the worst calamity that struck us. It disturbed me to think that Saskia would choose Dragomir over me, yet that conversation was only the first gust of wind that signaled the hurricane.

Here's a funny incident that I'll tell you about to take the edge off after hearing so many stories of treachery and disillusionment... It was a couple of weeks after the fateful conversation I just narrated. It was the beginning of fall, a time we were preparing to leave Siena to live in Florence... we were out for a walk together when we met a poet on the lawn of the University of Siena...

The poet was sitting in a bathtub on the lawn. He was bare-chested, garlanded with ivy and flowers, and while he sat in his tub, he recited lines from *The Iliad* with such a fervor that I had to approach him. I needed to see what kind of man this was who appreciated so much the eternal Homer—father of beauty and god of literature...

The poet greeted us with exceptional friendliness. He was slightly younger than me. He was handsome of figure, strong of build, and had such a heroic and noble way in his conduct, that I asked him if he was related to the hero Theseus. He replied to me with a great effusion of apology, saying that he was not in any way related to the hero Theseus, but that he was in fact a direct descendant of the immortal Sappho. Saskia had by now also taken a great interest in him, although it was not so much his beautiful appearance, nor the fact that he recited ancient poetry while seated in a bathtub on the lawn of an Italian university... rather, she was attracted to *one certain poem* he had written. After his Homeric soliloquy, I asked him for another verse. He leafed through his papers, tempted by his translations of Horace, until he finally settled on a poem he wrote to a girl he loved. Her name was Adélaïse.

It was a fine poem, and Saskia couldn't contain herself. She asked him a million questions... "*But what is this?! Who is your Adélaïse...?!*" The poet responded, "She is my English lady, Madame." But she has to be French," Saskia said, "with the name 'Adélaïse!'" To this, the fine poet said, "I know not. We only spoke English together. But she spoke such beautiful English... and with a wonderful English accent, that I was led to address her as 'my English lady.'"

"My, that is something!" Saskia then asked him where his Adélaïse was now, upon which, he wept tears of lament and said 'that she had gone'... simply... *'that she had gone.'* Saskia told him not to worry, that we ourselves would find her. She asked the poet then where we could find him again, once we found Adélaïse. He said that he would be here—in his bathtub.

"I was on my way to Rome to meet the pope," he told us, "I doubt in all truth that I could win his favor, faithful as I am to the almighty Zeus. Alas!, it's hard to find patronage in our time... Here in Siena, I am lucky. Like Diogenes, I have this bathtub to sleep in. Only the company of my English lady do I lack..."

"Don't worry, we will find her!" Saskia said, almost crying, so full of emotion was she. I then asked the poet how we were to call on him when we returned, and he told us his name. It turned out that our Homeric bathtubber was none other than the great poet, Pietros Maneos. Both Saskia and I greatly admired his poetry that was famous throughout Europe, and we told him so... and with that we were gone!

Chapter Thirty-two

We left Siena then with most of our worries behind us. I say "most" of our worries, because there were two black clouds on the horizon hunting down the sun, two things that threatened our relationship. The first was our conversation back in Siena where Saskia said to me in effect that her allegiance to me came *after* her allegiance to her fortune. The second came in an envelope whose sender and contents remained a secret that Saskia guarded from me the whole time we were in Italy. This envelope had been delivered through her estate and was given to her at her bank when we stopped on our way out of Florence to collect her income. She wouldn't tell me who'd sent the letter. I asked several times, and each time she said to me, "I'll not only tell you, but I'll give you the letter so you can read it yourself. All you have to do first is tell the driver to turn around and take us to the country where you were raised..."

"I'm sorry my love, but our driver is not capable of taking us to my country. We would need a boat for such a task."

"So you *are* from Malta!"

"No, not from Malta." We were back on this story once again.

"From where then?"

I kept silent.

"I see you're not going to tell me. Very well, forget it."

So we carried on, travelling northwards.

We soon arrived in a place called Staggia: a quaint little village with a magnificent castle, one third of the way to Florence. There we stopped and said farewell to our driver. It was a village recommended to us in Siena, a place to stop not only for the castle, but to stay at a certain travelers' inn: Il Focolare[1]. It was said to be a famous stopover for people travelling from southern Italy to Florence.

It was afternoon when we checked-in to Il Focolare. The inn was very rustic. Everything was made of wood. A little boy who appeared dim-witted came outside to fetch our bags. He brought them inside to the innkeeper who greeted us with his wife. Both were light-eyed and jovial, dressed in peasant clothes. Near the check-in counter, a fire crackled away in a giant stone hearth. It was now autumn and the air had become chilly. A number of elegantly-dressed travelers were gathered downstairs in the dining room which adjoined the lobby. They were eating, as it was still lunch hour.

The innkeeper only spoke Tuscan and Italian, so Saskia had to translate everything he and I said to each other. I checked-in with my real first name and an assumed last name, as I was now paranoid that word of my travels would get to Tripoli. Saskia used an entirely false name to protect her inheritance, since we were sharing a room.

When I said that my name was Saul, the innkeeper looked at me long and steady. There was something singular about his gaze. It wasn't *unfriendly*... it was just *singular*. He finally smiled,

---

[1] IL FOCOLARE: 'Il Focolare' is Italian for 'The Hearth.'

gave me our key, and explained to Saskia in Italian how to find our room.

In the hallway, we passed two Parisian ladies, they were dressed elegantly. They complimented Saskia on her beauty. She thanked them and gave equal compliments and asked if they liked staying here at this inn.

"Oh, it's very fashionable!" one exclaimed, "All of the best people come here. Of course it is very rustic, and the innkeeper and his wife are humble to the point of being eccentric… the innkeeper walks with a limp, and his wife makes her own clothes! …but all that goes to make this place as charming as it is!"

"That's very nice," we said, and left the two ladies and went to our room. Saskia wanted to visit the castle right away, then go for dinner in a restaurant in the village—we were only planning to be in Staggia one night and were anxious to get back on the road to Florence early the next morning. I pleaded with Saskia to stay with me at the inn that afternoon and evening, suggesting that we extend our stay in Staggia an extra day to visit the castle in the morning. There was something about the inn that attracted me in a strange way; it reminded me of my life from a long time ago; it reminded me of home. I'm not sure if it was a home I ever really knew, or a home I only dreamed of. Something, if only the way it smelled, urged me to remain close and not leave too soon. Saskia was urgent to travel on, for reasons I didn't know, but she agreed to stay a second night. I left the room and went to the counter to reserve for a second night; then I met Saskia and we went to the dining room to eat a late lunch.

Our two French ladies were not in the dining room, and it seemed that all the other diners were Italian. The talk of our neighbors grew lively. As I couldn't understand any of what they were saying, Saskia amused me by translating the gossip she heard around us. She then got into a conversation with two Italian girls of her age. They were from Rome, and they were with their mother; and none of the three spoke French—nor English, nor Spanish, nor any other language that I knew—so I quickly grew tired of this meeting and told Saskia I was going to go out to the yard of the inn to sketch with my new pastels that she bought me. She said she would be out soon.

I went into our room to get my tablet and box of pastels, and when I came down again, I passed the innkeeper who was staring at me with the most curious look. I proceeded out to the yard and entered the garden where I found a bench and sat to begin sketching a wild scene of all that I saw: the hills on the horizon the colors of fire and ash, the sun descending towards those hills where it would extinguish itself in a few hours. And in that garden, I sketched the flourishes of wildflowers; the strings of ivy, those necklaces of nature; and the vines of the red and green grapes, those succulent jewels of the gods.

I was lost in my picture. Only once did I look up from my work. I looked over to the inn and there I saw the innkeeper looking out at me through the tall window. He saw me notice him and made a faint smile, then bowed his head and turned and walked away. It may have been an hour after that when I heard little footsteps crunching the gravel on the path in the garden. I tucked my sketch away, I didn't want Saskia to see it until it was finished.

"There you are!" she laughed. She was cheerful. She told me that after she stopped talking to the family from Rome, she started heading out here to find me. While on the way, the innkeeper and his wife approached her and asked if we would accept an invitation to have dinner with them.

"Why us?"

"They said that they find us interesting."

"Where do they want to dine?"

"Here at the inn... but in their private dining room."

"Well, let's accept then," I said, and Saskia took my arm and we went back inside Il Focolare.

At dinnertime, the innkeeper led us down a long stone hallway to a circular stairway. We walked behind him and he limped as he walked, thus we walked very slowly. Atop the circular stairway, in a circular dining room with a vaulted stone ceiling, a table was laid for a meal for four. It was a massive table, and there was a stove in the room emanating heat. A pot on the stove erupted steam. The steam poured out of small windows carved in the stone; they brought in a comfortable breeze in that room, and it was not too hot. On the table was a decanter of white wine, another of red, some antipasti, fresh-cut flowers. Our hosts thanked us for giving them the honor of our company, and we responded that the honor was ours. Saskia told me she felt faint and needed to splash water on her face, then she whispered in Italian to the innkeeper and his wife. We asked if she needed to rest, but she said no, that she was hungry. While she was in the bathroom, I sat dumb, not being able to speak Italian. Our hosts looked at me with curiosity. When Saskia returned, her hair was tied back and her face was damp. She said she felt much better, and she ate the antipasti with great appetite.

"How did you both come to be innkeepers?" I asked. Saskia translated my question and then said to me, "They say that they are not really innkeepers. Or rather, that they didn't set out to become innkeepers. It all happened by accident."

"We are originally farmers," explained the man, "My wife's parents and my parents were all farmers. And this inn used to be a giant family farm that my grandparents built seventy years ago. We inherited it when they died, and we continued farming—mostly grains, root vegetables, herbs, and milk-goats for their cheese. Then, four years ago, the government closed the main road joining Rome to Siena and Siena to Florence; so travelers began taking the road that goes through our village of Staggia. Overnight, the whole village changed: our castle, for example, began to resemble an anthill in a desert, with all the visitors scurrying around it morning till night. At this same time, people started coming to our farm to ask if they could pay to stay the night ...you see, there are no inns in Staggia. So little by little, we started changing old barns and animal sheds into guest rooms. Then, before you know it, we had the town's one and only inn!"

"That is the way most things seem to happen in life," I said to the innkeepers, or 'farmers,' rather, "Our most interesting life changes seem to arrive by complete accident. A chance meeting will inspire a new venture that one would never have considered before."

"But you and Saul are in Tuscany for a reason..." the innkeeper said to Saskia, "I mean... *a very important reason.*"

"Yes," she smiled, "We are searching for my best friend. I haven't seen her since I was eleven. We were told that she is now living somewhere in Tuscany. Have you ever had a French girl stay here named Adélaïse?"

"Oh," the innkeeper frowned, "perhaps we have made a mistake."

"Why?!" asked Saskia.

"That is too bad," said his wife.

The innkeeper then excused himself to use the bathroom and limped out of the dining room. While he was gone, his wife made a comment to Saskia: "His limp is getting better every week. He used to barely be able to walk, right after his accident..." Saskia sat still looking frightened. The woman kept talking until, a few moments later, her husband reappeared and interrupted her... "What luck that whoever used the bathroom before me didn't pull out the stopper after splashing water on her face! *Look what I found...*" Everyone at the table peered into his hand. "Before I pulled out the stopper to wash my hands, I noticed a gemstone at the bottom of the sink. I think she would miss this!"

Saskia immediately felt in her ears for the earrings I gave her. She was about to take them out to see if the stones were missing until I informed her that all the diamonds were in place. None had fallen out. The innkeeper held up the stone and said, "It looks to be a very precious sapphire!"

Saskia made a loud gasp. She reached for her necklace: a gold heart-shaped locket she always wore—except for when she slept beside me. I had never seen inside the locket before. Now she opened it and showed the interior. It had two settings: one had a blue sapphire, the same size as the one the innkeeper had found; the other setting was empty. "I bought two sapphires when I traveled to Ceylon—sapphires are everywhere in Ceylon, and they are not expensive. One of the sapphires is for me, and the other is to give to Adélaïse as soon as I find her" She then turned to the innkeeper, "You saved my life by finding that... If I'd lost it, that would surely mean that I'd lost Adélaïse forever. I couldn't live with that truth!"

The innkeeper went to find a box to put the stone, as well as the locket, in—since the locket didn't shut correctly anymore. Saskia would need to find a jeweler to repair it, and return the stray sapphire to its setting. I thought about Saskia's statement: that she couldn't live with the truth should it be known that she would never see Adélaïse again. Don't we all say that, and isn't it an empty phrase: that we couldn't live knowing we could never have the other again. Saskia could certainly live if she knew she couldn't see me again, likewise I without her… but would I *want* to live, had I known the truth to be my life would be without her? Maybe the test of a man, or of a woman, is if he or she is *brave enough to refuse life*, were it a life without the beloved.

That whole story of the innkeeper finding Saskia's sapphire and returning it to her convinced me of one thing: that he was a noble farmer. He was a man of honesty and integrity. And that knowledge would prove important for reasons you'll soon find out.

The only time that evening when someone other than us four appeared in that dining room is when the head cook at the inn brought the plates of food in. We were by now on familiar terms with each other, so I ventured to ask the innkeeper why he limped when he walked. Saskia translated his response, saying that… "…he had a bad accident out in his fields last June… while he was fixing one of his farming machines…",

"You see, the machine jumped one of the gears on the wheel," said the innkeeper, "and the blade that cuts the grain struck my thigh. It made a deep gash… So I came back here to the inn. I bandaged my leg. I went to bed. My wife was visiting our son in a neighboring village where he lives with his wife and our grandchildren. She was spending the night there, so I slept alone here. I woke up in a lot of pain. My whole thigh was swollen, the pain was really bad. It was already infected. I was worried I was going to lose my leg—you see, one of my friends growing up, his father lost his arm because it got cut by a farming machine… it got infected and then turned to gangrene…

"Mid-morning, my wife was still gone. So I decided to get to a doctor myself. It took me hours to hobble to the nearest doctor. He's in another village. When I got there, I found out the doctor left that morning to deliver a baby somewhere. My leg was now so badly infected, parts of it that had been painful before started to grow numb. I had every reason to fear gangrene. I went to the apothecary in that village where the doctor lives and I asked for some medicine. They didn't know what to do other than clean the wound. But there was a woman customer there—a lady, a foreigner, about sixty years old, with long grey hair and kind eyes—who said she could help me—*and, she did help me!* She suggested we go to my house because I would need to lie down somewhere for several days without moving. Before we left, she bought some medicines and some herbs from the apothecary—medicines and herbs that I had never heard of...

"She helped me get back here to our inn. My wife still wasn't back, so this lady stayed to care for me, waiting till my wife was back so she could give her instructions on what to do. This lady, I tell you, she was a great healer! She stayed that whole day caring for my wound, having me take different medicines, tinctures of special herbs. My wife came back in the evening and she was very afraid for me. She was grateful to this lady who was helping me. By evening, the infection was under control. The good lady said that the risk of gangrene was gone as long as I continued the treatment. My wife admitted that she didn't know the first thing about treating such a wound. She asked the good lady if there was a way to convince her to stay a few days in case the infection came back. Since we run an inn, we offered her our best room to sleep in. We had our cook go to great lengths to prepare elaborate meals for her. After a few such meals, she told us she preferred simpler meals, as she wasn't demanding in her tastes.

"...And so," he continued, "to make a long story short, this woman, this lady, saved my leg last spring. She became a great friend to my wife and to me, and I am in debt to her forever. I may still limp, but I have my leg; and the limp is going away. She was back here a month ago and stayed with us, and she checked-up on my leg. She said the limp will soon be gone and I'll be like new. As for her, I pray that she'll recover just as I have. You see, she just suffered the most horrible shock. I'm afraid I'm partly responsible, although I was only trying to help her. She was the healthiest person I ever met, I know she will recover quickly. I pray to God that she will. She's back in Florence now, ill from shock. But tomorrow, early morning, my wife and I are going to set off for Florence to care for her as she cared for me."

Of course the innkeeper's story reminded me of how Saskia saved me in Barcelona, how she cared for me there just like the lady in this story cared for the innkeeper. And so I offered to tell the story of my meeting Saskia to the innkeeper. Saskia said she would have trouble being the translator of such a story, as she preferred to be humble, but I begged her, asking her to be proud for having saved someone's life. I wanted to tell the story also to remind *myself* of how Saskia saved me, so that my gratitude to her would never fade away. I know that retelling a story to others is the way to make a story immortal.

The innkeeper begged Saskia to translate it, saying that nothing could interest him more than to hear the story of how a couple such as she and I came to meet. And so, the innkeeper's wife cleared the dishes from the meal we had eaten. She put water on the stove for tea. And I told the story of our fateful night in Barcelona accurately and in full—except that I left out Penelope Baena, and I left out the opium. I kept the poisoning part of my story as vague as possible.

Once my story was told, we all realized we had forgotten about the tea. The innkeeper's wife brought the water to a boil once more. Her husband then took over, setting a large clay pot on the table in which a sack full of medicinal herbs was steeping. The innkeeper's wife set empty clay cups before each person at the table, and her husband lifted the heavy pot and poured out four cups of the herbal infusion to drink...

That was the moment I realized just *why* the inn smelled as it did, and *why* I was so drawn to its odor; I realized why it reminded me of my home. I sat looking at my cup of tea with the swirling herbs, smelling it; and I realized it was the *exact same tea* my mother made for me as a child and adolescent. I had a nervous stomach as a child, and she gave me this tea saying it would calm my stomach. The tea was an infusion of various herbs native to my country. At that farmer's-innkeeper's table, I sat in a sort of revelry of memory... a fog of nostalgia enclosing me... and then... down. I was plunged into melancholy. Then, up! I was lifted up in rapture. Then I was sent to walk in my mind. It was a strange landscape. I looked around me for clues as to where I was. My mind trailed off, while my voice too, it trailed off. Then I said to the innkeeper and his wife in a voice full of melancholy and rapture, *"Thank you... thank you both for this excellent tea."*

"Saul? Are you okay?!" Saskia looked frightened. I realized then that I was scaring her, and that I didn't *want* to scare her. So I put all my energy into smiling. And when she saw me smile, she sighed with relief... "Oh, goodness, Saul!... You're back... please, don't scare me anymore!"

"Saskia," I said to her with a very calm, steady voice, "Tell the innkeeper and his wife that I realize now why I couldn't bear to leave their inn today to go look at the castle with you. Tell them that I now realize why I suddenly feel like I'm at home. It was just like my mother told me when I was last with her: 'Saul, my son, once you have the chance to leave our country, take it... go to Italy... go to Florence... There you will find happiness, there you will find peace, there you will find joy. And there, come one day, you will find me, and we will be a family again.' Tell that to the innkeeper, and tell it to his wife, and tell them that I found her again; I found my home and my family... all in this cup of tea."

Saskia looked at me and said nothing. Great confusion displayed in her eyes. Those eyes, that mouth, that gently quivering face... She didn't know how to react to what I was saying.

"Tell him," I asked once more of Saskia.

With that she turned from me to the innkeeper and his wife. She placed her hands on the heavy wooden table and began reciting words in Italian. The two of them looked at me with alarm. I held my clay cup between my hands, and they their cups between theirs... and I looked down into my cup, into the dregs that the tea left behind once drunk. I looked over at Saskia. Then I looked back across the table at the innkeeper and his wife. Their looks of alarm had now turned into looks of infinite kindness. They now looked at me smiling radiant smiles, what kindness in their faces! While the innkeeper's eyes remained on me, he put his heavy, rustic hand on the hands of Saskia that were placed on the table. He turned to her and he spoke a string of Italian phrases...

Saskia listened to his words, and then looked at me with a look so tender—at once joyful and sorrowful—she then began to cry. Thus she looked at me while the tears toppled down her face, each one catching up with the last, each tear hunting down the tear before it...

As water is born high-up on a mountain spring, secreted from a hidden place within the rocks so as to tumble down in streams and waterfalls, to gather below together once again in the ocean, so were Saskia's tears born high-up on her perfect face, secreted from a hidden place within her eyes, so as to topple down in streams upon her cheeks, to topple from her chin... Then the tears gather whole to form oceans of hope in the cups of her hands.

"What is it Saskia?" I asked of her, I begged of her, pleaded, "What is it?!" She looked back to the innkeeper. Then to his wife, her eyes remained on me. While my own eyes remained focused on the empty tea bowl in my hands. All of this happened in one confused moment. Finally, Saskia said to me with tenderness in her voice... "They say it's true then, Saul. They say it's true."

"What is true?"

"They say that you are the one."

Chapter Thirty-three

We continued to sit in complete silence at that table: Saskia sobbed into her napkin, the innkeeper and his wife looked wide-eyed at me while whispering in Italian or in Tuscan together. I, meanwhile, didn't care why they were looking, or why Saskia was sobbing; I was busy musing on the phenomenon of nostalgia[1]. It is definitely an "aching," as the definition suggests. Part of the original sensation—in this case, the smell of the tea—is there. But the original elements of the scene when the experience first-occurred are long-gone. For me, this was at my home in our fishing village. I was but a child or adolescent; and my mother brewed this tea with the knowledge that it would heal all my woes—and it did. Now it was the source of my woes, although the smell remained healing. But *why* was this tea *here in Tuscany?* I would soon find out...

---

[1] NOSTALGIA: The etymology of 'nostalgia' is from the Homeric Greek νόστος (nóstos), meaning 'homecoming,' and ἄλγος (álgos), meaning 'aching pain.'

At first, I felt suddenly separated from all three of my companions—almost as though I were an intruder at the table. Saskia was crying, obviously about me, had I done something wrong? Apparently, I was no longer in their eyes the person who I was minutes before. Something was said about me in that language I couldn't understand… what was it?! Something powerful… Just look at the way the farmer-innkeeper stared at me! And his wife too! I felt incredibly uneasy all of a sudden. I wanted to excuse myself and go walk in the yard. They, however, quickly excused themselves for treating me strangely. But it didn't help. Now I too was a stranger to me. All because I was then ignorant of something which now—telling you this story—I consider essential to understanding myself. What was it? Well, it all began when I told Saskia and the innkeeper and his wife that "I found the home of my youth in the cup of tea they prepared for me." After they said, *"I am the one."* And so, impatient to know all, I implored them to know…

"I had guessed you were the one," the innkeeper told me, "when you came to our inn and said your name is Saul… And then when I saw you out in the garden painting with the pastels… Now with tea that put you in a sort-of trance, I know you are *the one.*"

"Which *one*?!"

Saskia repeated my question in Italian, and the innkeeper said something to her in a low, and serious voice. Saskia looked stunned, and instead of translating it, she began to cry more heavily than before.

"Translate what he said, Saskia."

"I cannot!" she cried, "Give me a minute…"

We all sat silent around the table. When Saskia cleared her voice from the crying, she said to me, "The woman who healed the innkeepers leg, and who became their friend… it is…"

"*Who*, Saskia?!"

"It is your mother!"

"My mother?!" Hearing this sent a freezing shiver across my body. I guessed that some very bad news would follow, since whatever they said to Saskia had made her cry. She insisted that

there was no bad news that I didn't already know. That she was crying because I had found my mother, just as I had hoped to do, although I didn't believe I could do it in a region as large as Tuscany. I told the three of them that I didn't believe them. "How do you know... Rather, *why did you think that she was my mother?!*"

"I don't think... *I know!*" said the innkeeper, *"She is your mother!"* As he spoke, Saskia translated sentence by sentence...

"The innkeeper says that your mother has stayed at their inn for at least three of the last six months, and that she is back in Florence now but when she left last time, she said she was planning to return to their inn this winter. She had never heard of their inn before she met the owner here at the apothecary after he injured his leg. You see, your mother, she was his nurse! The innkeeper and his wife begged her to stay with them, at least until his leg was on the mend. She hesitated though... she was busy trying to find you. But then she learned that Staggia—and this inn in particular—is a crossroads for people travelling south to north, or vice-versa, in Italy. And of the travelers from the South, she found out that a good portion are foreigners who land port in Civitavecchia... people that come from everywhere, from every country in the Mediterranean! And unless their destinations are Rome or Naples, they'll probably pass through Staggia on their way up to Genoa, or Milan, or Venice, or to Florence. Very often to Florence. Your mother lives in Florence, and has for years, although she travels—*too much*, they say—wandering endlessly throughout Tuscany, looking for her only son. When she comes to this inn, she talks with the guests. She inquires if they might have heard of you. Of course, she doesn't give your patronymic. She doesn't tell anyone who your father is, she just calls you Saul. The innkeeper was the only one in Europe, your mother said, who knew the real story about you. She and he have perfect trust in one another, and they have since the first day they met at the apothecary. She told him all about your childhood, and life in the village where you were raised. At her new home, in Florence, he said, she spends all day Sunday, every Sunday, walking around the Piazza della Signoria, and across the Ponte Vecchio bridge... she said that you knew that's where you could find her in Florence...'"

"The innkeeper is telling the truth," I said, "How else would he know about the Ponte Vecchio? It must be my mother."

"It *is* your mother," said the innkeeper, "and you are Saul, the son of Solarus."

"Enough!" I said, I stood up from the table, emotions were wrapped tightly around my neck, I could hardly breathe. All six eyes were upon me: Saskia, the innkeeper, his wife; they all sat with their teacups still in hand, and their eyes upwards at me. "Please," I said, "Everyone, let's sit quietly for a little while. I need to take this all in."

I sat back down and didn't say a word. I could tell the others wanted to speak, but they didn't. I had asked them for silence. I asked for more tea. The innkeeper's wife promptly poured boiling water into my cup over a fresh dose of herbs. I inhaled the scent again and thought of my home and my mother.

"Your mother made me this same tea each day when my leg was infected," said the innkeeper, "It is supposed to heal everything from infected wounds to infected souls to infected hearts. She bought the herbs at the apothecary where she met me, but they are herbs that are common throughout the Mediterranean. They are sold in the marketplace in the village where you grew up. Most of the herbs are common, but the mixture is important. Acacia honey is added for sweetness; but its secret ingredient—that which gives it a special flavor, and which is said to add years to a person's life, slow the body from growing old, heal wounds, create strengths and kill diseases, is due to a plant that grows only in your country. She brought several hundred grams of it dried when she came to Italy. She gave me some to make my own tea, and I've never been in better health. Your mother has a great talent for healing.

I fell silent after that. Yet my translator did not stay silent. I got up from the table and walked down the hallway to a room where a window looked out to the yard. It was dark, but the sky was clear and the moon almost full. 'To think that this man knows where to find my mother in Florence... To think that my mother spent three months in this inn... Well, what am I waiting for tonight?... I should leave now! Or better to be fresh when I reunite with her... thus, I'll leave at the first light of dawn tomorrow!' I rubbed my chin for a moment... Now what was it that my host said about my mother having suffered a shock? And her being ill?

I needed to find out more, and as soon as possible. I needed to get my mother's address in Florence, I needed to get on the road as soon as possible. I hurried back into the dining room to tell Saskia that we needed to leave first thing in the morning—and that it was a matter of life and death. The moment I arrived at the table, Saskia shushed up their conversation—as if I could understand Italian!—and it only took me another moment to realize that Saskia had deceived me. She had purposely worked in my absence to plot a way to sabotage the one reunion in my life that I considered as important as my life itself. Here is what happened...

I arrived back at the table and surprised Saskia in the middle of her discussion with our host and hostess. She looked at me with her mouth agape. She said to me, "So, you are from Tripoli, Saul!... from Libya!"

"Really!" I was stunned.

"Actually, you are not from Tripoli; but your father, Solarus, is. Your mother too, the niece of the Christian King of Tripoli, she too is from Tripoli. But you, Saul, you were born in a fishing village on the Mediterranean coast of Libya. Your mother had to leave Tripoli to go into exile as soon as she was pregnant with you. She found a home for you both in the humble dwelling of an old fisherman and his wife. Solarus had pleaded with her to leave Tripoli and find safety for their child. As for your father, *as you yourself already know*, he was executed: forced to drink poison hemlock, for having 'seduced' the king's niece. Since your father was an outlaw in the eyes of the king, your mother warned you throughout your childhood about the dangers of you going to Tripoli, and of using your real name—the name of Solarus—there... You see? I found out your secret without having to wait for you to tell me! Clever, no?"

"*A clever traitor* is what you are! I forgot to ask our good hosts to keep quiet about my origins... How did you get them to tell you all of this?"

"Your Saskia is good at getting information without letting her intentions known," she told me, "I simply made conversation, talked about this and that. They of course assumed that I already knew your whole story. And so they forgot themselves as they talked, and bit by bit your whole story leaked out."

"Well since you are not my enemy, Saskia, I hope you will forget about trying to get me to take you to my country."

She looked at me then with a look of sadness on her face. She just shook her head, whispering quietly, "No, I am not your enemy... I am not your enemy..." Meanwhile, the innkeeper and his wife were talking quietly to one another. All of our tea in all of our cups had by now grown cold. Just then, the young boy who carried luggage for the inn burst into the dining room. The innkeeper's wife shouted at him for disturbing our dinner. He said he was sorry but that he'd just come from the station and she'd told him to hurry if he had any news from their friend, the sick woman in Florence who turned out to be my mother. The boy cried-out a bunch of phrases in Italian. The innkeeper and his wife fluttered their hands, wiped tears from their eyes, and dismissed the boy who ran out with stamping feet and arms flailing.

The innkeeper looked at me consolingly, and as he spoke Italian to me in a rueful voice, Saskia translated what he said to me...

"You two will need to go to Florence at daybreak, no later." he said, "You cannot leave now because there is no one to drive you. A driver will come at dawn, I will instruct him to take you to Florence. I will follow tomorrow night."

"Why must we leave at daybreak, no later?" I asked, "What is going on?"

"I hate to be blunt, Saul, but I have been a farmer for so many years. One thing a farmer knows is how to be blunt and not afraid of dealing with life. What the boy said was that your mother is just barely hanging on to life—I think you need to not waste time in going to see her. You see, your mother has been full of despair for a very long time on your account. I thought that these things would iron themselves out and her despair would calm itself, but it just keeps getting worse and worse... Is it true that your mother hasn't seen you in over fifteen years?"

"It is true," I said.

"So you know, she moved from your home to Florence five years ago. It was right after she moved here that there started appearing these 'wanted-posts' in the newspapers, looking for you—apparently they were published in newspapers all over Europe—so your mother heard, at least. She was scared to death by these wanted-posts—why?, because, they were looking for you in order to execute you, Saul! (Saskia looked at me with extreme horror as she translated this to me... extreme bewilderment and horror.) ...I don't know, Saul," the innkeeper continued, "are you aware of these wanted-posts?"

"I was not aware of them. Although I heard rumors that my picture was circulating in the press; and that harm will come to me if I ever return to Tripoli,"

"*Harm* is right, my dear young man, in the form of twenty-five thousand gold louis. The government in Tripoli—*your government*—has that enormous price on your head, and it will go to the person who captures you and delivers your corpse, or else your body alive in chains, to the king of Tripoli."

"Twenty-five thousand louis?!" I laughed, exalted, "I am happy to learn I am worth so much!..."

All of this made Saskia cry... "You laugh, Saul?! My poor friend! What have you done?!"

"It was no crime committed by Saul," said the innkeeper, "Although it was never published in the newspapers *what* Saul had been charged with, Saul's mother knew. For although she was exiled from Tripoli nine months before his birth, she still always knew how to get news from the capital. It appears that the king of Tripoli heard a prophecy from a venerated old prophet—a man who they say is ninety-nine years of age...

"The prophet said to the king—to a king who had ruled since his adolescence—that he would continue to rule until the end of his long life. '*Except for one thing*,' the prophet said, '*The day is not far away, when the son of a wild-man will come to take your power.*'...

"Do you realize the effect that these words had on a king as superstitious as the one who rules Tripoli and all of Libya today?" said the innkeeper, "Remember, this king was the king who, as an adolescent, forced your mother to watch an execution at sea where family was made to kill family—your mother told me the gruesome story!—and he himself, remember, didn't even attend this horrible execution—who knows why?...

"This same young king was the king who ordered your father Solarus to be executed. He was also the king who made your mother flee in exile while you were in her womb.

"Today, this superstitious king is an old man. He has ruled a kingdom for almost his entire life—do you think he is ready to die, or lose power? The thought of this is more terrifying than any fear that a man born less-fortunate can have—oh, pity to all who are born kings!—yet this terrifying thought is his obsession: *'The day is not far away,'* said the prophet, *'when the son of a wild-man will come to take your power!'* ...Well, this king knew who the 'wild-man' was... When your father was alive, people everywhere referred to him as 'the wild-man'—a nickname owing to his exotic features mixing Slavic and Cherokee blood, and to his wild hair. Now, your king knew that your mother was pregnant when she went into exile—her pregnancy was the reason for which he executed your father—yet, he didn't know what sex the child was. Once he heard the prophecy, he sent spies out to gather information. They traced you and her to your small village on the Mediterranean. They learned that you were born a male. They learned that you grew up healthy. But they learned that you both were gone from the village... (fortunately for both your lives, you had left home for who-knows-where, and she had left home as well!)...

"The spies didn't learn enough to track you down. They reported what they knew: that your mother had recently left your country and was living in Europe somewhere; but they didn't know which country she had moved to, nor whether or not you were with her. But the fact that it was known that you were a male solidified the king's faith in the prophecy. It was known now that the 'wild-man' did in fact have a son, and that the son was alive; it thus became the king's highest priority to execute that son. That was all five years ago, yet the price on your head remains to this day, and you continue to be the subject of international newspaper articles that offer an enormous wealth to the one who captures or kills you. It is for this reason, that your mother has spent the last five years wandering tirelessly around Tuscany, visiting every city and village, trying to find you to warn you: 'Do not go back to Tripoli!' Fortunately for her sanity, she was informed that you had either left Tripoli, or were in hiding. As you were always a faithful son to her, she was sure that *if* you made it to Europe, you would come to Tuscany to try to find her. She thought there was a slight chance you would learn for yourself of the danger, that you would learn about these newspaper articles; yet she knew you always scoffed newspapers and journals, and hated the press in general; so she thought it more likely that you would only learn about the wanted ads from the man who killed you to collect his riches...

"And so your mother wandered everywhere. Then she wandered here last spring, and told me all about you while my leg was healing. That is how I recognized you... I saw you painting in the garden. She said you had always loved to paint, that you painted the boats of the old fisherman who raised you. She said you left home to become a painter in Tripoli. Everything about you was identical to her description. If only I had been more cautious before! It is my fault for the state your mother is in now!..."

"What state is she in now? ...Tell me!"

"Eight days ago, a young man—he was about your age, but he was a little younger—passed through Staggia. He was also from your country, born just outside of Tripoli. He had a light complexion, and your hair color. He also was a Christian. He was of European descent. You are much taller though; and now that I see you, I see how many differences there are. Never could it be said by someone who's seen you both that you two look similar. If I just could have known his name, that would have prevented this whole disaster... The man who called me down to see this gentleman from Tripoli was my friend who owns the café where the gentleman had lunch and a few drinks. I had a good look at the man and thought that he could be you: the son of Solarus. But when I tried to flag him down to inquire, he was already down the road and gone...

"I gave up all hope until I asked my friend the café owner if he could guess where he might be off to. He said that he didn't need to guess, he knew for sure... the gentleman told the owner of the café that he was headed to La Locanda Villa B*** in Petrognano. He mentioned this to ask the café owner if he thought it was a nice place to stay. The café owner knew La Locanda Villa B*** very well and said that it was one of the very finest country inns in all of Tuscany. The gentleman seemed pleased, and I was too. I quickly sent word to Florence to tell your mother that I believed I had just found her son, and that she should go quickly!... 'Look for him at La Locanda Villa B*** in Petrognano!...' Oh, if only I hadn't been so enthusiastic! Looking back I'm ashamed. I too went to the Villa B*** just after dinner. I was hoping to see her happily reunited with her son. Instead I found her there in Petrognano, collapsed in a fever!...

"I took her back to Florence. The shock slowly left her and her fever cooled. As soon as she was coherent, I begged her to forgive my rashness. I feared my rashness was going to cost her her life. When her fever dropped, I no longer feared that my rashness would cost her her life, but I knew it might cost her her sanity... your poor mother was raving!

"And so I came back here to the inn. That was four days ago. Now the boy comes in here tonight to worry us again. He said that your mother's nurse just sent word from Florence that your mother's fever came back and it is higher than it was at first, and that she is now in danger. She was at her residence in the centre of Florence. The nurse said she was delirious but awake; repeating often the phrase, 'Send for Saul.'"

"I tell you," I said, "we must leave this moment!"

"I know, but you cannot," the innkeeper told me, "No matter how badly you want to go, there is no one here who can drive you."

"We must find a driver!" I said.

"A driver will be here at dawn, that much is certain..."

"We will wait," I said to them both. Then, "Goodnight." Saskia and I bid them a sorrowful farewell and took leave of them to go to our room and wait for the dawn. They were good people, the innkeeper and his wife. I wasn't sure about Saskia, but I knew I would remember them always.

Chapter Thirty-four

Neither Saskia nor I slept that night. She lay on our bed with her eyes wide open while I paced the floor. At dawn we went out into the yard to greet the driver. The innkeeper also was there in his pyjamas; he woke to say another farewell to us and to instruct the driver to do as we told him. As we were leaving he told us once more that he would come to Florence that night, as soon as his obligations in Staggia were taken care of.

Saskia was quiet when we set off. For a long time, she sat rereading the letter that she picked up at her bank the day we left Siena. I asked her to please tell me who the letter was from and how they knew she was in Siena when she'd told me clearly before that no one knew she was in Siena, or in Italy for that matter, but she wouldn't tell me. I asked her what was in the letter that made her want to read it over and over so many times, but she said that it was of no importance compared to the health of my mother. She told me that after we saw my mother and had that worry behind us she would even show the letter to me so I could read it myself in its entirety, although she insisted that the letter would bore me. I found this statement of hers bizarre, but I didn't press the point. I was too worried about my mother. The innkeeper said that he feared for my mother's life in the beginning, and here the boy says that her fever was now worse than it was in the beginning. Now after fifteen years away from her, I would come to her new home in Florence to find her with whom? With a doctor?, or with a priest? Tears welled in my eyes, while my arms and legs trembled—both because of my mother and because I hadn't gone to bed the entire night before.

Saskia interrupted my gloomy thoughts to tell me that she planned to get off at the next town which had an inn, where she would wait for me. I asked her whatever for, and she told me that it was for the same reason that I refused to go with her to the Île Saint-Louis to look for Adélaïse: "So many years have passed since you were last with your mother, I want you to have some time to be alone together. If I were there, you both would feel as though I were an intruder."

"That is fine. I can meet my mother alone. But why do you want to find an inn along the way? We can get a hotel room in Florence. I can visit my mother and then come back afterwards."

"If only I could wait till Florence," she sighed, "I'm starting to feel really sick. Remember, I didn't sleep last night either."

"I know, kiddo. I'll ask the driver to find an inn for you." Looking back on what Saskia had just said, she was announcing the arrival of the two black storm clouds that had followed us from Siena. To be honest, I didn't really give the matter any thought at the time. I was only thinking about the health of my mother. I didn't care at that moment whether Saskia came with me to Florence, or stayed to sleep off her fatigue at some country inn while I made the voyage myself. This was one day that I didn't put Saskia above everyone else in my heart and my mind.

I asked the driver if we would be approaching an inn. He said yes, that the main road was closed this year, so we were forced to take the side road that went through the villages of Petrognano and Certaldo. I knew of Certaldo, at least by name; it is the celebrated birthplace of Boccaccio. But Petrognano I hadn't heard of—until I remembered that it was the village where the innkeeper said my mother fell ill when she went to see a man she thought was me, but who wasn't.

"We have one of the best inns in all of Tuscany in Petrognano," said the driver, "a place called 'La Locanda Villa B***.'"

'There you have it,' I thought, 'it's the same inn where my mother took sick. A perfect place for Saskia to sleep her weariness away while I go spend the day and night at the bedside of my sick mother whom I haven't seen in fifteen years.' I told the driver that it was perfect... "Please stop at La Locanda Villa B***!"

* * *

Saul stops his narrative...

As you know well, my dear friend, La Locanda Villa B*** is the place where you and I met for the first time. And you remember the state I was in?... clothes disheveled, my face torn with grief, tired as the devil, in short: completely ruined. And now you know why... I didn't sleep the night before. Between Siena and Staggia I was in despair over Saskia, then in Staggia I became a nervous wreck about my mother whom I believed to be terminally ill. The brief period of happiness I knew in Paris had slipped through my fingers, although I held my fingers like a net so as to catch the remnants of the world that was so beautifully falling all around me. Now apparently my fingers were spread too far apart to catch any beauty, all I caught now was those remnants of ugliness, the staple that makes up the daily meal of the unlucky.

Then you recall how Saskia was that day: in the yard of the inn in Petrognano, she cried more than was appropriate to see me off for the one day and one night in Florence I would be spending without her. She told me to kiss her one last time, and when she kissed me, she kissed me on the mouth, admitting to me that we were lovers. We never admitted to one another that we were lovers. We never kissed one another on the mouth—at least not as she kissed me that day you saw us in the yard of La Locanda Villa B***. I should have understood then that she was saying farewell to me. Yet how could she have said farewell to me then, when I needed her more than ever? Still, I didn't think of her that day. All my thoughts were with my mother.

Saul resumes his tale: "On the way to Florence..."

"And so I left Saskia there at the inn in Petrognano. I left her there with all of our money. We had just finished all of Juhani's money, and now our only funds were what Saskia drew from her inheritance in Siena. We paid the driver in advance to take me to Florence and back to the inn at Petrognano. When I left her, I only had enough in my pocket to pay a meal or two while I was in Florence. I planned to stay the night at my mother's, so I didn't see a need to ask Saskia for money. Thus I left her there with all her money and all her tears; and the driver and I went on to Florence.

I arrived in the city-centre of Florence and went to the address given to me by the innkeeper. I found my mother's residence. It was an inexpensive housing place for widows. I rang, my mother's nurse came to let me in. She wore a solemn expression on her bone-white face. She only spoke Italian, so she could not express herself to me. She motioned to me that my mother wasn't at home and gave me an address to where I could find her. I bowed my head to the nurse and went out to where my driver was waiting for me.

I handed the address to him, and we started off slowly. The road took us out of the city. 'Is it a country resting place?' I wondered, 'away from the noise of the city?' It was while on that road, void of landmarks and signs, that a gnawing fear began to eat at me. Call it the air, call it intuition, call it whatever you like, it was overall a fear that justified itself when we came to a large pastoral plain, a field of grass and stones. The grass was green, the stones were white. They were tombstones.

Thus we came to a graveyard. And there with my driver I broke down and wept. I didn't know how to react—does one ever know in this situation? With all the words I could muster, I told my driver to leave me... "Go, please," I said. I then followed the smell of incense. I saw a small group of mourners—four elderly women and one little girl—they were following behind a priest and an altar boy carrying incense. I went up to the priest and said the name of my mother. He signaled to a headstone that was some twenty meters away. The women mourners glanced up at me and nodded with respect. I took them for Italians, no doubt friends of my mother during the last five years of her life.

I watched the priest and the altar boy with his trail of smoke, together with the mourners. I watched my mother's small funeral procession disappear down the gravel path while I made my way to the headstone from which they came. And by a fresh grave, I fell down and wept. Her name was written clearly on the headstone, together with the epitaph:

She wandered and wandered, looking for her son.

She lies now buried, in a city close to her heart.

I lay on that grave for the entire evening and all of the night, sighing, crying, lamenting that I did not arrive sooner to prevent her early death. "Happily, she must have died," I said aloud for the earth to hear, "for she finished her life in Florence, the one city she loved." 'Why though did it take four days for the last message to arrive to the innkeeper?' I wondered, 'Well, it's for the best. If the innkeeper and his wife had received news the day after my mother's condition worsened, they would have gone to Florence while Saskia and I were still in Siena, and I would never have met them: they who led me to her. Ah, she must have died two days ago—so as to be buried today... So why did *I* take so long to come? What was I doing of such great importance? I know what my mother would say to that: "You were living, my son. You were living. Go on and live some more."

And so that is what I did, I went and lived some more; although that entire day and the night to come, I stayed and mourned by her holy graveside. The moon was half-full and growing, the sky was clear, the night was fresh, yet comfortable to the skin; thus, it was a wanderer's night. Where to was my mother wandering now?—I wondered this and wandered far into my memories as the night progressed and my tears bleached my skin cleaner and more white.

By morning, I was drained of tears, soaked in sadness, I considered my mother lucky for having survived this world until free of it. I too wanted to be free of it. I took the tea from my pocket: the tea that my mother had blended for the innkeeper—that which was called: 'Eternal Life,' and I sprinkled it on her grave, so that now my mother too could go and live some more.

I left then my mother's grave. I saw no other living souls as I made my way through the cemetery. I was surprised to see my driver parked near the road. He had been asleep, but the sound of the gravel crunching under my feet was enough to wake him. He said, "Oh, signore! I know you sent me away but I wondered how you'd get back to Petrognano... I know that Signora has all of Signore's money with her!"

"You are right, Signora does have all of Signore's money. I thank you... but tell me, did you stay out here waiting for me all afternoon and evening yesterday and all night too?"

"Of course, Signore. Where else was I supposed to go?"

"You're a good man," I said. And we started off driving back down the road to Petrognano.

Now is the part that you all recall: when I came back to La Locanda Villa B***, I let our driver go for good and went to the check-in desk to inquire which room Saskia was in. That was when the despairing news came: It was known that Saskia had definitely left the inn, and that she had left with another man, but nothing was known about the route she had taken, or destination to where she went. They were certain, however, that she was not coming back.

Chapter Thirty-five

Saul takes a break and fills our glasses for a last drink while he finishes his story...

"It is the part of the story when I met you," Saul said to me as he lit another pipe, "that the nobility of my tale begins. You heralded all the good that followed...

"It is when I came back alone to the inn in Petrognano... You found me as I was giving up on life. I was in despair to a degree that would have killed me had you not helped me. I'd just lost my mother *and* Saskia. The fact that you helped me to learn where Saskia had gone; that you drove me to Civitavecchia, bought me passage on that boat to Tripoli—you then lent me money for my journey, once I'd arrived in North Africa. All of this was—*and is*—extraordinary to me."

To this, I told Saul: "I was a witness to a scene of great beauty and tenderness between you and Saskia in the yard of the inn in Petrognano. I merely believed that you and Saskia each deserved the happiness of seeing the other one again. I didn't know then what was dividing you two. Now you've just finished telling me about your sojourn in Staggia where you learned from the innkeeper about the bounty on your head. I didn't know about that when I took you to the boat docks. I *did*, however, learn about it when I got back to Paris that next spring. I revisited an old newspaper article I'd saved that told of the magnificent bounty on your head should you or your corpse be sent to Tripoli... I had clipped the article out years before, as I found your case interesting. Had I remembered that clipping on the way to Civitavecchia, I would have never let you go to Tripoli."

"And so all this time, you must have thought you drove me to my death that day!"

"Precisely!"

"You know, though, I was fully aware of the money one would get for killing me—I knew that boat ride to Tripoli was a voyage to my own death... Even if you had remembered that newspaper clipping, I would have begged you to buy me a ticket for Tripoli. Why, you ask? You could think that I was going to Tripoli to save Saskia. After all, if any bounty hunters knew that I loved her, she would have been taken hostage. They would have beaten her, tortured her, and what have you, until I came to offer myself up for execution. Sure, you could think this was the reason, but it wasn't...

"While we were riding to the port near Rome, I thought about my reasons for going to my suicide. It wasn't to save Saskia—we kept our relationship such a secret, I didn't believe it was possible that anyone knew about her and me. How could they have known?! You see, I gave my enemies way too little credit. They knew about Saskia and me. At least *one* knew! You'll find this very interesting. I'm going to resume telling you the story of my life from the point where you got me to Civitavecchia and bought me passage on the boat to Tripoli—a favor for which I owe you my life..."

* * *

Saul's adventures in Tripoli, and all that followed until the end of his tale...

"The boat was crowded with passengers. Almost all were men, and by all appearances, of dubious character. Such it seemed was the Italian passage to Tripoli—a passage of scoundrels.

The voyage was very long, time dragged on and on. The Mediterranean is blown by chilly winds in the autumn, but this year the weather was hot and fierce. There were no cabins on the ship so we were forced to stand all crowded together on the deck under that pitiless sun. I kept a scowl on my face to avoid conversing with other men. When there was enough room to pace, I would think during that horrible pace about the worst things: my mother's death, Saskia's betrayal, and my own imminent death looming over me... "As soon as we reach the shore," I mumbled under my breath. Then I turned and saw a man standing in front of me, looking solemnly at me...

"You seem to be the only person on this boat who isn't speaking Italian," he said to me in French.

"That may be true, since I wasn't speaking at all."

"Oh well, I see we both speak French..." He then went on to ask me all sorts of questions, at which I grew hostile and annoyed. I didn't want him near me, couldn't he see this? I was a dying man, I wanted to be alone...

It was just before I grabbed his collar to threaten him, that I looked clearly at his face. I paled then with a feeling of great sorrow, and fear too. He was a desperate-looking creature—one to find on such a boat—he was the perfect portrait of the wandering failure, the itinerant outsider, a rejected traveler, lonely and cast down into the depths of a world that becomes everyday more miserable to live in.

...Yet it is not this that disturbed me. What gave me sorrow and fear when I looked at his face was the fact that he and I looked so much alike.

"My name is Alfred Pion[1]," he said, "I'm from Paris."

I shook his hand and looked curiously at him. His mouth and his eyes both resembled mine, although his showed a suffering that had never been a part of my features. But beyond the face, I saw we had similar clothes and hair, we were almost the same height, the same color of skin-tone... and yet he looked like a miserable wretch. Was it the suffering in his eyes?

"Why are you going to Tripoli?" he asked me.

"I'm from there. Going back home."

"Oh. I've never been. You should show me around. I keeping getting kicked around in this world. I moved to Germany and had really bad luck there, so I went to Spain—more of the same—then to Rome. Always the worst things happen to me, my luck is terrible. Oh, but don't worry, I still have a bit of money... don't think I'm trying to beg or get anything for free, I just wanted to talk to someone... You see, it's *travelling* that has dragged me down. I should have stayed somewhere and married. But here I am... after suffering in Rome for the last two weeks, I decided to give Tripoli a try. I hear it's cheap and the people are good. Do you want some tobacco?"

I said no, and looked more at the pathetic creature in front of me, at how ashamed he was to be alive. Then it occurred to me how much in vain *my own* travels in life had been, since in the end I lost Saskia. I looked at that wasted remnant of a man standing in front of me, and I knew that it was best to die in Tripoli without her. For if I went on living in hiding after she had betrayed me, I would come to resemble this pathetic soul standing in front of me...

And so, my meeting this Monsieur Pion gave me some courage to die in Tripoli that day. I hadn't had the courage before, only the necessity. Now I had the courage...

---

[1]ALFRED PION: "Pion" is French for "Pawn."

Still I've always been a dreamer who believes in impossible hopes—miracles that will never fail to guide me to paradise. I always believed that Fortune was on my side, and that she would stay by my side; and it is for this reason that I've always sacrificed my dear wine to the gods.

The captain announced we would soon arrive. The fear of execution then crept back into my belly. I turned to Alfred Pion, "Well, it was a pleasure talking with you... I have a feeling you're going to have good luck in Tripoli... Take care." I hoped he would leave me then, but he stayed close by my side.

From the waters of the Mediterranean, I watched the familiar sight of the African coastline enlarge and grow defined as we approached Tripoli, the city where my father was raised and was killed. Now that I was walking into my own execution, it of course occurred to me to go hide somewhere in the belly of the ship until we left port again, maybe then I could save my life. But I knew I wouldn't do that. There was nothing left of me at this point. I already lost my life my last night in Italy and I now had more than enough courage to die.

So I shuffled slowly across the deck as the boat was brought to shore. Alfred Pion begged me to meet him that night in town to have drinks, seeing as he knew no one in Tripoli, nor his way around. I said no, that I wouldn't be there that night, "I am only going to stay in Tripoli for a couple hours before I continue on with my travels." I didn't think I was lying. Doesn't a man's execution and death force him to continue on with his travels? 'Sure, death forces you to give up familiar things. And from then on out, it's languages you can't understand and nights sleeping in strange beds...'

We were finally docked at the Port of Tripoli. Now I had nothing to do but wait with the dirty herd of passengers while they led us through and checked our names off the registration to let us disembark. I looked out at that busy port with people everywhere—that city full of poor people, city full of people who would murder a man just for a meal... 'And just think, people!... Who is arriving in town but me: the jewel of the Mediterranean with the six hundred thousand franc price on his head!...'

And so I continued shuffling along, while Alfred kept his lost soul pinned to me.

We were part of the first herd of passengers to disembark from the boat. Alfred kept by me. As soon as we were on firm land, I looked around me, and soon enough I saw it: at the gates of the Libyan customs, some men had already spotted me: five Libyan guards, all armed to their teeth. They were approaching us.

"You are a poor man, my friend," I whispered to Alfred, "this is the price you pay for having chosen me for a companion. You're probably about to go to prison, you know..." Alfred didn't understand a thing I was saying, and in a moment we were enveloped by the five guards. They whisked us quickly away from the bustling port to some corridor nearby where no one could interfere with their business.

"Which of you is the son of Solarus?" asked a guard.

"I am."

"And he? Your friend?"

"Never saw him," I said, but he didn't believe me. "You two are friends of some sort."

"No, he's innocent," I told him. But the guard didn't believe me and ordered two of his men to chain Alfred and haul him off somewhere. 'The poor wretch!' I thought, 'the way he turned pale when they chained him and bobbed his head at me and cried like a child as they dragged him away—as though he were the one being executed! I had no doubt they would question him a while about me, hear only ridiculous answers, and then let him go on his way. But who cares!' I never did see Alfred de Pion again. You'll hear soon enough how he ended-up...

As for me, I was stuck in that corridor with the remaining three guards. The one who had given the orders to the others, I figured he was their chief. His uniform was a little cleaner than the others, his face wasn't as ugly, and he wore a moustache. The other two, his henchmen, were short, stocky beasts with necks that resembled the gnarled trunks of trees. They both smelled badly, and their faces were horribly pockmarked. It was these two who wanted to put me in chains before they led me wherever I was to go. The chief, however, said not to chain me...

"He will not run away," he told his men, "He gave his real name in the ship's registry when he arrived on that boat from Italy. He obviously came to Tripoli to be captured. Don't chain him... he won't try to run."

"Very well," they told me, "Walk in between us. Let's go."

Chapter Thirty-six

The Revelation...

For a long time we walked under the scorching sun. The guards and I were all silent. I didn't recognize the neighborhood we were in, which was strange as I thought I knew all of Tripoli by sight. Then came the birds of prey circling over in the sky, and the smell of brine, so I knew we weren't far from the beach.

"This is it," said the chief of the guards, pointing ahead to a very small palace with a gold dome. It looked like it used to be an embassy. I thought back to the time years and years ago, when I worked in Tripoli earning slave's wages, painting gold leaf on the domes of all the palaces around the city. I thought I'd seen every palace in the city, though I'd never seen this one.

They opened a side-door of the palace and ordered me into a dimly lit corridor. They ordered me to walk ahead of them. With the sudden shelter from the sun, and the cool air that blew down the corridor against my face, I felt my strength renewed. I actually fooled myself for a moment into thinking I was free, that I was alive and fortunate... then the chains were put on me.

"We're going to see the boss now. We'll have to put you in irons." They fastened cuffs on my wrists, and locked iron shackles on my ankles. "Continue on up here," said the chief guard, and I walked and clanked like a galley slave.

As we approached what looked like the main hall of the palace, the light in the corridor grew brighter and then came the odor of incense, and rich foods: roasting meats and red wine. "It seems my executioner is having a feast," I mumbled aloud. Then I heard a man's laugh. I stepped down a step and the light of the main hall filled my eyes. It was a small hall for a palace, big enough for fifty men, no more; and in it, I saw only a few scattered souls sitting on the far-side of a long wooden banquet table. And those souls, the image of that room that lay before my eyes, was a scene belonging to a drama that no madman's nightmare could even create. That scene could only have been written by the most evil of all gods.

Looking at that banquet table, at the people sitting behind it, facing me, I no longer wanted my freedom. I no longer wanted my life, but death for them, and then death for me, life erased from memory—for at the center of the table, seated in the head chair, smiling at me, his prisoner, was Dragomir.

"Saul!" he laughed, "So good of you to come back to Tripoli!"

I trembled in my humiliation. "I can't understand it," I said, "*You?, Dragomir?, a bounty hunter?!*"

"I said to you once in Málaga, I've worn many hats in my day. This is just another..."

I was stupefied... How, of all the assassins, special agents, and police in the Mediterranean, how could it have been a simple clairvoyant and opium dealer from Spain who managed to capture the son of Solarus? But this quandary ceased to interest me as soon as I saw the person who was sitting beside Dragomir...

She lifted her head and her hair toppled away from her face and I saw the portrait of a someone too inhuman to be of this earth—hell would have been a paradise for me then, rather than to have to look upon what I saw: for there at the table, seated at the right hand of the lord, my captor Dragomir, as if she were his mistress, sat my love, Saskia.

My entire soul died at that moment. As I looked at those two, I felt all who I was and had been molting away like the skin of a snake: my body and life had died and only my chains remained. So Saskia conspired to sell me for money! Was it for her love of money? For her love of Dragomir?! Or was it that she hated me?! I needed the answer then, my heart could beat not another time without it, yet I could not speak a word...

She looked at me a few times—oh, my eyes were fixed on her!—but each time she looked at me, she turned away again as though she were completely uninterested in my presence in that hall. Can you imagine?! ...after all we'd been through together!, and now, being brought in shackles and chains before her!, a prisoner, before the eyes of your beloved, while she sits at a banquet table to accompany the man who has sentenced you to death? To see your love attend your death as your executioner's maid of honor!

Moments of silence passed. Saskia no longer bothered to look at me. Soon I managed to say to her in a feeble voice... "Saskia... Why... Why are you sitting there?!" It was the most pathetic thing I had ever asked; but then again, *I was pathetic* at that moment—it had just been revealed to me, after all, that my entire life had been nothing but pathetic farce in which I was the dancing fool.

"Saskia! I crossed the sea for you!" My voice was bolder this time, although neither time I'd said her name did she bother to look at me.

"Saskia!" I called again, "But *why* if I call to you don't you run to me? Why don't you embrace me? We are on a new continent together! Am I not your beloved standing before you after a long absence? And now we are on a new continent together... why then don't you run to me?" Dragomir, all this while, sat with a smirk on his face as he watched me address her. I imagined it amused him greatly to watch me begging love from a marble goddess.

"I went for the day and night to Florence, Saskia... to see my mother. My mother... she died. So I spent the entire night in vigil by her grave, crying. Then at daybreak, I came back to Petrognano where you said you would be waiting for me, but you had gone. They said you went to Tripoli. Why Tripoli?! Because it was your fortune, no doubt? It said you would realize your destiny after entering the country of my birth and the city where my father was raised. Or did you come to be with Dragomir? You knew he was here, obviously. Did you know *why* he was here?... So wait... now I know!... *it was he!, wasn't it?* The one who sent you that letter... That letter you read a hundred times on our way up from Siena. You told me you would let me read that letter once we saw my mother... you said the letter was unimportant compared to my reuniting with my mother. Of course you knew that after I saw my mother, both you and that letter would be gone. Did I tell you that my mother is dead?..."

During all of what I said to her, the only times Saskia seemed to acknowledge that I was speaking to her were the two times I mentioned that my mother died. Twice I told her my mother died, and twice her lower-lip quivered, twice her eyelids closed solemnly momentarily. Was she actually feeling sorrow? So why then did she say nothing?! Why didn't she even look at me?... I had the crazy idea then that she couldn't even see me. Was I just a ghost standing in that room? I tried to find other clues to help me understand this incomprehensible situation. And can you believe that Saskia interested me so much that it was only then that I noticed there was a second girl in the room! There was another girl at that table, seated at Dragomir's left, a girl of about Saskia's age. I studied this other girl for a long time. And while I studied her, I sensed that *only now* Saskia was looking at me. I flashed my eyes back to my beloved and I saw that *she was in fact looking at me!...* Yet before our eyes even met, she looked away with an expression of... I would say scorn, or rather, shame...

'Shame?' I asked myself, 'Saskia ashamed of looking at Saul? Ashamed *of me* because I am no longer a man? Because I am just a prisoner in chains?, a caged dog? Or is she ashamed *of herself?* Ashamed of herself for betraying me?'

"All right, that's enough getting reacquainted, time is ticking..." Dragomir waved his hand and the chief of the guards obediently approached him and listened to what Dragomir whispered in his ear. The guard politely asked Saskia and the other girl if they would wait outside for a minute. Saskia stood up and took the hand of the other girl, and walked out of the palace hall. By the way they held hands, I knew then that the girl was the famous Adélaïse.

"You two can leave as well," Dragomir said to the two other guards. "But wait right outside the main door. I will need you in a few minutes."

The guards exited and I was left alone with Dragomir in the hall. My mind began to race as I thought of ways I might attack and kill him now that we were alone. Had my ankles not been fettered along with my wrists, I know I would have tried. But Dragomir interrupted my thoughts to begin giving me *the revelation*...

"Forgive me, my dear Saul, if I keep those chains on you. I know that you have a fiery temperament... You're the willful, capricious type of man. You are strong too. I don't want to give you any unfair advantages."

"Hmm, the willful and capricious type? And what type of man are you, Dragomir?"

"Me? I am the patient and resourceful type. The type of man who wins in the end. You know, Saul, I knew you wouldn't follow me here to Tripoli where these chains awaited you. No, I knew you wouldn't follow *me*... but you would follow *her*. Isn't that true?"

"That *is* true!" I agreed, "You are clever. But you're cheap as well. You're cheap because you could not bring me to Tripoli on your own. You had to get an innocent girl mixed up in this. Why?! Why did you have to involve Saskia?!"

"Saskia? ...Oh, you mean *Clara!* Nit-nit-nit, my poor, poor Saul, you really don't understand this whole thing, do you?... I'd say it's lucky for you that I involved her in this. Otherwise you would've never had the pleasure of meeting her! You are happy you got to meet her, aren't you?...

"You see, Saul, that is how very clever I am. I've been engineering this trap for you for the past five years. Five years! Can you believe it? Five long, patient years of work on a plan that will only reach its climax and conclusion today. *Do you realize what patience is required for such a task?...*

"You see, Saul, it was five years ago that I first read about you in a newspaper: 'Twenty-five thousand gold louis d'or to the one who catches the son of Solarus, first name: Saul, and brings him to Tripoli.' ...Twenty-five thousand louis! That's enough gold to make the wealth of five men! I knew that if I had this money, I would never have to tell another single fortune for the rest of my life. I could do whatever I want, I could live like a Sultan... like a god!...

"I told you when we met in Málaga that I'm no mystic. Remember what I said to you then?... 'I am no clairvoyant. I am just a charlatan who does what he can for money...' Life feeds on life, you know, and human life means relatively little to me.

"...It was just after I read in the newspaper about the reward offered for you that Clara came to me at my home in Málaga. It was her choice to come to me. She was a wanderer. Thirteen at the time, she was a mere child, out on her own in this mad, confusing world, and she was hoping that I could give her a roadmap to guide her through the labyrinth of life. The poor girl was so baffled. But how could a girl *not* be baffled at that age?, with no parents or relatives, wandering around the world alone because she doesn't know what else to do with herself!...

"She desperately wanted help to know what to do in life. So I took the liberty of choosing her path for her... I decided the best use of her life was to catch my prey for me!" Dragomir laughed a good deal after saying this, "You must admit, Saul, she did the job perfectly!

"...But in order to have her catch you, I first needed to get your two lives entwined; and this I did by planting the seeds of obsession. The first step was to get her to *really believe* that I possessed psychic awareness, which I did by guessing things about herself and her life—easy enough in her case, so much about her was transparent. Then, once she had complete confidence in my psychic powers, she didn't need any convincing that I knew her future and her destiny. She had complete faith in me. So this is when I told her what was needed to get you here standing before me in chains today. I told her *the key to her destiny was you!*

"...As for you, Saul, you were a lot harder to get a hold of in the beginning. And it wasn't until the summer before last that I managed to get you to my home, thanks to Pulpawrecho... may he rest in peace...

"Of course that tainted opium that made you collapse beneath Clara's balcony, that was actually meant for *you*, not for my old friend Penelope Baena in Barcelona. I lied to you about that in Paris. You see, I couldn't think of another way to make sure you would eat all of that poison the night of your birthday unless I planted the ruffians at her house to *make* you eat it—I know that wasn't the most 'elegant' part of my whole orchestration—but just so you know, Saul, that opium didn't contain enough poison to *kill you*, only to make you wander beneath Clara's balcony and fall unconscious. Don't think I wanted to *kill you!...* The proof: remember your girl told you then about some 'tall man in a black suit' who gave her a book once? It was a novel in which the character was poisoned with verdigris, and the novel had information on how to cure the poisoned person... Guess who that man was who gave her that novel! You see?! I didn't want you dead... I wanted Clara to heal you and make you nice and strong again."

Dragomir stopped his explanation and there was a moment of silence. Then I realized it all!... "So you weren't just *that* man!" I said to Dragomir, "You were *all* of these men! You were also the man in Barcelona dressed head-to-foot in black crêpe, weren't you? The one who told me I looked ill and pointed me the way to the hospital!"

"From the looks of you that night!" laughed Dragomir, "If I hadn't been the one who poisoned you, I would have given you up for dead! But everything was in order... a nice coincidence that the girl I'd chosen for you lived on the exact street that led to the hospital I sent you to find!...

"Although I didn't really want you to find it, of course. I didn't send you on a walk through the garden of Aphrodite just so that you might come out the other side at a public infirmary! You wouldn't have wanted to pass the night of your birthday in some public hospital, would you? No, I knew little Clara would be singing her gypsy songs on her balcony that night—the fortune I gave her told her to do so. Oh, Saul, there were so many reasons why I chose her for you... one being that she was so young. When we are young like that we are so easy to convince of fate and destiny. A simple fortune read to her in an eerie Spanish mansion and she was seduced! Yes, it was easy for me to seduce her, yet it wasn't easy for *her* to seduce *you,* no. That was one drawback of her age. Older women are much better than young girls when it comes to seduction. You weren't seduced at first, no... You even tried to *abandon her* in Barcelona, remember? That had me worried. I had to bribe the workers at the boat docks to lie to you and invent some departure delays. They told you that you were stuck in Barcelona for a while, do you remember that?"

"Quite clearly."

"I had to bribe quite a lot of people on your account. This was not a cheap five years for me. It will be good when I have the twenty-five thousand louis to cover my losses. I almost forgot, I still have to pay the guards who arrested you at the port today. You see, I had to pay a lot of people off to get you in these chains you're in today, Saul. I even had to kill! I had to get rid of that snooping 'Andrea' boy. He would have fouled everything up if he had stayed alive. Then there were the businessmen staying at the Hotel Sant Felip Neri in Barcelona... You see, it was important to my plan that you stay at that precise hotel. You wanted a suite when you returned there after abandoning Clara. But the only two suites were now occupied by two men who wouldn't take the hint I gave them—I *did* give them their chance to give up their rooms! But they were stubborn, so they each got knifed in the gut and thrown into the street. It was meant to look like a very suspicious and very absurd double-suicide. What an absurd death-scene that was!, it made me laugh... But what baffled me Saul, is that for all your brains, it didn't seem to occur to you to book one of the dead men's suites after that. Why did you insist on remaining at that cockroach farm up in Urquinaona? I had to go scrounge-up that old toothless guitar player and put him in that dirty tavern and tell him to talk to you about some scarf you dropped. *You see how you made me work to capture you?!...*

"Oh, then there was Paris... you absolutely loved Paris, didn't you Saul? You *are* a decadent soul... each night at the Comédie-Française, fashionable strolls in the gardens all day... You and your girl would still be there today if I hadn't ransacked your apartment on the quai to give you a scare. I still regret that I didn't get you to leave soon enough. I knew that your mother was dying of loneliness in Tuscany..."

"What did you know of my mother?!" I shouted. I trembled with fury at hearing my mother mentioned by this 'creature.'

"Her neighbors said that her one wish was to reunite with her only son. But truthfully Saul, I only knew the story of your dear mother from the gossip of the Florentines. I never once checked-up on her myself. And never did I hear any Florentine say a word about your mother that wasn't full of praise. I have a mother too, Saul. I know that they are holy. I never tried to speak to your mother in order to get to you. I may be a charlatan, but I have a mother too."

Dragomir sat a minute, quiet and pensive. He then resumed talking... "So while your dear mother was worrying herself to death in Tuscany, you were playing around in Paris—I wasn't happy about this; so in order to get you to Tuscany, I poisoned your wine. Again, it was not enough to kill you, only enough to make you sick—as you found out the next day when you tried to get that donkey drunk."

"Dragomir, bring Saskia in here. Let me talk to her."

"Saul, I'm almost finished sharing with you the organization of your capture... it's almost through, be patient...

"You remember Mademoiselle Lingot in Paris? The girl who told you and your girl that Adélaïse ran off to Tuscany with some older couple? She was telling the truth... the couple was Penelope Baena and me. We convinced Adélaïse to come with us to Italy; and then she gladly came here to Tripoli when we promised her a reunion with her best friend, Saskia. She is a very pretty, very sweet girl, this Adélaïse. Did you notice when she was just in here? Oh, no... you only had eyes for your Clara... Sorry, your 'Saskia.' I know how much you love her. Well, as we were leaving Italy to come here, we had Adélaïse write a letter to Saskia—Adélaïse calls her Saskia as you do. The letter contained personal clues, references to private secrets that only the two of them could know about... then we mailed the letter to Saskia's bank in Siena. Yes, it was a letter from Adélaïse, *not from me.* Adélaïse told Saskia in her letter that she would be waiting for her in Tripoli. This is what made Saskia abandon you in Italy. Your girl does love you, Saul. Believe it or not, she loves you as much as you love her. She didn't want you to see that letter from Adélaïse because, as you know, she knew from the innkeeper and his wife in Staggia that you are wanted in Tripoli, and that your coming here to Tripoli meant your death. As for herself, she had already made up her mind—and she even told you, don't forget!—she would travel any distance, and alone too, to reunite with her best friend, Adélaïse. And she *did* find Adélaïse, so now she is happy! ...You know, Saul, the life of a man with whom a young woman is intimate for a short while means relatively little to her where lifelong friendship is concerned." Dragomir broke once again into great laughter after saying that. "That's funny, is it not? But truthfully, Saul, she *does* love you, as much as you love her."

"She shows it very strangely," I said, "She won't even look at me or offer the slightest sympathy as I stand before her in chains, awaiting execution."

"Yes, Saul, you and I both know... Women have a strange way of showing their love!" Dragomir's witticism made him laugh all the more loudly, while I meanwhile cursed him, shaking with fury, my chains a rattling cacophony of clanging metal. The sound reminded me once again how heavy my chains were, I could never break them. And so I asked kindly of my executioner, "Dragomir, please... I request to speak to Saskia now."

"No requests, Saul."

"You are an unnatural creature! I am a man condemned to death, and I can make no requests? Damn-you, insect! Let me talk to Saskia"

"There will be time for that."

"When?"

"We are going on a little boat ride now."

"What do you mean *a little boat ride?*"

"A little boat ride in the name of your king."

'A little boat ride in the name of the King of Tripoli!' ...That horrible phrase sent my mind flashing back to the story my mother told me as a boy of *the execution out at sea*, when she was taken on a boat to witness the death of a young nobleman, ordered by the adolescent king. I would have nightmares of that execution when I was a boy... they were so vivid, I had given faces to all the characters: the sister who was shot in the head when she refused to kill her brother, the second son whom the condemned brother convinced to shoot him to save their family—he shot his brother, then he turned the gun on himself—I imagined all their faces, right down to the face of the condemned man himself. Now I was to enact my childhood nightmares for real... the thought sent me into convulsions, I admit I was seized with horror. And in my panic, I struggled to free myself from the iron handcuffs.

"Don't do that, Saul. You're just going to scrape up your wrists."

He then walked to the door and called the two guards back in. "Take the prisoner to the boat," he ordered, "Lock him in the cabin."

Chapter Thirty-seven

The chief guard, along with his two pockmarked henchman, led me from the palace down a deserted street until we came to a beach, where a jetty of sandy stones stretched out into the sea. It was an unpopulated beach and there were no boats or people or signs of habitations visible either up the beach or down... only in front of us, that single stone jetty with crystal blue water lapping gently around it. This view before my eyes had an unreal, dreamy quality, as though it were a pastel landscape painting. The only movement in the painting was the gently lapping blue water. So had it looked since I was a boy in my dreams and nightmares of that execution out at sea my mother witnessed. It was a scene painted in pastels. It was a day just like this day: clear skied, the sand bright orange, and the Mediterranean whose waters are often so wild, on this day were still and as calm as a puddle of glass.

At the end of the stone jetty stood a magnificent boat with enormous white sails puffed-up with wind. The guards escorted me down the jetty, and once we reached the boat, they slackened the irons on my ankles so I could cross the gap from the jetty to the boat deck. I was somehow not surprised to see that Saskia and Adélaïse were on the boat. I had begun to believe evil things by then. I believed that they themselves desired to be the ones to actually kill me, to spill my blood and watch me die. Saskia and Adélaïse were sitting together on the floor of the deck holding hands and whispering to each other. They looked so happy in their little white matching linen dresses, their feet dangling over the side of the boat. They might as well have been having a picnic together.

Saskia only glanced at me for a moment when I came onto the boat. She didn't look into my eyes. She only looked at my chains: at my bleeding wrists and my feet. There was a look of both reassurance and love in her eyes. I was sure she was reassured to see me bound in irons, that she could feel safe knowing that I could not escape to harm her, nor escape my death. But the love in her eyes was the most painful. I felt that even though she had sold my life for money or for whatever reason, she still loved me in some part of her. And with that thought, the most painful realization dawned on me: *that the only person living in the world who loved me, and whom I loved, wished me to die!*

And so that was the moment *that I wished the world to die: every memory, every creature, every breath that makes us creatures... every trace of life... to die and never be reborn!*

If ever I had been happy in this world, if I had ever admired the universe and all that was created within it, that admiration vanished the moment Saskia let it be known that her wish was for me to die in front of her... and for what sake? For the sake of her friendship with Adélaïse.

The guards escorted me into the cabin of the boat. In the center of the cabin room there was a table. On one side of the cabin were bunk beds. On the opposite side was a window looking out onto the deck to where Saskia and Adélaïse sat together talking. Finally, at the back of the cabin, next to the window, there was the bench to which I was chained. The guards attached each of my ankles to a leg of the bench. The bench legs were nailed solid into the wooden planks of the boat. The cuffs on my wrists were unlocked long enough for the guards to chain my hands *behind* me; thus if I decided after all to deprive the executioner of the pleasure of killing me by strangling myself, I was now out of luck. I looked out the cabin window then and watched Adélaïse and Saskia as they spoke to one another on the deck. I could hear every word they said...

Adélaïse was laughing. "We're finally together again, Saskia! I can't believe it! It's been a crazy long time!"

"I can't believe it either..." There was melancholy in Saskia's voice.

"Why are you sad?"

"I'm just nervous. I just want it all behind us. I just want it all to be over, so we can move on."

I repeated Saskia's words over and over again in my thoughts. Several times over and again, I repeated, *'I just want it all to be over, so we can move on.' ... 'I just want it all to be over, so we can move on.' ... 'I just want it all to be over, so we can move on...'* 'Yes,' I thought, 'After I'm gone, she will finally be able to move on...' I now truly feared death. Footsteps approached the cabin from outside. Then the voice of Dragomir...

"Clara, come now... we're going, it's time... Guards, see to the comfort of Adélaïse until we get back... make sure she's in want of nothing. Oh, and make sure the prisoner behaves himself." Through the window of the cabin I observed Adélaïse as she watched her friend walk off the boat at Dragomir's side. I could see Saskia and Dragomir walking down the jetty towards the city.

I waited in that cabin for what seemed about two hours. I struggled with my chains and tried to loosen the bench, but I knew it was no use. All my ideas were stupid... I thought to shout to Adélaïse through the window for help. But what on earth would I say to her?... *'Hey Kid! If you help me get untied, I won't tell anyone!'*...? She was busy sunbathing, she wouldn't bother with me. As you can see, I was facing the pathetic ending of an otherwise beautiful life.

It was late afternoon when Saskia and Dragomir came walking back down the jetty towards the boat. Dragomir was pushing some kind of a wheeled cart, from what I could see through my cabin window. The sun had fallen low, and all I could see outside were silhouettes. Yet as the sea was calm and quiet, I could hear every sound and word perfectly. Dragomir stopped at the end of the jetty by the boat, and handed something to each of the guards...

"One gold louis for each of you. Good work, boys. I won't need you for anything more. Just help me get this cart aboard. Then stay on the jetty and help me untie the ropes at your end, we're shoving off for a little boat ride."

The guards moved the cart onto the boat and I could see clearly now, the cart was carrying sacks of lemons—'Why lemons?' I wondered. Back on the jetty, the guards untied the ropes and pushed the boat adrift in the sea. The sails caught the wind, and the four of us: Dragomir and Saskia, Adélaïse and me, started sailing slowly but steadily out into the vast and fabulous Mediterranean Sea.

Now I could see Saskia clearly in the sunshine from my prison bench. She passed in front of my window and went to Adélaïse and hugged her and smiled. "Oh, Adélaïse! I'm so glad *that's* over with! Now we're sailing... Soon we will be all together and happy."

"Soon they will be all together and happy," I repeated in a mumble, "I hope Saskia pulls the trigger..." With the guards back on the shore, who else would do it? It seemed like Dragomir's style to give the honor of executing me to the woman I loved. Dragomir came into my cabin that moment followed by Adélaïse...

"Unfasten his chains from the bench," he said, "But leave his wrists chained together behind his back."

"Do we keep him in the cabin?"

"Please, no... Don't keep me here! Let me see the sun a final time before I die!"

"Alright, do as he says... bring him out to the deck to see the sun."

Saskia was standing at the bow on the deck. She was staring at the coast of Libya as it grew gradually fainter. One could still see the tiny dots that were people, milling around on the piers of Tripoli that jutted out from the stretches of beaches. One could still make out the palm trees, and the houses were still rather large.

"We are not that far away," Saskia said and turned around to face the cabin door from which I emerged, still in chains, led by Adélaïse. Saskia acknowledged me this time, but she did not look at me long. She seemed more fascinated with the landscape. She turned around to face the sea again and shouted, "Oh hurry up! Let that horizon disappear from sight forever!..."

Dragomir, meanwhile, seemed extremely gay of spirit. He was laughing, making boyish jokes, leaping around the deck. I stood stoically and gloomy, my back to the mast.

"It's time to taunt you, Saul!" Dragomir laughed. He tore the lemons out of the four sacks with joy—tossing them wherever they might land: on the deck or in the sea. After a while of that, I saw that in the sacks, underneath the lemons, were brilliant gold pieces. "The sacks are filled with louis d'or!" Dragomir laughed. Then he explained his ruse, "I covered the coins with lemons to look like a citrus merchant. Smart, huh? While we were walking through the poverty of Tripoli, all the people were staring at Clara here. No one cared about my lemons! Ah, but if they'd seen the flesh *and* the gold, those poor devils would have stolen both—there's enough here to make the whole city rich! Not to mention those greedy guards. Why do you think I didn't bring the guards on the boat? Who would be able to stop them from taking all!, what, with the pistols and swords they carry... "Look at all this money, Saul! *...You see what I get for killing you?* There are twenty-five thousand of these beautiful gold coins. All divided amongst these four sacks. Each sack weighs almost fifty kilos!—can you imagine that?! *Did you know that your head weighed so much?!...*"

Dragomir was euphoric with laughter. "Hey Clara!" he yelled over to Saskia, "Stop looking out at that sea and come feel this gold!" She didn't turn around or respond to him, she kept at the bow, staring out at the horizon. Adélaïse, at that moment, came to me where I stood at the mast and she stood beside me. She gave me a thoughtful and serious look. She seemed to want me to know something... but what? Was she sorry she had to execute me?

"Clara!" Dragomir yelled again, "You can come over here now. Leave off your watch! Tripoli is finally out of sight... the horizon officially shows water in every direction!" And with more loud laughter, Dragomir resumed playing with his gold. He was paying so much attention to his riches that I thought I *just might* be able to slip my legs through the chains on my wrists; I could then leap on him and try to strangle him with the chain joining my wrist. 'If I can't strangle Dragomir,' I thought, 'I might succeed at the very least to throw the sacks of gold overboard before he had the chance to kill me. I'd be dead, but they'd be poor...' And so I tried that desperate plan and began struggling with my chains, pushing my hands low enough to get around my feet; yet I stopped when I felt Saskia's hand touch softly my wrist. I hadn't noticed that she had come from the bow. I looked at her with malice and resumed struggling with my chains, but she now held both her hands on my wrists—not with force, but with tenderness, with compassion; and she said, "Stop, Saul."

"You stop, Saskia!" I cried quietly to her as cold sweat poured down my cheeks, "Stop *this* is what I mean... After all we have meant to each other, you owe me at least the decency of helping me to die right now. Don't make me stand here through all this humiliation. It is because of my death that you are rich, so treat me with respect: tell the executioner to do his work and quickly!" She didn't say anything to all this, she just looked at me.

"The way you look at me now, Saskia! It is compassion you have... You know that this is the first time you've looked at me for more than a second since I arrived in Tripoli? Please continue looking at me until I die. Look at me with compassion while the executioner does his dirty work. At least then, I can forgive for what you've done to me. With my forgiveness, you can live with a clean conscience after my death."

Dragomir heard me say this and he lost all interest in playing with his gold. Saskia looked at Dragomir at this moment and a tear rolled down her face. "Dragomir," she said to him,

"Please, Dragomir, the horizon is out of sight. No one can see our boat. Can we tell him now? He is suffering too much. Why must he wait so long?"

"My God, you both are so serious!" said Dragomir, "And you, Saul, you poor, poor man! What you must be going through in that head of yours. I think I'll give you the last revelation now, so as to make your burden less heavy. It all begins with a story that you will think is funny." So saying, Dragomir came close to me. I noticed Adélaïse stood only a few steps away, watching and listening. As for Saskia, she still had her hand affectionately on my wrists that were bound in chains.

"Saul... Do you remember that gentleman you met on the boat from Italy? The one who vaguely looked like you... Except he didn't have quite so nice of a face as you. What was his name? Alfred, I think it was. Yes, that's it, Alfred Pion. A Frenchman. Well, it's a funny thing about Monsieur Pion, you see. He couldn't manage to stay alive too long... I paid a couple ruffians to stab him with a dagger and then stuff his body in a coffin. After that was done, I had him brought to your king...

"'Voilà, Your Highness, Your Grace!' I said, 'You asked for him, and I brought him! The son of Solarus—stone dead!' That idiot king trembled with such delight as he looked at the coffin; and when he opened it, he exploded with pleasure, as though he were a child opening the world's greatest Christmas present. He saw his salvation in the dead face of Alfred Pion...

"The king never saw you, *the real* son of Solarus, not once in his life, consequently, he quickly turned to his court advisors and asked if the dead body was really you. The advisors looked at each other with embarrassment. They also were unable to respond in the affirmative or the negative—for none of them had ever seen you either!... They talked amongst themselves and then responded by saying, 'Your Highness, this man looks exactly like the portraits of the son of Solarus in circulation.'

"And the king had to agree," said Dragomir, 'And so much was true! The portraits in the press did resemble Alfred as much as they resemble you. The king was easily convinced—so much so, that I wonder why no one over these past five years ever tried and succeeded in bringing a corpse that vaguely resembled you to the king to collect the twenty-five thousand gold louis. I certainly lucked-out, because your king really is a fool!"

"He's not *my* king," I told Dragomir.

"That's right, you are exiled, aren't you. Right now, you have no country. But the king of Libya is one of the biggest fools I ever met. He was so happy once his advisors identified the corpse properly as being you, he cried to me, "You lifted the curse, Monsieur! You saved my life! No wild-man's son will take my power! I shall always be king!' The fool then took me in his arms as though I were his son... How do you like that!—and the best part of it was your girl here... Boy, this Saskia is a brave and clever little one! I had no idea! It is thanks to her that we got the money as easily as we did. I was expecting to have to resort to some risky tactics in order to leave that palace with even a portion of the twenty-five thousand louis. Here's what she did...

"The king's men closed the lid on the coffin, and began to talk about how 'that affair was solved,' and how now they could move on to other business. It was then I asked for my payment. I mentioned the reward offered not only in the press, but on documents carrying the royal seal. The king responded in a lukewarm tone, "Oh, yes, about that..." and he turned to his advisors, apparently to discuss the matter of whether I should be paid. Meanwhile they asked me to sit over in a chair a little ways away. I knew that kings are notoriously bad at keeping promises, especially when they involve giving money or property away, so I expected the worst and plotted my next move to get revenge and get my money...

"It was while I was plotting away, that I was surprised to see Saskia enter. Your clever girl managed to get into the throne room to see the king without an introduction! She walked right over to him and knelt to kiss his hand. The two then began talking. I don't know what her trick was to befriend him, but within minutes, she had him completely charmed! She then let him know all the details of her love affair with the 'deceased' son of Solarus: Your meeting in Barcelona, your life together in Paris, your trip to London together—although I know you two never did go to London together, did you?—as well as your romantic tour of Tuscany. All of that charade your girl was playing happened just a few paces from where I was sitting, waiting for the king. It was true she had him charmed, but I didn't believe it would lead to anything. But then she really stole the show...

"You should have seen your faithful girl when they brought the closed coffin before her and the king's men came and opened the lid. Saskia looked at the corpse of poor Alfred Pion with his lips all puckered in the most ridiculous way, and she broke down in hysterics... sobbing violently, beating her tiny little fists on the floor...

"'Oh, Saul!' she wailed, 'My poor, poor, Saul! My prince! My beloved! Whatever has happened to you?! This is the worst, etc....' Then she turned to the king, 'Oh, King! Most worthy King! Why did Saul of all men have to die?!' ...The effect this had on the king was perfect. Saskia's tears didn't move the king to pity. That nasty fool can't feel sorry for anyone. But the effect Saskia's sobbing and pleading *did* have on the king—and on his advisors as well—is that it left no question about the authenticity of the corpse: Saskia's tearful testimony was the proof they needed to know that I'd killed the right one. The king was so pleased and reassured by Saskia's violent sorrow, that he ordered the gold to be brought to me at once. Saskia all the while pretended she didn't know me, treated me as a complete stranger—worse, she treated me as the monster who killed the love of her life, she even spat in my face. That act alone convinced the king that, in addition to being beautiful, she was a daring and spirited girl, and so he begged her to come visit him at court anytime she wished. And so she has an open invitation to his throne room! So you see, Saul, all was conducted perfectly!...

"And the money came just like that... twenty-five thousand gold louis... equal to six-hundred-thousand francs! You see them here? Feel how much these sacks weigh! Look at the coins, they are beautiful, aren't they?! So that's the good news Saul. And now that you know the Frenchman died in your place, I don't think I'm risking anything by unchaining you now..."

"By unchaining me?!" I said, not understanding what those words meant, so in shock was I, "By unchaining me?!"

...Yet that is what he did!

...With the help of Adélaïse, Dragomir unlatched the iron chains and unwrapped those that had snaked around my arms every which way when I tried to free myself. I, all the while, remained in shock. I couldn't believe what a turn my story had taken!

Dragomir continued to describe with enormous pleasure the events of that day while Adélaïse and Saskia brought soap and a pail of water to wash the blood and dirt from my body. "Oh—the best is for last!" said Dragomir, laughing, "Your king told me how he'll be feasting tonight... to celebrate your death, you can believe. He will be drinking a lot of wine, he told me himself. I took precautions of my own in this regard. It's not so much that I hated the man, yet I had to prevent him from not paying me the bounty when I gave him your dead body—and you see by the events of our meeting that I had good reason not to trust him. (Kings are notoriously an ungrateful lot, you know!) So I had a trusted man of mine contaminate all the king's wine with our best poison—and don't think it was that harmless verdigris that I put in your opium, nor was it the scum I put in the wine that sickened your alley cats in Paris... no, no, this was the 'king-killer'—a real *death liqueur!* One drop of it will kill a god, let alone a king! I guess that's what the prophecy meant when it said: *'The king will lose his power when the son of a wild-thing enters Tripoli.'* He was already filling his chalice when we left. I'm sure he's not feeling so powerful right about now!—that is, if he is feeling anything at all..." Dragomir's cheeks filled up with joyful color as he cheered on all of us with his tale; he tossed his head back and roared with delight. Then he bowed low to me with respect—it was a gesture he had never done before, "Now how do *you* feel, Saul?"

"I don't know what to make of it, Dragomir. You *could have* sold me to the king today. If you'd stayed in Tripoli, in addition to the gold, you would have received enormous fame, a royal appointment, lands, titles..."

"Oh, I hadn't thought of lands and titles! A tempting thought, Saul! Yet think of it... my job was to kill a man—*you*—who, according to some crazy mystic's prophecy, was going to 'destroy the king' simply by entering a city. Do you think that during these five years I could have taken myself seriously if my only goal was to murder a man because he is believed by some stupid king to carry a curse around with him that will destroy this king? Saul, that is absurd! I may be a scoundrel, but I don't murder people to satisfy the whims of superstitious kings. And so now that you're unchained and free, take a walk with me around the deck. You need to get your blood flowing again."

Thus Dragomir and I began to take a walk on the boat deck... After we got a few steps, Dragomir said to me, "Oh, Saul! You're not walking too straight!"

"I admit, I'm in shock. I'm not sure what is going on. I think if I realize *that I am still alive*... I mean, *if* it occurs to me that *I am* still alive, and that *I will* stay alive... I will consider this the most beautiful moment of my life, this day the most beautiful day!... I am feeling dizzy, however. I think I need to sit down."

"Saskia!... Adélaïse!... Come help our dear Saul to sit down on this cask over here. Adélaïse, bring him some water to drink. Splash some on his head." This, the girls did, and as they attended to relieving my thirst, to cooling my skin, and easing my bewildered heart, I pleaded to all present to know the reason for *the one thing that made my soul ache above all else*...

"What I still don't understand is this, Saskia... When I was brought in chains before you in that little palace in Tripoli, *you would not look at me! Why?!* I pleaded with you! It was all I wanted!...

"And then on this boat... I was sure that at any moment I would be executed, by any and all of you... but all three of you knew that I would go free!—*right?!*"

"Of course we knew!" Saskia cried, "Do you think I could have kept my sanity if I thought for a moment you might be killed?!"

"But I was in chains! Dragomir spoke about the money I would earn him... You never let me think I might live, Saskia! You wouldn't even look at me on the boat either! And so I thought of everything I might do to kill myself first, to end this being near you but of having lost you. The only thing that saved me from leaping into the sea with my chains on to drown myself was a vague disbelief that you could hate me that much—and all of a sudden! But how unbearable was the sight of you and

Adélaïse at play together, sitting together, lounging on the deck, sunbathing, laughing!... and the worst of it all... *you wouldn't look at me!...* It was *that* that made my soul ache above all else! All the while I stood here in chains, I received no look from you whatsoever... No gesture to communicate to me that you felt badly for me—*or that you were even aware of my existence!* Instead, all the while we were on this boat, *you just kept looking out at the horizon!...* So I ask, *how come?!"*

"'How come?!'—you ask, 'How come?!'" While Saskia cried these words through her mouth damp with tears, she held her little fists so tightly together that her tiny knuckles turned all white, *"'How come,' you ask?!"* While she cried this, her eyes flashed back and forth so wildly, searching for meaning in my eyes, that we were both driven to the kind of grief only great love can inspire, and both fell together in tears.

"If you knew I would be saved," I said, *"Why didn't you tell me not to worry? Why did you keep looking at the horizon like that?—silent—silent!"*

When I said this, Saskia jumped into my arms and cried so freely, rubbing her hot face against me until every place on my body that had been dry was now wet. She gave me a hundred caresses and planted kisses in all the tender places. And then my little wanderess that I loved so much spoke to me in a way that only a wanderess could speak...

"You ask me why I looked at the horizon like that... It was because I knew that that horizon was the only thing that could destroy us. As long as I could see dots of men on the shore, and boats in the water, I knew we couldn't be happy; since at any moment you could be identified as a prisoner. Those three guards that we left behind on the beach, for a small price they could have been bought to identify you as *the real* son of Solarus. Only when the horizon was gone, did I know the threat that you would be taken from me was gone."

Still crying, she added, "And the reason I didn't look at you in the palace in Tripoli, where you first appeared before me in chains, is because Dragomir ordered me *not* to look at you. The moment I saw him in Tripoli, he told me his plan to save your life. He swore to me that he would save your life. But he told me that if I were to look at you, recognize you, or show you any kind of sympathetic or loving gaze, that that would ruin his plan to save your life, and he may be forced to let you be executed after all. He said to me, 'If you love Saul, and you want to live a long and happy life with him, then you will obey my orders: you are not to look at him, not to show you care about him, until he is free with us and our boat is safely out to sea. That is why I couldn't wait for the horizon to disappear. It was too painful not to show you I love you..."

"Saskia..." I mused, changing the subject, "it just occurred to me that you are eighteen now. You were only seventeen when we met. It's strange, because I never really think of you as having any age. For me, you are timeless—like a marble statue..."

"Saul," she suddenly pressed on me, almost whispering to not be overheard, "Listen, I know something about Dragomir that you don't know. So be careful before you make up your mind... What I mean is that you are stronger than you think you are ...in this situation especially. What I think you don't know about him is just how much respect he has for you. He would just about see anyone in the world die before you... *Yet, remember his loyalty is to himself above all else!...* if it had come down to somebody on shore recognizing you as you are: *the true son of Solarus*, you would have ended-up like the Frenchman."

"Saskia," I changed the subject again, "Just now it is true, you are eighteen years old; yet often when you speak you have a timeless air about you... you are as eternal as a poet."

"Saul, listen to me! Today, when I met the king who ordered your death, I met a man with only one thought in his demented, old head... Saul, don't underestimate the king's preoccupation with killing you... He wanted you dead at all costs. In his mind, your staying alive meant his loss of the throne and his loss of life. Yet also don't underestimate the risks Dragomir took to keep you alive. But remember, Saul... although Dragomir wanted you alive, he told me plain and simple that nothing on earth was going to come between him and those twenty-five thousand louis d'or."

"Ah, except for *love*, my dear Saskia—*except for love!*"

...It was Dragomir's voice that sang out to interrupt Saskia's urgent message to me. He had been standing unobserved near the cask where I was sitting as I talked to Saskia, and where my wounds were being attended to by Adélaïse and Saskia, and he had listened to all Saskia had said to me. He then raised his voice and addressed us all to say, "Saskia here said that although I want the son of Solarus to remain alive, that nothing on earth would come between me and those twenty-five thousand louis d'or. Well! She knows me by heart, but hardly knows my heart... Nothing could come between me... nothing *'except for love, my dear Saskia,'* and I meant it!"

"Very funny, Dragomir."

"Is he joking?" Adélaïse asked.

"Of course he's joking."

"I am *not* joking," said Dragomir, "*Love* is the only thing I would let come between me and these twenty-five thousand louis d'or. The only thing is *love.* And *love* is what I just heard expressed in the vows of these two victims of the hopeless chains of *love.* Oh, love is a terrible thing, and lovers deserve to be pitied. This is why I'm giving to Saul and Saskia, these two happy victims of the disease called love, half of my fortune. You two are to receive twelve thousand and five hundred gold louis d'or. May you build a happy home!"

Saskia didn't believe a word of this. Saul didn't either. Dragomir then seemed to realize what an outrageous thing he had just promised... *"Did I say, give half of my fortune away?! ...How absurd!*

Saskia didn't seem too crushed by the news; in fact, once Dragomir had finished his tears of lamentation, she let out a laugh so light and gay and so sincere, that in tears of joy she admitted that, *yes*, Dragomir would have been, in fact, 'clean out of his mind' to give away half of his reward money.

"No, no!" Dragomir then said aloud, setting things straight, "To give away half of my fortune! People would take me for a romantic. A fool, etc. After all, I received these twenty-five thousand louis for killing you, Saul. Now you and Saskia know that I didn't *exactly* kill you—that will be our little secret to tell at parties. We will have so many fun little stories to tell at parties, won't we, you two?... And now, back to the money... Saskia, are you still listening? You look a little, shall we say, 'absent.' 'No,' you tell me? You *are* here? Well, that is good!...

"So listen, you two... if I were *not* a charlatan, I *just might* give you half my fortune—split the money right down the center! Twelve-thousand five hundred gold louis for each—half for you two, and half for me (And I trust with this gift you wouldn't let poor Adélaïse starve!). But, *unfortunately for you both...* I *am* a charlatan. Therefore, I am keeping fifteen thousand louis d'or, while you and Saskia get ten thousand."

"Is he joking?"

"I am *not* joking!"

"Ten thousand gold louis!" we cried, clasping our hands together. Saskia put her arms around me, while I looked at this clairvoyant from Málaga as though I were looking at a saint, *"But Dragomir, that's a fortune!!"*

Dragomir simply laughed at this and asked me, "Is it not my job to give fortunes?! Fortunately, however, I won't need to do that anymore. With fifteen thousand louis d'or, I am wealthy for life! And you two are wealthy as well! ...as long as our boat doesn't sink." He then looked at Adélaïse, who stood looking up at all of us with admiration, "Don't worry, Adélaïse... you know that their money is your money. Just don't any of you forget your friend Dragomir when that day finally comes..."

"Which day?"

"'Which day,' you ask?! You know, Saul... You know, Saskia... I love many things on this beautiful earth, and I could spend the whole evening and night naming them... but there is one thing I love above all else! ...and that thing is a wedding feast!" Dragomir roared laughing at his own cleverness until he almost fell from the ship. When he caught his balance and calmed himself he said, "Sure, Saul... the adventurer's life is a fine thing, but what does a man need of that life when he has the love of a good woman? Although once he has found that woman, he's going to need plenty of money..." So saying, Dragomir picked up the sacks of gold one at a time, and he began dragging them into the cabin. “Heavy!” he said. Didn’t I say each sack weighs fifty kilos? I’ll be in the cabin dividing our shares!... Saul, do me a favor while I’m counting our money...”

“Anything you like.”

“Keep the boat on course for Spain. We wouldn’t want the wind to blow us back to Tripoli, *would we?!*”

Chapter Thirty-eight

The boat we were sailing was a beauty. It had left Tripoli with four passengers who were also the crew. Dragomir was the one who'd borrowed the boat for this quote, 'little boat ride'; and now, it being officially late in returning to Tripoli, the owner must have been furious. He was surely hunting us down by then, but what did we care? As far as we were concerned, the new owner of the boat was Captain Dragomir; and since he himself no longer needed to play the part of the fortune-teller, he gave that role to his boat. Thus, he named his boat: *The Clairvoyant.*

And so we sailed that day and kept course until we reached Málaga, meeting no hardship, undergoing no pain. Dragomir docked *The Clairvoyant* at the port and said to his happy crew that he wished to remain behind when we were to move on. He wanted to close-up his home in Málaga and transport his favorite possessions onto *The Clairvoyant*, which would then serve as his home while he sailed off in some direction or other, looking for the perfect place to begin a new life.

Adélaïse, Saskia and I spent the day in Málaga sightseeing. Adélaïse had never been to Málaga, although it was a city that had dramatically changed her life. Dragomir took that time to open a new bank account where he deposited fifteen-thousand gold louis in cash. He told us that after we parted ways, we could always find him by writing to his banker. We told him likewise that he could always reach us through Juhani's bank in Madrid.

"Where will you three go now?"

"Paris," I said, "But only until summer. After that we will all three go wandering together. I've convinced Saskia and Adélaïse to come with me to see the white nights of Saint Petersburg. Now that you made our fortune, we no longer need Saskia's inheritance money from her uncle. Now the two of us can begin a romance in the open; we can live together without hiding."

Dragomir smiled. "Another reason you don't need to hide anymore: There is no more king of Tripoli who wants to kill the son of Solarus. It appears you are a free man now, Saul."

"Maybe too free... I think I'm going to miss you following me from city to city, Dragomir. I'll miss you watching me from your box at the Comédie-Française."

"Don't worry, I'll still track you down," said Dragomir, "I've been worrying about you for five years now; and old habits die hard. Well, goodbye for now, all of you..."

"Goodbye to you, Dragomir," we all said. And so there in Málaga, Spain, we three wanderers: Saskia, Adélaïse, and Saul, all said goodbye to that singular man, Dragomir: the clever charlatan and gifted clairvoyant who made us find each other, who made us happy, and who made us rich. Before we parted ways, Saskia had a final question for her fortune-teller...

"Just one thing I could never figure-out, Dragomir... In my fortune, you said: *'Your fingers were not made for keys, but for strings. You love song, and you sing.'* ...How in the world did you know this? I didn't have my guitar with me that night. How did you guess I played a stringed instrument? How did you know I sing?"

Dragomir smiled and replied, "Your callouses, my dear girl. Those precious, little fingers of yours had the indentations of guitar strings on every one!"

"Oh!" Saskia thought about that a moment, and then she blushed to her ears. "...And that I sing? However did you guess that?!"

"I don't know," said Dragomir, "have you ever met a guitar player who didn't like to sing songs?"

To this, Saskia smiled and shook her head... "Boy, a thirteen-year-old will believe just about anything! You really played just as you fancied with my innocent little mind, didn't you, Dragomir? But today my life is perfect, so I'm glad you chose me for a victim." Saskia then exhaled her sweet breath. And let her eyes dance to each of our eyes, and she smiled that great, wide smile—that beautiful and sincere smile that could seduce the whole world: the smile of *The Wanderess*. **”**

Chapter Thirty-nine

It was evening now at the *Lion d'Argent* in Calais when Saul finished telling me the story of his adventures in Europe and North Africa, as well as the naissance of his romance with Saskia: that magical *Wanderess* whose image will always burn bright in my memory and imagination.

So, I wondered what happened afterwards: When Saul, Saskia, and Adélaïse parted ways with Dragomir in Málaga, it was still autumn-time. Still the same year and same season as when I first met Saskia and Saul in Italy, and drove each one separately to Civitavecchia. Now it was springtime; and two and a half years had gone by since then. Today that is long past.

"After we left Málaga," Saul began, "we all three... Saskia, Adélaïse and I... went to Paris, where we lived together in perfect happiness. Life was an idyll. Money of course was no longer an issue for us, yet Saskia and I lived in frugal simplicity, spending very little money at all; it was our mutual love and our hope for a happy future that made our lives rich. Likewise, our friendship with Adélaïse constantly renewed all the joy in our hearts. Saskia and I both looked on Adélaïse as on a daughter. She was much less worldly than Saskia. She was more vulnerable and naïve, more precocious, and was still a child in many ways. Although she confessed to us one day that she'd had a lover once. He was a poet, and the two spoke English together. She said that her time with him was the happiest time of her life, although the two separated by accident and, to her great sadness, she gave up all hope of finding him one day. We asked her if her lover-poet ever called her "My English Lady." Adélaïse blushed like a blooming garden of embarrassed flowers when we asked her this, and she begged we tell her if *all* poets call their muses their 'English ladies.' Saskia and I winked at each other and agreed that our Adélaïse was *the famous* Adélaïse who was the subject of the poem we were read by the love-struck gentleman in the bathtub in Siena.

Adélaïse's birthday was coming up, and for her present we took her to Siena and arranged for her to stumble one afternoon, all alone and vulnerable, on her past lover, the poet Pietros Maneos, who was still where Saul and Saskia left him: reciting Homer in his bathtub—'*à la Diogenes*'—on the lawn of the University of Siena. Both Pietros and Adélaïse, being now older and more mature of heart than when they first met, fell deeply in love with one another. And they, bless their romantic and innocent souls, agreed that this "accidental" reunion was proof that both their gods—Adélaïse's Catholic god, and Pietros' Greek gods—were either both the same god, or else they were great friends and approved of each other.

Since the two lovebirds were in paradise together and had almost completely forgotten that we exist, Saskia and I went ahead and left them in Italy. She and I went, just the two of us, to the top of the earth... to experience in the month of June what I'd always dreamed of experiencing: the white nights and eternal days of Saint Petersburg.

We loved travelling together so much that, after Russia, I took Saskia wandering for over a year. Or perhaps it was Saskia *who took me* wandering for over a year...

We visited places we had never imagined we would go: the cities of Prague, Kiev, Budapest, The Black and Caspian Seas, Macedonia and the sacked city of Troy, Constantinople: the gateway to Asia; we then explored Persia. We wandered on further yet, to India, to Nepal, to Tibet! I studied the origins of Sanskrit, and the complexities of opium smoke. Saskia studied yoga, and the Kama Sutra. She and I cooperated to smuggle a kilo of saffron out of India, into France, where we sold it at a tremendous profit. She and I both agree, looking back on all we did and saw, that the East had a good influence on us. Thanks to the East, Saskia was inspired to ingest oriental medicines and consider her body as a force of nature. While the Orient inspired me to inebriate myself with perfumed wine while reading the poetry of Omar Khayyám[1].

Saskia and I are happy to be back in France though. No country is sweeter! And we also get to see Adélaïse and her poet again... they also just returned from travelling—or from: *wandering*, rather...

They lived with gypsies in Romania. They wandered Europe like rustics, travelling as far north as Sweden; and they wandered like fortune-hunters to the equator, hunting diamonds in the rainforests of the Congo. Maneos in enjoying great fame from his latest book; and he's also encouraging Adélaïse to write a novel about her own wanderings. He is impressed by her literary talent. She is spending hours every day working on it—she says it will be a "romantic adventure" novel. Saskia and I need to make sure that Pietros and Adélaïse can concentrate on literature without having to worry about the "practical things" that get in the way, so we decided last month to sign Saskia's inheritance over to Adélaïse. That way, Saskia and I don't have to be discreet about our relationship, while Adélaïse will have that income to give her security for the rest of her life. So we immediately hired a team of attorneys to study her uncle's will to look for a reason why such a

---

[1] OMAR KHAYYÁM: 11th Century Persian poet and thinker, most famous for his collection of poems known as *The Rubáiyát*. Khayyám's poems are highly respected among scholars and often center around the virtues of wine and intoxicants, as well as the joys of drunkenness and the romantic advantages of being inebriated to the point of losing inhibitions. Payne read Khayyám's poetry with fervor during the brief time he lived in Muslim Morocco.

transfer would be impossible. The attorneys found nothing in the will that forbids such a transfer, and nothing that would afterward forbid Adélaïse from enjoying romantic involvement with a man. She will be free to marry whom she wants, or otherwise live as she pleases... Thus, it seems like a perfect arrangement to us all...

"So this is the reason we all came to Calais! Yesterday we arrived here and Saskia, Adélaïse, and Pietros took the boat to Dover where Saskia has arranged to sign the papers that will transfer her income into Adélaïse's name. As you know, I'm forbidden to enter England, so I'm waiting here in Calais for their return. Adélaïse and Pietros had the misfortune of catching food poisoning on our way here from Paris, so they went straight to bed in their cabin when the three got onboard. That's why you only saw Saskia when their ship left the port. But they'll be back this evening—according to the timetable at the pier, their ship will come in before nightfall. Oh, you must certainly wait! They'll be as thrilled to see you as I was!, for if it weren't for you, we would all be no doubt, alone, poor, and without love in our lives. When we are back in Paris, I would like to invite you to the Comédie-Française if you're free."

"I'm always free for the theatre," I said to Saul.

"You know, it's funny," continued Saul, "I used to have three ambitions: To visit Florence, experience the white nights, and then to let the earth swallow me up."

"You wanted to die after visiting Saint Petersburg?" I asked.

"Well, to be honest...

"...But I hope I'm not annoying you by talking about this. I just imagine that, as a novelist, you like to study man's character."

"I'm interested to hear it," I said.

"It's just that I don't believe in living a life in decline. Either one grows, one blooms, or one diminishes. I wasn't able to imagine any way after witnessing the white nights *to continue to live while growing*. And since I refuse to *live and diminish*, I wanted to die."

"But now *you've seen* the white nights. And you've chosen to live after?"

"With Saskia, I cannot diminish. When lovers are in love, they don't diminish. When wanderers wander, they do not diminish. The world lays itself out beautiful before them; a rich tapestry to explore; with love in abundance. But for this, a wanderer must be favored by Fortune. Fortune is *not* "riches," it is "Poetic Beauty" that comes by surprise!—like a ship coming in from Dover..."

And with those words, a ship came in from Dover. It came in as if summoned by the gods. A vessel emerged from the twilight and entered the port of Calais: A stately ship, with English flags fluttering. On the deck, a multitude of passengers: the ladies brightly-colored in their spring clothing, or else dressed in white; and the men in their white, or their dark, serious suits, all gathered for their arrival on the continent. Saul and I raced from our private dining room out to the great balcony overlooking the port below. I put on my eyeglasses to see more clearly the horde of passengers gathering to disembark.

"Saskia is on that ship," Saul mumbled calmly, "She is on that ship..." And then he cried out... "There she is!... the beauty wearing the yellow dress!" He turned to me, "You know how my heart is racing right now! It will stop beating all together if I don't hold her in my arms very soon!"

"Go and meet her, Saul!" I cried, "Don't wait here a minute longer. Don't wait for me. I will hurry down to the port, just the same. But I have to take it easy on my leg; I will watch you two from up here... but you run all the same! Saskia is coming ashore... This will be the first time I will see you and her *coming together...* and not *splitting apart...*"

"Okay, but we will wait for you below by the ship... We've been hoping to find you again for so long. Saskia won't be happy to hear how I spent these last two days until she gets to see you herself... she will insist you spend time with us! *What a perfect surprise!... À tout de suite*[1] *!*"

* * *

[1] ALORS, À TOUT DE SUITE: *(Fr)* 'So then, see you in a minute!'

Of course I wished to see Saskia again after all these years. From where I stood on the balcony of the *Lion d'Argent*, all of the port was lit-up and bright. She looked amazing. She disembarked from the ship, no longer like the clumsy young girl she was—albeit *she was a very beautiful* clumsy, young girl... No, now time had passed for the better, and she was a woman—sophisticated and alluring. She didn't skip or hop down the platform; she walked with the feminine perfection and grace that God, the sculptor, gives when he has created a masterpiece.

And from my balcony I saw him approach and greet her: the only man that God created worthy of this woman. Saul took her bags and embraced her in his arms; while I watched on with pride and with love. So why on earth would I want to go down to the port to be with those two? Was I not the author who helped create their happiness? Did Saul really think Saskia wanted me there at this moment, when on earth all she wanted was him?

As for me, I had all I wanted... I had their story. Saul and I spent all of two days together, separated by a night where neither of us slept, nor ever wanted to. For two days and one night, Saul narrated his story, while I set his soul to page for generations of readers and dreamers, of lovers, and of wanderers and wanderesses: those tossed among the continents on this, our pleasant earth. And so I ask you one more time: Do I really need to go down to the port—amid the travelers in their drab or colorful dress who grow fewer until gone—so that I can interrupt the eternal kisses Saskia is giving to Saul? No, I knew better than to go meet them. Saskia would thank me in her heart for not coming. Perhaps I will run into them again someday, in some unexpected place as usual... or perhaps at the Comédie-Française in Paris.

Until then, I can always read about their love in the novel I will write from Saul's story. The book will begin in Italy. And it will end right here: where Saul left me... I've changed my plans since my arrival in Calais... *Au Bras d'Or* and the gardens of England can wait. I have something more important to do. And so, I am finishing to pack my bags this instant, to leave Calais—and Europe altogether—to travel long and far, very far away. And so, the novel will end now, just as Saul left me to run down to the port, so he could leave every person, every soul, everything behind—so as to meet his love, his *Wanderess*, his life; the woman he himself had wandered so long to find.

CPSIA information can be obtained at www.ICGtesting.com
Printed in the USA
LVOW07s1935050116

469270LV00017B/1484/P